ALIEN WARS

Also by Vaughn Heppner

Fenris series:
Alien Honor
Alien Shores

Doom Star series:
Star Soldier
Bio-Weapon
Battle Pod
Cyborg Assault
Planet Wrecker
Star Fortress
Planetary Assault (with
   BV Larson and David VanDyke)

Invasion America series:
Invasion: Alaska
Invasion: California
Invasion: Colorado
Invasion: New York
Invasion: China

Ark Chronicles:
People of the Ark
People of the Flood
People of Babel
People of the Tower

Extinction Wars series:
Assault Troopers
Planet Strike
Star Viking

Lost Civilizations series:
Giants
Leviathan
Tree of Life
Gog
Behemoth
Lod the Warrior
Lod the Galley Slave

Other novels:
Accelerated
I, Weapon
Strontium-90
Death Knight
The Dragon Horn
Elves and Dragons
The Assassin of Carthage
The Great Pagan Army
The Sword of Carthage
The Rogue Knight
The Lost Starship

VAUGHN HEPPNER

ALIEN WARS

47N⬥RTH

Text copyright © 2015 Vaughn Heppner
All rights reserved.

Published by 47North, Seattle
www.apub.com

Amazon, the Amazon logo, and 47North are trademarks of Amazon.com, Inc., or its affiliates.

ISBN-13: 9781477828687
ISBN-10: 1477828680

Cover design by Maciej Rebisz
Illustrated by Maciej Rebisz

Library of Congress Control Number: 2014955283

Printed in the United States of America

To my wonderful sister, Bonnie Heppner

1

The Fenris System was two hundred and thirty light-years from Earth. The system's fourth planet—named Pulsar—was an enormous gas giant twice the mass of Jupiter. High clouds raced in Pulsar's upper atmosphere. The mists whipped past a teardrop-shaped warship, an Attack Talon. The methane winds howled, shaking the craft. At the same time, the planet's gravity *pulled*. It sought to drag the spaceship down into denser gases. There, the gravity would crush the warship out of existence.

As the vessel shuddered under the strain, it continued to fight this fate. For several weeks now, the Attack Talon had hidden from its searching enemies. It did so by staying under the clouds. The ship's engines strained while grav-plates neared overload. The human hijackers of the craft feared to take the ship into space. If the alien Kresh captured them, their punishment would be long and brutal.

Even now, the Attack Talon sank lower into the atmosphere. Slowly but surely, it was losing the fight against the planet's powerful gravity. Within the vessel, conditions had become critical. Interior bulkheads shook and metal groaned with a twisting sound.

Cyrus Gant of Earth held his breath as he waited for the horrendous gravity to crumple the ship like tinfoil. If that happened, Jana, his girlfriend, would die, together with Skar 192, Yang, and the others of Berserker Clan who had helped him hijack the spaceship.

If Cyrus died, he'd never get a chance to rescue Dr. Wexx or Chief Monitor Argon of Teleship *Discovery*. Cyrus had traveled the two hundred and thirty light-years from Earth with them. They had come to colonize the Eden-like planets here. Instead, dinosaur aliens—the Kresh—had attacked them, capturing the Teleship and interning the crew for study. Cyrus had managed to escape, finding human allies in the star system.

Inside the ship, Cyrus shook his head. The situation was bewildering. The Kresh controlled most of the Fenris planets, most but not all. They battled the ground-dwelling Chirr, intelligent insects with vast tunnel complexes sunk deep into the two planets they controlled.

The Attack Talon's crew waited under Pulsar's clouds for good reason. A cyborg fleet was coming, and the Kresh didn't know about it.

So, how did Cyrus know? For a moment, he grinned. His best friend was a psionic master born in the Fenris System. He was a young man named Klane. With his amazing mental powers, Klane had discovered the approaching cyborgs and a closer menace.

The Chirr had burrowed deep under the surfaces of Fenris II and III, named Heenhiss and Glegan respectively. For generations, hidden deep underground, the Chirr had constructed spaceships. Soon, possibly in days, the Nest Intelligences of the Chirr would launch ten thousand warships to battle the Kresh, trying to wrest control of the Fenris System from the dinosaurs.

When that happened, the crew of the hijacked Attack Talon could make its move.

Yet none of that was going to matter in about ten seconds. From an open access hatch, grav-plates howled with complaint and smoke billowed. The stench of electrical burning told Cyrus all he needed to know. Frightened curses rose next, and two unseen techs began to shout.

While holding his breath, Cyrus moved to the hatch, waving smoke from his face. He peered into the gloom. Flames flickered from a panel. Lower down, an exposed grav-plate glowed a dangerous orange color. One of the techs sprayed flames with foam from an extinguisher. The other held a heavy wrench, pointing at the glowing plate.

If the anti-G devices failed, everyone aboard the hijacked ship would die as the vessel plunged deep into the planet's gaseous interior.

"What's wrong with the machine?" Cyrus shouted.

The two techs looked up through the glass of their rebreathers. Fear burned in their dark eyes. The orange glow deepened, and a *screech* sounded from the plate. That whipped the techs' heads around.

The one with the extinguisher shouted incoherently, aiming his device at the radiating grav-plate. The second tech lowered his shoulder, shoving his mate aside. Then he raised the wrench and swung, striking a protrusion on the plate. A metallic cap popped off. The wrench-wielding tech dropped his tool, unhooked a long device from his belt, and shoved the stiletto part into the protrusion's narrow opening.

"No!" shouted the tech on the floor. "You'll kill us if you do that!"

The second tech never hesitated. He plunged the device into the slot until it *clicked* and twisted hard to the right.

The howling quit as the plate ground inside, the grating worsening by the moment. Around Cyrus, bulkheads buckled, and the deck shifted under his feet. He stumbled, and the metallic screeching told him the ship would soon twist open, letting in the methane atmosphere.

The tech holding the thin device yelled. He let go of the tool, shaking his hand. Then he grabbed the handle again and yelled even louder, snatching his digits away. The smell of cooked flesh rose with a trickle of smoke from his skin.

"What are you trying to do?" Cyrus shouted. "Maybe I can help."

The tech looked up. Through his grimace of pain, he shouted, "The sensor shaft has burned out! We knew it would in time. But if I can connect the Kami rod to the liberator spool—"

Cyrus stopped listening to the technobabble. He'd have to do this by feel. Grabbing the sides of the hatch, he jumped down into the smoke. He didn't wear a rebreather like the techs, but he pinched his nose and squinted. He was a lean young man with steely muscles. He was also a psionic Special from Earth. With his low-grade mental ability, rated Fourth Class, he'd helped power the Faster-than-Light drive that had allowed the Teleship *Discovery* to reach the Fenris System. The Kresh had captured the Teleship and now they attempted to replicate the sabotaged star-drive at High Station 3.

"We're doomed!" shouted the tech with the burned hand. "I'd thought to—"

"Shut up!" Cyrus shouted, coughing afterward. The smoke stung his throat. "Let me concentrate." Despite the electrical smoke and the burnt stench and his coughing, he closed his eyes and gathered his telekinesis. Reaching out with it, he sensed what the tech had attempted to do. A red-hot rod had fused in its chamber. If he could move it . . . ah, that must be the liberator spool . . .

A flare in Cyrus's cranium told him he'd have a headache after this. Clenching his teeth, he mentally freed the fused metal. He dissipated heat, and that made his noggin hurt badly. This was harder than he'd realized. Concentrating, he blasted the rod with telekinesis—nudging it—and automated sequences finally took over.

The grinding stopped. So did the torturous screeching all around him. The bulkheads quit shaking, and the cyclone sounds powered down. The override system took over, and the grav-plates began working again, dampening the gas giant's tremendous gravity so it no longer tore the spaceship apart.

A ferocious headache pounded to life, making Cyrus nauseous. He must have used more psionic strength than he realized. His fingers dropped away from his nose. He inhaled smoke and his head jerked back at the acrid bite in his nostrils. He began to cough harder than ever. Then the foul electrical taste reached the back of his throat. Doubling over, he coughed harder yet, and he shuddered. He was going to vomit.

Hands grabbed him. Someone shoved a rebreather over his face.

Cyrus breathed pure air. That helped. He swallowed, forcing his body to relax. His head still hurt, but he was able to open his stinging eyes. Through his tears, he noticed the tech with the burnt palm grinning at him. The man clapped him on the shoulder with his uninjured hand, making Cyrus stagger. The man pointed at the grav-plate. The orange glow had disappeared. It looked normal again.

"We're going to be okay," the tech shouted.

Cyrus nodded, which was a bad idea. He bit back a groan. He had to lie down. Soon now, he wasn't going to be able to see. The coming headache would be worse than any migraine. Probably, he wouldn't be able to hold anything down for at least a day.

"You saved us, at least for a little while longer," the tech said.

Cyrus managed a grin. He knew the Kresh were hunting for them, and the aliens had psi-adepts able to detect the use of his talent . . . if they were close enough. But he hadn't had a choice, right? Die now or die later. He'd chosen later. Besides, Klane had mind-scanned near space several hours ago. No Kresh vessel had been close to Pulsar. Thus, it was impossible anyone had been able to detect his use of telekinesis. He had nothing to worry about, nothing at all.

Cyrus vomited, and blackness descended over his vision. Using his minimal talent almost always cost him. Why couldn't he be powerful like his friend Klane?

No. Don't worry about that. We're alive, and we're safe for a little longer. Now, if I can just find my way to a quiet hall . . .

2

The raptor-shaped Kresh—Dagon Dar FIFTH—stood in the scanning chamber of his special Battle Fang *Whet Steel*. He was twice the height of an unmodified human, with gray scaly skin and a blue robe. He had a crocodilian snout and a long tail, and maintained exceptional decorum due to his fabled, coldly reasoned logic. Even in the Innermost Circle of the Hundred—the alien political entity that ruled the Fenris System—none could outthink him. It was why he held the rank of Majestic Interrogator, and it was why he knew that sooner or later he would find the Humanity Ultimates somewhere in orbit around Pulsar.

"Revered One," said a tall humanoid with an elongated cranium. A *baan* encircled the forehead, a silver circuit that extended the human's psionic range. The Bo Taw, for such his kind was named, sat up. That movement removed the *baan* from the amplifier discs, which were attached to twin prongs curving down into the larger machine.

There were seven other Bo Taw in the chamber, each in a cubicle near the bulkheads. Each wore a forehead *baan* pressed against amplifier discs as he or she mentally scanned near space, using psionic power. Kresh did not possess such talents, which was why they used gene-warped humans for the task, and why each human had been induced to love those of the master race. It was the best way to ensure obedience.

With deadly elegance, Dagon Dar turned to the Bo Taw who had addressed him. The human kept his gaze lowered in reverence.

"Report," Dagon Dar said.

"I detected a telekinetic impulse," the human said in a low tone. "It was of short duration and uncommonly weak. Therefore, I could not pinpoint its exact origin. Yet I believe . . ."

"Finish your thought," Dagon Dar said. He disliked excitement or rushing anyone needlessly. He desired full data before acting, and thus exhibited great patience even for a Kresh.

"Revered One, as unbelievable as it may sound, I'm sure the thought originated somewhere in the gas giant's upper atmosphere."

Because Dagon Dar wanted truth, he hadn't told the servants his suspicions. Psionic talents were unreliable at times. Worse, such individuals were prone to fabricating mental mirages. Therefore, at his orders, the Bo Taw searched around Pulsar, but they didn't know for what. It was unlikely any creature subsisting in a one-G environment could be within the atmosphere of Pulsar. Certainly one could rely on grav-plates for a time, but that would be risky. Pulsar's intense gravity would soon burn out such devices. Not even Humanity Ultimate fools would be so rash. That, in any regard, would be the unspoken consensus. Dagon Dar did not care to deal in those, however. Facts about reality and those alone were his passion so he could add to the *Codex of All Knowledge.*

The Kresh now felt the faint stirring of the other Bo Taw in the chamber. None looked up, of course. That would be a breach of protocol and might warrant punishment. None wished for that, nor did they care to lose face before him or their peers. Bo Taw were the highest-ranked among the human herd and prickly about their status.

"Was there anything else you wished to add?" Dagon Dar asked.

"No, Revered One."

"Continue to monitor the ether."

With a *click* of metal against metal, the Bo Taw pressed his *baan* against the amplifying discs, closing his eyes as he searched near space with a combination of telepathy and telekinesis.

The man had given him interesting data, and it was exactly as Dagon Dar had foreseen. Where else could the rebels hide? Nowhere else made any sense, given the stolen Attack Talon's origin point on the moon of Jassac. Therefore, logically, the rebels must have risked Pulsar's high gravity, attempting to hide in the upper atmosphere.

Yes, yes, his search was starting to come together.

Dagon Dar knew himself as the most logical and rational being in the Fenris System. Yet it was gratifying to see his deductions playing out as expected.

Am I not the Majestic Interrogator? Did the FIRST not request my direct participation in solving this mystery?

Dagon Dar took two steps toward the main screen. The claws of his large hind talons scraped against the flooring. Pulsar showed on the screen, a blue-green gas giant with banded colors swirling with a multitude of high cumulous storm clouds.

He'd arrived at this reasoned position after three weeks of study, speculation, and questioning. Yes, over three weeks ago a ripple of discontent had spread throughout the Fenris System. Humans had slain high-ranked Kresh, one of the Hundred itself, Zama Dee the 73rd, in fact. That was a crime against the ordered structure of reality.

Kresh ruled because of their superiority. Humans served with love in their hearts due to their inferiority and easy malleability. A few isolated subjects showed aberrant behavior, becoming . . . yes, becoming Resisters. None of those had ever possessed the means to inflict deadly damage, not on the scale shown on the moon Jassac.

The unbelievable had intruded upon the thoughts of the highest philosopher kings, the Innermost Circle, those ranked ONE through NINE, the single-digit Immaculates. They discussed the anomaly and came to a swift decision, sending *him* to the scene of the terrorism. Question: Did the murders originate in the minds of Humanity Ultimates or did it have something to do with the escaped Earthling?

As he studied the screen, Dagon Dar used a claw of his upper limb to scratch his jaw.

Three weeks in Pulsar's gravitational system had taught him many interesting facts. The moon Jassac orbited the gas giant. The reddish moon with its uplands and chasm valleys held spectacular vistas, to be sure. Zama Dee the 73rd and others had set up terraforming stations on the planetoid, attempting to remake it into the lost Kresh home world of long ago.

The ecosystem, at present, allowed the Kresh and unmodified human servants to live in the deep valleys. The air had congealed thickly enough down there to breathe unaided. Perhaps as interesting, Zama Dee and others had released wild humans onto the sparse uplands. The *wilds* lived like primitives and indulged in ancient superstitions. A quick study of the situation on Jassac had taught Dagon Dar that some of the human tribes possessed psionic-able shamans.

Dagon Dar scratched his jaw harder. Allowing psionic individuals among the primitives struck him as rash. Yes, the thirst for understanding, to fulfill the *Codex of All Knowledge*, drove every right-thinking Kresh to a lifetime of diligent study. But to give unleashed humans such an edge . . . it struck him as wrong.

What propelled Zama Dee to do such a thing?

He hissed, telling himself he had other quarry. There would be time enough to delve into the . . . the stupidity of Zama Dee and her compatriots.

During the past three weeks, Dagon Dar had scoured Jassac, collecting data. He had visited Zama Dee's city, seen the destruction to the Operant Tower where her technicians and mentalists had attempted to pry open the intellect of this Anointed One.

The humans certainly develop complicated myths. It must be a byproduct of their emotion-driven reason.

Because of their emotions, the rebellious humans had driven a captured shuttle into the tower. As commandos, they jumped out and slew many, apparently freeing the key specimen. Soon thereafter, they took the shuttle into orbit. There, it appeared, they captured Zama Dee's Attack Talon. The vessel had promptly disappeared.

As Majestic Interrogator, Dagon Dar began asking questions, probing, searching. Where had the attacking humans originated? He had found the wreckage of a grav-sled in the Jassac uplands. The sled's design pointed him to High Station 3. The artificial habitat orbited Pulsar several million miles from Jassac. A quick search through Zama Dee's Orbital Central records showed him that Chengal Ras the 109th had trailed a stealth vessel from High Station 3 to Jassac. Presumably, Chengal Ras destroyed the craft. Some of the craft's occupants obviously used the grav-sled to escape onto Jassac. In any case, Dagon Dar had backtracked for information, traveling to the habitat. At High Station 3, he interrogated the Earthlings, those that still lived. He had walked through the Teleship named *Discovery*. The name implied curiosity among the Earthlings. Clearly, they were intelligent. They had invented a star-drive, where the Kresh had not.

Dagon Dar could give credit where credit was due. He prided himself on the rare ability. Kresh had captured the Teleship several cycles ago when it first appeared in the outermost asteroids of the Fenris System. The humans had fought with cunning, and the captured crew had provided interesting specimens for study and later, for dissection.

Yes . . . he had probed and questioned the Earthers, and questioned captured High Station 3 Resisters and then—

He had found two facts of amazing utility. One, a Special named Cyrus Gant had escaped confinement and later escaped from High Station 3. He had piloted the stealth-craft to Jassac. The Earthling had also no doubt recruited upland Jassac primitives, using them as soldiers during the tower attack in the city. That was the origin of the deadliness: the Earthling.

A new problem asserted itself. According to Earther records, this Cyrus Gant possessed weak psionic abilities. How then had he masked himself sufficiently from routine Bo Taw mind probes to perform these prodigies? The answer had given Dagon Dar priceless information. He believed it might propel him from FIFTH to FOURTH.

Among the High Station 3 Resisters was a red-haired female. She practiced a mind trick called a null. That null allowed a psi-able sentient to disappear from psionic tracking. Clearly, the woman taught Cyrus the trick, and Cyrus must have taught the freed Anointed One. That's how the hijacked Attack Talon had remained invisible these past few weeks.

Resister lore told of a human savior. What a conceit indeed. The Anointed One would possess fantastic extrasensory perception great enough to defeat every so-called enemy. As if humans could live well-adjusted lives on their own. Study after study proved they needed Kresh guidance to lead meaningful lives of worth. Still, the one named Klane seemed to have extraordinary psionic abilities, and he must have used the null to make the stolen Attack Talon disappear long enough for the rebels to reach a hiding place.

The logical place of hiding, given the various parameters, was in the highest clouds of Pulsar.

Dagon Dar grinned, revealing gleaming teeth in a crocodilian snout. Others could practice the null. Yes, his strongest adepts took turns on each spaceship, rendering them invisible to the Anointed One. Surely, as a precaution, the so-called savior human kept watch around Pulsar for Kresh ships. Now, because of the null, Klane would not find them, even if he were many times stronger than the most powerful Bo Taw.

Dagon Dar eased upward onto his hind claws, a sign of eagerness. He had many questions, many tests he wished to perform on Klane. And oh, he had devised gruesome punishments to practice on this

Cyrus Gant, the Kresh Killer. That one would face many agonies before he expired in hideous payment for his crimes.

As the cylindrical Battle Fangs approached near Pulsar orbit, it would simply be a matter of time until someone visually spotted the stolen craft. Yet he had to do this precisely or the gas giant would claim the Humanity Ultimates. Well, the actual killer would be the massive gravity. He had to keep the humans from diving deep into the planet in a last act of rebellious suicide.

Dagon Dar hissed. He would not allow the rebels such an easy death. Oh no, he had too many streams of data he wanted to tease out of the interesting specimens. And what he wanted, the Majestic Interrogator got.

3

Cyrus opened his eyes with a start. He sweated as he lay on his pallet. His mouth was parched, and a terrible sense of doom filled him.

Clenching his teeth, he sat up and swung his legs off the bed. He must have slept for hours. With the rest, he could now see after a fashion. A few splotches were in his vision.

He noticed that he still wore his boots. Jana must not have come in. She would have tugged them off his feet for him.

His was a small chamber, about the size of his sleeping quarters aboard *Discovery*. The journey from Earth to the Fenris System seemed to have taken place a lifetime ago.

He stood, and his head throbbed. Probably, the best thing would be to continue sleeping. He couldn't, though. Staggering to a box, he rummaged in it and took out a clean shirt. He needed to shower, but water was limited aboard the Attack Talon.

How much longer can we hide down here?

He would have shaken his head, but that would have hurt too much. The dream, the vision—

He looked up and suppressed a groan. From his early days in the Latin Kings gang, he'd learned to hide weaknesses of any kind. That was so long ago those times in bottom-level Milan, in Italia Sector. Would he ever see Earth again?

Cyrus wondered if he'd just had a precognitive dream or vision. Those often came true. He'd never shown an affinity for those, but maybe his strange adventures on Jassac had rattled something loose in his mind.

He couldn't remember his dream, the details. An overpowering sense of doom filled him. It was vague and unformed, but it was there. Doom . . . death . . .

Yes! He felt the immediacy of death. That constricted his throat. He'd faced death many times, and he'd cheated death on each of those occasions.

Am I doomed to die soon? Is that what I'm sensing?

He tried to swallow but couldn't. His mouth and throat were still too parched.

Digging in his box, he picked up a bottle. Using his teeth, he eased out its cork. He took a swig, swallowing alien whiskey. That made him cough, and it warmed his throat, his chest, and finally his stomach. He took another, longer swallow.

This was good stuff. He corked it, shoving the bottle under his clothes. Jana hated him having whiskey because she didn't like him drunk. He searched inside the box until he pulled out a knife.

The sheath was some kind of alien leather, the handle, bone. He drew out the blade. Inspecting its razor sharpness, he grinned. Sure, it wasn't a vibrio-blade, but it was a good knife. He used it to cut people in Milan when they hadn't paid on time.

Flipping the knife, Cyrus caught it by the tip. Yeah, he felt groggy and unsteady, but knives were an extension of his reflexes. Most people liked guns better, and for distance work, pistols were superior. But a knife could often beat a gun in close quarters. For one thing, most people became nervous when faced with a knife. It had psychological advantages, and it took a certain kind of fighter to go blade-to-blade against someone else.

Cyrus twirled the knife for two rotations. He caught it neatly by the handle, and he flipped it again. He began doing it unconsciously, twirling it three rotations and catching it by the handle.

The premonition of death returned. It throbbed in him like a heartbeat, and he knew the sense was true. Could he beat a precognitive dream?

I mean, what good are they if you can't fight them?

Cyrus snarled, and he twirled the blade four rotations, catching it by the handle. He'd flipped knives thousands of times, maybe ten thousand, one hundred thousand.

As he flicked the knife, he tried to remember the dream. No. All he got was darkness, black doom, death.

He spun the knife and it twirled as he tried to catch it. The razor tip slashed the tip of his thumb. With a jerk, he yanked his hand away. The knife clattered against the deck plates.

Cyrus stood there, watching bright red blood ooze from his fingertip. He didn't love getting cut, but it wasn't a big deal. Missing the catch, though—

Is that a sign of bad luck? He snorted. *Of course it is. I'm going to die. I've dreamed of my death. That's why I can't remember it exactly.*

He could find Niens the mentalist and ask the man if that was right. Niens would know. Yet that would be cowardly, right? It would admit he was scared, and Cyrus never admitted that to anyone. He'd learned long ago that a man had to face his fears head on, or he had to run to fight again another day. What he never did was let others know he was frightened. That was the great sin against survival down in Level 40.

Cyrus wiped the blood on his pants, picked up the knife, and shoved it into its sheath. Then he opened his shirt and tied the blade against his side. It was always wise to have a hidden weapon.

He needed food, water, maybe a talk with Jana. How much longer did he have to live? No. That was the wrong question. If he'd been marked for death, did that mean the others would necessarily perish? He had to figure that out and make sure they lived.

Yeah. He wanted to get back to Earth. Well, he wanted to save Jana and the others. He wanted to free the humans under the Kresh tyranny. He also wanted to warn Earth about the Kresh, the Chirr, and most of all, about the cyborgs from one hundred years ago who had escaped into space. Earth needed to know about these enemies.

Stepping into the corridor, it occurred to him he should talk with Klane. If anyone could figure out his dream, maybe help, it would be the Anointed One.

The walk helped clear his head a little. Few people were aboard, so it didn't surprise him the corridors were empty. There was the shuttle crew, some Attack Talon techs, a handful of Berserker Clan warriors, a soldier, Klane, and Cyrus himself.

While he walked down the Attack Talon's corridor, Cyrus heard groaning. Concerned, he rushed into the nearby chamber.

As if he were a priest kneeling before a pope, Klane knelt before a holoimage of the Fenris System with his face buried in his hands. The youth—he was a few years younger than Cyrus—was naked from the waist up, although he wore black pants without shoes. Klane was thin and pale, with reddish, puckered scars crisscrossing his frame. A greasy junction-stone dangled from his throat, held by a twist of Tash-Toi hemp.

Long ago, in a Bussard ramjet generational ship, Klane's ancestors had come to the star system from Earth. The Kresh had captured the vessel and the colonists within. The aliens had then availed themselves of every female egg. Some they'd gene-warped and others had only been slightly altered, fertilized in test tubes. The people on Jassac's uplands had been slightly modified with rugged bodies and cavernous lungs.

Klane had been something different, possibly a failed Kresh experiment. As a baby, the Kresh had deposited him on the sands near Clan Tash-Toi. He'd grown up as a seeker's apprentice, weaker than the other children, but possessed of psi-powers. The junction-stone had been a crutch to help him focus his abilities. Maybe that's why he still wore it now.

As Klane knelt with his hands pressed against his face, he groaned once more.

Cyrus wondered if he should back away and leave the man in peace.

"No," Klane said.

Cyrus's head swayed. "You're reading my thoughts?"

With his face still buried in his hands, Klane nodded.

Cyrus understood that he had a weak talent. But he hadn't thought anyone could read his mind without him being aware.

"It's easy once you know how to do it," Klane said.

"Sure, if you say so."

Klane looked up. His blue eyes were dry. Yet even as he stared at Cyrus, a grimace twisted his features.

"What's wrong?" Cyrus asked.

Klane thumped his chest.

"Did you exercise too much? Overdo it, maybe?" asked Cyrus.

Klane shook his head.

"What do you think—"

"I'm still linked with Timor Malik."

"You mean the soldier on Heenhiss, on Fenris II?" asked Cyrus. "The one whose body you inhabited a while ago."

"Yes . . ." Klane groaned, and he collapsed, hitting the deck plates with his chest.

Cyrus rushed to him. He knelt—

"Don't touch me," Klane said as he pushed up to a sitting position. He breathed deeply and he exhaled. "It . . . it's happening. It's really happening. The sights, they overpowered me for a moment."

"What sights are you talking about?"

Klane's head snapped higher, although his eyes became unfocused. He moved his lips, but no sounds issued.

Cyrus glanced at the holoimage of the Fenris System. The blue-white star burned hot. It was bigger than Sol by twenty percent.

Around it circled a Mars-sized planet in a Mercury orbit. The sphere was burnt nickel-iron, mountains and valleys of it. Heenhiss and Glegan were Earth-like planets in a temperate orbit. The Kresh used hundreds of millions of modified human soldiers to battle the Chirr underground in their tunnels on Heenhiss. Timor Malik was a soldier there, a gene-warped Vomag; Klane had inhabited his mind and body several weeks ago.

With his unfocused eyes, Klane blinked slowly. His lips moved again. "I can't believe it," he whispered.

"What do you see?" Cyrus asked.

"Not me," Klane whispered. "Timor Malik is seeing this."

"And you see what he sees?"

"That, and feel what he feels . . ." Klane said, lapsing into silence.

4

Timor Malik was a Vomag solider in Cohort Invincible. A First Rank in charge of a squad, he was short and stocky with arms dangling almost down to his knees.

He wore a helmet, a torso plate, and tough synthetic breeches. Today, he had perimeter duty, carrying a heavy repeater, with extra ammo in his pack. He led a squad, ten soldiers much like him. They guarded testers, a trio of technicians with long seismic devices, searching for secret Chirr openings.

The spires of tall, equatorial jungle trees towered in the distance, darkly green with purple trunks. Buzzbirds circled, occasionally dipping down, no doubt trying to spear howlers gathering spire-nuts. Closer to the squad were gigantic sand towers blasted in half, former Chirr vents that had helped cool the deep nest.

The 624th Army to which Timor belonged had dropped onto an equatorial nest. Heavy crawlers and five-man attack-cars—flyers—had sprayed death-chemicals first. Then special jumpers in battle armor had cleared the jungle zone of warrior Chirr. Afterward, the troop dirigibles arrived from the northern polar region. Timor had debarked, part of the Tenth Underground Assault Division. They had lost thousands battling their way deeper into the tunnels with sister divisions doing likewise in a circular area. After that—Timor had a gap in his memories. The gap troubled him. He'd led soldiers deep into secondary Chirr tunnels. He could remember that much. Then, nothing: blank, and he'd awoken on the surface, having no idea how he'd gotten there.

Naturally, the commanders had processed him through endless inquires, mind-probing by a Bo Taw until he stood before a loud high-officer demanding answers. Timor must have satisfied them, because the high-officer had assigned him to a new squad that had perimeter duty. Well, this was an equatorial nest raid. If he'd been in a polar region, they would have put him in confinement for sure. In the equatorial regions, every soldier carried a weapon, even those under punishment duty or arrest.

At the moment, the majority of the 624th Army's one hundred thousand soldiers rushed deeper underground, battling toward a Nest Intelligence. The rumors coming out of the hole were that the Chirr had grown thicker in numbers and more ferocious, a sure sign the assault divisions neared the Nest Intelligence. There had even been some surface attacks. The Chirr had come up somewhere. This patrol was one of hundreds to discover the location.

A roar of sound in the sky caused Timor to glance up over his shoulder. A squad of flyers raced somewhere, sleek attack-cars with flamer canisters underneath.

Timor shook his head. The Chirr must be crazy to attack above-ground. They never won a fight on the surface. Why did they bother now when they could do more decisive damage underground?

"First Rank!" a soldier shouted.

"Keep it calm," Timor said.

The soldier nodded. "I spied movement ahead."

"Formation C!" Timor shouted in a voice filled with authority.

The squad deployed as the testers picked up their locators, racing to the rear. They barely got there in time.

A Chirr squeezed out of one of the wrecked vents. The black creature had glistening chitin with six scuttling legs. Two serrated pincers clicked and a long, thin flexible tail whipped behind. The Chirr squealed and its eyestalks surged forward, focusing on them.

Timor's lips curled with distaste.

The Chirr, as long as a man was tall, bobbed up and down on its six legs. Then it leaped, landing thirty feet farther on the ground. Timor could hear claws scratch against the stony soil. With deceptive speed, the Chirr raced at them, its six legs a blur of motion.

"Engage by the numbers!" Timor shouted. The first soldier sighted the creature. Everyone in the squad had a number. The first soldier squeezed off a three-bullet burst from his repeater. Exploding slugs struck the creature's upper torso, blowing apart chitin and causing black gore to rain on nearby tremor stalks.

The Chirr squealed with pain and it toppled sideways, sliding to a halt. Another trio of shots in the braincase killed the thing.

Maybe that was the signal for the others. Chirr boiled out of the old vents, squeezing up with unnatural speed.

"Grenadiers!" Timor shouted. Each squad had two. "Give the Chirr a second to gather below the vents. Then lob a pulse bomb down on them."

The secret to battling Chirr on the surface was keeping your head. If soldiers did that, it was hard to lose. Well, until the Chirr brought up the heavies. These were the sweepers, pure bio-creatures without any modern weapons.

Like fleas, the sweepers leaped onto the ground. As they gathered, they squealed and clicked their pincers. In seconds, they turned, focusing on the soldiers. The bugs surged toward them, and tiny black objects sailed overhead.

The pulse bombs detonated, flattening the Chirr, blowing apart their chitin-armored bodies.

Timor aimed his heavy repeater, and he shot individual sweepers that escaped immediate destruction. The attack intensified as more and more Chirr boiled out of the vents.

"Fall back by sections!" Timor shouted.

Three-man sections leapfrogged back as the pulse bombs and exploding slugs continued to devastate the bugs. Then dirt erupted where the squad had first been. Chirr exploded out of the ground, looking for someone to shred.

Timor grinned viciously as he took a small box out of his breeches. With a stubby thumb, he pressed a button. A previously hidden detox bomb ignited, and Chirr parts rained.

He hated bugs. It was part of his conditioning. To kill them brought intense satisfaction.

Timor waited, and he expected to call division and request mortar fire. If the bugs came up too fast and thick, he could ask for a bombing run. Instead, the Chirr attack ceased.

The squad hunkered down behind chitter sage and waited.

"Where are they, First Rank?" a soldier asked Timor.

"Don't know," he said, but he thought it was a good question.

Suddenly, the ground shook. Timor could still see the broken vents. They crumpled, toppling over, burying the Chirr parts around them.

"The heavies are erupting!" a soldier shouted.

That's exactly what Timor expected to see, but the trooper was wrong. Instead, maybe several miles away, dirt and jungle trees blasted into the air. They blew upward, and he realized the junk must have been flying high indeed for him to see it from here. There was a lot of it, too. That would take extreme explosions, enough to cause the quake here.

Then, solid columns of light blazed into the sky, clawing upward into the heavens.

A soldier crashed down beside Timor. The man panted before asking, "What are those things, First Rank?"

As the soldier asked, a shrill whine made Timor wince in pain. The distant beams of light intensified in color. More dirt and trees exploded upward, closer this time. Again, heavy columns of light speared into the heavens. The whining sounds grew worse until every soldier clapped his hands over his ears. The whine came from the beams, or perhaps the hidden beam projectors.

"Those are rays!" Timor shouted.

"Shooting at what?" the soldier asked.

Timor craned his head, looking up at the clouds. The beams burned through them. "Shooting at spaceships, I guess."

"The bugs are shooting into space?"

The question put a cold knot in Timor's gut. The Chirr had never done that before. He didn't like that they did it now while he was stuck at an equatorial nest.

Then the earth rumbled and shook so badly that Timor's teeth rattled. An even louder explosion threw him upward into the air. He landed hard with the breath *oofing* out of him.

"Was that a bomb?" a soldier shouted. "It sounded like an atomic bomb."

Timor nodded. It did indeed sound like one. Then huge black objects appeared in the sky. More nuclear ignitions thundered with noise. Blinding light and vast flames roared behind the black objects as they jerked higher into the air.

"Are those Chirr spaceships?" asked a soldier.

Timor stared at the soldier. First, the Chirr had fired beams into . . . what, into orbital space? Maybe the bugs tried to clear away Kresh laser platforms. That made sense. Now the Chirr launched spaceships into orbit. They didn't launch atmospheric flyers to clear the air. No, they sent warships into low orbit. If the bugs could clear space of Kresh laser platforms and spaceships, what would happen to all the soldiers on the ground and in the tunnels?

A sick feeling spread through Timor's chest. The bugs might cut off the 624th Army from resupply. That would mean they were all alone at an equatorial nest with thousands of miles of jungle between them and the nearest polar region.

5

In the stolen Attack Talon cruising the high atmosphere on Pulsar, Cyrus listened in awe as Klane gasped out Timor Malik's story.

Would the new Chirr space fleet defeat the Kresh around Heenhiss? How well could the bugs operate in space? They were used to three-dimensional warfare in the nests. Certainly, they could adjust to space. Of course, they *could*. The question would be how quickly they would do this.

Cyrus noticed that Klane had become quiet.

The Anointed One opened his eyes. He looked at Cyrus.

"You've been telling me what Timor Malik sees," Cyrus said.

With an effort, Klane climbed to his feet. Left-handed, he grasped the junction-stone dangling from his throat. He spoke in a thoughtful voice.

"I used to think the Kresh were demons, but not anymore. The Chirr are the demons. They're long, black, glisten with evil, and climb out of the hot ground. If they defeat the Kresh, what will happen to the clans on Jassac? Becoming protein for the bugs is worse than living in subjection to the Kresh."

"Don't forget the cyborgs," Cyrus said. "If they win, they'll turn everyone into monsters."

"That is why we must reach High Station 3," Klane said. "We must use your Teleship and flee to Homeworld. They can return with a battle fleet and destroy the aliens."

"That might take too long," Cyrus said. "By the time we travel to Earth and come back again, all the Fenris humans might be dead."

"What other choice do we have? If we attempt to help the Fenris humans with our lone warship, we'll fail. The people here will lose to whatever race is victorious in the coming struggle."

"Yeah," Cyrus said. "That's the problem; that, and we lack a Teleship."

Klane's eyes widened as he searched Cyrus. "That isn't why you come to me: to discuss our objective. You've had a precognitive dream."

Cyrus wanted to tell the Anointed One to stay out of his mind.

"I can't help it," Klane said. "You project so strongly."

"No I don't. I was trained to hide my thoughts behind a mind shield."

"Trained by weaklings," Klane said. "I don't mean any offense by that, but Earth's Specials are inferior to the Bo Taw and to the seekers on Jassac."

"Earth humans built a star-drive, not the Kresh."

"True," Klane said, "and completely immaterial to our subject. Fenris psionic humans are superior to Sol psionics. That's going to change everything one way or another."

Cyrus thought about that. "Okay. So . . . can you teach me a proper mind shield?"

"Maybe . . ."

A chill made Cyrus's shoulders shake. "You mean you could if I lived long enough, but seeing as how I'm going to die soon, it doesn't matter."

"No. I can't pierce your dreams. The memories . . . something hides those from my view."

"So I *do* have a strong mind shield."

"I think it's something else. Maybe you don't want to remember the dream. You've rejected it."

"Because it was too awful to think about?" asked Cyrus.

"I'm not a trained mentalist. We could ask Niens."

"I'd rather not."

"As you wish," Klane said with a disinterested shrug.

"So . . . if I have long enough left for you to teach me, why can't you show me the proper techniques for a powerful mind shield?"

"I will be blunt: because you're too weak."

Cyrus felt the familiar heat rise in him, and he stuffed it away. Klane was only speaking the truth as he saw it. Cyrus pursed his lips. "Okay. I asked for that, I suppose."

"I meant no disrespect."

Cyrus studied the young man. Klane had open features and a likeable way about him. Cyrus believed he had a sense about people. It wasn't a psionic gift, but an ability to read character. He realized Klane truly didn't look down on him. On Earth, the variously ranked psi-classes looked down on those weaker than they were. Seeing that he belonged to the bottom class, other Specials had always looked down on him, and Cyrus resented it.

"I have a question," Klane asked.

"Shoot."

"Do you mistrust Mentalist Niens?"

Cyrus wanted to say, "Why don't you just read my mind for the answer." Instead, he said, "Maybe a little."

"So do I."

"Can't you read his mind?"

"Not as easily as . . . as I can others."

"You were going to say, 'Not as easily as I can read *your* mind.'"

"Since you are correct, I could accuse you of reading my mind."

Cyrus grinned. "Sure. What's your point? Why are you asking me about Niens?"

"Don't you want to know why I mistrust him first?"

"Okay."

"I'm uncertain his loyalty conditioning for the Kresh has been fully broken," Klane said.

Cyrus nodded. That was one of the ways the Kresh kept the telepathic Bo Taw under control, by brainwashing them early to love their masters. The Kresh also wore mechanical mind shields, protecting them from their psionic slaves. With those shields, the dinosaurs were safe from mind attacks.

"Can't you just break the conditioning for Niens?" Cyrus asked. "Simply enter his mind and fiddle around with it?"

"I might strip away his loyalty conditioning that way, but in turn, I might make him . . . I'm not sure what the right word is for the concept. Ah, I might turn him into a killer."

"A soldier?" Cyrus asked.

"No. Into a man who hates so strongly that he enjoys destroying lives."

"Oh. You could turn him into a homicidal maniac."

Klane stared at him—and Cyrus realized the Anointed One was reading his thoughts.

"Yes, exactly," Klane said, "a homicidal maniac."

"You can do such a thing to a man's mind?"

"I believe so. It would be delicate work, but after what happened to me on Jassac . . ."

"Too bad you couldn't turn individual Bo Taw into homicidal maniacs against the Kresh," Cyrus said.

Klane became thoughtful. "Yes. I might be able to do that."

It was Cyrus's turn to stare. He snapped his fingers and began to pace with excitement. "Maybe that's how we can defeat the Kresh. You could start a rebellion among their Bo Taw."

Klane pursed his lips. "Should we attempt such a thing as the Kresh fight the Chirr for control of the star system?"

"We can't worry about the orbital battle around Heenhiss right now. My idea is to use the Kresh's strength against them. Have you ever heard of the Trojan horse?"

"No, but I see the story in your mind."

"Yeah, go ahead. Scan it."

Klane was quiet for a time, until he said, "I have it. The Greeks tricked the Trojans. But by your memories, the gods helped them do it."

"Yeah, yeah," Cyrus said, waving that aside. "The point is the Greeks used an inside job to defeat the Trojans. We can use the Bo Taw against the Kresh."

"By having them trying to murder their masters?" asked Klane.

"Not exactly," Cyrus said. "Maybe it would be wiser to reroute the conditioning. Listen. You're supposed to be the savior of Fenris humanity. Great visionaries of the past had precognitive dreams about you. Doesn't that mean you need to use your psionics in some new, clever fashion?"

"I do not know."

"The mind is like a computer," Cyrus said. "Well, it is in certain ways. Sometimes on Earth, hackers made a programming virus, a worm in the code. You've suggested that you already know how to fashion a mind virus that turns Bo Taw love into hate, or mentalist love into hate. What if you altered the conditioning a different way? Make it so the Bo Taw love you or love the idea of humans rebelling against the Kresh."

"Interesting," Klane said. "I cannot guarantee I could do this, but if I probed a Bo Taw mind, it's possible I could discover how to do this."

Cyrus snapped his fingers. He was on a roll. "And since the Bo Taw are psi-adepts, maybe you could reroute their thinking so they would send impulses to others that would change them, too. That would make it even more like a computer virus."

"Explain the concept to me," Klane said.

"Read my thoughts," Cyrus said. "It will be quicker."

Klane stared at Cyrus. "Yes," he said shortly. "Your idea has possibilities."

"We would have to make certain the Kresh continued to fight the Chirr," Cyrus added. "We can't let the insects win."

"Agreed," Klane said. "I will ponder the idea. Yet I think in the end I will have to talk to Niens."

"Why him?"

"He is a mentalist," Klane said. "He will have insights into the brain I will have overlooked."

"First you'd better make sure about him," Cyrus said.

"Then you have no problem with me tampering with his mind?"

Cyrus hesitated. That was a big step. Niens had thrown in his lot with them. It would be wrong to tamper with his mind without telling the man first. "First see if Niens is totally with us, and then let's decide what to do next."

"Very well," Klane said. He promptly sat down cross-legged and closed his eyes.

Cyrus waited, but Klane kept his eyes closed. Finally, Cyrus backed away. He'd leave the Anointed One to his task. He needed to talk to Jana. And it would be wise to check on the grav-plates. If a space battle had begun around Heenhiss, it would soon be time for them to leave Pulsar and make their strike for High Station 3.

As Cyrus walked down the corridor, he wondered if the Kresh were slaughtering the Chirr or if it was the other way around. The best outcome would be if the two alien species obliterated each other.

"I can always hope," Cyrus said, but he feared for the future.

6

In reptilian silence, Dagon Dar watched the holo-vid footage.

He stood in his private quarters aboard the Battle Fang *Whet Steel*. The laser-fired news was more than two hours old, the time it took light to travel from Heenhiss's present orbital position around Fenris to Pulsar.

As dry hot air swirled around him, Dagon Dar witnessed the catastrophe. Gigantic beams rose from subterranean chambers in Heenhiss's planetary surface. Chirr rays destroyed orbital laser platforms. Psionic shields held for several minutes on a larger, inhabited satellite. Finally, the Bo Taw adepts must have wearied from the strain. Then, massed Chirr beams obliterated the station, cutting away swaths of satellite. Metal pieces spun into space.

One after another, the Kresh defensive stations disappeared or became molten slag. The extent of Chirr ordnance—the unrelenting beams—staggered Dagon Dar. How had the insects been able to keep it secret all this time? The mass showed years of preparation, possibly decades.

Not only was this a disaster for the military effort on Heenhiss, but for the entire Fenris Kresh. The bulk of the star system's population lived on or around Heenhiss. Three hundred habitats orbited the second planet. Some of those now came under the planetary Chirr beam assault.

That in itself was mind-numbing enough, but there was more to the tragedy.

Dagon Dar leaned forward. Could this be correct? Chirr space vessels launched from underground ports? By the data, it would appear they were nuclear-pulse craft, notable for their ability to lift hundreds of thousands of tons into near orbit. Only antimatter explosions could hurl heavier vessels into space with greater efficiency.

It would appear then, the Chirr lacked antimatter engines. Good. That gave the Kresh a chance. It might be time to use vast antimatter bombs on the Chirr-held planets.

Dagon Dar watched the unfolding assault. The hologram of Heenhiss appeared in its glory before him. Bright objects lifted from the surface. The vessels came from Continent I, from II, III, and from Continent IV. Only the polar regions failed to produce Chirr spacecraft.

A few Kresh Attack Talons had been in orbit, along with individual Battle Fangs. As far as history showed, the Kresh had never needed unified space fleets in the Fenris System. Conceivably, Kresh had practiced such fleet maneuvers in the distant past, but Dagon Dar did not know.

I must rectify the lack of knowledge, or we must learn it if we never have.

In mute astonishment, the FIFTH watched swarms of Chirr violator-ships rise to do battle. They came in their thousands, these nuclear-pulse craft. The orbital laser platforms that should have annihilated them had been turned into disassembled molecules or floating hulks.

Dagon Dar hissed, bobbing his head. Attack Talons grouped together. Good. Compared to other species, Kresh could learn a lesson astonishingly fast. As a unit, the warships targeted enemy vessels. Heavy Kresh rays struck one pulse-ship after another, causing debris to shed like shavings from a totem carving. Often, the beams destroyed a pulse-ship with a spectacular blast.

Then the subterranean rays countered the daring group. The psi-shields persisted for seconds before one Attack Talon after another winked out of existence.

"At last," Dagon Dar hissed, not because of Kresh losses, but now one of the true military craft entered the fray.

A large Kresh hammer-ship decelerated into near orbit, a cube-shaped deep-space vessel. They weren't suited for atmospheric combat, but for gaining strategic control of a star system. The situation was obviously dire for the colossal craft to come this near a planet.

The hammer-ship launched hell burners. The massive torpedoes' heat shields glowed red as they descended into the atmosphere. A titanic explosion annihilated a dozen Chirr pulse-ships. The same blast likely murdered millions on the planetary surface below. But those would mainly be Vomag deaths—soldiers, humans. They didn't count in the larger scheme of things. One could always breed more of them.

Ah-ah, glorious, glorious indeed, he thought, as more hell burners ejected from the hammer-ship. Now the insects would learn to fear. Except . . . what was this? Chirr planetary beams struck the descending objects. Despite the bi-carb casing, hell burners actually broke apart without exploding. Then one of them ignited. Once again, a white-hot nova annihilated vainglorious Chirr. Yet even as that took place, other planetary beams chewed into the ultra-armor of the hammer-ship. Surely, the vessel couldn't sustain such rays for long.

With a weary spirit, Dagon Dar saw he was right.

Almost majestically, the hammer-ship broke into drifting sections. Tiny armored pods jetted away, but it was too late. A red explosion within the pieces of the hammer-ship ensured that none of the Kresh military crew survived the vessel's destruction.

Dagon Dar absorbed the data. Even a second hammer-ship dumping gravity waves—attempting to slide into near orbit—failed to lift his spirits. There was a reason for that. Dagon Dar always had a reason for everything.

Nuclear-pulse ships exited Heenhiss's atmosphere, finally reaching orbital space. The Chirr lifters began to launch true spacecraft.

Dagon Dar subvocalized, creating a holo-board before him. He clicked his claws on holo-pads. Yes. This was depressing: an analysis of the new Chirr vessels. They boasted regular fusion drives. Had the insects used crashed Kresh vessels in the past as their models? He believed that probable.

The alien spaceships were incredibly small. Using swarming tactics, they moved en masse like insects onto the attack.

Dagon Dar slid his hind talons across the deck plates, inching closer to the main hologram. What would these tiny warships use as weaponry?

This is vital.

What would the Chirr mind conceive? What would Chirr technology allow?

Ah! Fusion-powered missiles slid from the outer hulls of these craft. The missiles zeroed in on the hammer-ship, the surviving Attack Talons, and scattered Battle Fangs.

The Chirr outnumbered the Kresh ships a thousand to one. Kresh beams reaped a bitter harvest. But it proved too little. One Chirr missile in one hundred reached its target, but that was enough.

Soon, no Kresh spacecraft orbited Heenhiss, not even the heavily armored hammer-ship.

Dagon Dar swallowed. The Chirr ships now began attacking the nearest space habitats. That was a crime against rationality. The Chirr destroyed Kresh homes, murdering a superior race.

With a hiss of triumph, Dagon Dar witnessed a unified Kresh squadron swinging around the planet. Ah, now, now, there would begin a proper annihilation of the nest aliens. These Kresh ships moved fast, with ultimate precision, murdering many individuals within the enemy swarms.

The Chirr had done damage, but—

A weird, sad cry issued from Dagon Dar's fanged jaws.

The Kresh spaceships began to drift in different vectors from each other. They no longer moved like a school of razor fins. It seemed as if the Battle Fangs and hammer-ships simply stopped functioning rationally.

Was there a nefarious Chirr tactic at work to produce such a result?

Dagon Dar turned away and his long tail whipped back and forth. This was a disaster of epic proportions.

In silence, he faced the hologram. He was the ultimate rationalist. He observed reality with true clarity.

I must catalog the Chirr vessels while I have this opportunity. Anything else is a sin against logic.

The Chirr possessed nuclear-pulse-bomb motherships. They had small swarming craft. Another species might call them fighters. No, they were perhaps bombers, larger than mere fighters. Even so, there were larger Chirr spaceships of an odd, polygon design. Those hadn't launched missiles or fired rays of any kind.

No. That is an imprecise thought. I did not observe them firing any beams. Could the Chirr have used psionics? Our Bo Taw project mind shields that can stop beams for a time. Maybe the Chirr have found an offensive, perhaps even mechanical, mind weapon.

Dagon Dar clicked his claws together. He remembered reading a report on the Kresh-Earth ship fight. The Bo Taw had used mind control on the Earthers. Could the Chirr have used something analogous on the Kresh vessels?

He brought up a larger image of a polygon-shaped craft. It had fantastic arrays of antennae. Those must help project something. The question was: What?

"FIFTH," a Kresh comm expert said over the speakers. "I have an incoming message from the FIRST of our Race."

"Relay it at once," Dagon Dar said, cocking his head.

A smoothly rational voice began to speak over the comm. It was indeed the FIRST. Dagon Dar would recognize her voice anywhere. She spoke with serenity and modulated perfection.

"Dagon Dar FIFTH, Majestic Interrogator," the FIRST said, "I will not attempt a dialogue with you. The simple reason is that I do not believe I will live long enough for your message to reach me. Thus, I will give you my final monologue. I charge you to accept it as my will and political testament for our Race."

"Done," Dagon Dar said.

"Alas," the FIRST said, "the Chirr have caught us by surprise. It was a brilliant ploy, and they have carried it through with their customary brutality."

Dagon Dar's tail swished in agitation.

"I will assume you have acquired footage of the carnage. You will have seen their tactics and seen how we attempted to defeat them with inferior force. The Chirr have reached space, but they continued to act in their customary manner—except in one particular way. I wish to address this facet in my monologue.

"First, it must be obvious to you, Dagon Dar, that you alone of the Innermost Circle will have survived this sneak attack. The others are dead, slain by the Chirr. That means you will have been elevated to FIRST. You are now the most superior. With the destruction around Heenhiss, no Kresh will come close to your intelligence and breadth of knowledge. You must guard your person with care. You must continue to expand the *Codex of All Knowledge*. Once we have pierced the mysteries of life, we shall find the Creator and present Him with our codex as a gift of love for His benevolence."

"To His benevolence," Dagon Dar recited the ancient creed.

"I charge you to guard our Race, Dagon Dar. We are the ultimate in Creation. We alone of all species love logic and rational thought. We perceive as none of the inferior races can hope to emulate."

"You speak truth," Dagon Dar whispered.

"That is why this attack is monstrously vile. Yes, I suppose one could suggest a thesis: the Chirr strive for life as every race attempts. I reject that out of hand. They have survival instincts, but they lack perception. Thus, they are inferior to us."

Dagon Dar paused thoughtfully. This present attack: might it suggest a superior intellect? Survivability might be the ultimate test of a race's utility. It would make for an interesting thesis. Then he realized that he would no longer compete against his equals, but against rough Kresh of the lower ranks. He had no need of a rarefied thesis.

No. On that path lies arrogance and dull rationality. I owe to the Race to continue to strive for excellence. If nothing else, I must begin to model perfection for those below me.

"These things are likely self-evident to you," the FIRST said. "We are attempting a mass evacuation of the Heenhiss gravitational system, but it will fail. The Chirr loathe us. They attack with the accumulated bitterness of generations. This is their hour in the sun. My calculations show a seventy-eight percent chance of total Heenhiss annihilation of us. I have already alerted the Kresh forces around Glegan. The Chirr will undoubtedly send their fleet there. Perhaps the Glegan Chirr are ready to launch another fleet. You will have to decide on the optimum course of action, Dagon Dar. It is possible the survival of our Race rests with your intellect."

Yes, he could see that.

"I will not counsel you on your course," the FIRST said. "Rather, I will tell you a secret. It is unfathomable in scope, and you may reject my thesis out of hand. I accept the possibility, and I believe that if you do reject this thought, your probability of survival will shrink by half."

Dagon Dar swished his tail. The FIRST had always been insufferably sure of her ideas. Yet here she died and he lived. Survivability was everything.

"Attend my words," she said. "The Chirr vessels approach my habitat and I will not live much longer."

She paused before starting on a new track. "There is a strange anomaly in the Fenris System, Dagon Dar. The humans came to us long ago in their colony vessel. It proved to be a great boon to our Race. The humans make wonderful slaves. Now, another colonizing vessel from Earth has crossed the depths of space to reach Fenris. So, too, have cyborgs attacked our system. The Chirr lived here and we, too, reached the star system many, many cycles ago. My question is this, Dagon Dar. Why have several spacefaring races congregated here? Is it chance that has brought this about?

"I reject such simplistic thinking. I am FIRST. I am Kresh. Reason and logic are my finest tools. I have concluded that some other agency is at work among us, drawing us here in some subtle fashion beneath our cognizance. Yes, each species lusts for Heenhiss and Glegan. Yet I believe the odds of each of us arriving here points elsewhere for the reason. I suspect that you must discover the agency at work. If you do not, it is possible that we will continue to be pawns in a process we do not understand or even conceive.

"That is my legacy to you, Dagon Dar. I will transmit my findings to your craft. You have little time, I believe. The forces working against us—"

The message ended abruptly. It left Dagon Dar staring at the holo-globe of Heenhiss. It also meant the FIRST hadn't transmitted her findings.

Two colossal thoughts invaded his thinking. One, the Chirr had won a space victory around Heenhiss and brought devastating loss to the Kresh. Two, it was possible a great mystery surrounded the Fenris System. Could the former FIRST have been correct? Or was it more likely that her unhinged thinking had caused a lapse in Kresh security to allow the insects this monumental success?

It was time to think furiously and reach a working conclusion.

What is the correct course of action? I must discover one before it is too late.

7

Klane tossed on his pallet as he dreamed. It felt like the time he'd left his body and went traveling through the Fenris System. He knew his soul, spirit, whatever made his self-identity, remained within his physical form. Yet he saw . . .

Is this the future or is this now?

A squat vessel, a beaten cargo hauler—no, this was an ice hauler. The ship traveled the run to Jassac's outer asteroid belt going to the edge of the star system to bring space ice to the moon. Once at Jassac, heavy rockets would lower the iceberg to a planetary convertor. The machines devoured the ice, feeding water into the atmosphere as vapor. In this way, the Kresh thickened Jassac's life belt around the surface.

In his sleep, Klane kicked off his covers. He needed to know . . . to know . . .

He groaned. Something operated deep within his subconscious. He hardly knew it was there. From time to time, he sensed unease. This feeling had been building lately. It seemed as if his mind . . . his mind . . .

The sensation lessened. It almost felt as if the intruding thought recognized his awareness of it and ducked lower, waiting.

After a time, the dream, vision, farseeing, solidified once more. Yes. This was like his . . . *understanding* of Timor Malik.

The Vomag soldier fought for his life on Heenhiss. What Klane saw now took place far from the second planet, in the distant outer asteroid belt. Here, ice objects drifted in eternal night. The Fenris asteroid belt contained the farthest bodies of the star system.

Klane's awareness entered the battered ice hauler. Five crewmembers lived in miserably tight quarters. Three slept while two worked in the pilot module.

Senior Darcy Foxe ran the hauler, and she quarreled with Jick, a troublesome sex addict. Of course, Jick lusted especially after Darcy's long legs. The little man yearned to run his hands up and down her thighs. He wanted to tear off her spacer uniform and make her perform lewd acts with him.

Darcy piloted the hauler onto a dirty snowball. As the hauler settled onto the ice, Jick floated to her chair and put a hand on the back of her neck.

Darcy reacted with startling speed, almost as if she'd been prepared for his unwanted caress. She turned and slapped the back of Jick's hand with a prickle-pad. Such a weapon was illegal to own. The longest prickle broke the skin.

Jick yanked his wounded hand against his thin chest. "What have you done?" he cried. "Look at this. You've drawn blood."

Darcy laughed. She was sick of his advances and his coy touches and brushes against her side. She had hoped to refrain from doing anything extreme, but his final caress had pushed her over the edge.

"Look, look!" Jick cried, showing her the back of his hand. A spot of blood welled there.

Now Darcy twisted the knife, as it were. She smiled sweetly and told him, "The prickle was coated with poison. I infected you, Jick."

"What?" he cried in a shrill voice. "This is outrageous!"

"How many times have I told you to keep your hands to yourself?"

"You but joked with me!"

"No, Jick. I meant what I said. Now you are infected."

"I'll report you!" he shouted.

"Oh. Well, I suppose I'll have to keep the antidote to myself then. I'll let the poison work through you as a toxin. I hope you survive long enough to make your report."

Jick blinked at her with his overly long eyelashes. "Darcy, you'll let me die?"

She scowled, angry with herself. She should just let him believe that, but it wasn't in her. Still, she could let him hang for a while in order to terrify him. "No, I'm not a murderer. Nothing of the kind will happen. But I fear I must tell you that the toxin will make your member shrivel."

"What?" Jick shouted.

Darcy nodded. She lied. She hadn't coated the pricks with poison because she didn't have any. The sentinels would have detected her carrying poison aboard the hauler. Because of the poison, they would have marked her for elimination. The Kresh were strict concerning spacer protocol aboard a hauler.

"Darcy, darling," Jick said. "Have mercy on me. Give me the antidote."

She shook her head. "You've been a nuisance the entire trip. Now, you'll have to change your ways. Remember, *it* will shrivel and you will never enjoy a woman again. It's possible if the antidote isn't given in time that you'll contract testicular cancer."

Jick wailed in despair. "Don't you understand? I can't help myself. Your body draws me, calls to me. Have mercy on me, Darcy. Give me the antidote and lie beside me so my sorrows will drain away."

"If you keep talking like that, I'll double the toxins."

Anger soaked into Jick's eyes. He studied the screen. It showed some of the asteroid's surface and then a profusion of stars. "Perhaps we should unload the engines onto the ice," he said in a sulky tone.

"Murdering me won't solve your problem," Darcy said. "Remember, if I die, you'll never find the antidote."

Jick began to breathe harder. Finally, he pointed a quivering finger at her. "Witch! You scheme with malice against me. You flaunt your body throughout the ship, gliding sinuously here and there so my mind seethes with desire. Now, I learn that you're vile and conniving. I thought you but tested me, to find the strength of my passion. Instead, like a fox, you torment me. I hate you, Darcy. I will now call down a curse upon you to—"

Darcy held up a hand. "Have a care, Jick. If you curse me, I'll summon the others for an inquiry. It's possible we'll space you."

Jick's face drained of color. His shoulders slumped. Finally, he pushed away, heading for his cubicle.

Feeling guilty for lying but resolved to make Jick stop harassing her, Darcy returned to her controls. She measured the snowball, its volume, weight, and percentages of frozen water. They had performed an analysis while braking, but there were always subtle variations. Small robots scurried over the surface, taking samples.

For the sleeping, psi-watching Klane, time passed with a dreamer's speed.

Perhaps two hours later ship-time, Darcy sat up. She scowled and bent forward. With several taps of her long fingers, she ran a diagnostics on the sensors. They reacted smoothly, without fault.

This was odd. According to the sensors, a metal object lay buried in the ice.

On his pallet aboard the Attack Talon in Pulsar's upper atmosphere, Klane groaned in his sleep. Deep in his subconscious, an iota of intelligence knew great excitement.

What is that? Klane asked.

The alien iota muffled its excitement and lowered its mental radiation. Perhaps as camouflage, it heightened Klane's awareness of the farseeing.

In the ice hauler, Darcy donned a vacc-suit. She should wait for others. Hauler customs and Kresh laws were strict on spacewalking alone. She knew that, but decided to check this while Jick sulked in his cubicle. It was conceivable he might enter the command module while she was out and discover her disobedience. Darcy decided to risk it anyway. Something about the metal object in the snowball seemed to call to her.

With the vacc-suit sealed and oxygen cycling, Darcy entered the tiny airlock. Atmosphere hissed away, and the outer hatch opened with a *clack*.

She should have latched a line to the door bolt. Darcy broke more spacer customs and plain common sense. Instead of hooking a safety line, she settled a thruster pack onto her shoulders.

The sun looked small from here, far away in the center of the star system. None of the planets registered on her regular vision. The only one that might have was giant Pulsar, and it was on the opposite side of the sun.

Darcy sighed. The sun, the stars, the emptiness of space affected her. She had wanted to be a mother many years ago. Now, she didn't know. The Kresh were harsh taskmasters. They laid down strict rules for the spacers. Did she want to bring a child into that?

No. She wanted serenity, ease, and to be left alone. Lately, even that had begun to pale. Surely, there was more to existence than luxury. Many spacers lived like Jick, indulging their appetites. Why not? Life was hard and then you died. She wanted a reason for existence. *Who will remember Darcy Foxe, senior aboard Ice Hauler 266-9?*

Maybe that's why she'd donned a vacc-suit and now traveled alone across the snowball. With expert control, she jetted hydrogen particles from her pack. Behind her, Hauler 266-9 rested on the asteroid. The vessel was oval with extra engines attached to the hull, along with other equipment.

The journey to this icy rock had taken almost two years. It would be another two before the asteroid reached Pulsar.

Darcy jetted over the curve of the small planetoid so the hauler disappeared behind the horizon. She watched the helmet's HUD. A beep sounded in her headphones and a black dot appeared on the interior screen.

Rotating so her back faced her direction of travel, she squeezed thrust from her pack, slowing her velocity. Finally, barely drifting above the surface, she unhooked an anchor rifle. She aimed, fired a metal hook, and reeled herself onto the snowball's surface.

A smile curved onto her long face. She walked on an asteroid, bounced really. With smooth practice, she glided to a crevice. There, she climbed down thirty meters into the asteroid.

Unhooking a flashlight, she clicked it on and peered at the frozen substance. Was that a metal object back there? She couldn't tell.

Her heart raced and her lips had become chapped. What did she look at? She didn't know why, but the feeling came to her that this was incredibly ancient.

Is it alien?

By that, she didn't mean Kresh. They weren't aliens, but the masters, the Revered Ones.

Demons, Klane thought to himself as he psi-observed Darcy. He, too, knew excitement, and this time he sensed the foreign intelligence buried deep in his subconscious. Even in his sleep, he strove to uncover its identity.

The thing slithered free of his psi-senses, burrowing deeper, out of perception.

I will uncover this mystery, Klane promised himself. First, he yearned to know what the metal object was in the asteroid.

He looked through Darcy's eyes, as she stared through her helmet.

I should get back to the hauler, Darcy told herself.

Just then, her headphones crackled into life. To her dismay, she heard Jick clear his throat. Then he said over the headphones, "What is this, my dear? I find you're out on the asteroid."

"Jick," she said in a dry voice.

"Yes," he said. "What are you doing out there, my dear?"

You can't tell him, Klane said. And he made it a command in her mind.

I don't want to sleep with him to keep him quiet, Darcy said, as if arguing with herself.

You don't have to, Klane told her.

How will I keep him quiet then?

You'll think of something, Klane said.

"Darcy," Jick said over the headphones. "I think it's time you and I had a *long* talk."

Darcy frowned, and she finally pulled herself from the alien thing hidden down in the ice. As she climbed out of the crevice, Klane's farseeing withdrew from her mind.

His awareness seemed to leap back toward the Attack Talon in Pulsar's upper atmosphere. For a fleeting second, Klane's powerful psionics saw what looked like Kresh Battle Fangs gliding down into the atmosphere.

Shock filled him—Kresh spaceships were already at Pulsar? Why did the Battle Fangs enter the upper atmosphere? Only one reason seemed possible. In some fashion, the Kresh knew he was down here hiding and they hunted for him.

I have to warn the others.

On the pallet in his chamber, Klane's blue eyes flew open. The knowledge of his dream filled him. The awareness of nearing Battle Fangs caused him to swing his legs off the bed. He rose with a lurch, shouting.

Meanwhile, deep down in Klane's subconscious, an alien psi-parasite mentally sighed with relief. The selected body of destiny—this Klane—had sensed its presence. Now, the Kresh intruded on the Chosen One's thoughts. Yes, the approaching Battle Fangs came at the perfect moment. It must mean that fortune aided its great and noble task.

8

Cyrus swung around as Klane barged into the control room with his naked feet slapping against the deck plates. The Anointed One wore pants, but that was all except for the greasy junction-stone around his throat.

Cyrus stood behind Jana's pilot chair.

She was his woman, a reddish-skinned native of Jassac with brown eyes, long brown hair, and a full figure. When he'd first met her, she'd worn fur garments and lived like a primitive in Berserker Clan. Now, she wore an Attack Talon uniform for one of Zama Dee's crew. Down on Jassac, she had received old memories from her seeker, a powerful psionic. Some of those memories had taught her about modern life.

Through protected windows, they could see Pulsar's harsh winds blowing clouds around the ship. Cyrus and Jana had been touching and discussing their approaching marriage. Well, Jana had been doing most of the talking and Cyrus the touching.

"Listen!" Klane shouted. "The Kresh know we're here. They're coming!"

It took Cyrus a moment to understand what the shouting was about. When he finally got it, he asked, "How far away are they?"

"Minutes from entering the atmosphere," Klane said.

"What? That doesn't make sense. How can they be so close? Wouldn't you have sensed them a long time ago?"

Klane scowled. "That's right." He closed his eyes as a look of concentration came over him. Just as fast, he opened his eyes. "They're gone," he said. "I can't sense their ships anywhere."

"I don't understand. You said they're entering the atmosphere. They're here."

"I did."

"Then—"

"I had a dream."

"Wait a minute," Cyrus said. "You just *dreamed* the Kresh were here?"

Klane nodded.

"I know Specials have precognitive dreams sometimes," Cyrus said. "Heck, I think I had one. But I don't think that means your dream—"

"No! You don't understand. It wasn't a precognitive dream. I used farseeing in my sleep."

"What's that?"

"Exactly as the name implies," Klane said. "I see things far away as they take place. I saw Timor Malik earlier, but that was less farseeing and more a . . . a connection between the two of us. What I saw in my sleep just now took place in the opposite direction, in the outer asteroid belt."

Cyrus glanced at Jana.

She shrugged. "This is beyond me," she told him quietly.

"Yeah," Cyrus muttered. He eyed the Anointed One. Klane looked ragged around the edges, maybe even a little wild. It was a surprise they didn't all have nightmares about approaching Kresh. Yet Klane had amazing psi-powers. It would be rash to ignore the man's warnings.

Cyrus gripped the upper edge of Jana's pilot chair. He recalled his death premonition earlier. He'd never had precognitive dreams. Was that anything like farseeing in your sleep? What had Klane seen that

made him think of Kresh warships? First you see it and then you
don't. Something strange seemed to be going on.

"Agreed," Klane said. "I'm sensing that, too."

Jana eyed Cyrus, her look saying, *What's wrong with him?*

"I'm reading his thoughts," Klane told her. "It saves time."

She gasped and clutched Cyrus's hand.

Cyrus noted her reaction. Nobody liked to have his or her thoughts
sifted through. It made the person uneasy.

Klane rubbed his face, an agitated gesture.

"Maybe it's time we poked up out of this thick atmosphere like
gophers," Cyrus said. "You know, sort of take a look around and see
what's what."

"No," Jana said. "The clouds and radiation shield us."

"True," Cyrus said. "But they're also making us blind."

"That's why Klane's farseeing is so useful," Jana said.

"I thought I explained that," Klane said. "Farseeing is different. I
have to be out of body or dreaming to do it over stellar distances. Not
with Timor Malik, though. He's the exception because of our former
link. When I scan around Pulsar, I do it through a process of TK and
telepathy. I search for receptive minds."

"I got that," Cyrus said. "But maybe I don't understand the farseeing. You claimed to have seen the Kresh through a dream."

"My farseeing saw an event in the outer asteroid belt. When my . . .
awareness, I suppose you'd call it, returned, I saw the Kresh Battle
Fangs descending into our atmosphere."

"But now with your regular way of doing it, the Kresh ships are
gone?"

Klane nodded.

"And you trust this . . . farseeing?" Cyrus asked.

"I do."

"Hmm," Cyrus said, rubbing his chin. "You just said something
interesting. Your normal way of scanning has you searching for minds."

"Exactly."

"There could be a simple explanation then," Cyrus said. "You and I shield ourselves from their mind scans as they search for us. Could the Bo Taw have learned to shield themselves from you?"

"You mean with a null?" Klane asked.

"Or something similar to a null," Cyrus said.

Klane appeared to think about that. "It's possible."

"Yeah," Cyrus said. "The more I think about it, the more that seems like the answer. If they've learned about the null, we doubly need to take a look around with the Attack Talon's sensors."

"Agreed," Klane said.

Cyrus turned to Jana.

"Shouldn't we ask the others first before we leave our protection?" she asked. "This is a big decision."

"No," Klane said. "I'm in charge. I'm telling you to take us up into space."

Jana glanced at Cyrus.

Cyrus thought about it. They'd never had a knock-down, drag-out discussion about authority. They should have. Everyone looked to Klane, though. He was the Anointed One, so it made sense he should know what to do.

"You mistrust me," Klane said.

Cyrus scowled. "Are you back to reading my thoughts?"

"Listen to me. I sense danger. It's coming. We have no more time to dally."

"I don't know, Klane. We don't have to rush the decision that fast. Let's think about this for just a minute." There was something odd to Klane's behavior, something *different*.

Klane opened his mouth as if to argue. Then he shut it. "Yes. Perhaps now *is* the time to debate this."

"Should I call the others?" Jana asked. She meant Yang and those of Berserker Clan who had received memories from the seeker. The inner group also included the Vomag Skar and possibly Mentalist Niens. It did not include the shuttle crewmembers or the Attack Talon's people they'd captured while taking over the vessels.

"No," Klane said. "This is between Cyrus and me."

"Yang might think otherwise," Jana said. "Skar might disagree, too."

"Skar will agree with whatever Cyrus thinks," Klane said. "The soldier considers himself the Earther's guard. Yang has pretensions to leadership, but he is Berserker Clan and I am Tash-Toi."

"You can't bring that into it," Jana said with heat. "We're all beyond Jassac's philosophies. We each have seeker knowledge now. We understand the greater danger."

"We're still who we were," Klane said.

"You think you've always been this forceful?" Jana asked. "I've been watching you, Klane. Our weeks aboard ship have changed you. Do you even remember some of the stories you told us about your youth? I think you've changed a lot more than you realize."

Klane pursed his lips.

"Okay. Everyone is different," Cyrus said. "Klane is still the Anointed One and I'm the man from Earth. I'm the only one besides Skar who thinks like a modern person."

"You misjudge yourself," Klane said. "You primarily think of yourself as a Latin King, an enforcer for your Milan gang."

"Okay, whatever," Cyrus said. "The point is, who's in charge, you or me or a mixture of it? We need a captain. I sense doom, and you are getting edgy. Likely, one way or another, we're going to be in combat before this is through."

"You know I should lead," Klane said.

Cyrus wanted to laugh. The man little older than a teenager wearing nothing but scruffy pants figured he should lead, huh?

I have the memories of many people, Klane told him telepathically. *They speak to me, using the wisdom of accumulated lives. You are resourceful and brave, but you lack my deeper insights.*

"I know you're the supposed savior of the Fenris System." Cyrus cleared his throat. Klane was starting to intimidate him. Cyrus realized the man should lead them if he was the Anointed One. Yet something was off about Klane, and that troubled him. Cyrus put up a mental block, thoroughly tired of the psionic intrusion. "Do you have any idea how you'll do that saving?"

Klane appeared to mull that over. Maybe his many memories had a brain hall meeting. Suddenly, the Anointed One's eyes widened with apparent understanding. "My farseeing must have something to do with it. Yes. The alien artifact in the asteroid is the key. I'm sure of it now."

"Whoa, whoa, whoa," Cyrus said. "What artifact? You're not making sense. Does this have anything to do with the farseeing in the asteroid belt?"

Klane told them about Darcy Foxe, Jick, and the ice hauler.

"So this spacer found an object, an ancient alien thing," Cyrus said. "I don't know, Klane. Finding it now seems to be a little too coincidental. There's something odd going on and I can't quite pinpoint it. I'm sensing—"

"Danger," Klane said. "I'm feeling it, too, waves of danger. We must take the Attack Talon into orbital space. Despite what I didn't see with regular psi-scanning, I fear Kresh Battle Fangs may be entering Pulsar's atmosphere."

"I'll tell you what," Cyrus said. "In the interest of time and ship safety, let's make you temporary captain." He didn't see what he could do to stop Klane if the man decided to start moving them like pawns. So, if Klane wanted to be in charge, they should do it for now. "Afterward," Cyrus said, "we should hash this out with the others. By that I mean, Yang, Skar, Niens—"

"I no longer trust Niens."

"No problem. But I think we should at least bounce this off Yang. The man has experience running a tribe. He would probably add a few things we're forgetting."

Klane's blue eyes seemed to shine for a moment.

Cyrus found that unsettling.

"Agreed," Klane said. "I will captain our vessel. Now, take us up, Jana. Let us see if the Kresh have discovered our secret or not."

The three of them took their places in the command module. The Kresh Attack Talon only needed a few crewmembers to run. The rest helped with damage control or were along as ground fighters.

"Attention," Cyrus said over the intercom. "We're about to take off, so buckle in and wait for orders."

Klane sat beside Jana while Cyrus settled in at the weapons panel.

The Attack Talon's engines began to thrum with power. Slowly, Jana lifted the ship higher. Pink and yellow clouds whipped past the vessel. Without the grav-plates, the Attack Talon would have rocked wildly.

Cyrus's nostrils widened as nervousness bit. They'd hidden down here for weeks already. Boredom and then stir-craziness had threatened everybody. One thing he remembered from the institute was psi-echoes. Those with ESP could play mental tricks on themselves. That's why reality therapy was part of the curriculum. If for no other reason, Cyrus thought it was a good idea to pop up and look around with sensors instead of *solely* trusting Klane's psionics to see what was nearby.

"Shouldn't we bring one of the Attack Talon's former crewmembers onto the deck?" Jana asked.

"We know what to do," Klane said.

"They've taught us and we have memories," Jana said, "but they're actually trained to run these particular ship systems."

"No," Klane said. "This is too important to leave to them."

"Because Niens is untrustworthy?" asked Cyrus.

"That's a shrewd question," Klane said.

"So what's the answer?"

Klane glanced over his shoulder, giving Cyrus an unreadable stare.

For an instant, Cyrus felt as if an alien watched him. It put a cold feeling down his spine.

Cyrus waited for Klane to say something. Was the Anointed One able to break through his mental shield to read his mind?

Hey, do you hear me? Cyrus projected the thought. He'd never been much of a telepath, and it appeared he still wasn't. Klane didn't even react. That seemed odd.

Just what was going on inside of Klane's head?

9

Dagon Dar brooded as he studied a hologram of the Fenris System.

Confusion reigned among the Kresh. Long-distance arguments meant warships remained at the third planet. The personnel in the Glegan orbital platforms were on high alert. How would that help the satellites against massive planetary-based beams if the Chirr down there tried to do what had happened at Heenhiss?

All the while, the Chirr continued to attack the Heenhiss space habs.

Earlier, Dagon Dar had given orders for every Kresh spaceship in and around Heenhiss to flee into deep space. The vessels could redeploy later. The logical act was to save what he could instead of trying to defend the indefensible. The strength of the Chirr armada staggered his imagination.

If that fleet reached Glegan, the Kresh there would sustain crippling losses. If the Chirr underground on the third planet launched an equally large space fleet as they had at the second, at the right moment, the Kresh forces there would perish.

Should the Kresh fleet withdraw from Glegan, leaving millions to die? Or should the Glegan fleet fight and possibly face annihilation?

What kind of Chirr force lay under Glegan's planetary surface?

Many Kresh argued that Dagon Dar should take the Pulsar fleet, such as it was, and add their ships to the Glegan fleet.

The new FIRST tore himself away from the holo-globe and stalked out of the chamber. He began to move along the corridors of his Battle Fang. He had to ponder the evidence and make the most logical choice for the Race.

Half of the remaining Kresh vessels orbited Glegan. Roughly one quarter resided in the Pulsar gravitational system. One fifth of the remaining Kresh warships were far away in the outer asteroid belt, scattered around the periphery of the star system. The rest of the warships either journeyed between planets or waited at out-of-the-way locations.

If that wasn't enough of a logic puzzle, there was the strange and final warning from the old FIRST. That's why Dagon Dar strode down the corridor, trying to make sense of her odd advice.

Human crewmembers fled from his path. They recognized an agitated Revered One when they saw him.

As he stalked through the largest corridors of his ship, Dagon Dar issued commands. Battle Fang *Whet Steel* increased velocity, along with its sister ship. They would join the other warships gathering at Jassac. From there, in several hours, he would make the fateful decision concerning the Pulsar fleet.

What should I do about the former FIRST's suspicion? Dagon Dar had never entertained the slightest notion of an alien entity softly pushing the various species to come to Fenris. It was a staggering idea. Yet there was more. The former FIRST supposed a foreign entity might be guiding . . . what? The alien intelligence pushed *Kresh* into taking selected actions?

That is preposterous!

Dagon Dar stopped, and he cocked his raptor head. Why should that be a preposterous notion?

That isn't how my intellect deals with a troublesome idea. I do not reject it out of hand, but consider every possibility.

As he stood on his speeding Battle Fang, Dagon Dar began to think deeply. The former FIRST should have laser-beamed her articles to him, outlining her suspicions and giving him full data on the thesis. What had led her to her conclusion anyway?

It might have been the very fact of three distinct intelligent species living in one star system. She had also pointed out a fourth species, the metal creatures called cyborgs. That four very different species had each came to the Fenris System during their years of advanced technology . . . what would be the mathematical odds of that?

According to the data he'd examined, the crew of the latest human colony ship had not known about the first attempt. Why did the humans journey so far to reach this particular star system?

Did that objection a few moments ago—that is preposterous!—occur in my brain from my own thoughts, or did a telepathic creature plant the thought there?

No. The idea had not originated within him. Dagon Dar knew himself well enough to realize that. If nothing else, the thought proved the former FIRST's thesis.

Several postulates naturally derived from the thesis. Had the Heenhiss Chirr struck when they did because the former FIRST had stumbled upon the amazing truth? Could the meddling alien subvert Kresh thoughts? Or did the alien use the much more moldable humans and Chirr to do its bidding?

Dagon Dar stopped, becoming rigid. He began to *think*, really cogitate, using the full extent of his amazing Kresh intellect. With extreme logic, following the reasoning wherever it led, he correlated data and ideas. His mind wrestled with the concepts and examined ratios and probabilities. Finally, he roared as his tail lashed, thumping against a bulkhead.

How could he have not seen it sooner? It was highly improbable that the humans could ever have gained an Anointed One. Klane had originated in the Kresh labs. Zama Dee had instructed others to put him among the primitive humans. The Kresh as good as gave the humans their supposed savior, as told to Dagon Dar by the Resisters on High Station 3. What's more, the primitive tribes had ready-made seekers to guide the humans.

And in our labs we created the Bo Taw, superior telepaths.

Given these facts, this alien presence must have worked an exceedingly long time to prepare for the Anointed One. Yes, yes, the Chirr fleet had broken out of the tunnels the same month the Anointed One gained space freedom. The two events were connected. It was obvious.

The connection had to be the hidden alien meddler. Logic dictated the entity's existence. There was no other rational explanation. The alien's reality changed the Fenris equation.

All Kresh must wear our anti-telepathy devices at all times.

Swiveling around, Dagon Dar strode for his communications chamber. Glegan must be a trap meant to annihilate Kresh space power for good. The alien meddler must hate the Kresh because only they could detect it through heightened reasoning. Therefore, the entity used the Chirr to attack them. That would give the Anointed One time to do whatever he was supposed to.

I must gather the fleet in the Pulsar system. I must cogitate with extreme exactitude and discover the abode of the meddling alien. Somehow, I must extinguish them or it before the hidden one destroys the Kresh.

10

Cyrus Gant sat before the weapons panel as the Attack Talon rose from Pulsar's atmosphere.

Jana pressed tabs and adjusted controls. Klane sat beside her, avidly watching the window portal.

As the ship climbed out of the immense gravity well, the gas giant's multicolored atmosphere thinned out. The clouds lessened and it became darker outside. Soon, stars began to appear.

"Better seal the viewing port," Cyrus said.

Jana tapped another control. Blast doors slid before the window. With another tap, she brought the viewing screen online.

"I suggest we use passive sensors at first," Cyrus said.

"I agree," Jana said.

Cyrus grinned to himself. He knew Jana was proud of how much she'd learned these past few weeks. Even with the memory transfer, her piloting the Attack Talon wouldn't have been possible without the simulator. She'd sat before it most of her waking hours. The former crew had taught her. With ancient seeker knowledge buried deep in her mind, she had quickly gained a pilot's rating.

"Sense anything unusual yet?" Cyrus asked the Anointed One.

Klane said nothing, although he closed his eyes and bent his head. It meant that with his psionic abilities he was studying the void outside the ship.

With his fingertips, Cyrus rubbed his other palm. His hands were sweaty. He was nervous all right. The journey from Earth to the Fenris

System had been okay. Ever since he'd arrived, though, it had become a nightmare. Did Chief Monitor Argon still live at High Station 3? If anyone could survive the Kresh interrogators, it would be the High-born. He hoped most of the space marines were still alive. Yang and his Berserkers, and especially Skar 192, were good soldiers. But they were nothing like Earth marines.

A loud and ominous *beep* alerted him that the ship's sensors had spotted something.

Cyrus studied his board. He still had problems reading the Kresh symbols. "What are you picking up?" he asked Jana.

"I think it's a Kresh Battle Fang," she said, her voice quavering. "It's heading straight for us, Cyrus."

Cyrus's chest hardened. So, the Anointed One *had* spotted some-thing before with his farseeing. He should have trusted the man's dreams.

"Klane, can you sense them with your psi?"

"No," Klane said bleakly. "I can't see them."

"You know what to look for when I use the null," Cyrus said. "Do you sense similar mental vibrations out there somewhere?"

Klane was silent for a time. Then he said, "I do. They've tricked me. The Kresh have definitely learned about the null."

Sweat beaded on Cyrus's forehead as he bared his teeth in a silent snarl. Their one ace had been the null. Now the Kresh knew about it. Worse, the dinosaurs had used it to sneak up on them.

Jana moaned as a series of beeps came from her panel. "They're hailing us," she said.

"What do you say, Klane?" Cyrus asked. "What should we do?"

"Maybe we should answer the comm," Klane said.

"What?" Cyrus asked, turning toward the Anointed One in shock. "Are you crazy? Radio connection strengthens the Bo Taw's psi-abilities. I've told you about that before."

"We must survive," Klane said as he sat stiffly in his chair. "That is the central issue. Hence, surrender is the safest option."

"The issue, hence?" Cyrus asked, his brows furrowed. "When did you start talking like that?"

Klane turned around, and he stared at Cyrus. His eyes seemed to burn with power. "Down on your knees!" the Anointed One shouted. "Bow before me."

Before he knew what he was doing, Cyrus gave Klane the finger. It was so automatic that it surprised him. He realized in that moment that Klane was different. The Anointed One didn't even seem like the same person.

A moment later, psionic pain struck his mind. Cyrus gasped. He felt the power trying to shut down his consciousness. He fought back, concentrating, using lessons taught back at Earth's institute. The attack mind was too powerful. His eyelids began to flicker as he fought to keep them open.

Cyrus snarled and sweat began to drip down his face. He had to do something. Klane, or whatever Klane had become, would soon put him under. Inspiration struck. Cyrus slapped the weapons board, launching several missiles at the enemy.

"You fool!" Klane shouted. "Go to sleep—now!"

Cyrus fought back with everything he had. It was like a man trying to stop a bulldozer with his hands. So, instead of engaging the psi-attack head-on, he kept mentally skipping back. Soon, though, he would run out of room and would fall asleep.

In a hazy manner, Cyrus watched Jana swivel around to face Klane. They sat side by side. She started to swing at him, aiming for the side of his head. Klane must have sensed that. His head whipped around. The Anointed One glared at her.

For a moment, the mind attack against Cyrus lessened.

Jana's arm lost motive power. She struck the side of Klane's head a glancing, harmless blow. Then she crumpled as if her bones had dissolved. She slid from her chair onto the floor, out cold.

Immediately, the psionic pressure against Cyrus resumed.

"I can kill her," Klane said in an emotionless voice.

"What's wrong with you?" Cyrus shouted. "Why are you doing this? We're your friends. You're the Anointed One who's supposed to save humanity."

On the main screen, a bright bloom showed a Battle Fang destroying one of the missiles. Cyrus had managed to launch three.

"They'll kill us," Cyrus said past gritted teeth. "They'll dissect you to see what makes you tick."

"No," Klane said as if he were a recording. "It is too late for them. I have found it at last, at long last."

"What are you talking about? Is one of the Bo Taw controlling you?"

Klane's eyes seemed to smolder. "How can you conceive of the long eons I've spent—"

Klane closed his mouth, and lines appeared in his forehead. "Cyrus?" he asked, sounding normal again.

Cyrus knew the truth then. His friend hadn't acted as if he'd been Bo Taw controlled. This was someone else.

"Klane! Something alien is manipulating your mind. You have to fight it."

The Anointed One nodded slowly, as if it took great effort to do that. "I know," he said. "I feel it inside me. Just a minute ago, I pulled back on the strength of my mental bolts aimed at your mind. It keeps forcing me, though. I don't understand how it can do this."

Inside the ship, a klaxon began to wail.

With a seemingly rusted neck, Klane turned and studied Jana's panel. "The Kresh have launched missiles at us," he said.

"We have to fight them."

Klane shook his head.

"Do you *want* them to capture us?" Cyrus shouted.

Klane's voice and demeanor changed once more, becoming more mechanical. "You do not understand. I cannot risk destruction. We will surrender."

Another bloom appeared on the main screen. Another of their missiles exploded to an enemy Battle Fang's destroying laser.

"What are you anyway?" Cyrus shouted. "How did you take over Klane's mind?"

"It doesn't have all of my mind yet," Klane said through gritted teeth, seeming like his old self again.

"Whatever you are," Cyrus said, "you'd better release your grip on Klane's mind." With his limited Special powers, he tried to help his friend. It was like hitting a steel wall. He couldn't do anything. He was too weak. He had to reason with the thing, trick it maybe.

"If we can't fight them," Cyrus said, "the Kresh might accidentally destroy us."

"We will wait now," the mechanistic Klane said. "They will autodestruct the missiles aimed at us."

"You must be the reason why I sensed doom earlier," Cyrus said. "We had the Trojan horse here among us. I wish I knew how this happened."

With a wooden motion, Klane tapped a panel, opening channels with the Battle Fang. A Bo Taw appeared on the screen. The modified human wore a *baan* around his elongated forehead and a red robe around his body.

"You will surrender," the Bo Taw said.

"Kill him, Klane," Cyrus pleaded. "Use your powers on the Bo Taw."

"Surrender," the Bo Taw said on the screen.

"Fight him," Cyrus said.

Klane appeared not to hear either man. He sat frozen, perhaps the two entities fighting inside the Anointed One's mind.

For Cyrus, this felt too much like the last hours aboard Teleship *Discovery*. Through mind control, the Bo Taw forced most of the Earth crews to fall alseep. For a time, only Cyrus had resisted them.

The man from Milan resisted now, and he realized a moment later that no one attempted to control him.

"We will surrender," Klane told the Bo Taw.

Cyrus snarled silently. He rose and activated the main laser control. The engines revved and a bright red beam appeared on the main screen. It lanced outward from the Attack Talon and burned into the enemy Battle Fang.

The Bo Taw on the screen shouted in terror. Harsh raptor-like words sounded behind the modified human. Then a Kresh appeared on the screen and swept the Bo Taw out of the way. The dinosaur stared at them. It was like looking at an intelligent, two-legged crocodile.

"Stop your attack at once or the other ships will retaliate," the Kresh said.

Cyrus cursed the alien. He planned to go down fighting.

"Stop what you're doing," Klane told him. Then the Anointed One frowned at Cyrus.

Red-hot pokers of pain broke through his mind block, stabbing Cyrus's thoughts. He groaned. *What a crock.* Klane kept switching sides—one second he helped; the next he attacked.

Stunned by the mental assault, Cyrus slid off his chair onto the deck plates. He hadn't turned off the laser, however. It still beamed at the enemy ship.

Maybe because of that, Klane stood up, moving toward the weapons panel.

On the main screen, the Kresh Battle Fang exploded spectacularly. At almost the same moment, two more Battle Fangs rose up out of Pulsar's atmosphere. They beamed the Attack Talon.

"Shield us," Cyrus whispered from the floor.

Klane whipped around, staring at the bulkheads.

Cyrus heard bubbling sounds: the enemy lasers chewing through their ship's armor.

Then something incredible happened. A Kresh ray sliced through the ship's exterior armor, boring through the ablative foam underneath. The beam burst through the command module bulkhead. Klane stood in the ray's path. His left shoulder and part of his side melted away. Blood exploded out of Klane, and he collapsed onto the deck plates.

The mental assault trying to put Cyrus to sleep evaporated. His eyes flew open, and he realized the Anointed One who was supposed to save the Fenris humans either was dead or would be in the next few seconds.

11

In the Attack Talon, automated hatches clanged shut, sealing the hull breach from the rest of the ship. In the command module, air now violently escaped into space.

As the air pressure rapidly dropped, Cyrus found it difficult to stay awake. Klane lay on the deck plates. Despite his missing left shoulder, arm, and a frightful chunk of his side, he only seeped blood. It should have poured out of him.

Cyrus was vaguely aware that Klane used his telekinetic powers to pinch off the exposed blood vessels. How long could that last?

The enemy Battle Fangs no longer beamed their Attack Talon. The comm line was open. A Kresh spoke, demanding their immediate surrender.

Jana was closer to the hull breach than anyone else. The air pressure had to have been less there. She lay on the floor with her eyes closed, although she twitched, indicating that she still lived for a little while longer.

This was a disaster. How could Klane survive such a horrible injury?

I cannot. I will die soon enough.

Sluggishly, Cyrus tried to decipher the thought.

It is I, Klane. I'm speaking with you.

From on the floor, they locked stares. The Anointed One looked at him with glazed eyes.

I must transfer.

"Take over my consciousness?" Cyrus whispered.

A moment, please; this is no good.

A piece of metal lifted from the floor and flew to the hull breach. It slapped against the opening. The sides bubbled, melted by intense heat caused by Klane's TK, no doubt.

It was a fantastic example of Klane's abilities. He held death at bay by the power of his psionics. Now, he repaired the command module.

I will die. My life is over. But my thoughts and abilities will live on in you as I transfer my memories into you.

"I don't think I want that," Cyrus said.

You must. I perish. I must still use what I have to save humanity.

"Fenris humanity?"

All humanity, both here and in your solar system.

"I must be me, Klane. I refuse to let anyone control my mind. Something in you controlled you."

Klane ignored the last comment, apparently focusing on the first. *I want you to be you. Now relax. I must transfer fast. I do not have long enough to make this an easy adjustment.*

Before Cyrus could say anything more, he arched his back as waves upon waves of memories and thoughts slammed against his mind. A torrent, a river, a tidal current of thoughts hammered his mind and confused him. He saw Klane's life in brief flickers of images. He saw the seeker's life, and the seeker before him and him and him. It bewildered Cyrus.

Then something cold and dark, alien and slippery, tried to glide past without notice. Maybe it would have worked, but Cyrus had been waiting for the alien thing that had controlled and killed his friend.

Wait! What are you?

I am nothing.

How does nothing tell me, it's nothing, Cyrus asked. *You're not human. You're something else.* And he blocked the alien thing.

Do not resist. I can teach you much.

Screw off. I'm me and nothing is touching who I am.

You do not understand. You are so primitive it hurts to communicate with you.

So piss off.

No. I will burrow—

Cyrus used a mind bolt as Jasper had taught him to wield long ago. The old Cyrus Gant couldn't have done much. But he had already absorbed most of Klane's psionic strength. The bolt caused the entity to squeal with pain.

Stop! I can hurt you more than you know.

Words, Cyrus thought. *Fight me for control if you dare.* And he struck at the entity with another mind bolt.

Wait, the entity seemed to gasp. *Don't you understand what I'm offering you?*

Yes! Slavery. Earth government tried to put a lock on my mind. I fought them and won. I'm going to fight you, too.

I have found the ship. It is here. I can go home again and heal fully. In exchange for your help, I offer you any star system you wish to rule.

An exchange for my soul doesn't interest me.

You have no soul.

I beg to differ.

You are a clod of dirt, a nothing in the expanse of the universe. Yes, become my Steed and I will give you power, more than you can conceive.

Slaves don't wield power. Now piss off, you little mind prick.

You'll die without my help.

We'll see. Cyrus concentrated and battered the entity. It cried out and attempted to shield itself. Silently, Cyrus laughed. He was never sure or not if his mockery enraged the thing. But icy power emanated from the entity. It fought back.

In his body on the floor of the Attack Talon, the two battled for control of his mind and person.

You will be my Steed and I the Rider.

Let's go, you alien mind bugger. Let's get it on and fight it out.

The command module of the Attack Talon disappeared to Cyrus Gant. He went somewhere deep in his mind. Then that, too, seemed to fade away. Slowly, a different venue coalesced in his thoughts.

Cyrus found himself in Level 40 Milan. Somehow, he'd come home again. This was marvelous. He sprinted as air burned down his throat. Obviously, he fled from something. What was it?

Before he turned around to look, Cyrus was aware he wore a Latin King synthi-leather jacket. It felt good, and he knew once he zipped it up that it would afford him some protection. He didn't think whatever chased him had a slugthrower, but a knife like him.

Cyrus's fist tightened around the handle of a vibrio-blade. He was a master at this. Once he clicked it on with his thumb, the blade would vibrate many times a second, giving him cutting power.

He ran in a dimly lit area, with tall blocks of machinery on either side of him. He must be in the guts of the processing center, the air recyclers. Did that mean he'd come here for a Dust shipment?

This was also cannibal territory. A weird cult group hid out of sight down here. They had bizarre rituals and indulged in eating their fellow humans. They used pounds of Dust, not just grams. So, the Latin Kings sold to them. But no one liked to make deals with the cannibals. Maybe that's who he ran from.

Why can't I turn around to look?

Unreasoning fear filled Cyrus. That made him angry, and he gripped the knife handle harder than ever. With a shout of rage, he twisted his neck and looked back over his shoulder.

An inky cloud floated behind him. Out of the cloud peered an ivory eye without a pupil or iris. The eye seemed blind, and then he realized the being used the whole orb to sense with.

There was nothing in Level 40 like that. Cyrus knew it in his gut. Something wrong had happened.

Am I having a Dust nightmare?

Before he could figure that out, he tripped. With a cry, he sprawled onto the slick paving, skidding headfirst. The knees of his pants tore through, and he friction-burned the palm of his left hand so it began to bleed. Worse, much worse, his vibrio-blade skittered away from him across the paving.

Cyrus scrambled to his feet, turning, and he saw something completely different. The blockiest man he'd ever seen scuttled toward him with an odd shuffle.

The man had a bullet-shaped shaved scalp and lacked eyebrows. The eyes were weird white like nothing he'd ever seen. The man wore silky garments like a holo-porn star, and his arms and thighs bulged with muscle. His muscle shape seemed off, though.

As Cyrus watched, the muscles under the silky garments seemed to melt and rearrange themselves into something more normal.

That was so freaking weird that Cyrus heaved, and a thin dribble of vomit splashed onto the paving.

"You must submit," the man said. He stood twice as tall as Cyrus and easily twice as wide. No one had shoulders like that; no one.

"I can crush you if you resist."

Cyrus had no doubt about that. "Are you an enforcer?" he asked.

The man stopped, and he looked around. With a slow nod, he regarded Cyrus again. "I see. You have reverted. It doesn't matter. I am the master of whatever domain you choose."

"Are you high?"

The man's lips spread in a parody of a smile.

Cyrus scrambled fast for his knife. He heard the man's heavy shoes striking the paving. The freak rushed him. That was okay. Cyrus knew how to deal with big guys. He'd been doing it his entire life.

"Submit!" the man shouted from behind.

Cyrus's right hand closed on the handle of his vibrio-blade. His thumb moved. *Click!* The blade vibrated at high speed.

A crushing hand gripped his left ankle. The man began to pull, yanking Cyrus's body along the paving.

"I will crush the bone until you scream for mercy."

Cyrus cursed the man, and he twisted like an eel. He did one thousand sit-ups some days, which made him strong. He twisted, turned, and slashed the knife.

It whined higher than Cyrus had ever heard a blade go. With a grunt, he forced the blade through the man's leathery flesh and into the bone. The pitch hurt his ears, but Cyrus kept pushing, and the blade sliced through bone and flesh, neatly lopping off the offending hand.

With a kick, Cyrus launched the hand off his ankle.

The man jerked his arm back, and he held it up before him as if he'd never seen something like this before. Maybe he hadn't.

Cyrus expected blood to jet and the man to howl. Neither event occurred. A vicious black substance oozed out of the severed wrist while smoke began to trickle.

"You're not human," Cyrus said while scrambling to his feet again. He shuddered with loathing, hating the alien creature that bled such black glop. He didn't want that thing to touch him again.

The alien with the white eyes regarded him.

"I don't think we're in Milan," Cyrus said.

"In the real world you are dying," the alien said.

Despite the loathing he felt, Cyrus forced himself to grin. "No. I don't think so. Klane died, or *he's* dying. I'm very much alive, though."

"Your spaceship is burning up around you."

"I don't believe it."

The alien snarled, and he waved his smoking wrist back and forth. "We will try this again, you stinking human. You will submit to me or know the bitter cost of resistance."

"Life's a bitch and Cyrus Gant will never do what you want."

"Do not believe it. For all submit to me in the end."

Before Cyrus could ask what the alien meant, darkness fell as all the lights went out. The whine of machinery stopped.

12

One second Cyrus hardly knew that his thoughts drifted in limbo. The next moment the left headphone in his helmet crackled to life. The right speaker hissed as if the helmet had sprung a leak.

What's going on? Where am I? Why am I wearing a helmet?

Then Cyrus realized that First Sergeant Mikhail Sergetov shouted at him. That was weird. The last time he'd seen the space marine, they had been aboard *Discovery*. He had thought Mikhail was dead. But the marine hollered at him.

"What do you think you're doing, Cyrus? Get your butt back on the A-couch and buckle in."

Despite his delight at hearing Mikhail again, Cyrus ignored the words as he floated through the laser chamber, heading toward the outer hatch.

Am I back on Discovery? *How is that even possible?*

Cyrus looked around in wonder.

A large structure taller than a man held the laser's focusing mirrors near the collapsium blast doors. The mirrors were at the top of the combat dome, the one they were in.

Okay. This is very cool.

Around the chamber were computer banks, data links, laser coils, and emergency repair gear. Five acceleration couches were installed in a circular marked area behind Cyrus. Two combat-suited marines lay there, strapped in for shifting. On the third couch, Cyrus's straps lay askew like dead snakes.

The marine NCO speaking to him through the suit comm wrestled with his last buckle.

"Get back to your couch!" Mikhail repeated.

Cyrus reached the hatch, catching the release bar. He twisted toward Mikhail. Despite his throbbing headache—Cyrus wasn't sure why he had one—he grinned through the helmet's faceplate.

"There's nothing to worry about," Cyrus said. "I'm going to look at the stars."

"Are you mad?" Mikhail asked. "We're about to shift."

The grin tightened. Cyrus understood something about this journey. A BAD THING waited around the corner of time. Maybe it waited outside among the stars.

"I have to do this," Cyrus said.

"It's too dangerous out there," the first sergeant told him.

Something glinted in Cyrus's eyes. "You taught me what to do."

"Don't pin this on me!" Mikhail shouted as he finally freed himself of the straps. He swung his armored feet onto the deck plates.

"You'd better buckle in. We're about to shift." Cyrus turned to the hatch as his gloved fingers tapped in the override code. He was surprised that he still remembered it.

"Listen to me," Mikhail said, launching himself from the A-couch. "The Chief Monitor won't overlook it if you go outside. He can't because Dr. Wexx will hear about it. They'll mark my profile with demerits, and the colonel will be forced to bust me down to private. What do you want to do anyway, die out there?"

The grin disappeared from Cyrus's face. He didn't *always* follow the rules, because sometimes the rules killed. Life was rigged and something always went wrong as the BAD THING reached out to destroy. His eyes shined with a haunted fear, just as they used to shine as a knife boy in the slums of Milan.

Wasn't I just in the slums? Something is wrong here. I'm . . . reverting to who I used to be, not who I am now.

In the combat dome on *Discovery's* outer hull, Cyrus hooked the tops of his booted feet against a metal lip. Anchored, he applied pressure to the bar. Ignoring the curses in his headphones, he opened the hatch.

"I'll break your bones for this!" Mikhail shouted, sailing toward him.

Cyrus stepped through the portal and closed it behind him. That would slow the NCO. Cyrus leaped, floating onto the surface of the giant Teleship. Look at the stars. Their pattern . . . he'd never seen them like this because they looked different from the solar system.

Inside his helmet, Cyrus grinned. He couldn't help it. The stars spread out in a glorious panorama. He couldn't get enough of this. As a kid growing up in the bottom level of Milan, he'd never seen the stars. He'd never seen the sun, touched a tree, played in open fields, or swum in the sea. On Earth, most people lived in the kilometer-deep cities that often reached forty levels down. The nearly fifty billion souls of Earth made such living arrangements necessary. Only rich people lived a natural life aboveground.

All that had changed once he joined Psi Force. Now, he hated confinement with an even deeper loathing than before and he loved—needed—open spaces.

Cyrus winced as the buzzing in his skull intensified, like razors slashing his thoughts. He gritted his teeth, enduring. He began to pant, and his suit's conditioner hummed as sweat appeared on his thin face. It hurt to blink and it hurt—

I'm outside on the ship's surface. I have to ground myself or risk flying off if they change heading.

He looked around. The skin of the Teleship was like any meteor drifting in space. Well, almost. The surface lacked mountains or valleys. It was uniform but made of asteroid-like rock, with dust where he could leave his boot prints if he so desired.

Twisting his supple body like a gymnast, Cyrus spotted the black dome he'd exited. Several similar domes dotted his vision. Some held mirrors to focus combat lasers. Others contained missile launch pits.

Discovery was like an old-style dreadnought from the Cyborg War of over one hundred years ago. Combat ships had used particle shielding then, hundreds of meters of thick rock to withstand enemy lasers or nuclear-tipped missiles.

Below the shielding minerals of the Teleship were the gigantic AIs, the fusion engines and acres of stasis tubes for the frozen sleepers. Over fifty thousand superior individuals waited to begin a colony in the New Eden system. Below stasis was the core structure of life support for *Discovery*'s crew: one hundred and seven men and women.

"Cyrus! Get back here!"

He saw Mikhail shine a powerful beam from the open hatch. The light tracked across the surface and finally reached him.

"We have a few minutes until the shift," the first sergeant said through the helmet's headphones.

It hurt to blink, but Cyrus did it anyway. He wished he could rub his head. He'd been wondering lately if the trouble came from out here. It was against the rules to be here during a shift.

"Do you want to die?" Mikhail asked.

"Not really."

"The shift—"

"I need to see it," Cyrus said.

"You're mad," Mikhail said. "No one is supposed to look at a null opening. It will smash your mind."

That couldn't be any worse than the buzzing in his head. Cyrus frowned. He sensed something . . . It seemed terribly important.

"Mikhail, strap in. We're going to accelerate."

"I don't see—"

"Get down on the deck plates!" Cyrus shouted. "Do it now."

The beam shining at him went away. The first sergeant finally got it. Sergetov needed to get back to his acceleration couch before the ship's engines started.

Cyrus adjusted his suit, aiming thruster nozzles at the stars and his faceplate toward the ship's surface. Using his index finger, he gave the gentlest of squeezes to the throttle. White hydrogen fog sprayed from the nozzles, propelling him downward. He released the throttle and took out grappling hooks, readying them for impact.

Jabbing the hooks onto the rock, he used his gloved thumbs. Each grappler shuddered as it thrust an anchoring spike into the rock. Cyrus rotated his body so his back floated just above the surface. Quickly and nearly as efficiently as a space marine, he attached filament lines to the hooks so they crisscrossed his suit. He didn't have official combat training, but he knew how to do some things now. Mikhail had been teaching him. In trade, he'd shown several of the marines a trick or two about vibrio-knives.

Such combat sparring between a Special like him and space marines would have horrified Dr. Wexx if she'd known about it. Likely, it would have horrified everyone aboard ship.

Cyrus's breath went out in a whoosh as the Teleship accelerated, the surface rushing up several millimeters to meet his back and push him. In seconds, he felt the one-G acceleration. He liked it, as floating weightless in the ship for nearly three standard days had heightened his headache.

He blinked several times. The razor pain in his mind receded with the one G. His eyes had become scratchy and dry. This felt better, and his breathing began to even out.

"You okay, Mikhail?" Cyrus asked.

"You're a bastard," the marine radioed.

It was technically true, but Cyrus didn't believe the first sergeant had meant it like that.

"Acceleration should stay at one G for a while," he told Mikhail. "You can probably walk back to your A-couch if you're not there already."

"Meaning you can walk to the dome and get your butt in here," Mikhail said.

"Yeah, but I'm not going to do that."

"I should come out and get you."

"Sure," Cyrus said, "but no one is ever going to find out I floated outside during a shift unless you report it."

"They could be monitoring our comms, you idiot."

"They aren't."

"Yeah?" Mikhail asked, with a sudden lilt to his voice.

Cyrus heard the unease, and he shook his head. He knew better than to do that. *Don't show the Normals you're different. It always upsets them.* That's what his instructors in Psi Force had drummed into him, into all of them, weak or strong.

"I don't know for certain," Cyrus amended. "But I sure don't think they're going to stop accelerating anytime soon."

"If that's true, why don't you come in? If something happens to you out there, *I'm* the one who's going to bite it."

This was a poor way of repaying the marine for letting him into the laser dome. But sometimes when taking matters into your own hands—

A chrome ring suddenly appeared around the Teleship. The light caused the nearest stars to fade away and others farther away to lose their luster. The ring was awesome, and it had been there all along, although with a black-matted color. The chrome appearance meant a shift opening—a null portal—was about to occur.

It was too bad it had to be this way: him coming out during a shift. He got along better with the marines than anyone else aboard ship. They were a band of brothers, in many ways just like the Latin Kings of his youth. They looked out for each other, never leaving one of their own on a battlefield. As a knife boy in the slums, living by his wits like a wolf surrounded by a million hyenas, Cyrus had learned similar values.

The ring pulsated with light, with an intense chrome color. It was beautiful, it was an illusion, and for some reason, the razor pain in his head lessened.

Teleships were a relatively new invention, Cyrus knew. Seventeen years ago, there had been a serendipitous occurrence near Neptune. It happened in a miles-long science lab where people had created the first "discontinuity window" in the solar system.

Since the marvelous accident seventeen years ago, work to exploit it had proceeded feverishly. The Teleship *Discovery* was the latest and most important result.

A discontinuity window now appeared before Cyrus and before *Discovery*. The null space blotted out the stars, and it might have appeared black, but motes of gray light danced in it. One of those motes grew incredibly fast and strange colors blossomed, brightened, and—

Special Fourth Class Cyrus Gant began to rave like a lunatic. The pain in his mind shut off, but a new agony struck. He closed his eyes and that helped a little. His visor darkened and that likely saved his sanity. The impression on his mind of the hole in time and space caused him to writhe and flop like a landed trout. Fortunately the filament lines kept him secure. He groaned and his consciousness attempted to reject what he'd seen. The sheer nullity of it—

Under the filament lines, Cyrus curled into a fetal ball and he tried to press himself into the surface of the ship. He never wanted to see something like that again. It felt evil and vile, much as that time he'd broken into the S&M Palace to peek at what they did there. The brutality he'd witnessed . . .

"I'll win through," he whispered, repeating a childhood mantra taught to him from an ancient book.

Think, Cyrus, he told himself.

What he'd seen was a discontinuity window formed through a combination of powerful AIs merged with human clairvoyant and telekinetic abilities. Together, they had joined two widely separate points in space. And—

Although his eyes were screwed tight, Cyrus knew the Teleship sped at the DW and passed through it . . . *now.* A sudden icy sensation in his head accelerated a terrible feeling of loneliness. A rasp of sound caught in his throat. The grim feeling—it snapped into blazing heat, which told him they were through again, thank God.

During the momentary opening, a ship passed through the discontinuity window, shifting from one location to the other. In this instance, the jump occurred between two points 8.3 light-years apart. Cyrus knew because he could feel that Venice had done it.

Venice is dead. What's going on? Why am I reenacting all this?

Abruptly, the one-G acceleration quit.

Cyrus eased open his left eye. The tele-ring had changed back to black. It no longer shone like chrome. That meant the discontinuity window was behind them. Likely, it had already closed. That meant *Discovery* was 8.3 light-years closer to what everyone—news corps and citizens alike—called the star system of New Eden.

Cyrus unlatched the filament lines crisscrossing his body. Gingerly, he sat up.

The black dome was still there. The stars still shined, although in a slightly different pattern as before. And the buzzing headache had vanished.

It was time to get into the dome and placate the marines, particularly Mikhail. For a battle-hardened veteran, the man was a worrywart.

"Cyrus?"

A light shined from the portal. The circle of brightness sped along the surface until it reached Cyrus.

"Are you all right?" Mikhail asked.

"I'm feeling—" Cyrus winced and he suddenly gasped as he felt something new. This was different from the agony earlier. It was a lance of pain rather than a blanket of buzzing. This mind lance, this drilling sensation, was human in origin. Reflexively he blocked as they'd taught him in the Psi Force. The mental attack, the strength and uniqueness of it—it had to be Venice that did this.

"Mikhail?" Cyrus asked.

The marine groaned as if someone had shot him in the thigh.

Understanding lit Cyrus's eyes. This attack didn't make sense; it had come from nowhere. Was it the trouble? The thing that he'd been sensing was coming? Venice had just shifted. She shouldn't have the strength to hurt anyone with a mental attack. So what was going on that had changed the rules?

A stronger and more concentrated drill of purified hatred struck his mind. It was Cyrus's turn to groan even as he struggled to deflect the mind bolt.

Over the headphones, First Sergeant Mikhail Sergetov howled with madness in his voice.

If Venice was doing this to the marines out here on the surface, what was happening inside the core of life support in the tele-chamber?

Cyrus shoved off the surface, propelling himself toward the dome's portal. He used his index finger, triggering the thruster throttle. Hydrogen spray blew from the nozzles, pushing him faster, even as he prepared himself for the next mental attack.

Yet as he flew for the combat dome, the stars began to disappear, winking out one by one.

Submit to me or you will fade with the universe.

That didn't feel like Venice. It was alien—

Yes! The *alien* tried to trick him.

It's no good, Cyrus telepathically told the entity. *I'm on to you.*

Do you believe that?

I sure do. This is the second time you've failed.

Let us test your theory one more time. Then you shall submit and I can begin the great work.

13

As Cyrus Gant fought his strange mind war with the alien entity, Darcy Foxe aboard Ice Hauler 266-9 fended off Jick's latest advances.

She had returned from her excursion on the snowball, put away the vacc-suit, and showered.

That was the one luxury in taking these icebergs to Jassac. Once they landed on the chosen asteroid and hooked up the lines, they could shower to their hearts' delight. She had spent an hour letting hot water pummel her flesh. It had felt glorious.

She exited the tiny stall, dried herself before the vents, and heard pounding on the hatch.

Ice Hauler 266-9 was a small place to spend four long years with each other. They had a rec room, a library or reading chamber, and tens of thousands of holo-vids. Exercise, reading, and watching holo-vids all began to pale after two years. So they wouldn't murder each other, Spacer Command enforced staggered rosters. One third of the time, three crewmembers worked together. One half of the time, two crewmembers worked as a team. The remaining stretch awake was spent alone.

That meant each of them had to enter stasis tubes during part of the journey. Putting them in storage saved on food, water, and energy. Soon now, everyone would wake up and help install the engines onto the asteroid. Then they would ride the snowball back to Jassac. That meant this would be the last rotation this cycle Jick and Darcy would work alone together. She just had to endure him another day.

"I know you hear me!" Jick shouted as he hammered on the shower-room hatch.

"Go away," Darcy said.

"I ran my hand under an analyzer, you witch. You lied to me. There aren't any toxins in my system."

After tucking the edge of the towel so it was as secure as it was going to get around her, she looked up. "Are you that daft? The analyzer can't pick up the toxins I used."

"More lies!" he shouted, sounding outraged.

She was the one who should be angry. Jick tracked her with his eyes wherever she went. Sometimes, she'd thought about spacing him. The punishments were too gruesome, however. The Kresh always discovered the crimes through the hated Bo Taw, the mind rapists.

The spacers were one of the few human groups that thought of the Kresh as Kresh. On some occasions, certainly, they called a Kresh overlord "master" or "Revered One." Normally, however, the crew of the haulers thought of them as Kresh. Perhaps the aliens didn't feel a need to subject the spacers to love conditioning.

Darcy now moved closer to the hatch. "Think about it, Jick. How do you think I got the toxins past the inspectors in the first place?"

"Because you made it all up!" he shouted.

"Right," she said, deciding she'd have to use psychology on him. "Tell me this, then. How come your member hasn't stiffened since you've ingested the toxins?" She was guessing here, hoping his fears had made it impossible.

"You're lying about the toxins!" he screamed, pounding on the hatch.

Her eyebrows rose. He sounded demented. Then the hatch clicked open. It astonished her. She backed away as her stomach clenched.

The hatch opened wider and Jick stood there. He had an override switch in his hand.

"Well, well, well," he said, licking his lips obscenely. "This is very interesting."

"It's illegal to use an override code for personal situations."

"Ah-ha!" he said, triumphantly. "I'm here to enact ship law. You violated the codes, going outside alone. Now I've come to violate you, Darcy."

She backed away.

Jick stepped over the portal opening. He was thin and unappealing, with long features. Unfortunately, he had wiry strength because he spent an inordinate amount of time in the exercise room.

"I'm warning you, Jick."

"No!" he said. "I have come to warn you. Lie to me again and I will rip away your towel and expose you to my gaze. Then I will unbuckle my pants and mount you to my satisfaction."

"Rape, Jick? Are you threatening me with rape?"

He grinned so wide that his back molars were visible. "While you floated outside against custom, I opened the recording panel. I tinkered with it, Darcy, and I've shut it off."

"And you claim I broke custom?"

He scanned her ill-clad form. "Rip off your towel," he said in a husky voice. "Let me view your naked beauty."

A greasy feeling writhed in her stomach. His lecherous gaze sickened her. She felt faint. If he attempted to rape her—

No. You must think clearly, she told herself. Going alone outside was forbidden. Tampering with the recorder would bring the death sentence. *Does he mean to rape and then kill me?*

Each of them had passed psychological tests by mentalists. They were each supposed to be able to withstand the pressures of long space voyages. Had Jick snapped?

No. His lusts have gotten the better of him. All he does is watch porn. Now, he finally wants the real thing.

The sick feeling in her stomach made her nauseous, and that stole some of her strength. It wasn't fair that a geek like Jick was stronger than she was. If she kicked him in the groin and failed to reach her room . . .

"Go away, Jick," she said, trying to keep the quaver out of her voice. "Fix the recorder. Otherwise, when the others wake, I'll tell them what you've done."

"You'd let them hand out a death sentence against me?" he asked in a thick voice.

"Leave, Jick."

"No," he said. He moved toward her.

Darcy backed up until she bumped against the shower stall. The pit of her stomach throbbed.

Jick reached out. She slapped his hand. He snarled and slapped her across the face. It whipped her head to the side, dazing her. Jick reached out again, grabbed her damp towel, and yanked hard.

She yelled as the towel moved away, and she realized Jick stared at her naked body as he held the towel in his hand.

For a moment, he stood with his lips parted and eyes glazed.

Darcy covered her breasts and lower area as best she could.

Jick chuckled nastily. He grabbed one end of the towel and began to spin it. Then he flicked the towel like a whip, snapping it at her side.

She cried out. The wet end hurt as it snapped her. "Stop it, Jick."

He flicked it again, snapping it at her face. She swatted it away, and her breasts jiggled free.

"Nice," Jick said in a husky voice. "Those are very nice."

The greasy feeling worsened in Darcy, but now anger bubbled in her. Lousy, freaky Jick toyed with her. She was in charge of the ship. He was nothing but a tech, tagging along to make sure the equipment worked. How dare he do this to her.

She covered her breasts, and she plotted.

Jick laughed. "This is fun, Darcy. I'm going to make you dance for me. I want to see your tits again."

She slid away sideways, trying to keep from staring down at the floor. It looked slick to the side of Jick. She'd been dripping water there. If she could maneuver him onto the spot—yes. He followed her.

"Show me your tits again," he said in an ugly voice.

She shook her head.

"I'll snap out your eyes," he threatened.

"Your member will shrivel."

"Are you looking at my pants?" he asked. "I'm as hard as a rock, Darcy. You're in big trouble."

She stood glaring at him, covering herself.

He flicked the wet towel again.

With a shout, Darcy lowered a shoulder and charged. The end of the towel struck her in the face, but she was too determined to let it stop her. She collided against him. Jick cried out, and his feet slid on the wet tiles.

He crashed onto his rear. His shoulder blades struck the floor and the back of his head knocked with a thud.

Darcy almost stumbled onto him. She jumped at the last second and landed on the other side of him near the portal. Another hop took her into the corridor.

Jick groaned.

Darcy didn't look back. She ran down the corridor, twisted into another, and reached her room.

"Darcy!" he shouted.

Her heart beat wildly. She heard him running down the corridor. With trembling fingers, she punched in her room's code. The hatch unlatched.

"I'm going to have you!" he roared.

She opened the hatch, stepped over the portal, and shut it behind her. He had the override switch, so she only had a few moments to get ready. Flinging herself to her closet, she chose a T-shirt and slipped it on. It covered her breasts. That was good enough for now. With a hop, she reached her drawers, flung one open, and grabbed an emergency prober. It was long and thin, meant for testing nexus nodes. Jabbed at a gut or in someone's face, and it could do harm. It was better than trying to fistfight Jick.

She hefted the prober. Jick might be groggy from hitting the back of his head. He also might be even more enraged.

"Darcy!" he shouted, banging on the hatch.

She squealed as she started, and that made her angry. This was Jick.

"I'm coming in," he said, "and I'm going to do you."

"Go away!" she shouted. "Fix the recorder and quit joking."

"Joking?" he shouted. "You think I'm joking?"

"I don't want to hurt you anymore."

He chuckled evilly. A moment later, the hatch clicked. Jick pushed the portal open, and he stared at her with bloodshot eyes.

"I like what I see," he said. "Nice legs, Darcy."

She refused to cover herself. During her times portside, she had taken a few self-defense courses. She would attempt to jab out one of his eyes. It would be a difficult thrust, but worth everything if she succeeded. Then she realized he'd shut off the recorder. There wouldn't be anything to prove why she'd murdered him.

The queasy feeling returned. Why did the crazy person always have the advantage? It was utterly unfair.

"Oh, Darcy," Jick said, entering her quarters. "You can't imagine how many times I've fantasized about coming into your chamber like this. We're going to have such a good, good time."

That decided it for her. She would kill him. A Bo Taw could also read her mind later and see she'd had no other choice.

Jick advanced another step. She set herself. He eyed the prober in her hand.

"Do you think you can hurt me with that?" he asked.

"I hurt you once already, and I'll do it again."

"No. I'm the one who is going to do the hurting. I'm going to be very rough, Darcy, and I'm going to try many, many different variations."

Darcy drew a ragged breath. She needed to trick him again. Then—

The ice hauler's warning klaxon began to wail. The pulse sounds were unlike anything she'd heard before.

Jick cocked his head, and he scowled.

The klaxon blared louder than ever. It was a primary emergency.

"How did you do that?" he asked.

"I had nothing to do with it."

"What's the emergency?"

"I have no idea," she said.

He snarled. The klaxon noises were becoming painful to the ear.

"Let's check it out," he said.

"You first," she said. "I plan to get dressed."

"Do you hear that? It's a primary emergency."

"Yes," she said, amazed at this. What was causing it?

Then the hauler's AI came online. "Warning," it said. "A foreign spaceship is approaching. A collision is imminent. Warning, a—"

With an inarticulate howl, Jick spun around. He jumped through the hatch and raced to the command module.

Darcy Foxe heaved a sigh of relief. The klaxon continued to blare, however. She set aside the prober and rushed to her drawers. It was time to get dressed, wake the others, and see what kind of vessel planned to ram the ice hauler.

14

Silence filled Ice Hauler 266-9. The klaxon no longer wailed. With a slow step, Darcy entered the command module to see Jick hunched over the sensor screen.

He glanced back at her. Worry lined his thin face. "What is that?" he asked. "Do you have any idea? I've never seen its like."

She glanced at the command screen. A giant spheroid majestically approached on a clear collision course. It was still several kilometers away and seemed to be slowing. A visible hangar bay opened. Two smaller vessels poked out, each of them headed for the hauler.

"I've already woken Glissim," Darcy said.

Jick appeared not to hear. He fiddled with sensor controls. Nothing visibly changed.

"I don't think it's a Kresh vessel," Jick said. "According to this, the outer hull is made of an unknown material. If I had to guess, it's some sort of collapsed matter."

Darcy shook her head. They had heard rumors of a Chirr attack in the inner system. It was amazing to think the insects had spaceships. She didn't think the vessel out there belonged to the Chirr, though.

"Collapsed matter is very dense," Jick explained. "I believe the vessel has heavy shielding is what I'm saying."

"A warship," Darcy said.

"A probable non-Kresh warship," Jick amended.

"You heard the news earlier, right?"

"You mean about the Chirr space fleet?" Jick asked.

Nodding, Darcy asked, "Could this be a Chirr vessel?"

"I doubt Chirr ships could make it this far unnoticed. I think the vessel came from outside our star system."

Darcy edged deeper into the chamber. Like every other room aboard the ice hauler, it was cramped and far too cozy.

"I don't like this," Jick said, straightening. "I've heard rumors of invaders before."

Darcy remembered hearing something about that, too.

"What do you know about that?" Jick asked.

Darcy took another step closer. Frowning, she examined the alien vessel on the screen. It was bigger than a Kresh hammer-ship.

"There's something I don't understand," Jick said.

"What?"

"We're at the edge of the Fenris System. The alien ship is black, but doesn't appear to be radar-resistant. Surely, the Kresh would have spotted it long ago and brought warships to intercept the vessel. So, why haven't they done that?"

Darcy sucked in her breath.

"What?" Jick asked. "You know something."

"Remember the report about an alien ship simply appearing?"

"Now that you mention it," Jick said, "I do."

"Maybe this ship has a star-drive."

"You mean hyperspace?" asked Jick.

"Something that would have kept it off Kresh sensors," Darcy said. "If it traveled through hyperspace, the vessel wouldn't show up on radar until it reentered normal space."

"If such a thing as hyperspace even exists," Jick said.

"Do you have a better explanation?"

Jick stared at the screen. "What I don't understand is why it's coming at us."

One of Darcy's hands flew to her mouth. She moaned. Maybe she knew exactly why the alien vessel approached them.

"What do you know?" Jick asked.

She hesitated telling him. What difference would it make now? She almost blurted the news, and found it difficult to utter the words. Why was that?

"Darcy?" he asked.

This made no sense. *Tell him.* Finally, she stammered, "I-I found something in our asteroid."

"What do you mean, 'found'?"

"Something ancient," Darcy said.

"An ancient alien thing?"

"Maybe."

Jick's mouth dropped open. He studied the ship. "Do you think they're here to retrieve the ancient thing?"

As Darcy thought about that, she frowned. "It doesn't make sense, though."

"The alien ship is out there. That ought to be enough proof."

"I know. But the thing I saw was embedded in ice, in an *asteroid*. It must have been there a long, long time. Why would this ship show up now?"

"You think it's a coincidence that it arrived at the asteroid at the same time we did?"

"Maybe, maybe not."

Jick put both hands around the sensor panel, staring down at it.

"We have to warn the authorities," Darcy said.

"You mean warn the Kresh?"

"Of course," she said. Then his words struck her. She couldn't believe it. Jick? "Don't tell me you're a Humanity Ultimate."

"Why should the Kresh rule us?" he said. "Humans used to be free, you know."

"Oh yeah right," Darcy said. "A few minutes ago you showed why the Kresh should rule. Without their guidance, humans run amok, turning into rapists, for one thing."

Jick's facial muscles tightened. "I played a little joke. It's possible it was in poor taste."

"You weren't joking," she said. "You told me you weren't."

"Darcy, Darcy, Darcy, you never have understood me. Of course it was a joke."

"You're a Humanity Ultimate."

"Not really," he said. "Can I not have a few of my own thoughts, though?"

"I should report this."

"No. We should figure out the right thing to do. Look. The smallest alien shuttlecraft is slowing down."

"We must report this," Darcy repeated. "Whether you like the Kresh or not, our people belong to them. These are invaders."

"They might fire on us if we try to radio anyone."

"Jick, we're spacers. We must report this."

He stared at her, and he couldn't help looking at her breasts. "Okay," he said.

It angered her that he still lusted after her body. And it made her even madder that she'd argued to gain his permission to call. She was in charge of the ship, not him.

Darcy moved to her seat, sat down, and opened channels for Spacer Command Outer Asteroids. Harsh growling sounds came out of the speakers.

The two of them exchanged glances.

"The aliens aren't going to let us call anyone," Jick said. "They're jamming us."

"Should we attempt to hail them then?"

"Go ahead," Jick said.

Darcy Foxe scowled once more. *Don't ask him to do something. He's Jick. He just tried to rape me. I'm the commander. I don't need his help.*

She opened channels, directing communications toward the approaching shuttlecraft. "This is Ice Hauler 266-9. It appears you plan to board us. I must inform you that we are part of the Kresh Imperium. We are under their protection. I request that you speak with us so we may come to a peaceful solution."

"They're jamming us," Jick said. "That means they're not peaceful."

"Maybe they could be," she said.

"Really?"

"They're just being cautious," Darcy said.

Jick grew pale, which seemed like a strange time to become frightened if he hadn't been before this. "I hope you're right. I don't think you are, but I want you to be. I'm . . . I'm worried."

So am I, but what can we do? Nothing. We have to see what happens.

The big spheroid came to a halt two kilometers from the asteroid. The larger shuttle took up station half a kilometer from them. The smaller one kept closing.

"Look at that," Jick said, using an indicator on the screen. He circled an area of the triangular-shaped shuttle, the small one. "That appears to be a laser port, and it's aimed at us."

New, harsh sounds emanated from Darcy's panel.

"What is that?" Jick asked in a quavering voice.

Darcy adjusted her panel. "I'd say our sensors picked up their scanners. They must be studying us, and they're being very rude about it."

After a full minute, the sounds stopped. Now, the smallest alien shuttle approached even closer. Extra tubes poked out and aimed at the ice hauler.

"They're not trusting," Jick said.

"We could launch off the asteroid and try to ram them," Darcy said.

"Why?"

"To show them we're dangerous and that they have to talk to us."

"I'd say they're going to talk once they're here."

"Maybe we should see them first. There are worse things than dying."

"No," Jick said. "Once I die, it's over. As long as I live, I have hope. So, we won't be ramming them today."

"I've heard strange stories about the Chirr."

"These are not Chirr," Jick said.

As he spoke, the shuttle began to make the final braking maneuvers. The ice hauler trembled as the alien vessel landed on the asteroid. A tube snaked from the other craft to their outer lock.

"Let's go," Darcy said. "We might as well greet them as they enter our ship."

Glissim joined them in the small chamber. She was petite, blonde, and usually full of smiles. Today, worry creased her face. "Who are they, Darcy?"

"We're about to find out," she said.

Beyond the outer lock came clangs and the hissing of atmospheric pressure.

"That is against all regulations," Darcy said.

"We can't stop them," Jick said. He gave her a leer, an up-and-down study. "So we might as well sit back and enjoy it."

Darcy focused on the inner airlock and straightened her uniform as she waited. A new clang told her the outer hatch opened. The aliens were almost inside the ice hauler's pressurized quarters.

"I hate the waiting," Glissim said. "What if they eat us?"

"They're not Chirr," Jick said. "It's impossible they're Chirr. The bugs are at Heenhiss, not the outer asteroid belt."

The inner entrance began to slide open. The aliens from the giant warship were almost inside the ice hauler.

Darcy couldn't help herself. She stood at attention, frightened and curious of what she'd see. Beside her, Glissim moaned. Jick waited behind them.

The airlock slid open, and a human strode onto the ice hauler.

Before Darcy could exhale in relief, she saw her mistake.

Underneath the black uniform, the alien had polished metal parts and plastic flesh. His face was as lifeless as a mask. He had silver-metal orbs for eyes in black plastic sockets.

Behind him was an elongated monstrosity of flesh and graphite bones. It was too long-limbed to be human. With every motion, the thing made faint whirring sounds. Did it have motorized joints? It certainly possessed an armored body.

Glissim gasped, and she might have staggered backward. Darcy grabbed her elbow, steadying her crewmate. Then Darcy stepped forward and saluted as if the black-clad metal man was an inspector.

"Welcome aboard Ice Hauler 266-9. I am Senior Darcy Foxe, the commanding officer of our ship."

"I am Toll Three," the metal man said in a modulated voice. It only hinted at machinery, but it lacked emotive inflection.

"Welcome, Toll Three," Darcy said. "We see you've come in force. I mean your massive warship. Is there a reason for that?"

The alien smiled, revealing steel-colored teeth. He unlatched a device from his belt, clicked it, and waved the thing before Darcy and Glissim. The creature watched the device, finally clicking it off and returning it to his belt.

"You are human," Toll Three said. "Facts dictate that your species originated at Earth."

"Homeworld," Darcy said. "You're familiar with Earth?"

"Of course," Toll Three said. "Our origin point is also the solar system, but from a science hab orbiting the planet Neptune. We are cyborgs."

"We're related?" Darcy asked in a weak voice. As she spoke, she refused to look at the other thing behind Toll Three. Cyborg . . . Didn't that mean a meld of man and machine?

"Your query is immaterial to the project at hand," Toll Three said. "The battle fleet has arrived in the Fenris System. We are here to conquer and submerge your flesh into the whole."

An icy terror worked along Darcy's neck.

"First, the Prime Web-Mind desires knowledge concerning the alien construct."

"What construct?" Darcy asked.

"Subterfuge will gain you agony, Senior Darcy Foxe. We have sensed the machine buried in the ice. The Prime Web-Mind has no records of it. What is the construct's function?"

"I don't know what you're talking about," Darcy whispered.

Toll Three studied a device embedded in his left wrist. "My sensors indicate you are lying. Therefore, a demonstration is in order." He crooked a finger. Without another word, the tall cyborg behind him whirred forward with deceptive speed.

Glissim screamed, stumbling backward.

"No!" Darcy shouted.

The cyborg reached for Darcy. She flinched. It made no difference. Impossibly strong hands clamped onto the flesh of her upper arms. The thing pulled her near Toll Three as the others watched in horror.

Toll Three held a small, round object. "This is the agonizer. Observe." He touched it to her neck.

A sizzle of pain lanced through her. Darcy screamed as she writhed in the cyborg's grip. Toll Three removed the agonizer.

"Let me restate the question," he said. "What is the construct in the asteroid?"

"I don't know," Darcy gasped. "We just found it."

Once more, Toll Three studied his wrist device. "This indicates that you spout more subterfuge. This is an error."

"Please," Darcy whimpered. "I'm telling you the truth."

"Then why did your vessel land on this particular asteroid? There are over ten thousand asteroids to choose from."

"We're hauling ice to Jassac," Darcy said.

"For what reason?"

"The Kresh are terraforming the moon around Pulsar."

Toll Three's silver orbs remained motionless. "That is a clever deception, but unsuccessful. The probability of you choosing this asteroid at random means you are likely lying."

"No, no," Darcy said. "It just proves that coincidences do happen."

"I have not come to argue," Toll Three said. "The Prime Web-Mind desires information."

"Can I ask a question?" Jick said.

Toll Three's head swiveled. He regarded Jick standing in back. "Speak."

"You really want to know what this object is, don't you?"

The cyborg said nothing, waiting.

Jick swallowed nervously. He was scratching his left palm. "Look, it's clear you're honest. I give you something and you give me something, right?"

Again, the cyborg said nothing.

"I want preferred treatment," Jick said.

"Explain your statement," Toll Three said.

"If I give you what you want, you need to give me what I want."

"What is your desire?"

"Good treatment to begin with. We can talk about what else you can give me."

"You know about the construct?" Toll Three asked.

"Of course," Jick said. "I wasn't supposed to say. Senior Darcy doesn't know anything. I'm the one you want to talk to about this thing."

Darcy knew Jick was lying. He had his lying look. The weasel didn't want the agonizer to touch him. That's what this was about.

Toll Three studied his wrist device. The cyborg nodded. "You will report to the Prime Web-Mind."

Whatever that thing sensed, Jick was such a good liar that he could beat it. Darcy found that interesting.

"Sure, sure," Jick said, blinking rapidly.

Toll Three turned to the airlock. As he did, the other thing holding Darcy released her. The meld of human and machine reached for Jick.

"Hey," he said. "What are you doing? I'll come peacefully."

The cyborg grabbed him by the upper arms. Then it followed Toll Three to the airlock, marching Jick along.

"Good-bye, Jick," Glissim called.

He looked back at them. Sweat glistened on his face and fear swam in his eyes.

Darcy was ashamed that she felt relieved seeing Jick go. What would the cyborgs do to the rest of the crew? What would the Kresh do later? Oh, this was awful.

The cyborgs and Jick entered the airlock. They squeezed together tighter than people would do. Jick stood between them, and Darcy could hear him groan.

The inner airlock slid shut, and the cyborgs and Jick disappeared from view.

"Will he be okay?" Glissim asked.

Darcy doubted that very much.

15

Far away from the outer asteroid belt, Cyrus Gant panted with exhaustion as he journeyed through a dark and dreary realm. He had no idea where this place existed. It seemed as if he'd walked forever in pitch darkness. He had a searing headache as he searched for an exit from this realm.

Yes, and then where will I go? I don't belong here. This is—not a dream. But there's something I'm not remembering.

In the dark, he trod over sand, dirt, rocks, and slime. Hideous fumes accompanied the last. He slid and fell until slippery mud coated him. He continued walking. The foul substance eventually dried in his hair. For a time, he waded up to his ankles in squishy mud. He bent low and tasted the water. With a grunt, he spat it out. He wasn't *that* thirsty, not yet, at least.

Soon thereafter, he heard a slithering sound behind him.

He froze in horror. What was out there?

He heard a distant wheeze such as a sea cow might make. He'd watched a video on them in the institute on Crete. A strange wet slapping sound caused him to start. Whatever was out there headed toward him.

Cyrus carried a hand-sized stone. At times, he'd scraped the stone against others, putting an edge to it. A Berserker Clan primitive would have sniffed in disdain at his tool. To Cyrus, it was his cherished possession.

He paused. *Berserker Clan primitive? I should know what that is.*

The slithering sounds increased, and Cyrus heard grunts timed with the wet slap of mud.

Carefully, he moved away from the thing. Each time his foot lifted, however, there was a slimy sucking sound.

A terrible laugh came out of the darkness. It chilled Cyrus's flesh. The nearing thing shouted with incomprehensible words then. Others farther away took up the cry.

Cyrus bit his lip in indecision.

The slithering sounds drew nearer. So did the scoop of mud, and then a low muttering. Cyrus stood utterly still, although he began to tremble.

The slithering thing laughed and made a terrible lunge. It was closer than Cyrus realized. A cold hand grasped his ankle. It had incredible strength and ground his anklebones together. Cyrus bellowed with rage and horror. He swung, and the rock cracked against a skull. The thing groaned, although its cold grip tightened painfully.

Cyrus hacked repeatedly. The fifth blow caused the rock to slip out of his slimy grasp. With desperate strength he kicked his ankle free.

There was something terribly familiar about this, but he couldn't place it.

Distant shouts became frantic. There were many of these things out there. The splashing said so.

Cyrus floundered in the mud as he searched for his stone. He felt along the length of the dazed creature and discovered a bloated, man-shaped torso with arms and a head, but lacking legs. It was as naked, as sleek as a seal. He felt blubbery lips and pointed teeth like a cannibal.

What is this thing?

Cyrus's searching fingers touched stone. He gripped it, tearing it out of the mud.

The bloated thing muttered slurred words. Cyrus slipped and slid in the slime as he ran away from it.

I will defeat you.

Never, Cyrus thought.

You must submit.

A ragged laugh tore out of Cyrus's parched throat.

Don't you understand what's at stake?

No, Cyrus said through telepathy. *Tell me.*

Submit and you shall learn.

Vaguely, Cyrus realized he'd been through tests like this before. Something tried to dominate his mind, his thoughts. An alien fought him. Yes, that's right. The alien entity had put him here in the dark.

The understanding retreated from his awareness as Cyrus ran from the croaking creatures until the air burned down his throat. He ran until his side ached as if daggers thrust into him. His legs wobbled, and sweat washed away the coating slime. Then he bashed against a wall. It sent him reeling backward. Far in the distance, creatures hooted with glee.

Sobbing with effort, Cyrus felt along the wall, wading. Here, the slime deepened into water. Soon, he stood up to his waist. If only he had a flashlight, clothes, and good boots. What had happened to his courage? Didn't he used to be brave?

It was hard to be courageous in the dark, he realized, while naked and chased by slithering, cannibalistic monstrosities. He waded up to his chest and his toes squished between rubbery growths. The stench was worse than a dung pit.

He felt along the wall the entire time. Finally, a protrusion pushed against his hand. His exhausted mind took several heartbeats to understand what he held. It was a rung. He tapped his stone against it. The rung was metal. He pulled himself upward, reaching with his other hand, and touched another rung.

How high did they go? To find out, he would have to release his stone.

Indecision filled him until he grew aware that the chasing things no longer slithered, but splashed as if swimming.

Cyrus dropped the rock and began to climb. There were more rungs, about fifty of them. They led to a hole in the wall. He hoisted himself into the hole and immediately found a grate blocking his way. He had no time for this.

Cyrus tested the grate with a shake and then banged his shoulder against it. Metal groaned. With furious haste, Cyrus redoubled his efforts. He bent the metal bars back enough for him to squeeze through. It cost him a nasty cut in the shoulder. He was beyond caring. He crawled. He crawled until exhaustion forced him to sleep in the tunnel perhaps kilometers away from where he'd broken in.

He awoke in a cold sweat and with a raging thirst. He listened, expecting evil chuckles from patiently waiting half men. There was only silence. He began to crawl. He did so for hours, maybe for days. When his hands and knees became too tender, he stood and waddled in a painful, bent-over crouch.

There were side holes and holes in the ceiling. He felt a breeze sometimes. Once, he heard a distant clank from a hole. Much later, light shocked him. He'd rounded a bend, and far in the distance, a bright light confounded him. He stood blinking at it with tears in his eyes. He broke into a shuffling trot and soon grew aware that the light was far away.

He slept two more times before he reached the light. It flooded down from a chute in the ceiling. He examined the main chute. It was constructed of worn-smooth bricks. Filth stained them. Filth stained his arms, torso, and legs.

Cyrus stood in the light and wondered if he detected a waver in it as from a fire. He stood gazing upward until he felt a crick in his neck.

Reluctantly, he continued his trek. It was many sleeps before he took a side tunnel and exited onto a plain. Because it was dark, he had no idea if he left a giant castle or a hole in a mountain. He trudged several more steps before he spied another flare of light.

He crouched on the plain of darkness. His lips cracked and his tongue might have begun to swell. His legs ached and a cut on the side of his left foot refused to heal properly. He yearned for sandals or boots and longed for even the barest loincloth. A tunic and jacket, he'd trade a year of his life for those, and another year for a gun.

He realized the tiny point of light came closer. Then he saw the light flicker and knew it was a torch.

A shock of recognition filled him. A big man with a shaved scalp neared. He had white eyes without pupils. Yes. Cyrus had seen the man in Milan.

Milan?

That's right. He'd been born and raised there, and he'd joined the Psi Force on Earth. In fact, this was a psionic battle between him and the . . . the entity that had screwed with Klane there at the end on the Attack Talon.

"This isn't real," Cyrus said in a hoarse voice.

The big man had moved closer much too fast, as often happens in a dream.

"I want a vibrio-blade," Cyrus said. He concentrated and held his hand just so. As if by magic, a power knife appeared in his hand.

So, that's how things worked in this realm.

"Let's give myself clothes, boots, and a Latin King jacket," he said.

Seconds later, Cyrus wore clothes again. He should have done this a long time ago.

The big man halted three meters away. The torch flickered oddly, casting blue shadows on him.

"Who are you?" Cyrus asked.

"I suppose you've earned that much," the man said. "I am an Eich."

"That means you're not human, are you?"

"Sometimes I am," the Eich said, his lips twitching into a smile.

"What does that mean?" Cyrus asked.

Those horrible white eyes studied him. "You've wearied me. I admit that. You own a stubborn core. But that won't help you in the end. I have finally found the vessel, and I believe that it will come to me."

"What are you talking about?" Cyrus asked.

"Submit to my will. If you do, I will guide you to power. Resist and I will finally break you here and now."

Cyrus studied the big man, the Eich. "I don't think so. You haven't been doing too well so far."

"Neither have you done well."

"Yeah? I'm still in charge of my thoughts."

"That is true. But the Kresh have captured your body. They're returning you to High Station 3."

"You're lying," Cyrus said.

"I never lie."

"So speaks the liar with false sincerity," Cyrus said. "Sorry, Mr. Eich, but I grew up in the slums. I know the depths of human depravity, which means I likely know the worst of alien actions."

"You are wrong."

"Yeah? How so?"

"This is your final chance."

Cyrus clicked the knife so it whined with power. Then he shouted and charged.

"You fool. I need your cooperation. I need you to realize—"

Cyrus thrust the vibrio-blade, and it parted flesh as if the being was made of smoke. That caught Cyrus by surprise. He staggered, and then he tensed. He'd figured this guy must be heavy. Instead, Cyrus's head and right shoulder passed through the big man.

"You will never succeed," the Eich said in a hollow voice. Then he faded like rising smoke from a fire.

In that instant, Cyrus broke free of the alien entity's mind lock. The man from Milan opened his eyes, and it took him several seconds to realize where he was.

Cyrus's head lay on soft flesh. He looked up into Jana's concerned face. Her wonderful odor filled his nostrils.

"He's awake," Jana said.

Another face hovered over him. Cyrus recognized the blunt features of Skar 192.

Cyrus heard someone else snoring. He heard the thrum of a spaceship's engines. Then the lean features of Mentalist Niens peered down at him. Those cunning eyes tightened.

"You're yourself," Niens announced.

"Yeah," Cyrus said. "Who else would I be?"

Then it hit him what had been happening. In his own mind, he'd fought the alien entity that had tricked Klane.

Klane!

"Where's the Anointed One?" Cyrus asked in a hoarse voice.

"He's dead," Niens said.

"What?" Cyrus asked. "That's impossible. He's supposed to save Fenris humanity."

I still will.

While on Jana's lap, Cyrus cocked his head. *Who just said that?*

I did, Klane said.

You're dead.

Yes, but my memories and identity transferred into you.

"We're losing him," Niens told the others. "He's going inward to his mind again."

"No, you're not losing me," Cyrus told the mentalist. "Where are we?"

"In a Kresh Battle Fang," Niens said. "They took us captive. We're on our way to High Station 3."

With a groan, Cyrus sat up. His head throbbed with pain.

It is time, Klane inside him said.

Time for what?

For me to teach you how to destroy the Kresh.

16

I've been listening while you've been battling the singing god, Klane told him.

"Whoa, whoa, whoa," Cyrus said. "Slow down. Let me get my bearings first."

"Who are you talking to?" Jana asked him.

"What?" Cyrus asked.

"He's still confused," Niens said. "He's in shock. He may be hopelessly insane."

That was too much for Cyrus. He sat up and looked around. They were in a storage vault, around twenty of them. Skar sat nearby, the tough Vomag soldier. He was shorter than everyone else but had wider shoulders and long, dangling arms. Not even square Yang, the former chieftain of Berserker Clan, was as strong. Yang had leathery features and big hands. Others of Berserker Clan lay, sat, or stood nearby. Each of them had partaken of the seeker's memories. The last group, the shuttle and Attack Talon crew, appeared the most forlorn.

Cyrus spun around and stared at Niens.

The mentalist was tall, thin, and wore a rumpled white coat to his knees. He had narrow features, a beak of a nose, and spidery fingers.

"You have deduced a fact," Niens announced.

"You're right," Cyrus said.

"Do you believe you're sane?"

"Sure."

"Ah," Niens said. "You're not positive?"

"I'm very positive. I've—" Cyrus paused. Maybe this was another trick. The alien entity, the Eich—

This is no trick, Klane said inside Cyrus's mind. *You're now viewing reality.*

Cyrus held up his hands as if he could forestall Klane's thoughts. Then he rubbed his forehead. He had to think this through. The last he remembered of the Anointed One—

"The laser beam burned down Klane," Cyrus said.

"Ah," Niens said. "It's good you remember that."

"The Kresh in the Battle Fang killed Klane?" Cyrus asked.

Niens nodded solemnly.

"And the Kresh boarded and took us captive?"

"Precisely," Niens said.

"That means everything we're saying is being recorded."

"A reasonable deduction," Niens said.

Be careful, Klane said. *Don't let the Bo Taw know you're psionically powerful.*

That was interesting. "Listen," Cyrus told the others. "I'm, uh, feeling off right now."

"You must be hungry," Niens said.

As if on cue, Cyrus's stomach rumbled. "I am hungry," he said.

"Feed him," Niens told the others. "Then we must let him sit alone as he gathers his thoughts."

Cyrus wasn't going to worry how the mentalist knew that. He had too much to think about just now to worry about it. He accepted wafers from the others, wolfing them down. Then he drank metallic-tasting water.

This felt all too much like his original capture by the Kresh when first taken off *Discovery*. Then, everything had felt so alien. He was used to the differences by now, but didn't like them any better.

Cyrus sat apart from the others, perched his elbows on his knees, and bent his head. He rubbed his forehead, trying to piece things together. Klane was dead. That was difficult to accept.

My memories transferred to you, Klane told him.

So you're speaking from inside me?

Yes, Klane said.

Are you still alive in me?

That isn't a good question to ask. The answer is . . .

I think I get it, Cyrus said quickly. *You're not alive, but your memories are. Somehow, you're using the me of me to pretend you're alive. But if you say that you're dead, say it to your memory, you might disappear.*

You'll find that you have many . . . personalities in you now.

Because of the transfer? Cyrus asked.

Precisely.

Did you go through this?

Everyone who has received a full transfer has gone through it.

So, Jana, Yang, and the others don't know about this.

They do not, the memory of Klane said.

I think I'm starting to understand.

Good, because we don't have much time.

This talking back and forth between you and me is really a schizophrenic thing. Niens could be right in one way. I am insane.

No, the memory of Klane told him. *You are very sane. You must rest a moment and I will instruct you in using our powers. Because we didn't have time to transfer properly, I'll now have to teach you what you would have learned instantly if we could have done this the right way.*

Wait a minute, Cyrus said. *You're implying that I inherited your Anointed One psionic powers?*

I am saying exactly that.

Do the Bo Taw know about this?

They do not, Klane said.

So the trick here is to learn how you did stuff and then hit them from out of the blue.

This is like a raid, Klane said. *We must strike hard and fast. Kill them. Help the others kill everyone else. Then kill the Kresh.*

I can't kill the Kresh with my psi-power?

No, Klane told him. *The Kresh keep mechanical mind shields on their persons. That and the love conditioning keep them safe from their Bo Taw slaves.*

Cyrus had forgotten about the mind shields. *Okay. After we do this, we capture another spaceship?*

Afterward, the memory of Klane said, *we will head to High Station 3.*

To pick up my old friends?

We need the Teleship. With it, we will escape to Earth.

Cyrus raised his head. He could feel the others watching him while trying not to stare. Did they realize he could use Klane's powers? Well, he couldn't yet. Frankly, he didn't see how it was possible to transfer psionic strength from one person to another. But it was worth a try. Otherwise . . . humanity was screwed.

Yet there was a different being in him, the alien entity, the Eich. What was that? The Eich had known about a ship, something found elsewhere in the star system. Apparently, this ship could have a profound impact on the coming war.

Can I convince the Eich to tell me about the lost ship? Cyrus asked.

It's dangerous to bargain with the singing god, Klane said. *I tried that once, and in the end he controlled me.*

He didn't control you all the time, though, Cyrus said.

I still fought him, you're right.

But now you're free of his influence.

Cyrus could almost hear a chuckle in his mind.

I am the memory of Klane. The Eich has no hold over my memories. You must keep him separate. That is my advice to you.

What is he? What is a singing god?

I don't know exactly, Klane said. *I think the entity is a psi-parasite. The Eich hid much from me. For eons, I think, it's lived in the metal tube under the mountain. Why it chose now to come out—it must have something to do with the ship I sensed in the asteroid.*

Cyrus nodded. He'd keep the Eich separate as he tried to escape from within the belly of the beast. The Kresh had them. The Anointed One had died, and nothing stood against the dinosaurs gaining *Discovery's* star-drive. How soon would it be until Bo Taw–powered, discontinuity-window technology allowed a massive Kresh fleet into the solar system?

You must regain your freedom, Klane said.

I know. But what do we do once we're free?

As I've always suggested. You must fix the Teleship and escape back to Earth.

Do you think the Kresh have been rebuilding a new AI system for the Teleship?

I think that's extremely likely.

Cyrus turned away from the others and studied the nearest bulkhead. How could he learn to do what Klane did without the Bo Taw mind watchers knowing everything? He didn't feel any stronger than before. How did he know the memory of Klane spoke the truth about new psionic powers?

I urge caution, Klane said. *If you practice before you're ready, the Bo Taw will know and put you in a mind lock. Since they know you're here, you can't use a null to shield yourself.*

Okay. This sounds like a problem. How do I get better if I don't practice?

First, you must let me outline what to do.

Go for it, Cyrus said.

Sit down. Close your eyes and compose yourself.

Cyrus picked a spot, leaning against a bulkhead. He could feel the ship's thrum against his back. They traveled back to High Station 3. It seemed like a lifetime ago that he'd slipped away from it.

Closing his eyes, Cyrus listened as the memory of Klane instructed him in high-level psionics. He observed as the Anointed One took him to places in his mind, showing him what he'd have to do. Finally, Cyrus asked the memory how he could possibly have the power or strength of the Anointed One.

I altered your brain, Klane said. *In my last minutes of life, I stamped much of myself upon you.*

How does that work?

I cannot show you what I don't understand. An older seeker's thoughts guided me then. I do not know where his memory lies in your mind.

The information made Cyrus nervous. *The Eich could have tricked you and shown you what to do. In fact, maybe the singing god did something like that to you in the caves.*

Ah . . . yes, I think you could be right. That would explain much.

I doubt the psi-parasite would go to the trouble of showing you all that if he didn't build a few fail-safes for himself in the altered mind.

That is more than likely. Still, you are stubborn. You proved too difficult an adversary for him. He may have underestimated you.

Or it means he's simply looking for another way to get what he wants.

What do you suggest? Klane asked.

Seems as if I should be asking you that, Cyrus said. *You're the memory and I'm the real thing.* He pondered the problem, but didn't have an immediate solution. *Okay. We'll continue the training in lieu of anything else for now.*

The memory of Klane showed him more. Time passed. Finally, after several hours, the regular noises in the vault intruded upon Cyrus's concentration.

You're tired, Klane said. *You need to rest. Afterward, you can attempt the first live practice.*

Cyrus's eyelids were drooping. The psi-training was far more exhausting than he would have thought from his days at the institute. He yawned. Sliding onto his side, he laid his head on his folded hands. Ah, this felt so good. His mind felt numb. A long sleep would help him recuperate. Likely, it would also help him sort out these memories.

Cyrus slid into unconsciousness. Then shouts woke him, he didn't know how much later. He sat up, groggy. "What's going on?" he asked.

A large door opened. Seven Vomags with drawn guns entered. The soldiers forced the others against the far wall.

With a grunt, Cyrus rose to join the others.

"No," a Bo Taw said. A thin human with the tallest cranium Cyrus had ever seen stood at the entrance. Behind the Bo Taw were more of his kind with *baans* circling their foreheads.

The first telepath pointed a thin finger at Cyrus. "He's the one we want. Now that he is weak, the Revered One wants to begin the interrogation."

Three of the Vomags aimed their guns at Cyrus. He squinted at them. If the Bo Taw knew he was tired, did that mean they'd been using telepathy to spy on him? And if that was so, just how much did they know of what went on inside his head?

This was bad.

17

Compared to the Attack Talon, the Battle Fang had narrow corridors and worse vibrations when the engines ran strongly. A recycler in the wall clattered as Cyrus passed it. The vent blew oily fumes into the air. Was something wrong with the ship? Maybe entering Pulsar's immense gravity had strained the vessel.

The Vomags leading the way ignored the fouled air. They were too busy marching, letting their boots crash against the deck plates.

Cyrus had never felt more helpless. Fenris humanity's great hope was dead. Only the memory of Klane lived on, and in this instance, that had a strange truth to it. Now, Cyrus Gant was supposed to fill the Anointed One's place. Maybe the memory of Klane had shown him how to do it—if he had the psionic strength to go head-to-head against the Bo Taw.

The problem is that I'm a Special Fourth Class. I can shift a Teleship a measly 1.8 light-years. My psi-strength is a joke. Now, I'm suddenly supposed to rise up like a superhero. No, I don't think so. And yet, what do I lose by trying?

As he followed the modified soldiers, Cyrus wondered how Jasper had died. It had been a long time since he'd thought about his friend from Earth. Good old Jasper—he hadn't much liked the man when he'd lived, had he?

The Vomags halted at a bulkhead. It vanished.

With a resigned sigh, Cyrus entered a spacious room. He stopped short. Instead of a Bo Taw to question him like last time, a Kresh regarded him.

Shifting a boot, Cyrus found sand underfoot. That was odd, right? Hot, dry air cycled through the vents, making Cyrus sweat. What kind of room was this anyway? He noticed alien murals of sharp angles and dark colors on the walls. A post rose in the center of the chamber. A glowing red crystal pulsated on top.

"Fall on your face before the Revered One, Mingal Cham the 3012th," the tallest Bo Taw said in a sonorous voice.

The Kresh lashed its tail. "We will forgo the ceremonies," the dinosaur said. Cyrus had to strain to make out its words. "Time is pressing upon us."

Cyrus shivered. Watching the Kresh talk was so odd. It had a large, pink crocodile tongue and sharp teeth. How could it form words with those jaws? If he walked into a zoo and heard a polar bear greet him, it would have felt as surreal. He'd had little direct contact with any raptor-like alien. This one was big: twice his height. The Kresh looked as if it could lean forward and bite off his head. According to everything he'd learned, the creature was incredibly smart.

Mingal Cham wore metallic silver streamers. They fluttered in the hot air, tinkling like giant Christmas tinsel. Various devices hung on a leathery belt. His horse-sized eyes were the worst, so dark and round, filled with reptilian intelligence.

"Attend me, Bo Taw," the Kresh said. "What is the Earther thinking?"

Cyrus straightened from his listening to Mingal Cham. He barely strengthened his block in time. The mind probes struck. Like needles pricking a balloon, each threatened to pop his defenses. With a technique taught him by Klane, he hardened his block. Their telepathic pressure grew.

"He resists us, Revered One," the chief Bo Taw said.

It was then Cyrus got a whiff of the reptilian reek. Mingal Cham the 3012th smelled like a crocodile that had eaten too much gamy meat. Cyrus noticed that the creature panted. The Kresh's breath struck him in the face.

Cyrus turned his head away sharply.

"What does his action signify?" Mingal Cham asked.

None of the Bo Taw spoke up.

"Are you lacking in ability?" Mingal Cham asked his servants.

The Bo Taw closed their eyes. The attack on Cyrus's mind intensified and his psi-block weakened.

Did they attempt to discover the extent of his strength? Or did they suspect he could do more than before? If he summoned the memory of Klane to help him now, what would that mean for later? Yet, if he let them probe his thoughts, wouldn't they know everything?

For the briefest flicker of an instant, Cyrus could have sworn he felt the Eich offer his aid. Cyrus rejected it. Either he would rule his own mind or nothing else mattered.

We shall see if you always feel that way, the Eich whispered.

Then the memory of Klane surged to the forefront. With his help, Cyrus strengthened his block.

The chief Bo Taw's eyes snapped open. "Revered One, something happened in his mind. It weakened under our combined assault. Then it strengthened by several factors."

The Kresh lashed his tail. "Dagon Dar has proven correct concerning the subject. He predicted this would happen. This is most interesting. Intensify your efforts. Break open his mind."

The chief Bo Taw bowed with exaggerated reverence. Then he peered at each of his fellows. In their long gowns, with folded hands and serene countenances, they bent their elongated heads toward Cyrus. The gene-warped humans surrounded him, and their power surged at his mind.

Cyrus grunted as waves of psionic strength struck against his mind. He was already weary, and it made his eyes water as he resisted them.

"Vomag, strike a blow against him," the Kresh instructed.

A squat soldier marched to Cyrus. The man raised a hand and swung in a controlled fashion. Cyrus ducked. As he did, he tried to grab the Vomag's hatchet, the one dangling on the belt next to his pistol.

The soldier knocked Cyrus's hand away. It was clear the Vomag was stronger and faster. With speed, the soldier slapped Cyrus across the face.

Pain flared. His eyes watered and Cyrus's mind shield slipped.

Perhaps the chief Bo Taw indicated that the slap had helped.

"Strike the subject again," Mingal Cham said.

Once more, the Vomag swung.

We'll teach him, the memory of Klane said.

Cyrus squinted. With Klane's help, he knew he could do this. The hand stopped an inch from his cheek. Cyrus reached out for the Vomag's sidearm.

An angry hiss alerted Cyrus. He barely released the butt of the weapon in time, rolling as he was taught long ago in the Latin Kings. The Kresh's swishing tail harmlessly passed where he'd been standing.

Cyrus's back thudded against the bulkhead.

"Smash his mind shield," Mingal Cham hissed. "We will put an end to this buffoonery."

"He's . . . strong," the chief Bo Taw whispered.

"He is an Earther," the Kresh said. "The records indicate he is a weak psionic."

"Not . . . anymore," the Bo Taw said.

Mingal Cham lashed his tail in agitation, studying Cyrus. "How did your psi-strength increase? You will tell me."

Cyrus panted as he lay against the bulkhead, striving to keep the combined Bo Taw mind assaults at bay.

"He's weakening, Revered One," the chief Bo Taw said.

"We know something occurred to you," the Kresh told Cyrus. "We have discovered your legends about an Anointed One."

"Not mine," Cyrus said.

The reptilian tail lashed. "The Fenris humans have a hope—the Humanity Ultimates do. It was a vain hope. The Anointed One came from Kresh labs. We gave them their savior. Now, we want to know what motivated us to do so."

Cyrus cocked his head. "What . . ." he panted. "What kind of question is that?"

"I am Kresh," Mingal Cham said. "I am the superior. You will answer my questions, not query your master."

Cyrus laughed dryly. "I know what you're after. I have the answer."

No, the Eich said. *You must not reveal me to the Kresh.*

Yeah? Cyrus asked.

"He speaks to another," the chief Bo Taw said. "I do not understand this."

"What other?" Mingal Cham said. "How is that possible? Aren't you shielding his mind from other telepaths?"

"The other lives inside his mind," the Bo Taw said. "I do not know how that is possible, but it is reality."

Cyrus finally got it. Maybe it was Klane in him. Maybe this particular knowledge came from other memories. The Kresh were the ultimate scientists. Mingal Cham had set up a laboratory situation in this chamber. In some manner, the Kresh knew more than they should about what had happened to Klane and now to him. These mustn't be ordinary Bo Taw. These must be some of the strongest around. Why had they been concentrated in one Battle Fang? Easy. They were here to test him.

We have to do something now, Cyrus said.

I can help you, the Eich said.

Nope. Don't want your help. The price is too stiff.

This once, I will give my help for free.

You're a lousy liar, Cyrus said.

114

You must remain a free agent, the Eich said. *The Kresh know too much. I distrust them.*

What do you say, Klane? Cyrus asked. *Can we fry these bastards?*

Let me show you what to do, the alien psi-parasite said. *Everything I know and am is under assault.*

"Revered One," the chief Bo Taw said. "I don't understand what I'm sensing. We may all be in danger."

"From a lone human?" Mingal Cham asked in doubt.

"There is wild power in him," the Bo Taw said. "I have never sensed this before."

"How can that be possible?" Mingal Cham asked. "You did not sense the psionic strength in him before."

"Nevertheless, Revered One," the Bo Taw said, "I respectfully request that you leave for your safety."

"Negative," Mingal Cham said. "The entire star system hangs in the balance."

Cyrus's head snapped up. This was the first he'd heard about that.

"Revered One," the Bo Taw said. "Now, please."

"I rule here," Mingal Cham said. "I set the parameters. You are the strongest adepts in the Pulsar gravitational system. You will corral his mind."

"Yes, Revered One."

Do you hear? the Eich asked the memory of Klane.

Something in Cyrus seemed to nod.

Cyrus groaned, and he clutched his head. All the thoughts, memories, maybe minds bouncing around inside him—he must be going crazy.

If you don't strike with fury, Klane said, *the Kresh will dissect Jana and remove all her organs.*

Cyrus shook his head. That was a lie.

"Break down his mind barrier," Mingal Cham instructed his Bo Taw. "Show me the alien entity in him."

The Bo Taw assaults became even heavier. Their psionics pressed down upon Cyrus. The reptilian reek disappeared from the room, at least for Cyrus it did. The thrum of the Battle Fang vanished. Cyrus's eyesight dimmed and his world became silent. Still, the psi-attack pressed down from all sides.

I can't resist them much longer, Klane told Cyrus. *You must use the psi-entity's stratagem.*

Never! Cyrus said. *I am me or I am nothing.*

I will aid you, the Eich said. *We can bargain later.*

Cyrus thought he shook his head. He could no longer tell.

The Bo Taw psionic attack reached the control of his lungs. A new foreign thought reached in—the chief Bo Taw—telling him, *I can make you choke to death.*

Cyrus knew it was true. Either he bargained with the alien entity or it was over for him. *Show me your trick,* he told the Eich.

It did.

In desperation, Cyrus unleashed the Klane power in him. Cyrus watched the Eich, ensuring the psi-parasite didn't take over his mind. That allowed the memory of Klane to strike with fury and the hatred of dying. Only at the last second did Cyrus realize there lay the alien trickery. The memory of Klane used too much psionic power. *No!* Cyrus howled at Klane, attempting to halt the rage of the Anointed One.

It was too late to stop the initial onslaught. With masterful cunning, the memory of Klane wielded the full power of Cyrus's altered brain. He swatted aside the individual mind shields of the Bo Taw. Where they had tried to bludgeon with psionics, he snipped the critical link between mind and body.

In the chamber, the Bo Taw simply collapsed onto the sandy floor, dead. The Vomags who raced in trying to get a shot off at Cyrus also crumpled to the floor, equally dead.

Throughout the Battle Fang, humans died by the score: techs, mechanics, and pilots.

At that point, Cyrus reached the memory of Klane. He was able to soften the expanding atomic-like psionic blow. The memory of Klane blasted people into comas, dropping them, but not instantly killing them. Cyrus didn't want to kill everyone aboard the Battle Fang.

A reptilian roar alerted the minds in Cyrus that the Kresh still lived. The mechanical mind shield protected the alien dinosaur from the psi-assault.

Cyrus opened his eyes. The creature twice the height of a man charged him, leaping with its hind talons ready to slash him to ribbons.

Rolling, Cyrus dodged the first strike. The talons screeched against the bulkhead. Then the Kresh rebounded from the wall, landing on its back. Mingal Cham scrambled fast. Kresh were as quick as lizards.

Cyrus held out his hand. With telekinetic power, he lifted a Vomag pistol off the floor. It flew through the air and crashed against his palm, twisting one of his fingers that got in the way. Mingal Cham the 3012th bellowed. The reek of his breath washed over the man from Milan. Cyrus aimed. The Kresh charged again.

As fast as he could pull the trigger, Cyrus sent exploding pellets into the Kresh's leathery hide. Then he rolled once more. Mingal Cham crashed against the bulkhead. He staggered back with blood pouring down his ruptured body.

Using TK again, Cyrus collected another pistol. He deliberately took aim. Mingal Cham turned his raptor head, looking at him with dull comprehension.

Five shots to the head did it. Chunks of flesh and skull blew away. Then Mingal Cham thudded onto the deck plates.

Panting, his head hurting—but the voices silent for once—Cyrus straightened. He checked the pistol, went to a soldier's corpse, and reloaded. Taking a hatchet, Cyrus began to march down the empty corridor with it in one hand and the loaded pistol in the other.

He passed dead soldiers, dead techs, and dead Bo Taw.

I did this. I'm more than a Special Fourth Class now. I'm more powerful than Venice ever was.

He remembered how terrified everyone had been of her on the journey to Fenris. Tentatively, he mind-scanned the ship. There didn't seem to be any more Kresh on the Battle Fang. That was good.

Cyrus still didn't know in what manner the Eich had tricked him, but a premonition grew. After a half hour's search, he found the vault. Opening the bulkhead, he peered in. His chest hitched as he saw everyone lying on the floor.

Rushing to Jana, he found her unconscious. Nothing he could do could wake her.

Is she dead?

She will be, the Eich said, *unless you do exactly as I tell you.*

Finally, Cyrus discovered the alien entity's latest trick to control his actions.

18

The good news—if Cyrus could call it that—was that most of the others woke up. A few of them were dead; those who lived included Skar, Niens, and Yang. The living armed themselves from the dead Vomags and searched the Battle Fang from one location to the next.

"Everyone else aboard ship is dead," Skar said a half hour later.

Niens turned to Cyrus, who stroked Jana's forehead.

Cyrus became aware of the mentalist's presence, but he ignored the man. Finally, Niens crouched beside him, causing one of his knees to creak and then pop with sound.

"I'm not as limber as I used to be," Niens said.

Cyrus didn't bother looking up.

"She's barely breathing," Niens observed.

At first, Cyrus didn't think he was going to answer. He had done this to her because he didn't know how to wield his new power. Therefore, he had let the memory of Klane and the alien psi-parasite do this.

Cyrus shook his head. If he couldn't control the power, what good was he?

"Cyrus?" Niens asked.

"She's in a coma because I put her there," Cyrus whispered.

"Is the coma physically or mentally induced?" Niens asked.

"Both."

"How did it happen?"

Cyrus touched his chest, indicting he'd done it.

"I'm not sure I understand how that's possible," Niens said.

"Me neither," Cyrus whispered.

"Yet someone killed the Kresh and his attendants."

Cyrus squeezed his eyes closed. He'd become a monster. He had killed people with his thoughts, his psi-power. He couldn't control it properly, though.

I've destroyed friends, possibly my lover. How could he look in a mirror again?

Cyrus balled his hands into fists, squeezing with all his strength. Had he slain Jana? If it was possible, he had to save her. Yet he had to do it without playing into the Eich's hands.

Cyrus looked up. In bottom-level Milan, he'd seen Dust buyers like Niens, rich men with shifty backgrounds. The mentalist knew how to run with the crowd. Could he trust the man?

"Do you still love the Kresh?" Cyrus asked.

Niens lofted his plucked eyebrows. "I have thrown in my lot with you. I can hardly love them."

"That's not an answer."

"You're right. I'm curious, though," Niens said. "Why don't you simply probe my mind and find out?"

It was hard to say. *Am I a murderer?* "Not sure I trust my psionics anymore," Cyrus muttered.

"Ah. Because of the girl?"

"Woman! Jana is a woman; my woman."

"Of course, of course," Niens said smoothly. "I did not mean any disrespect."

"But yeah," Cyrus said. "That's the reason I'm not probing you. I just killed everyone, or the—"

"Or the what?" Niens asked.

Cyrus decided to talk about something else. "You're a mentalist. You're used to dealing with Bo Taw, aren't you?"

Niens nodded.

Cyrus turned away, and he stroked Jana's forehead. *How can I have done this? No. I have to get it together. Wallowing in sorrow never helped me in the slums. It won't help me in the stars, either. Time to get on task.*

He cleared his throat. How far could he trust Niens anyway? The mentalist had thrown in his lot with them. That was true. Yet Niens wouldn't answer about loving the Kresh or not.

"If it helps to settle your thoughts," Niens said, "Yang has taken control of the vessel. At the moment, none of the other Kresh have radioed our ship. We're still heading for High Station 3. Until we decide on a course of action, I suggest we continue on our path to the habitat. Traveling in this manner helps to camouflage our actions from the other Kresh."

Cyrus continued to stare at a bulkhead.

"Does Yang's decision meet with your approval?" Niens asked.

Cyrus regarded the mentalist. It surprised him to see the deference on Niens's face.

"Clearly," Niens said, "you are the leader. Without you, none of us will remain free or alive for long."

Cyrus grunted his acknowledgment of the words. They hardly registered, though. How could a woman killer be the leader?

"You are tired," Niens said. "You are also distraught. Sleep is a great healer. I suggest you avail yourself of it while you can."

Cyrus didn't say anything. He felt the weariness tugging at his body. He *was* tired. Had he killed Jana? They were supposed to get married. She was the woman of his dreams. Now, he finally got his secret wish of life—to be a great Special. But he couldn't control the power. It had gotten away from him.

No. The psi-parasite had done this to him. Cyrus scowled. He wasn't going to let the alien entity get away with this.

He mumbled that under his breath.

Niens leaned forward.

Then Cyrus couldn't help himself. He slid onto the floor beside Jana. Crossing his arms, he laid his left cheek on them and fell asleep.

||||||||||

Cyrus woke feeling like crap. His head hurt. His tongue was puffy—

He sat up and moved beside Jana. Nothing had changed. Her chest rose and fell slowly. Her features remained frozen. How long could she last in a coma?

A snort told Cyrus someone else was here in the vault with him. Niens sat up, pushing a blanket off him. The mentalist lay on a mat.

"Feeling better?" Niens asked.

Cyrus shook his head.

"Nevertheless," Niens said, "I see greater understanding and alertness in your eyes. Do you believe you could wrap the entire Battle Fang in a null?"

"Probably not," Cyrus said.

"Hmm . . ."

"Why would I bother to do that anyway?" Cyrus asked.

"While you've been asleep, we've received several calls."

"From whom?" Cyrus asked.

"A Kresh named Dagon Dar."

"Is he important?"

"It would appear he controls most of the warships in the Pulsar gravitational system. Otherwise, no."

Cyrus realized Niens had attempted a feeble joke. It didn't help. His inability to control his psionics might have killed the one person he really cared about.

"We're still heading for High Station 3," Niens said.

"Where is this Dagon Dar?"

"I believe Yang said the Kresh's ship orbits Jassac."

"Have the Kresh launched any drones at us?" Cyrus asked.

"None that we can detect," Niens said. "By the way, are you hungry?"

Cyrus was going to lie and say no. His stomach growled.

"It's as I thought," Niens said. He indicated a tray. A series of concentrates lay on it, along with water.

Instead of torturing himself—that had never been Cyrus's way—he slid his butt to the tray and began to eat. He'd survived in the slums because he looked at life as it was. He'd never been able to afford emotions. Yeah, he'd put Jana in a coma, but she wasn't dead yet. The Eich had a plan. Well, there had to be a way to beat the alien at its game.

Cyrus eyed the mentalist. Maybe he could use the man's professional knowledge or wisdom—if a slippery eel of a man could ever be called "wise".

"You've reached a decision," Niens said.

"Are you showing off?" Cyrus asked.

"I am a mentalist. You, I believe, are in need of one. But you mistrust me." Niens held up a long-fingered hand. "One need not be a genius at my trade to see the signs. Nevertheless, I am a genius. It was why Zama Dee employed me in such a high-level capacity."

"Blowing smoke, are we?"

"I do not understand the idiom."

"It doesn't matter," Cyrus said. He eyed Niens, and he saw wrinkle lines at the edges of the man's face. The mentalist was older than he'd realized. Was that good or bad?

"Klane didn't trust you," Cyrus said.

"I know."

"Why do you think he didn't trust you?"

"Because of my conditioning," Niens said. "I have remnants of Kresh-love in my psyche. Since I know it's there, I battle it."

"How do you do that?"

"By desiring freedom, of course," Niens said. "Also, I know the Kresh will use their worst punishments on me."

"You say 'freedom' because you know that's what I most value."

"It's possible."

"How can I trust you if you're already lying to me?" Cyrus asked.

"I fear recapture by the Kresh," Niens said. "It is my strongest motivator."

"What if Dagon Dar offered you a reprieve for helping to capture us?"

"Zama Dee once offered me something similar," Niens said. "No. I will cast my lot with you, and with the humans of Earth."

Cyrus wondered if he dared to trust Niens. If he didn't, who else could he talk to that made sense? Skar? Yang? The memory of Klane?

"Are you ready to hear a story?" Cyrus asked.

"Most assuredly," Niens said.

As Cyrus opened his mouth, a klaxon rang throughout the ship.

"Now what?" asked Cyrus.

The ship speakers came to life. Yang spoke in his heavy voice. "Dagon Dar FIRST is about to make an announcement to all the Pulsar gravitational ships."

"That's odd," Niens said.

"What is?" Cyrus asked.

"That isn't the FIRST's name."

"Meaning what?" Cyrus asked.

"The old FIRST is dead and Dagon Dar has taken over," Niens said.

"That must mean the Chirr surprise attack at Heenhiss proved successful," Cyrus said. "I wonder if that has anything to do with the message."

"The communication is incoming," Yang said over the speakers.

"Kresh of the Pulsar gravitational system," a reptilian voice said. "The cyborgs have appeared in the outer asteroid belt. The Imperium now faces two highly viable space races. Both appear to be on war footing. All Pulsar ships will immediately head to Jassac. There, we shall hold a council of war to decide on our strategy. I expect all Pulsar ships to reach Jassac orbit within thirty hours. This is a binding order to every ship in the gravitational system. Attend now. Any commander who disobeys must be taken into custody and replaced immediately. Dagon Dar FIRST has spoken."

As the speakers quieted, Niens turned to Cyrus. "Now what are we going to do?"

Cyrus scowled. That was a good question.

19

Cyrus paced back and forth, his head bent and his face creased with worry and guilt. Jana lay on the floor in a coma as she barely breathed.

"How long can we keep her alive?" Cyrus asked Niens.

The mentalist took his time answering. "The Battle Fang has medical facilities. We could put her on life support."

"You know how to do that?"

"I do," Niens admitted. "Our problem lies in other areas."

"We'll get to that," Cyrus said. "If she's gone . . ."

"You are a fighter," Niens said.

Cyrus glared at the mentalist. "I'm not sacrificing her for the greater good."

"I doubt her trouble is physical as you first surmised. My initial examination leads me to believe her problem is entirely mental."

"So, I have to risk entering her mind to save her?" Cyrus asked.

"Who else can do so?"

"I think the Eich did something to her."

Niens coughed discreetly. "Perhaps you could explain to me what you're talking about."

"Okay. What do I have to lose? I need somebody to bounce this off of." Cyrus told Niens what he knew. He told the mentalist about the transfer, the memories talking to him as distinct people, and the alien psi-parasite.

Niens's eyes glowed with fascination. "Yes, I see. Very interesting," he said. "I wonder how the psi-parasite came to attach itself to Klane."

"There was something under one of the atmospheric converters on Jassac," Cyrus said. "It lived in a deep cave complex. Klane referred to them as singing gods, but now I think there is just the one. Klane went to the singing god once as a young lad. There, the seeker told him to reach out with his mind. The Eich gave Klane psi-power, the ability to teleport. The psi-parasite also altered Klane's mind to give him greater psionic strength.

"Klane went there once more after the Kresh captured his friend, the seeker. Klane spoke to the so-called singing god and then blacked out. I have hints in Klane's memory of what happened. As before, I believe the Eich altered his mind further, strengthening him, turning Klane into the Anointed One. That's when the psi-parasite must have transferred from the tubes under the mountain and into Klane."

"Is the parasite composed of flesh?" Niens asked.

"I don't think so, no. More likely, he's some form of energy."

"You know this for certain?" Niens asked.

"No. It's a gut feeling."

"I imagine it's something more," Niens said. "But we won't worry about that for now. Hmm, do you think the Kresh don't know about the singing god?"

"No."

"What is the parasite's goal?"

"The Eich keeps referring to a ship. I think the parasite lost its ship. I don't know how or why that happened, or how a parasite happens to own a ship. It wants to go home and heal, I think it told me."

"What ship?" Niens asked.

"I have the feeling it's in the outer asteroid belt."

"Chirr, Kresh, cyborgs, and humans," Niens said as he rubbed his fingertips. "Now, it appears there is another alien race. This being is crafty and hidden, wielding grave mental powers."

"What are you implying?" Cyrus asked.

"The Eich altered Klane, you said. It is more than possible it has been altering the primitive seekers, as well. I noted a few anomalies in Klane's former seeker when I operated on him under Chengal Ras's direction."

"Operated?"

"A technical term," Niens said. "I, uh, attempted to adjust the seeker's mind. The Kresh have certain tools to, um, train stubborn brains."

"Does the Battle Fang carry such tools?"

"No," Niens said. "I looked. In any case, the things the Kresh do with tools and additional Bo Taw tampering, it appears the Eich can do with psionic power alone. Yet it would seem the being has critical weaknesses. Otherwise, why does he or it not rule the Fenris System?"

"Maybe the parasite rules as much of it as he desires to," Cyrus said.

"What does that mean?"

"I'm not sure. It's a feeling I have. Maybe it's a stray thought I picked up from the parasite."

"Can you describe these thoughts?"

Cyrus shrugged.

"No," Niens said. "We are in desperate straits. If we continue for High Station 3, Dagon Dar will send drones after us. If we obey his orders, we will deliver ourselves into Kresh hands, or talons would be more accurate to say. For the moment, we are free. We must use everything we have in order to remain so."

"Okay, okay," Cyrus said. "What do you want me to do?"

"Think," Niens said. "Bend your thoughts to these conjectures. Why do you believe the Eich might rule Fenris?"

Cyrus massaged his forehead. He'd had impressions really, not thoughts. But he was willing to think this through if he could, and if it would help save Jana. "Well, I feel as if the Eich might have tampered with the Chirr."

"This is interesting. Tampered how do you think?"

"The Chirr have psionic creatures among them, right? They've also managed to collect psi-energy in almost physical balls."

"How do you know this to be true?" Niens asked.

"Klane went there while he was mentally absent from his body," Cyrus said.

"Ah . . ." Niens said. "That is where his consciousness went. How could I have known?"

"I have the feeling the Eich doesn't like the Kresh. In fact, I believe it fears them."

"Do you know why?"

Cyrus shook his head.

"What does the ship do, the one just found?"

"Don't know," Cyrus said.

"Can you probe Klane's memory to find out?" Niens asked.

"I can ask him."

"It," Niens corrected.

"Excuse me?" Cyrus asked.

"The memory is an 'it,' not a 'he.'"

"You're wrong," Cyrus said. "I talk to the memory all the time. It's definitely a him."

Niens waved his hand. "It hardly matters. The point is the psi-parasite resides in your mind and yet you don't seem to control it or it you. Perhaps as important, the something or someone altered your mind in those seconds or minutes as the Anointed One made the mind transfer. I suggest therein lies the problem—and the hopes of our salvation."

"What do you mean?" Cyrus asked, looking bewildered.

"I'm guessing," Niens said, "you have great powers. Do those powers come because your mind is different? Or do they come because Klane's memories know how to tap the human mind better than anyone else has ever done?"

"I never thought of it like that."

"I'm inclined to believe the altered mind is the key, although maybe Klane's memories know how to use the alteration better than anyone else."

"Does it make any difference which way it is?" Cyrus asked.

"Oh, yes," Niens said. "I should think it would make considerable difference."

Cyrus waited for Niens to explain. Instead, the mentalist plucked at a button on his coat.

Noticing the scrutiny, Niens said, "The mind is a labyrinth. Because of your descriptions, an old article I read some time ago has resurfaced in my own thoughts."

"What descriptions?"

"The nature of your mind battle with the Eich," Niens said. "You saw Milan again and other realms. There, you battled one another as if in a real world with real-world parameters. Except, at times, you could materialize weapons and boots. The paper I just spoke about theorized such a situation. It called the mind battles 'conceptual authenticity engagements.'"

"What the heck is that psychobabble?" Cyrus asked.

"To find and defeat the Eich, I believe you must delve into your mind. You must go to the altered areas. There, I suggest, the parasite resides. If you can defeat it there, you might submerge the alien's thoughts into your stream of consciousness and subconsciousness."

"Do you hear what you're saying?" Cyrus asked.

"The man who wrote the paper was brilliant," Niens said. "The Kresh did not believe his thesis, however. They destroyed him as hopelessly insane."

"You mean they killed him?" Cyrus asked.

"That is what I said, yes."

"If he was insane, why kill him?"

"Obviously, because he had become useless," Niens said. "He served no more purpose."

"He was a man."

"Yes," Niens said, "to us. To the Kresh, he was simply a mad beast. Here is my belief. The Kresh will destroy us soon. To save us, you must become the Anointed One in deed as well as in name."

"Who said I'm him in name?"

"No one else can hold the title," Niens said. "You hold the memory of Klane. Someone has altered your mind. For some reason, the Eich seems to desire that Fenris humanity have a chance in the game of aliens. Perhaps you should trust the parasite."

Cyrus laughed.

"If you do not," Niens said, "soon, the Kresh will burn us down."

Cyrus stepped closer to Niens, jabbing a finger against the man's skinny chest. He jabbed once, twice, thrice, knocking the mentalist backward each time.

"Do you want an alien to run my mind?" Cyrus shouted.

Niens shook his head.

Fighting for self-control, Cyrus said, "The Earth authorities once put an inhibitor in my mind. I did everything in my power to get rid of it. I know what it's like having a leash. Never again, Niens! I'm Cyrus Gant or I'm dead. There are no other options."

"Even to save the life of the woman you love?" Niens asked.

There might have been a second's hesitation. Then Cyrus blurted, "No! I'm not willing to sell my soul for anyone, and that's final."

"I see, I see," Niens said. "You have convinced me. I will not suggest such a course of action again."

Cyrus stepped away. He could feel the anger struggling to rerelease. Why could no one understand how horrible mental domination was? Breathing deeply, he began to pace.

"May I suggest a different course of action?" Niens asked in a soft voice.

Cyrus threw a hand into the air that could have meant anything.

"As I said a few moments ago, you must delve into your mind. You must return to the conceptual authenticity engagements."

"Go onto the Eich's turf, eh, and hunt him down?" Cyrus asked.

"That is colloquially spoken, but succinct nevertheless."

"Do you think I can win?"

"It's not really a question of winning," Niens said. "We have no other options. Either you become the Anointed One or we will perish by drone or by claw on Jassac."

"Yeah, I'm beginning to believe you. So, I go into his world—his mind turf—and I beat the knowledge out of the Eich on how to heal Jana."

"And how to produce a ship-wide null so we can escape Kresh detection," Niens added. "Yet I wouldn't think of it as beating knowledge out of him. You must subdue the alien, make his knowledge part of your regular memories."

Cyrus stared at Niens. "Do you realize what you're saying?"

"I believe I do, yes."

"You want me to understand the Eich. With its knowledge . . ."

Who could stop me then?

Cyrus frowned. Was that his thought, or had the psi-parasite slipped it in just now? The alien entity was crafty. A grin spread into place. He liked the idea of chasing down the Eich. The thing had screwed with him. It had stolen his woman. Now it was time for Cyrus Gant to track it down and make the alien pay.

"Okay," Cyrus said. "I'm ready. What do I do?"

"One word of caution," Niens said. "What you're attempting sounds dangerous. It is more than possible the alien parasite has set up the situation to lure you onto his home ground."

"How could he do that?"

"By being shrewder than you realize," Niens said. "He may have studied you and learned your weaknesses. If he can subdue you in his territory, he might gain full control of your mind: in essence, taking over."

Cyrus squinted. "You think that's possible?"

"Very much so," Niens said. "I must caution you once more. This isn't a lark. This is incredibly dangerous."

"And if I don't go?"

"Then you may never learn to control the full extent of your new psionic powers. You will be the last hope of humanity in theory, but never in practice."

Rubbing his jaw, Cyrus studied Jana. He could hang back, and everything would be lost. He could risk his soul to win his woman and possibly save humanity from the Chirr, the cyborgs, the Kresh, and this Eich parasite.

Maybe this is why I came to New Eden. Cyrus Gant was born to roll the dice for the biggest prize anyone ever chased.

"Let's do this," Cyrus said. "I want to hunt me down an alien psi-bugger."

20

The Battle Fang drifted at its present velocity for High Station 3. Under Skar's piloting, they attempted to move as deftly as possible.

Other Battle Fangs, Attack Talons, and two hammer-ships accelerated for Jassac. The Pulsar gravitational system burned bright with hot engines. For a time, this Battle Fang might slip unnoticed for the habitat. Soon, though, Dagon Dar would learn about the disobedient warship. Then questions would fly, and possibly fast-accelerating drones.

Cyrus lay down on a pallet in medical. Jana lay beside him on another couch. Mentalist Niens made preparations. Yang stood guard. The old chieftain stood in a corner with his arms crossed, one fist gripping a Vomag hatchet, the other a pistol.

"Are you ready?" Niens asked Cyrus.

Cyrus licked his lips. He'd been listening for some time to Niens's explanations of how to do this. He figured he knew the procedure, at least in theory.

"Let's get it done," Cyrus said.

"Then relax," Niens said. "Listen to my voice and concentrate."

"Relax and concentrate?"

"I've already explained that. If you can't do it—"

"It's nutty," Cyrus said, "but I'm game. Start talking."

Mentalist Niens did, softly, bent down beside Cyrus.

He closed his eyes with Niens's hot breath tickling his left ear. Cyrus turned his telepathy inward. Slowly, his consciousness sank, sank, sank . . . His eyelids grew heavy. It felt as if he were falling. With his mind, he twisted around, spying a dark land. It had to have been part of the altered area of his mind. He had to go down there and find the Eich. It didn't sound easy.

He continued down, and his conscious mind receded into the background.

||||||||||

Deep within Cyrus's mind, a ghostly red wheel rotated in the otherwise dark sky. What made it worse was that the wheel remained in the same spot. After a time, its crimson light became like a burning eye, watching every slip of Cyrus's foot or silently mocking his need for knowledge.

Fortunately, through his Klane-taught psionics, Cyrus gripped a thin baton. It tugged toward the Eich, and in that direction he went.

In his mind, Cyrus scrambled over brittle crusts and rocks that crumbled like dirt clods. Later, he climbed tall blue crystals and slid down their sides. He had no idea what that represented in his thoughts. He doubted Niens would know either.

In the dim light of the spinning orb, he often saw his reflection. Twice, rain left him soaked. Each time, he tilted his mouth toward the cool drops and drank until his belly stretched. Lacking a canteen, he'd returned to the primitive expedient of bloating himself. The rain from the second squall had a bitter, metallic taste.

As he huddled under a crystal outcropping with rainwater trickling past his boots, Cyrus wondered if the Battle Fang could slip unnoticed to High Station 3. As he waited, he noticed the wear to his boots. When he moved his toes, he saw how thin the leather had become, how he could make out each individual digit. What did that mean?

It's all symbols, right?

Hunger gnawed at his belly, and his limbs were limp with fatigue. He wasn't able to make food or new boots, and he wasn't sure why. Did he need to be in mortal danger to make that part of his powers work?

A mournful wind blew through the crystals, interrupting his thoughts. Cyrus listened until he shivered. Without a fire, he might catch a cold or fever. He drove himself to his feet. The wind, his wet clothes—he walked, letting the motion warm him. Now that the rain had stopped, walking helped dry his garments.

Time passed as the tug toward the Eich increased. Thoroughly exhausted and with his stomach a grinding knot, Cyrus slumped against a twisted girder, which sprouted from the soil like an obscene tree. The beam had spaced holes. There were similar struts and the shells of blasted dwellings, as if long ago some atomic detonation had shattered the area.

Yawning, he lay down and slept.

Upon waking and still very much in his mind, Cyrus grabbed his baton and continued his lonely trek through the bleak land.

In time, he climbed and shoved past spiky leafless bushes, the tallest reaching to his chest. Red globs like teardrops hung from some spikes. Smiling, he noticed ants. It was good to see Earth creatures in the alien landscape. The outsized ants climbed into a teardrop glob and out again, each carrying a tiny piece of fruit down the spike bush.

Feeling ravenous, Cyrus picked a red teardrop and popped it into his mouth. It was sour and left a bitter aftertaste. Yet he could swallow it. Crouching beside the spike bush, he waited fifteen minutes or so. He felt no ill effects. So he proceeded to pick handfuls, shoveling the teardrops into his mouth like berries. After stripping all he could find, with his stomach still demanding more, inspiration struck. He plucked ants from the ground and ate them. It was tedious work, and he grimaced at the squiggling legs against his tongue, but he was famished.

I wonder why I'm so hungry. Does it mean something? Probably.

Later, with his stomach comfortably full and after a nap, he climbed up and down progressively higher hills. Then he trudged up the steepest hill and blinked in astonishment at the top. The hill gave way to a deep valley. There were lights like lanterns in the vale, and there was movement. Across the gorge, a city glowed with an eerie blue radiance. It was beautiful, and yet the glow struck Cyrus as poisonous in a way he didn't understand. He studied the city and soon perceived it was ruined. Vast twisted girders, shells of fantastically tall buildings, crystal rubble, and other glowing debris united to give the ruins its powerful radiance.

Cyrus rubbed his cheek. Some of the valley lights moved upward toward the ruins. They moved in a long procession.

Cyrus expanded his chest. His baton tugged toward the ruins. That's what he'd been trekking toward, huh? It was clearly an alien city.

If you fight the Eich and lose, you could become his mind slave. This isn't a game, Cyrus.

Hardening his resolve, he began to work his way down the spike bush–covered hill.

As Cyrus climbed downward, he was able to see more within the valley. A river meandered through the narrow bottom. Occasionally, golden motes flashed within the water. Whether the flashes were fish or something else, Cyrus was too far away to tell. Rocks or crystals lined the shores, except for a sparkling sandy area. There, exceptionally tall tents rose like exotic trees. Chimes tinkled faintly whenever the wind blew.

A cold feeling bloomed along the front of Cyrus's body. He stopped. The coldness intensified and he became acutely aware of someone studying him. It unnerved Cyrus. He darted behind a boulder-sized crystal. His neck tightened. So did his grip around the baton. Cautiously, he peered over the crystal. The cold feeling pressed against his face.

Cyrus scowled. He was tired of acting like a mouse in his own mind—his altered mind. Surely, these were some of the worst changes.

In any case, spike bushes crackled below him. The noise came just beyond a shelf of stone that concealed whoever made the sounds.

Cyrus's mouth dried out as he hunkered behind a different crystal and peered around it. More crackling sounds focused his gaze.

A hand appeared on the stony shelf. Several of the fingers were crooked. A grunt heralded a harsh bearded face with wild eyes. Another grunt brought a naked reddish man into view. Was he supposed to be a Jassac primitive?

Scars on the man's chest seeped blood. The scars were shaped like Kresh letters. Cyrus believed someone had carved them into the man's flesh. The primitive was large, wore a loincloth, and clutched a rock as if it was his weapon. The primitive stared down the hill he'd climbed and then slunk for a spike bush.

Cyrus became aware that both of them had chosen the easiest path up and down this part of the mountain. On either side of the path rose sharp crystals and impossible-to-scale cliffs. The terrain had funneled their passage. Was that by design? Despite the man's furtive manner, he carried himself like a warrior, ready to use his rock in a fight to the death.

Who chased the man? Was he a slave or something even more degrading?

"Up here," Cyrus whispered.

The man froze, and for a moment terror washed across his harsh features. Then the warrior—for his actions declared him one—clutched a pendant dangling from his throat. His lips writhed, in an oath perhaps. He overcame his terror and rushed in a crouch toward Cyrus's crystal.

Cyrus gambled by stepping out, showing himself. "I'm a friend," he said.

The warrior raked his gaze across Cyrus. It felt nothing like cold pressure. Even in the murk, Cyrus saw the subtle change in the man, a lessening of tension. The warrior kept rushing toward him. Was the primitive another of the many memories in Cyrus's mind?

"Hide," the man said.

Cyrus darted back behind the crystal boulder. In a moment, the large warrior couched beside him.

The primitive reeked of sweat, blood, and barely suppressed fear. Grim lines streaked his bearded face. The warrior seemed unpredictable, like a wounded tiger. He panted and used a forearm to wipe sweat and grime from his face.

"Are you in league with the Saurians?" the primitive growled.

Cyrus had no idea who they were supposed to be. Ah, he had an idea. "Are those the owners of the tents?" he asked.

The primitive spat on the ground. He examined Cyrus, noticed the baton, and grunted.

"You're a *psionic*?" Cyrus asked.

The warrior shook his head, saying, "The Saurians hate human psionics. They'll use knives to slay you, skin your hide, and fashion their evil flutes from your bones."

"How long have the Saurians hunted you?" Cyrus asked.

The primitive glared at Cyrus. Then he gripped his pendant, his lips writhing in a silent curse.

As the primitive's hand dropped away, Cyrus's curiosity betrayed him, and his eyebrows rose. The disc hanging from the man's throat showed an image of a junction-stone.

"Klane," Cyrus whispered to the primitive.

The man exploded with a startled oath. He clutched Cyrus's sleeve. "You've spoken with the Anointed One?"

"I have indeed. How do you know him?"

The primitive opened his mouth, perhaps to answer the question. Then a weird warbling horn cut him short, the sound coming from farther down the hill. Panic entered the warrior's eyes. He fought to control it, began to tremble, and then snarled a bloody oath.

"The Saurians?" asked Cyrus.

"The Sa-Austra," the primitive said bitterly. Maybe he noticed Cyrus's incomprehension. "The Eich's lost slave—the Sa-Austra is their champion in this place. We're as good as recaptured and headed for the vats."

"Does vat mean death?" asked Cyrus.

"I escaped their bloody altars," the primitive said, ignoring the question. "Maybe I should have stayed, helped them restore their glory. Anything is better than the vats."

"Death is forever," Cyrus said.

"Are you daft?" the primitive shouted. "They would have slain me on their altars and used my blood."

"Tell me what that's supposed to mean," Cyrus said.

The warbling horn sounded again, closer than before.

The wild-eyed primitive said, "The Saurians capture any who wander into this evil land. They seek to cleanse the blue poison from every ruin. Then they will rebuild the ancient machinery."

Cyrus scowled. He was thoroughly confused by these things. He never should have listened to Niens. His altered mind had become a madhouse of things he didn't understand. What did the blue poison have to do with the Eich? What was ancient machinery supposed to do down here in his mind? This seemingly made no sense. He began to hate the psi-parasite even more than before.

Heavy panting sounds from below the cliff along with clattering rocks became quite distinct.

The primitive's muscles tightened. He rose, clutching his rock. "The Sa-Austra comes," the man said, his features bleak. "I will never be his Steed. Better a warrior's end than changed in the vats."

Steed? Cyrus remembered the Eich boasting that someday he, Cyrus, would be the parasite's Steed. It must mean the Eich would ride and control him, a master-and-slave affair.

"We must work together," Cyrus said. "I must capture the Eich and make him reveal his secrets to me."

The primitive howled an ancient battle cry and launched himself downhill.

Cyrus stood and the sight shocked him. On all fours, a naked giant climbed up the steep slope. The giant had a spiked bit in his mouth attached to reins, and he had a high arching back and a saddle.

What must have been a Saurian—with red scales like a dragon and shaped like a man, although with a greatly elongated torso—crouched on the saddle. The Sa-Austra carried a bone-white sword of immense size.

The Jassac primitive recklessly plunged downhill. He hurled his rock. With a *clink* of metal, the Sa-Austra neatly parried the hurled rock with his blade. The primitive had already launched himself airborne, diving, recklessly seeking to knock the Saurian off his mount. The Sa-Austra's sword was out of position. The creature hissed a powerful word, a psi-force.

A meter before the primitive's bold plan would have borne fruit, something knocked him aside. The man thudded onto the rocky ground, his neck at a grotesque angle, broken.

So much for that memory, Cyrus thought. *I wonder if the primitive had once been a seeker on Jassac.*

The naked giant—the Steed—gave three short barks, laughter possibly.

That angered Cyrus, although he wondered if that was why the primitive had thrown away his life. Would the vats have changed the reddish seeker into a mount for the inhuman thing that rode the other?

A cold pressure pushed against Cyrus's body. The Saurian, the Sa-Austra, noticed him. It had white eyes all of one color. The creature flicked the reins. The giant mount hooted and began to scale the steep grade.

Cyrus's pulse quickened. Scalps flopped on the sides of the saddle, grisly trophies of human skin and hair.

The naked mount gathered himself. Like a giant cat, he leaped onto the outcropping that the primitive had scaled only a few minutes before. The Sa-Austra drew rein. Twenty paces separated the Saurian from Cyrus. Small, bony ridges ringed the creature's scaly head. Is this what the alien had once looked like? It seemed very possible. The Saurians were similar then to the Kresh. That was interesting. Was sentient reptilian life more common than intelligent mammalian life?

"The beast destroyed itself," the Sa-Austra hissed. "Its flesh is wasted and the blood soaked where it is of no value. You will take its place."

"How do I wake my woman?" Cyrus asked.

The Sa-Austra stiffened. The mount must have noticed, for he glanced up at his master.

"Give me your name!" the Sa-Austra demanded.

Was this the Eich? Cyrus didn't think so.

"It frightens you that I don't quiver at your presence," Cyrus said. "Why is that?"

"Your name, I demand it!"

Cyrus turned sideways toward the creature and held his baton aimed toward the ground. Mentally, he fanned through his options like a gambler through a deck of cards.

"Psionic creature," the Sa-Austra hissed, as if spitting poison.

"I noticed you're handy with ESP yourself," Cyrus mocked, seeking to goad the Saurian into a foolish move. "It shows a wise lack of faith in your sword skills."

The Sa-Austra raised the immense bone-white blade. "You shall weep on the altar as I sing the songs of cleansing. Your blood will boil, and the Family shall be another step closer to returning home."

"Do I hear a dead lizard speaking to me?"

The Saurian kicked its ridged heels into the mount's flanks. The giant moaned and charged on all fours across the stony soil.

Cyrus stood his ground. Then he, too, bounded, running uphill, moving across from the mount's left side to his right. The Sa-Austra likewise began to move his sword cross-body. Before the Saurian could complete the movement, Cyrus aimed his baton. Just as he had once made a vibrio-knife appear in his hand, he caused the baton to grow, and he gave it a point. Before the white sword could parry it, the point impaled the Sa-Austra like a spear. The Saurian hissed in agony, and the sweeping sword snapped the elongated baton. Sparks erupted, momentarily blinding the creature and its mount.

As they swept past him, Cyrus ducked out of the way. The mount crashed against a crystal boulder. The wounded Sa-Austra tumbled out of the saddle. Cyrus dashed there. He fumbled at the Saurian's belt, drew a curved knife, and held it to the Sa-Austra's throat.

"Tell me how to wake Jana."

The creature glared at him.

"I can kill you easily enough," Cyrus said.

"Do you think I am the one? No. I am the Eich's servant. Kill me and your woman dies."

Cyrus clenched his teeth. "So be it," he said. He applied pressure.

"Wait! I will speak. I will tell you how to cloak your vessel. I do not know how to repair your woman."

"So tell me," Cyrus said.

The Sa-Austra did. It made sense after a fashion. "There," it said. "I have relayed the message as the Eich told me I must do if you could defeat me. Now release me."

"Yeah, right," Cyrus said. "You'll just head back to your tents and get another mount. I'm not sure I can get out of here quickly enough."

The creature watched him. Something about it troubled Cyrus.

He thought about the stakes. Fenris humanity was doomed. One of the three alien races would win the coming war. If the Chirr won, humans would likely become food or psi-fodder. If the cyborgs won, people would become machine-flesh melds. If the Kresh won, humans would remain as slaves.

I'm the only chance we have. That means I have to play the game more ruthlessly than a Dust dealer would.

"Remove your knife from my throat," the Sa-Austra said.

"Sure thing," Cyrus said. He sliced, cutting the throat and jumping back. Blood jetted. The Saurian hissed, and it attempted to rise. Cyrus watched coldly.

The Sa-Austra slumped back against the crystal stone. "You are doomed, liar."

"Yeah? How about your master playing his little trick earlier. We're even, I'd say."

"You are doomed."

Cyrus decided he'd talked enough. So he headed back the way he'd come. It was time to leave his mind, return to reality, and see if he could slip the Battle Fang away without Dagon Dar noticing them heading for High Station 3.

21

Across the Fenris System in the outer asteroid belt, Senior Darcy Foxe of Ice Hauler 266-9 sat in the control module with Glissim.

The cyborgs had left them alone for the last twenty-six hours. That meant she'd heard nothing about Jick.

During that time, Darcy and Glissim had watched the cyborgs land three heavy lifters onto the asteroid. That had shaken the ice hauler each time. From the lifters jumped suited cyborgs. They carried mining equipment. Soon enough, ice and rock flew into space. Then the lifters rose with a strange silvery craft tethered to them. The lifters took the alien vessel to the main cyborg warship.

"Is that what you saw in the ice?" Glissim asked.

Darcy nodded silently. The cyborgs had the ancient treasure. What would they do with it? What did Jick pretend to know? Did it help him? Or did the cyborgs torture the fool?

Darcy didn't have any love for him—he'd tried to rape her. But he was human. They weren't. A terrible thought made it hard to sleep afterward. Would the cyborgs turn Jick into one of them? That was terrifying.

During the twenty-seventh hour, the message panel lit up.

Glissim turned to her. "What do we do?"

"Move aside," Darcy said. "I'll answer it. I'm the senior."

Glissim drifted from her chair, hovering just out of sight of the screen.

Taking the vacated spot, Darcy strapped herself down. With a tap of her finger, she opened channels. Toll Three peered at her on the screen.

"Prepare for boarding," he said in his monotone.

Darcy wanted to ask about Jick. Her tongue cleaved to the roof of her mouth as she stared at the cyborg. In her fear, she couldn't speak.

"Do you comprehend my words?" Toll Three asked.

Darcy could only nod.

The screen flickered off.

"What is it?" Glissim asked. "What's happening?"

Darcy turned around as she trembled uncontrollably. This was awful. She didn't know what to do. She didn't want to become a cyborg.

Minutes ticked by and became an hour. Finally, outer clangs foretold the cyborgs' return to the ice hauler.

With fear and trembling, Darcy and Glissim waited in the airlock chamber. The same procedure as before produced similar results. The inner airlock slid open and Toll Three with another freaky cyborg stepped into the chamber.

"H-Hi," Darcy stammered.

"You are the senior?" Toll Three asked.

Her tongue froze again. Darcy could only nod.

"You are the one who originally discovered the alien vessel?"

"Yes," Darcy whispered.

"You will come with me."

"W-Where are we going?" Darcy asked with a moan.

"Don your suit," Toll Three said.

"Is Jick all right?"

The cyborg stared at her in silence.

The trembling intensified so Darcy's teeth rattled against each other.

"I'm scared, Darcy," Glissim whispered.

"So am I."

The two women hugged. Tears leaked out of Darcy's eyes. "Glissim, I-I—"

"You've been an excellent senior," Glissim whispered, patting Darcy on the back. "I'll miss you very much."

"Please," Darcy whispered. "Don't say that. I'm coming back."

"I don't think any of us are ever going home again."

Darcy released Glissim. Was that true? It was too horrifying to consider. She faced Toll Three. "What are you going to do with me?"

"The Prime Web-Mind wishes to speak with you," the cyborg said.

"Who is that?"

For the first time, Toll Three showed a modicum of emotion, that of slight surprise. "You do not know the Prime Web-Mind?"

Darcy shook her head.

"The Prime is the ultimate construct in the universe," Toll Three said, sounding proud. "The Prime guides the Conquest Fleet and will begin the liquidation of the humanoids and their reptilian masters."

"You mean kill us?" Darcy asked.

"Liquidation does not mean death. It is a rebirth into the cyborg machinery. We are the future of the universe. Our conquest and assimilation is foreordained."

"H-How do you know?" Darcy stammered.

"We are superior. We shall liquidate each species in turn and rebuild in our perfection."

"Does he agree with that?" Darcy asked, pointing at the other cyborg.

Toll Three didn't turn to look. He peered at Darcy, waiting. Finally, he said, "Don your suit. Time has become a factor."

The trembling had stopped, but Darcy felt drained. Without energy, she climbed into a vacc-suit. She slipped a laser torch onto the equipment rack that acted as a belt. Just before Darcy put the helmet on, Glissim broke into sobs.

The helmet clunked into place and Darcy snapped it tight with a twist. The tall cyborg whirred near, grabbed her vacc-suit sleeve, and pulled her into the airlock.

It closed, air escaped, and the outer lock opened. The former cyborg tube was gone. The three of them walked on the surface of the snowball with stars glittering everywhere.

Her earphones crackled. "Can you hear me?" Toll Three asked.

"I can," Darcy said.

"We will journey to the warship."

"With what?" Darcy asked.

Toll Three stepped behind her, wrapped his arms around her torso, bent down, and leaped.

She cried out as they catapulted into space. It was a small asteroid with almost zero escape velocity. Darcy looked around wildly. The cyborg lacked a thruster pack. She saw no space lines either.

"How are we getting there?" she radioed.

"Do you see the warship?"

She looked up. She saw it all right. "You mean you just jump there?"

"How can you ask me that? You are witness to the event."

That was about right. Toll Three's jump was an event. Did the cyborg really have that kind of precision? Or would the cyborgs on the ship catch them in a giant net?

"Can I ask you a question?" Darcy said.

"You just did."

"That was to get your permission to ask about Jick."

"Who is Jick?"

Darcy felt cold inside. "He was the human who went with you the first time."

"Jick is gone," Toll Three said.

"Did you kill him?"

"No."

Darcy exhaled with relief.

"The Prime Web-Mind ordered his conversion," Toll Three said.

"What does that mean?"

"Your fellow human will become a model 6 cyborg in another fifty-three hours."

"Are you a model 6?"

"No," he said, sounding insulted.

Darcy couldn't think of anything more to say. How did the machines turn a human into a cyborg? Jick, Jick, Jick, he had been a fool to volunteer. He always tried to game the system. In the end—

Shivering with dread, Darcy fell into a frightened torpor. The rest of the journey passed in silence.

Finally, the giant spheroid loomed larger and larger. She couldn't see any net. Then her entire world was the cyborg warship. She noticed an open hangar bay. Light glowed there. They aimed for it.

Again she wondered if the cyborg could really leap with that kind of precision. Why not? A computer could do it. Theoretically, so could a human. It seemed crazy, though.

Toll Three passed through the portal and landed on the deck plates. Because he held her, Darcy landed with him. He released her torso. They walked across a magnetized floor.

They must not have grav-plates. That means the Kresh have superior technology. At least our side has an edge.

Toll Three took her through a hatch and stood on a large round disc. "Hold on to the rail," he said.

It took a moment. Then she spied the object. A pole rose from the middle of the disc. A rail radiated outward from it. She wrapped her gauntlets around it.

The disc lifted. Soon, bulkheads flashed past. Her fingers began to slip off. Maybe that would be for the best. She didn't want to die, but she didn't want to become a cyborg either.

One of Toll Three's hands clamped onto hers, keeping her fingers from flying off. The ride lasted five more minutes, possibly a little longer. Finally, the disc landed with a jar.

"Come," Toll Three said, tugging her hand.

They marched down a dim corridor. She didn't see other cyborgs or ship machinery, just smooth steel corridors. Finally, they reached another hatch. A portal slid down, and the two of them entered a small chamber with several chairs.

"Disrobe," Toll Three said over the radio.

Reaching up, she twisted her helmet. Soon, she stood in her ship clothes with the vacc-suit on the floor.

"Disrobe," Toll Three said over his suit speakers.

"Why?" she asked. "What difference does it make?"

"Disrobe," he repeated for the third time.

Feeling helpless, with a knot tightening in her stomach, Darcy Foxe stripped off her garments.

"You are an excellent specimen," Toll Three said, his metal orbs going up and down as he gazed upon her nude form. "Jick was right about you."

"He's really alive?" she asked.

"I've already told you he lives. He is waiting for conversion."

"So he'll no longer be human?"

"Not fully," the cyborg said. "Before he left the Prime's presence, Jick suggested the Web-Mind leave you as breeding stock."

She frowned. That sounded ominous.

Toll Three pointed at a chair. "Sit," he said over the suit speakers. "The Prime Web-Mind is about to address you."

Feeling horribly exposed, groaning at the coldness of the plastic chair on her butt and the back of her legs, Darcy gingerly sat down.

Toll Three moved beside the hatch.

She hoped he wouldn't leave. Being all alone on the alien ship seemed more terrifying than having a leering cyborg for a companion.

The wall before her flickered with light. Then an image appeared of growing triangles. They expanded but grew fainter until they disappeared. Smaller ones kept reappearing and going through the same sequence. She had no idea what it signified, if anything.

"You are the human, Senior Darcy Foxe?" a loud computer voice asked.

"I am," she whispered.

"I am the Prime Web-Mind of the Conquest Fleet."

Darcy had no idea what that meant.

Klane had seen the Prime Web-Mind before when his consciousness had roved stellar space. He had found a complex cyborg, a thing or meld of man and machine. There had been rows and rows of clear biodomes. In the dozens upon dozens of domes were sheets of brain mass, many thousands of kilos of brain cells from as many unwilling donors from a war fought over one hundred years ago.

Green computing gel had surrounded the pink-white mass. Cables, biotubes, and tight-beam links had connected the endless domes to computers and life-support systems. The combination made a seething whole. It was an empire of mind. The biotubes had gurgled as warm liquids pulsed through them. Backup computers made whirring sounds as lights indicated ten thousand things.

Of those things, Darcy knew nothing. The voice, screen, and room were her only conception of it. Moistening her lips, she said, "I'm pleased to meet you."

"This is interesting," the Prime said. "I had not anticipated such awareness among a worker human such as yourself."

Darcy tried to decipher what that was supposed to mean. She was too frightened, though.

"I notice heightened stimulation," the Prime said. "Faster heart rate, quicker breathing, and sweat secretion. You are excited to communicate with me, I see. That is another mark in your favor. Yes, Senior Darcy Foxe, I am the ultimate in construction. Other Primes exist, but I alone control the Conquest Fleet. It means that after the victory, I will begin constructing yet another cyborg base."

"Ah," Darcy managed to say.

"Your solemnity gratifies me. Your fellow human flooded the chamber with verbose and grandiose promises. He profaned the occasion with his chatter. Your aspect is the correct one when addressing such a superior construct as myself."

Darcy managed to bow her head.

"Interesting, interesting, you show me reverence. This was unsought on my part. I have a nation of slaves. They must obey my slightest whim. That is merely an expression of speech. I lack whims. My thoughts are dictates of perfected planning. Thus, if I order, my minions follow the action to the letter, to the dot."

Darcy nodded. The Web-Mind's flow of words startled her. It made the construct less intimidating.

"Perfect," the Prime said. "My speech has helped to put you at ease. I am the ultimate. Thus, if I desire a thing, I gain it. Senior Darcy, I have found an ancient . . ."

"Ship?" she asked.

"You speak without leave?" the Prime said.

Darcy realized her mistake. She shook her head.

"You did speak. I heard you. Listen. I will play back your words." And it did. Darcy heard herself, and she wondered why her voice sounded different when played back like that.

"What did you mean by 'ship'?" the Prime asked.

She took a gamble, shrugging.

"You have grown faint again. I presume it is in awe of my intellect." She nodded.

"Yes. I understand the problem. It is difficult for an unmodified human such as you to commune with a superior construct like me. I do not sense envy in you. No. I analyze fear, dread, and awe. I am certain you are in awe of me."

She nodded vigorously.

"In this instance, Senior Darcy Foxe, I am going to request speech on your part. I wish to have a dialogue with you."

"Thank you," Darcy said. "You are most . . ." She almost said "kind." Instead, she said, "You are most gracious."

"Indeed, indeed. This is a marvelous dialogue. The other Primes believe such communication sullies our logic programs. I hold to a different creed. I expand my knowledge base through such dialogues. It is unfortunate Jick proved untruthful. What about you, Senior Darcy Foxe: Are you truthful?"

"Yes."

"I knew you would say that. I have video cameras watching you. They are hidden, so don't bother looking for them. I find that some of my brain cells delight in seeing you. Stand up, Senior Darcy Foxe."

She did.

"Stand straight," the Prime said.

With a sniff, she squared her shoulders.

"Walk across the chamber, Senior Darcy Foxe. Strut for me as you would for a lover."

Revulsion swept through Darcy. She almost let that twist onto her face. That would be a disaster, she was certain. So she forced a smile and sauntered across the chilly chamber.

"You are a wonderful specimen of a woman."

"Thank you, Prime."

"Do my words make you proud?"

"They do," Darcy forced herself to say.

"That is the nature of a beautiful woman, is it not?"

"Yes," she said.

"Walk more. Let us see your buttocks jiggle."

Darcy blushed. She couldn't believe this was happening.

"Jick was right about you," the Prime said. "The Conquest Fleet does not yet have a breeding herd. Perhaps I should save you for it.

This is an interesting puzzle. I cannot fathom defeat in this star system. But it is well to remember that war is an uncertain endeavor. The Conquest Fleet might have to retreat. If we do, it would be good to add such a fine specimen as yourself to the greater herd."

Darcy stopped.

"No," the Prime said. "You will continue to strut through the chamber as we speak. I find watching you to be a soothing delight."

Darcy kept walking in the nude, trying to ignore Toll Three watching her as well.

"Do you know what the ancient ship does?" the Prime asked.

"No," Darcy said.

"Yet you found it."

"I did," she said.

"Were you looking for it?" the Prime asked.

"I do not think so."

"You're not sure?" the Prime asked.

This was her one lie. She hadn't known anything. Yet she was sure the Prime wanted to know what this thing did. Likely, Glissim was right. None of them was going home again. Yet she would try to stay alive as long as she could. She would attempt to remain human, too.

"Do you think your subconscious might have been searching for it?" the Prime asked.

"I do not know."

"But it is possible?"

"Yes," she said.

"Interesting. You begin to perspire more. Why is that?"

"I'm . . . strutting very fast," she said.

"Yes?"

"That causes perspiration."

"You are human. Do you think you're perspiring because of your strutting?"

"Partly," Darcy said.

"The other part?"

"It may have to do with finding the ship."

"A hidden or subconscious need?"

"Yes," Darcy said.

"Sit, Senior Darcy Foxe," the Prime said.

She sank onto a chair. It was no longer cold.

"We will save you for now," the Prime said. "I have found this conversation highly stimulating."

She nodded.

"Toll Three."

The cyborg stood at rigid attention.

"Take Senior Darcy Foxe to the alien ship," the Prime said. "We will watch her. If she had a subconscious thought before, she might have another while inspecting the vessel. Go. Do this at once."

"Question, Prime," Toll Three said.

"Speak."

"Should she don the vacc-suit first?" Toll Three asked.

"The alien vessel is in a secure chamber, but accidents are possible in a war zone. Yes. Have her don the vacc-suit."

Toll Three pointed at the crumpled suit on the floor.

Darcy jumped up from the chair, put on her clothes, and slid back into the vacc-suit, sealing the tabs.

22

Cyrus stood in the control room of the Battle Fang. Skar leaned against the cushioned captain's board where Mingal Cham the 3012th would have lounged.

Kresh didn't sit like humans. They stood, leaned, or lay down on their sides.

Several crewmembers from the Attack Talon sat at the various stations. Everyone studied the main screen. It showed the moon Jassac. Around it were parked nearly one hundred warships: darters, Battle Fangs, Attack Talons, and the mighty hammer-ships. The last vessels to arrive at Jassac showed up brightly on the screen. Their engines burned hot as they decelerated into near orbit. The rest of the Pulsar gravitational system was devoid of spaceships except for theirs.

"I've done everything I can think of to shield us from detection," Skar told Cyrus. "We're on minimum life support. I've shut off the engines so we're traveling on accumulated velocity. Spacewalkers went outside and sprayed black construction foam around the Battle Fang. The hardened foam presently dims any heat and radar signatures. I do not know about Bo Taw psi-sweeps."

"We're too far from Jassac for that," Cyrus said.

"Do not underestimate a FIRST," Skar said. "They are cunning beyond reason. Besides, couldn't Bo Taw still be in High Station 3?"

"You're right about that. Would they think to psi-scan from there, though?"

"I would," Skar said.

"What about Heenhiss?" Cyrus asked. "What's the situation there, as far as you can tell?"

"We've used long-range scopes to study the situation. The Chirr have swept the Heenhiss spaceways clean of Kresh habitats. The main bug fleet presently heads for Glegan. The computer estimates their arrival in five days."

"That's fast," Cyrus said, thinking of solar system travel times. "Have the Chirr living underground on Glegan launched their own space fleet?"

"Not yet," Skar said.

"The Kresh at Glegan are still keeping their warships there?"

"So far."

"Excuse me for interrupting," Niens said, "but isn't shielding our Battle Fang the first priority?"

Cyrus and Skar glanced at the tall mentalist.

"Skar has done what he can," Niens said, "but I doubt it will be enough. Once Dagon Dar spots our ship . . ."

Nodding, Cyrus composed himself. "I learned a trick from the dying Sa-Austra."

"That is the Eich?" Niens asked.

"No," Cyrus said. "The Sa-Austra is an old memory. It belonged to the Eich, but it was also separate. I'm not sure how that's possible. I've begun to wonder, though, if the Eich taught the seekers on Jassac how to mind transfer."

"Why would the psi-parasite do that?" Niens asked.

"That's a great question," Cyrus said. "If we learn the answer, I think we're closer to understanding just what the psi-parasite is and why it's been hiding in the tubes all this time."

Niens grew thoughtful. "You say you slew the Sa-Austra, a memory in the Eich. Did the psi-parasite lose that memory once you slew it?"

"I would think so," Cyrus said.

Niens stroked his chin before asking, "Do you feel up to making a null?"

"You ask me that now?" Cyrus asked.

The mentalist actually looked abashed.

Cyrus took a calming breath. "Before we reached this star system, the Kresh kept those on Earth and us aboard the Teleship in the dark concerning Fenris, or New Eden as we on *Discovery* knew it then. Our first battle was against a habitat in the outer asteroid belt. The habitat's function caused us to tele-shift near it. Somehow, the Bo Taw working aboard the habitat broadcast a false image of the entire star system."

"That is what you're going to attempt to do now?" Niens asked.

"No."

"Then why bother bringing it up?"

"The Sa-Austra had a different version of that," Cyrus said. "I'm going to cloak our Battle Fang. The Bo Taw in the Kresh habitat needed to broadcast their psi-image all the time. What I'm going to try is a single application of psionics for camouflage that will remain in effect."

"Is it dangerous to do?" Niens asked.

"Not for you," Cyrus said. He closed his eyes before the mentalist could ask more questions. Niens wanted to know too badly. It became annoying after a while.

Soft whispers surrounded him. Cyrus concentrated. Fear constricted his chest. He told himself he didn't have to worry. He wasn't attacking anyone. This was passive psionics.

The Sa-Austra had opened its memories about what it knew during the last seconds of its life. Cyrus hadn't been able to glean everything, but he had gotten this.

The whispers around him stilled as the noises faded. Cyrus heard nothing now, but he still felt the thrum of the fusion engine. Soon, he wasn't aware of breathing, smelling, or even standing. With psi-senses, his thoughts roved outside the Battle Fang. This was similar to creating a discontinuity window. He was always exhausted after doing that.

Concentrate, he told himself.

He sensed the Battle Fang of steel, titanium, foam insulation, wires, coils, nuclear fusion, plastics, and crew of humans. The ship was a capsule of life in the void. Skar had done wonders with the construction foam. Vomags were masters of improvising on the spot.

Cyrus began to erase. *The vessel is not here.* The hiding process would not last for a long time, several days perhaps. That would be more than long enough to reach High Station 3. He didn't know if it would shield the Battle Fang during braking maneuvers. The heat signature would be too strong to hide.

Worry about one thing at a time.

It was crazy that his mind contained these memories from others. Even worse was that these memories had their own personalities. He would have to return deep into his mind and conquer them so he could use the memories. If Klane had had more time for a proper transfer, none of this would have happened.

Well, that wasn't exactly correct. Klane could have smoothed out the other memories, submerging them into his mind. The Anointed One couldn't have done that with the Eich. The psi-parasite was the joker in the deck. The alien entity also had other unknown treasures of ancient knowledge. Cyrus wanted those.

I'm really doing this. I'm cloaking the Battle Fang.

As Cyrus used his increased psionics, something began to change. He thought he had everything under control. The knowledge from the Sa-Austra made *the* critical difference. He could cloak them from the Kresh. Then something new pulled at his mind. It was a gentle tug at first.

What is that? Cyrus wondered. *It feels like a psi-magnet.*

The gentle tug glued against his mind, making an inseparable bond.

Hey! Cyrus struggled against it. No good; he was stuck. It yanked, drawing his concentration away from the lone Battle Fang and across the star system.

At the speed of thought, Cyrus's concentration passed a gas giant and raced for the outer asteroid belt. In seconds, he reached a snowball asteroid and spied a huge metal craft nearby. Whatever did this to him was inside the alien vessel.

Cyrus's thought zipped through collapsium plating and to a hangar bay. He realized several cyborgs stood around a small silver ship. The thing was teardrop shaped and lacked any means of entrance or exit. At the bulbous part of the vessel was a human, a woman. She didn't wear a helmet.

The hangar bay has a breathable atmosphere.

Cyrus had time to marvel at the beauty of the woman's features. Then he saw her hand. She didn't wear a gauntlet. Her bare fingers touched the silver craft.

That's what had drawn his thoughts across space. Why should that be so?

Something in Cyrus cried out in anguish. *The ship!*

The woman turned her head. Had she heard that? Cyrus launched a psi-probe at her. She lacked the power to shield herself. Her name was Senior Darcy Foxe. She belonged to Ice Hauler 266-9. Darcy had spoken to the Prime Web-Mind of the Conquest Fleet. It had wanted her to look at the alien object they had torn out of the asteroid.

I get it. This is the Eich's ship. The parasite must have cried out a moment ago. How was that possible, though?

She sullies the ship. Stop her!

Before Cyrus could stop the Eich, the alien entity blasted a psi-bolt at Darcy Foxe.

You bastard. You're not getting away with it this time. Cyrus partly blocked the punch, the psi-blast.

He saw Darcy Foxe faint, dropping to the floor. For a brief second, the cyborgs did nothing. Then the blockiest cyborg rushed to her, picking Darcy up in his arms.

Cyrus wanted to look inside the ship.

Never!

The Eich caused Cyrus's mind to recoil from the ancient silver ship. His concentration fled from the cyborg warship, fled from the snowball and the outer asteroid belt. As fast as he had come, his mental consciousness journeyed back even faster. It was like a stretched rubber band allowed to snap back.

Cyrus Gant grunted. Sounds rushed upon him. Smells burst into flavor. Noises, odors, sensations bludgeoned him as he opened his eyes aboard the Battle Fang.

His knees gave way. Skar caught him, dragging him to a chair.

"Are you well?" Skar asked, worry etched across his blunt features.

Cyrus blinked, confused. How had the Eich done that?

"What happened?" Cyrus whispered.

"Explain," Niens said, stepping near.

"Sir," one of the crew said.

Cyrus breathed deeply. His head hurt. This wasn't as bad as coming out of the AI after creating a discontinuity window, but it was close.

"Sir," the same crewmember said, becoming more urgent.

"What's wrong?" Skar asked.

"I think you should look at that," the crewmember said. The woman pointed at the main screen.

Cyrus looked up. So did Skar. So did everyone in the command room. A Kresh peered at them from the screen.

"Turn up the volume," Skar ordered.

"This is Dagon Dar FIRST," the Kresh said. "We have spotted your errant Battle Fang. By the registry, it is one of mine, commanded by Mingal Cham the 3012th. Put him on immediately."

"What should we do?" Skar asked Cyrus.

He slouched in the chair, staring at Dagon Dar. Once again, he'd failed in his mission.

"My Bo Taw have told me about your psionic flash," Dagon Dar said. "You wanted me to see you. I find that interesting and arrogant."

Cyrus groaned. What flash? Couldn't he do anything right?

"Since you fail to put Mingal Cham the 3012th online," Dagon Dar said, "I must assume the Earther took control of the vessel. How this could have happened, I have no idea. Since you remain silent, we cannot engage in bargaining. I am FIRST. You have disobeyed a direct command. While I am curious about you, I cannot tolerate such insubordination. Who will obey me then? Thus, I am launching five Tal drones at your ship. You have several hours at best. Make your peace with the Creator, for you are all about to die."

Dagon Dar disappeared from the main screen.

One of the crewmembers manipulated her controls. The screen showed Jassac. From it, five bright points of light appeared.

"They've launched the Tal drones," Skar said. He turned to Cyrus. "What do you suggest we do next?"

23

While Skar and the others attempted evasive maneuvers and thought out battle plans, Cyrus returned to the altered part of his mind. He needed to know more. He had to break the Eich and figure out how to use the full extent of his Klane-given powers. Without Anointed One psionics, the humans weren't going to be able to affect the coming three-way alien war.

The descent into the dark part of his mind was different this time. He flashed like a meteor across the sky. In moments, he reached the location of his fight with the Sa-Austra. There, he found the Saurian's bleached bones.

That was odd. Time must work strangely down here in his mind.

What am I thinking? What time? I'm inside my thoughts. Cyrus didn't like how real everything seemed. This wasn't like his original mind fights against the Eich. The farther he traveled in the altered part of his mind, the more tangible everything became. It was harder to remember the truth. Was there a danger in that? Would he reach a place in the altered region where he couldn't simply zip out again?

Cyrus studied the seemingly ancient corpse. The Sa-Austra's garments and items had remained with the bones. Squatting, he pulled a ring from a finger bone and picked up a pouch. Then he spied a knife in a sheath. He had to have that, and he did, taking it. Afterward, he continued his trek.

Soon, a troop of Saurians riding vat-altered humans scoured the hills for him. Had they seen him flash through the darkness like a meteor?

I have to act as if everything is real. If I fail here, I'm going to fail in the real world. Everything depends on me.

He heard warbling horns and occasionally felt a flicker of psionics. Did the Saurians have that, or did the Eich help them?

Cyrus put distance between him and the Saurian patrols. He decided to keep his thoughts as neutral as possible. He walked in a measured tread, never hurrying, always suppressing panicked thoughts.

In time, he reached a desert of faintly shimmering shale. The flattish rocks clattered and often slid out from under his feet. It proved a desolate region, with only the black sky and the slowly rotating wheel for company. He drank twice from brackish pools and rationed the dried pellets in the Saurian's pouch. The ring had weight. The knife was razor sharp.

Each stop, Cyrus checked his baton. The original one had broken. He'd had to fashion a new directional-finding baton, seeking the Eich.

More time passed. He wished he could hurry this up. Why couldn't he fly to his destination? He tried, envisioning wings sprouting from his back. Since that didn't work, he ran and jumped, willing himself into the air like a superhero. Nothing happened.

Soon, though, a leathery creature wheeled overhead.

Cyrus crouched, watching it. Had he created the monster by his thoughts of flying?

I have to be careful what I envision.

The creature flew elsewhere. Alone with his thoughts, Cyrus walked until he reached a towering mountain.

What happened aboard the Battle Fang? How close were the Tal drones to the ship? Cyrus shook his head. Thinking about it would only worry him. He needed to find the alien parasite.

Out of the corner of his eye, Cyrus spied red glows. They detached themselves from the mountain, from a cliff face, it seemed. The ghostly wheel's crimson light was dimmer here. He had no idea why.

The red glows soared in the darkness, dipped and climbed. One screeched and dived at Cyrus.

He waited, knowing that running would prove useless. The thing closed. In the dim light, he saw that it had fiendish, horned features and leathery wings, and its abdomen glowed. Its stomach seemed transparent. Worms or intestines shined with wicked light in there.

Cyrus waited with his knife. When it closed with him, he'd slice it into ribbons of flesh.

The fiendish thing screeched and veered sharply. Its leathery wings flapped heavily as it climbed. Apparently, it recognized him as dangerous.

Heartened by the encounter, Cyrus hurried onto the plain of darkness. It wasn't true dark, but the ghostly wheel shed a quarter of the light it once had. Cyrus trudged until the flying red glows dimmed and disappeared altogether.

Thirst began to weaken him. He tried to mind-conjure water, but that didn't work here. He didn't know why. Cyrus kept walking, and what might have been an hour later, he spied a sudden flare of light. Cyrus rubbed his face. He saw flames, not just light. The fire seemed near, on a hill of sorts. Did Saurians camp there? He had to risk it. He needed water; could use food, too.

After a time, he came to a hill. His boots pressed upon spongy grass. He passed low rocks, threaded up a narrow path with a sheer drop on either side, and advanced onto a rocky plateau. He stopped, and realized he'd staggered in a daze. A fire crackled. Beside the fire was a rock big enough for someone to sit on. What appeared as part of a splintered door lay near the fire.

A door? That's weird.

Other hacked parts of the door burned in the blaze. He spied a water bag, blankets—

The softest of footfalls alerted Cyrus. He began to turn and froze.

Out of the corner of his eye, firelight shimmered off a long blade. He silently berated himself for being a fool.

A gruff voice spoke in a strange tongue. It sounded like a question. Too bitter to care, Cyrus continued turning, but a strong hand gripped his hair and jerked his head back the way it had been aimed. With a hand reaching from behind, the blade touched his throat. The person spoke again, harshly.

"I can't understand you," Cyrus said.

Seconds passed. Then lips brushed Cyrus's right ear. The person spoke slowly and deliberately, with a harsh accent. "I said: Who are you?"

"I'm Cyrus Gant of Earth. Who are you?"

The person shoved Cyrus, making him stumble.

Cyrus whirled around. The man was short, with reddish skin and thick shoulders. He had to have been a native of Jassac from the highlands. The primitive wore furs but clutched a saber, while a short-handled Vomag axe hung from his belt.

"Where did you come from?" the primitive asked.

Cyrus listened closely. It was an atrocious accent. "I'm from Earth like I said."

The primitive shook his head. It was a quick, dismissive move.

"May I ask where you're from?" Cyrus asked. There was something familiar about the man, but he couldn't place it.

The primitive considered the question as his gaze flickered over Cyrus. Finally, with his saber, the man pointed at the fire.

Cyrus moved beside it, his thoughts awhirl.

The primitive sat erect on the rock, as if ready for action. He muttered as he studied Cyrus. Then he pitched him a heavy waterskin.

Gratefully, Cyrus guzzled, aware of a faintly sour taste. He was about to guzzle again when his dignity reasserted itself. He pulled the skin away and lifted an eyebrow.

"You can drink more," the primitive said.

Cyrus nodded his thanks and guzzled.

"You are a fugitive?" the primitive asked.

"No."

"A sacrifice then?" the primitive asked.

"Not from the Saurians."

The primitive spat into the fire, where his saliva sizzled. "May their eyes rot in the trench," he muttered.

Refreshed from the water, Cyrus noticed the primitive's eyes. They were blue just as Klane's had been. For a moment, he thought it was the Anointed One. But no . . . it was just the eyes.

"Are you a seeker?" Cyrus asked.

"What?"

"A seeker to the Clan Tash-Toi," Cyrus said.

"Yes! I serve Sion Trumble. How could you know?"

Cyrus nodded gravely. That hardly sounded like a Jassac name. Maybe this seeker, this memory, came from a long time ago: different age, different customs and names.

"Sion Trumble is the hetman of Clan Tash-Toi," the primitive said.

He's from the same clan as Klane. Does that signify anything? Why are the eyes blue?

Cyrus cleared his throat. "How did you come to this land?"

The man scowled, which drew his heavy features downward. "The Saurians invaded, changing the very features of things."

Cyrus rubbed his hands before the fire, feeling its warmth. "Earth is two hundred and thirty light-years from Jassac."

"I know where Earth is," the man said. With his blue eyes feverishly alight, the primitive asked, "Do you wish to reshape this land, returning it to normal?"

"No! I seek the Eich that caused all this."

Troubled, the seeker sat back, looking away.

Cyrus cleared his throat. "Do you have a name?"

The man shot to his feet, the saber almost magically appearing in his hand. The look on his face was stoic, seemingly blank. Yet Cyrus was certain the man seethed with suppressed rage.

Cyrus held up a hand. "Will you listen to me?"

The man hesitated and then nodded.

"I do not know Sion Trumble." Cyrus chose his words with care. "I am ignorant of you and your ways. By your actions, it seems I may have insulted you. I did not mean any insult, and I apologize if I have."

"You apologize to a primitive of Jassac?"

"I apologize to you," Cyrus said. "You have given me water and let me share your fire. I thank you for both."

"You said you were from Earth."

Cyrus nodded.

"Yet you thank a Jassac primitive, a toy of the Saurians?"

"I have thanked you."

With a faint look of astonishment, the man sat down. He sheathed his saber and pointed at the waterskin.

Cyrus pitched it to him.

The man sipped and capped it. "Call me Braunt for now. I am . . . I am the right armguard to Sion Trumble the hetman of Clan Tash-Toi. I also have a talent, a psionic gift. That makes me the clan seeker."

"Did you fight Saurians?"

Braunt peered into the darkness. "The others are gone," he said, ignoring the question.

"I'm sorry," Cyrus said.

Braunt sat erect like a statue.

In the fire, a burning splinter cracked and sparks exploded upward.

Braunt studied Cyrus sidelong. Finally, the man said, "I know why you are here."

Cyrus said nothing.

"You wish to cross the barrier," Braunt said.

"Why would I wish to do that?"

"Because the Eich lives beyond the barrier," Braunt said. "There, you can defeat the parasite."

Cyrus kept a poker face, although inside he seethed with excitement. "How do you know this?"

"I am a seeker. It is part of my gift."

The feeling that Cyrus knew this man grew stronger. He believed he could trust the primitive, at least in this. "Okay. I think you're right."

Braunt breathed deeply through his flattish nostrils. He stood and sat back down. "You look exhausted. You should sleep. I will stand guard. Then we can march to the barrier." Braunt examined Cyrus. "First you should eat. I have some meat. It is very tough."

"Anything sounds good," Cyrus said.

"We are agreed?"

"You mean about reaching the barrier?" Cyrus asked.

Braunt nodded.

"We are agreed," Cyrus told him.

Braunt grinned fiercely. "I knew there was a reason I had survived. It has been a long time since I have dared slink near the barrier."

"Is it dangerous?" Cyrus asked.

Braunt made a harsh sound, which was all the answer Cyrus needed.

24

Senior Darcy Foxe sat naked in the same chamber as before. Toll Three stood guard at the hatch. Her clothes and vacc-suit were in a heap behind her chair.

She felt groggy as if hungover from a long shore leave. *Have I been asleep? Why don't I remember more?*

The appearing and disappearing triangles on the wall showed the Prime had returned.

"Senior Darcy Foxe," the computer voice said from hidden speakers in the bulkheads.

Her shoulders straightened. Would the thing demand she strut back and forth again? She didn't feel well, and didn't know how long she could keep that up.

Remember. This thing can order your death at any second. You must placate it, and trick it if that's possible.

Darcy wished she could talk to Glissim. She didn't dare ask for that, however. It could mean Glissim's end, and Darcy didn't want that on her conscience.

"I have analyzed your conduct before the alien ship," the Prime said. "I find it odd."

Darcy waited. She wasn't sure why, but the Prime didn't sound as pleased with her as earlier. What had she done wrong?

"Why did you collapse?" the Prime asked.

"I didn't mean to," she said in a quiet voice.

"Do not evade the question."

"I'm sorry. My head hurts. I don't know why I fainted. I don't even remember doing that."

The big triangles faded away. New smaller ones appeared.

Finally, the Prime spoke. "Your body functions prove your statement. It is good for you that you're not telling lies."

Darcy debated telling it she was too in awe of him to lie. Some interior warning kept her from opening her mouth.

Jick died—or ceased being human—because he spoke too much. I have to remember that.

"It is time for you to make a decision," the Prime said.

Darcy's stomach tightened. *I hate this. I'm too tired. My head hurts. I don't know what to do.*

"You worked for the Kresh. Are you surprised I know their race name?"

"Your breadth of knowledge awes me," Darcy said carefully.

"Yes. That is the problem with such superiority as mine. We Primes are beyond anything in the universe. I combine hundreds of human brains with AI computer circuitry. My speed of thought is matched only by my reasoning power. It is why I control the Conquest Fleet."

Darcy kept reverently silent. She was beginning to think most of the brain donors must have been men. The Prime had a gigantic ego, something one would expect from merging so many male brains together.

"Because you continue to speak the truth as you know it," the Prime said, "I will continue the analysis. I believe this star system holds hidden enemies. These hidden ones are the true danger, not the paltry fleets I see gathering to meet us.

"Ah," the Prime said, "you remain quiet, perhaps even confused. You are a worker for the Kresh. We have captured several of them before, Kresh, I mean. They proved an interesting species. The Prime of Kal has suggested we integrate Kresh brain tissues into us. I and others vetoed the idea. We are distinctly human cyborgs, and we shall remain so for quite some time. I suspect dangerous crosscurrents of thought would occur if we attempted to merge alien and human minds into one."

The Prime fell silent. Darcy waited. The air was too cold in here and she detected a faint odor, a cross between old meats and burnt electrical wires. She pushed the smell aside. Well, she tried and failed. Finally, she raised her right hand, rubbing her nose, smelling herself.

"You grow agitated in the silence," the Prime said.

He surprised her by speaking again, and she gasped aloud.

"You are easily frightened," the Prime said.

Darcy nodded.

"Clearly, you lack my perfect composure. I must remember that as I deal with you. I have been replaying files of Jick to myself just now. During our conversations, he annoyed me. In fact, I have halted his conversion into a model 6 cyborg. It will be my pleasure to torment the bothersome creature as he is. The coming days of battle may prove stressful. I will relieve those stresses by toying with him. Does that surprise you?"

"W-What part?" Darcy whispered.

"Excuse me. Are you claiming I lack clarity? Is that why you don't know what I mean?"

"N-No," she stammered.

"Then you admit to lacking wit?"

A gut feeling warned Darcy. "Neither of those things, Great Prime," she said. "To answer your original question, I touched the alien ship. I remember that much. Something struck me then. It has left me dazed, maybe somewhat confused."

"Oh. Let me recheck the file. Yes, I'm replaying it to myself now. Ah. It is just as I suspected. Nothing visible struck you."

"No?"

"You simply slumped. Right! That is how I deduced the hidden one. No. Let me rephrase. One approached the Conquest Fleet several jumps ago. We had a short dialogue before he escaped. The identity possessed mental powers. One with such abilities must have struck you before the alien ship. I correlated the two incidents and realize now the original must have come from this star system. That would also explain why the aliens of this star system have gathered their fleets in battle readiness. After our first meeting, the mental alien returned here to warn them. In their distress—realizing the extent of cyborg might—the two alien species have grouped together to face us. I wonder if the hidden one is their ultimate ruler."

What two groups?

"Your facial patterns are open to me, Senior Darcy Foxe. I analyzed them earlier and now understand your interior thoughts much better than you realize. You are confused. It may be that as a worker in the far asteroids you are unaware of the inner system maneuvers. I will show you and you will comment to me."

The triangles disappeared. In their place, the world of Heenhiss appeared on the wall. Darcy recognized some of the continents.

"I use long-scan teleoptics," the Prime said. "It is a passive system, using ambient light. Notice the destroyed space habitats. I find that odd. I can only conclude certain elements in the Kresh culture refused to side with the others. Yes. I notice the difference of craft. They are substantially diverse, indicting a dissimilar thought process. Do you understand me so far?"

"I do," Darcy said. The Chirr must have launched an annihilating fleet. They had destroyed the Kresh habs around Heenhiss. That was amazing. It was awful. In the past, she'd watched many programs about the war in the tunnels against the bugs. Why did the Prime think Chirr and Kresh worked together? It was an odd idea.

"The hidden one probed our fleet," the Prime said. "I spoke to him—by his thought patterns I deduced him to be male. He used psionic abilities similar to our shift mechanisms, our star-drive. I imagine his information about our fleet devastated the rulers of this star system. It has brought great upheaval. Yet in the end, the others and the Kresh united. Notice how the others travel with speed to the third planet. There, they will join forces to face the cyborg juggernaut."

The wall showed the others—the Chirr fleet—accelerating for Glegan.

They're not going to join forces, Darcy thought. *The bugs mean to wipe out more Kresh. Should I tell the Prime that? Might I gain my freedom that way?*

"You sit enraptured at the sight," the Prime said. "Ah, Senior Darcy Foxe, you give away so much by doing that. I understand you have a glimmer of hope. It is the worst aspect of the human condition. I will use Jick's hopes against him, providing myself with much amusement as I ready the Conquest Fleet to jump into battle."

If I tell him the truth, Darcy thought, *the Prime will make wiser plans. Can I do that to humanity? I'm probably going to die or lose my humanity one way or another. Maybe I can buy myself a few more hours of life. But if I tell the Prime the truth, the thing that is going to torment me will have gained an advantage from me. Jick would speak. I have to be better than Jick. Otherwise, I'm the same as a rapist.*

"The pitiful creatures of this star system don't understand my capabilities," the Prime said. "I recognize their strategy. It is elementary. They seek to combine their ships into one super fleet. It is the correct tactic. But it will fail. Do you know why it will fail, Senior Darcy Foxe?"

She shook her head.

"I believe you when you indicate that you don't know. Good. It will come as a surprise to you as much as to them. Now, we will begin a different line of inquiry."

The wall image of the bug fleet vanished. In its place was an image of the silver ship in the cyborg hangar bay.

"You touched the skin of the ship with your bare hand," the Prime said. "What compelled you to throw off your glove to do that?"

"I don't remember."

"Senior Darcy Foxe, we are about to enter a new phase of our relationship. So far, I have refrained from the regular methods of persuasion. Do you know why I've done this?"

She shook her head, too afraid to speak.

"Your form pleases me. It is that simple."

Darcy realized then the Prime definitely was made only of male brains. Did the cyborgs construct their Primes out of all male or female brains? In a sense then, a crowd of men interrogated her. A crowd of men stared at her nude form.

She wanted to hide, or at least to cover herself. *You have to think, Darcy. You have to use what you have.*

Suiting thought to action, she cupped one of her breasts, fondling it, flicking the nipple.

"Do you itch, Senior Darcy Foxe?" the Prime asked.

"I do," she said in as sexy a voice as she could muster.

"Scratch your other breast next," the Prime said.

She did so, and she arched her back.

"Yes," the Prime said. "You please me. I will reserve you for the breeding herd. In time, you will bear the cyborgs many babies. Does that gratify your female nature?"

"Yes," she said. *Somehow, I don't know how or when, I'm going to help to destroy you.* It was such a breathtaking thought, that goose bumps appeared.

"Indeed, indeed," the Prime said. "You are breeding herd material. Look at your skin. This is simply marvelous."

I suppose it is.

"Yet let us return to our discussion of the alien vessel," the Prime said. "Why did you want to touch it?"

Frowning, Darcy tried to remember walking into the hangar bay. The silver ship had stood there, gleaming. Then an atmosphere had hissed around her. Toll Three told her she could remove her helmet. Darcy had dropped it onto the floor. Mesmerized, she'd approached the craft. It had seemed to call to her with a siren song in her mind. Hardly realizing it, she had removed a gauntlet and touched the vessel. Delightful shocks had run down her arm. Then . . .

She frowned.

"What are you thinking?" the Prime asked.

"Someone spoke to me," she said.

"In your mind?" the Prime asked.

Darcy rubbed her forehead. "Yes. In my mind."

"Where did the other mind originate?"

"I'm not sure what you mean."

"The question is basic enough. What was the origin point of the hidden mind?"

Darcy scowled, rubbing her head harder. She might have—she looked up.

"What have you remembered?" the Prime asked.

"The other mind."

"Yes?"

"It originated on Earth."

"What?" the Prime asked. "That is preposterous. Earth doesn't possess a star-drive. You are lying to me, Senior Darcy Foxe."

"No. I'm telling you the truth."

"You have made me very angry," the Prime said. "I am rescinding my order. You will not go into the breeding herd. I will turn you into a model 6 cyborg. Toll Three, take her to the conversion chamber at once. Prepare her."

"I'm telling you the truth!" Darcy shouted. "Please, don't turn me into a cyborg."

"You insist on your lies. Now, you will suffer the consequences."

Before Darcy could say more, Toll Three wrapped his steel arms around her, lifting her off the floor and heading for the hatch.

25

Deep within his own mind, in the altered areas, Cyrus and the one who called himself Braunt slunk through a forest of towering cactus plants. Purple lizards froze whenever they passed. The tiny creatures flicked red forked tongues and watched them with eyes like burning coals. Braunt slew several and they roasted them, using dried-out cactuses for fuel.

Eventually they entered an ominous land of crusted fire pits and lava that occasionally bubbled in a spreading pool. The cooled areas of porous rock crunched underfoot and too often gave way like ice. Cyrus would have plunged into one breakage, but Braunt grabbed his arm and dragged him out of danger. For an instant, Cyrus glimpsed a red lava river fifty feet below his hole. The lava churned and bubbled with brimstone fumes.

Later as they moved through the altered areas of Cyrus's mind, they trudged along a high rocky shelf near a raging sea of fire. Instead of waves, giant flames shot up. They flickered, sometimes reaching forty feet. Less frequently, molten balls catapulted out of the inferno, whooshing in gigantic arcs before exploding back into the sea of fire. Yellow gases billowed. The stench brought tears to their eyes and made them cough.

"How much longer until we reach the barrier?" Cyrus shouted. The sea's constant roar forced them to yell. He had no idea what this signified in his mind. Maybe these were memories the psi-parasite had brought with him.

Braunt bit his lip with indecision.

The mannerism startled Cyrus. Klane used to bite his lip like that. There was something else. Cyrus could have sworn Braunt had been shorter before, the man's shoulders broader. Now, the seeker's shoulders were the same width as his, and the man was almost his height.

Can Braunt be . . . changing?

"I should warn you," Braunt shouted. "Many of the creatures beyond the lake of fire are huge beyond belief."

A large molten ball flew out of the raging flames. It whooshed so close to them that Cyrus felt its crackling heat.

"We cannot rest here," Braunt shouted.

Cyrus nodded, increasing his pace, following the man. As he did, he studied Braunt. Yes, the man was taller than before. The man *was* growing.

Into what? Cyrus wondered. *Is this some sort of metamorphosis? What is that supposed to signify? Maybe I'm supposed to change.*

With an explosive impact, another molten ball struck the sea of flames much too near them. Cyrus flinched at the sound. A billowing cloud mushroomed upward from the sea.

Braunt began to run. Cyrus ran after him. He'd be glad once they left the lake of fire far behind.

||||||||||

They slept in a cave, the sea of flames some distance away. Cyrus wondered why he needed to sleep in his altered mind. This was a mental journey. These things didn't exist as reality, but as concepts in his mind. Maybe because they seemed real, he slept in imitation of reality.

I should simply refuse to sleep. I don't have time to waste.

He turned to Braunt. Cyrus's head swayed in shock.

"Trouble?" Braunt asked.

There was, but Cyrus didn't know what to say. Braunt's skin wasn't as red as before. It was lighter tinted. He opened his mouth to ask the man about that. Then he hesitated.

Before when I asked him his name, he said to call him Braunt. He didn't say that his name was Braunt. Was that an important distinction?

"No problem," Cyrus said, deciding to let it go for now. He set the pace, traveling briskly, ignoring the need for sleep.

What seemed like hours later, he scrambled up a rocky incline. Braunt waited for him up there. On the ledge, the seeker oiled his saber. The man held the curved blade up to his eye lengthwise. With his oiled rag, he flicked a spot before sheathing the gleaming weapon.

In the distance towered gutted hulks of buildings. It was another ancient city, but of greater extent than anything Cyrus had seen so far. With a start, he realized something moved among the wrecks.

Cyrus gasped. The mechanism was huge, although the gutted buildings dwarfed it. The thing moved on treads that plowed over rocks and glittering chunks of glass. It gleamed metallically like Braunt's saber, had a tubular body and a multitude of metal appendages. Some ended in scoops, others in points that glowed red. The rest had pincers.

"The metal warrior is ten meters tall," Braunt said. "It crushed a friend of mine and sliced two others. Afterward, it carried the bloody remains to the sea of flames and with its scoop flung them in one at a time."

"A hunter-seeker," Cyrus whispered.

"You have heard of such metal warriors before?"

Cyrus wondered what the thing symbolized. Thinking about it, a new thought struck. This was an alien situation. He believed, then, it was a memory of a far planet the psi-parasite had been to in the past. Just how old was the Eich? He was beginning to think hundreds, possibly thousands of years. What had the Eich seen in that time?

"Come," Braunt said, "we must hurry. The metal warrior travels in rounds. Now is our chance to reach the ruins without being seen."

How can all this be in my mind? Cyrus thought. *I've never thought such things. I know this is the Eich's memories. He must be overlaying them into the altered part of my mind.* Cyrus blinked rapidly. These strange realms and creatures must mean the Eich was spreading out through his subconscious. If he didn't move fast enough to stop the Eich, he might wake up and find himself a prisoner in his own body. Cyrus shuddered. That was an awful concept.

They descended the rocky expanse and hurried across a plain of brittle grass. The wrecks of gargantuan buildings slowly drew closer like a mountain range. Halfway there, Cyrus recognized the extraterrestrial quality of the architecture.

That both excited and repelled him. He didn't need to travel to other star systems to find differences. He could travel his own altered mind and see what the other star systems held, or had held. Unfortunately, seeing all this had to mean that less of his mind belonged to him, Cyrus Gant of Earth.

Cyrus bared his lips, more determined than ever to find and defeat the psi-parasite.

The alienness of the city became even more apparent when they reached the outer edge of the ruins and walked through streets that seemed to stretch forever. Cyrus arched his neck. The gutted buildings soared higher than the Kresh towers he'd seen in the city on Jassac. Entire walls had slid away, exposing the levels. Other structures were mere metallic frames now. Glass shards, rubble, and swirling dust littered the streets. Old cables snaked here and there. Holes in the stone-hard streets showed cavernous areas that seemed to stretch to the world's core.

Eventually, they entered a different area. Here stood crumbling pyramids, broken plinths, and grotesque idols. They passed plazas cobbled with shimmering bricks. They walked past spike-filled holes and pits full of bones. They clambered over blocks twenty, thirty, maybe even sixty tons in weight.

ALIEN WARS

It seemed to Cyrus they invaded the heart of the city. The ruins towered even higher and the extent of the damage grew.

Many blocks later Braunt held out an arm to halt Cyrus. The seeker knelt and examined gravel.

"What is it?" Cyrus asked.

"A handprint," Braunt whispered. "Look. There is another. Saurians have ridden here. We must remain alert." His features hardened. "The Saurians have slain those like me before, although we have slain them in turn. They are dangerous." Braunt drew his saber and picked up a rock.

They slinked in shadows and darted across open areas. Braunt often paused, listening, scanning the streets. Cyrus became tense.

Braunt hissed in warning.

Cyrus stopped.

The seeker moved beside him and pointed across a crevice.

Four humanoid mounts trotted there with Saurian riders. The lance-armed Saurians peered everywhere as if searching.

"They hunt," Cyrus said, a cold feeling squeezing his spine.

"Why don't the giant men buck off the Saurians and beat them to death?" Braunt whispered.

Cyrus felt another inner jolt. Braunt now spoke with Klane's voice. He eyed Braunt sidelong. If once the seeker had been red-skinned, the man wasn't anymore.

"I would buck my rider off," Braunt said.

"Are the giant men still human, or has their time in the vats turned them into beasts?"

"Vats?" asked Braunt.

"Look," said Cyrus, "they're gone." While he'd studied Braunt, the Saurians had ridden away.

Braunt hesitated and then started walking. Cyrus followed him.

In this way, while avoiding other hunting parties, they reached a wide plaza with broken fountains. In the center of the least damaged

181

fountain coiled a granite snake-like statue with vestigial wings and a bony crest on its serpent head.

Is that what the Eich looks like? Cyrus wondered.

"There," Braunt whispered. He pointed at a monstrous dome in the distance. It was nestled between other large buildings. A fierce blue radiance set it apart from the others. Underneath the radiance the dome seemed intact.

"The barrier," Braunt said in a quiet voice.

Cyrus frowned. It wasn't a barrier, but a dome. Why did everyone call it a barrier then?

"Did the dome glow last time you saw it?" Cyrus asked.

Braunt frowned. "That's strange. I can't remember."

Cyrus tried to puzzle that out. The man had known before. Why would he lose the memory?

"Is your name really Braunt?" Cyrus asked.

The man raised his eyebrows. "I think so. Yes. That's my name. I am Braunt."

Cyrus rubbed his chin, deciding to let it pass. He considered the dome with its blue light. The Saurians had cleansed a blue glow from other ruins. What did the blue glow signify?

"Now," Braunt said. He had been scanning the plaza and side streets. They hurried across the cobbles.

"Maybe we should have gone around this area," Cyrus panted.

"No," said Braunt. "The last Saurians—" He slid to a halt beside a fountain.

Two Saurian riders trotted into view on a nearby street. Braunt and Cyrus eased behind the fountain. One of the mounts must have seen them. It hooted and pranced grotesquely about on all fours.

"At least there are only two this time," Braunt whispered.

The riders, smaller Saurians than the Sa-Austra and bearing lances instead of swords, turned their mounts toward the fountain. The first rider raised its lance. A black pennon fluttered from it.

"Cyrus Gant of Earth," the Saurian hissed, "come forth."

The second Saurian raised a bone-white horn and blew a warbling sound.

"How do they know your name?" Braunt asked.

"An excellent question," Cyrus said. The Sa-Austra had demanded to know his name. These two Saurians knew it. That seemed like a bad omen. He peered at the dome. It was still many streets away. "We must surprise these two," Cyrus said.

"How?" whispered Braunt.

"Remain here," Cyrus said. "Be ready to attack at my signal."

"Attack mounted Saurians?"

"They won't be moving fast when you do," Cyrus said. With a twist of his head, he cracked his neck. Then he flexed his hands and strode from behind the fountain, walking toward the approaching Saurians.

"Cyrus Gant?" the Saurian hissed.

"You have me at a disadvantage, I'm afraid," Cyrus said. "I don't know your names."

With a talon-like hand, the Saurian stroked a red pendant dangling from its throat. "We know you're a psi-wielder, Cyrus Gant. You should have told the Sa-Austra your name and come with him. For daring to raise your hand against our champion, you have gravely offended the Family."

"How do you know I didn't tell him my name?" Cyrus asked, still walking toward the creature.

"We questioned the Sa-Austra's mount."

Sweat beaded on Cyrus's neck. The Saurian unnerved him. With its long torso and short arms and legs, it looked like a lizard, more primitive than a Kresh. The unblinking eyes, the flickering forked tongue—he found the alien revolting. Maybe just as bad was the giant human mount with the spiked bit between his teeth and the shaggy hair in his eyes. The mount's only clothes were the demeaning saddle and reins.

Cyrus put that out of his mind. He needed to get a little nearer.

"Ask him," the second Saurian hissed.

Another, unseen, horn warbled a distant cry. It caused the two Saurians to glance in that direction, which made their saddles creak.

Cyrus strode faster as he began to ready himself.

"You bear us a message, psi-wielder," the first Saurian hissed. "We demand you relay it to us."

Cyrus's gaze had locked onto the lead Saurian. The alien had coin-sized scales that became almost black under its arms, while those on its long belly were faded to a pinker color. It hissed, and it slotted the lance into a holder. At the same time, it yanked a capture net from a different saddlebag.

"Resistance will be punished," the first Saurian hissed. "You think to change the land, but we will not allow it."

Cyrus paused. "What are you talking about?"

"We know your plan, psi-wielder."

"You couldn't possibly know," Cyrus said.

The first Saurian stood up in the stirrups. "You are the One. Obviously, you are walking through the damaged areas of your mind, healing them. At least, so you undoubtedly see your journey. You make the un-Cyrus areas Cyrus. But we refuse to go down to the dark night of oblivion. The Family will live again through the Eich."

Okay. Cyrus could understand that. It was a weird concept, though. These memories fought to exist. If the Eich died, would they die? That might give them reason to fight.

Cyrus realized, though, that here in the city he could use his talent. He could feel it flowing through him. As the Saurians watched him, Cyrus raised his right hand with the palm aimed at the creatures. Psi-power flowed from him.

The rear Saurian hissed with rage. Both urged their mounts to charge. As the mounts leaped to the attack, they slowed as Cyrus dimmed their reaction time.

The lead Saurian threw its net, but the psi-slowing of its arm marred the cast. Cyrus ducked the spinning net.

Braunt charged from behind the fountain. Left-handed, he hurled his rock. It sped like a sling stone and struck the first Saurian on its low forehead. With a squeal, the creature sprawled backward onto the cobbles. Moving like greased death compared to the other's slowed reactions, Braunt reached the fallen lance before the creature could grab it. The man skewered the Saurian through its chest as the lizard squealed horribly.

The second alien, realizing it was in danger, jerked the reins. The spiked bit caused blood to well in the mount's mouth. It turned and began to flee.

Braunt unhooked the short-handled axe from his belt. With cold efficiency, he hurled it after the retreating Saurian. The hatchet spun three times and crunched into skull bone. The Saurian with a blade sticking from its head swayed in the saddle. The giant mount bawled in woe and bounded away with his master.

Braunt's nostrils flared. They were no longer flat, but looked just like Klane's had once. In fact, Braunt looked exactly like Klane, with pale skin and blue eyes.

"That was a killing strike," Braunt/Klane said. "The Saurian should have fallen."

"Are you Klane?" Cyrus asked. "Or are you a shape-shifter who merely looks like the Anointed One?"

Braunt/Klane examined himself with surprise. Finally, he regarded Cyrus. "Hello, my friend. It's good to see you."

"Yeah," Cyrus said, finding it hard not to choke on his words. He stuck out his hand. They shook.

A warbling horn blared nearby.

"Come on!" Cyrus shouted. "We have to reach the dome before they do."

||||||||||

"Cyrus Gant, you must come back!" a Saurian called from across the wide street.

In Cyrus's mind, the two dozen mounted aliens milled beside a marble plinth. Golden hieroglyphs were etched into it. The speaker used a horn that amplified its voice. It shouted, "You must align yourself with reality, Cyrus Gant, not indulge in these vain fancies. You cannot fix the altered areas of your mind. It is an impossible task. Accept what is."

Klane heaved against an outsized door. It was massive and glowed with the same radiance as the dome. Huge arches ringed the dome. Alien bas-relief images had been chiseled into the masonry. Cyrus had randomly chosen this arch, running under it to the mighty door.

Cyrus watched the Saurians. It seemed as if it should have been easy enough for them to swarm and hurl their lances at him. If that failed, they could draw knives and follow him into the dome. Yet the Saurians did neither of those things, but carefully stayed across the street.

"Your actions will be remembered," the Saurian hissed through its far-speaker. "When the day of retribution comes, we will step forth and accuse you of malice. Your punishment will be long and terrible, Cyrus Gant. No one can defeat the Eich. He belongs to the invincible race."

Cyrus scowled.

"Cyrus Gant—"

Ahead of him, Klane squeezed through the barely open door. Cyrus followed. The door was metal and immensely thick. It had to weigh several tons. That Klane had moved it—the hinges had to have been well oiled.

As soon as Cyrus eased into the dome and shut the door behind him, the Saurian's words stopped as if cut by a knife. For more than one reason, Cyrus found that ominous.

"Look," whispered Klane.

They were in a short but large tunnel. It led toward an immense area. The field contained a circle of six blue crystals, each at least thirty meters tall. A blue beam shot out of a single mineral monolith. That ray speared at the middle of the domed ceiling. Before each structure was an open pit like a grave. Small gas flames flickered around the perimeter of each grave. In the center of the crystals was a metal disc. Between the disc and the mineral monolith lay twisted swords, crumpled helmets, rotting clothing and chewed boots, torn belts, and bones, heaps of bones.

"Why bones and swords?" Cyrus asked. "That doesn't seem very modern."

Cyrus took a deep breath and immediately regretted it. A rotted stench hit him. As he advanced, the foul odor made his skin feel greasy and caused his stomach to twist.

Blue light filled the interior of the dome, the illumination coming from the beam. Cyrus grew aware of a faint vibration and a whine. Both came from the ray.

Cyrus swallowed with a dry throat. He didn't like this place. If the Saurians belonged to the Eich now, why did they seem to fear the dome?

Am I really cleaning out the damaged parts by passing through them? That would be nice to believe. I need some evidence of it, though.

Cyrus walked toward the crystals, toward the mass of defiled bones. The stench of rotted death was powerfully rank. The area between the crystals was soaked with blood.

"We must cross the barrier while we can," Klane said.

"How exactly do we do that?" Cyrus asked.

"In the open pits—"

"The graves you mean?"

"The open pits," Klane said. "Inside them are portal openings. One of them leads to the Eich's fortress."

"How do we know which is the right portal?"

Klane turned to Cyrus in surprise. "I thought you'd know."

Cyrus considered that. Finally, he strode toward the nearest crystal. Klane trotted beside him.

At that moment, the giant disc in the center of the grisly mass began to dilate open like an obscene metal eye. Something made *whirring* sounds. There were *clanks*, a faint *chugging* sound. The metal disc dilated completely open and something began to rise out of the opening.

"We must flee," Klane said.

"Flee where?" Cyrus asked.

Klane gestured weakly toward the doors.

"No," Cyrus said. "The Saurians will capture us if we go back outside." He swept his fingers through his hair.

"We should climb down into a pit before whatever is coming comes," Klane said.

Cyrus stared at Klane for just a second. "Go!" he shouted. "Run!"

Cyrus sprinted for the nearest pit as the tusked head of an impossibly gargantuan creature poked out of the metal hole. Fast eyes opened. The creature spied them, and it bellowed with rage.

Flames roared from the sides of Cyrus's chosen pit.

"Jump!" Cyrus shouted, deciding he must have picked the right one if the guardian creature was trying to stop them.

Klane never hesitated, leaping into the pit. Cyrus glanced over his shoulder. The creature's warty neck appeared, a neck bigger than any sky vehicle. Once the monster's shoulders cleared the dilated opening, it would be able to grab them with long arms. Cyrus jumped into the pit.

It was time to find and slay the psi-parasite on its home ground. As Cyrus moved to a shimmering portal, the tusked creature boomed words.

"You fools!" the monstrous creature bellowed. "It has never been my task to guard the route into the Eich's realm, but to make sure no one can ever leave it. If you try to come back, I'll devour you on your return."

26

Dagon Dar stood in his private chamber aboard a hammer-ship.

As FIRST, he had commandeered the best warship as his head-quarters for the coming struggle. The circular chamber was strewn with charm, a reddish substance that grated comfortably against his talons. A padded acceleration board stood to the side. Prized chard posters hung on the walls, showing ancient scenes of his home world.

This was an elegant room, fraught with hot fragrances. It would be easy to become lost here in contemplation of arcane mathematical formulas.

I am FIRST. I have an obligation to my Race. I must bend my superior intellect to the great task.

He was of two minds on the correct course of action. Without the cyborgs in the outer asteroid belt, he would have traveled down to Jassac and questioned human primitives of the uplands. He would prefer to hunt down these hidden aliens and discover their agenda. The existence of the primitive seekers proved the aliens' hidden influence. No doubt the Resisters of High Station 3 and elsewhere had also originated with the hidden aliens. The Anointed One and—

Dagon Dar hissed. Klane, the Resister's famed Anointed One, had died. The human-hijacked Battle Fang meant nothing now. In a few more hours—possibly more because the Battle Fang accelerated away at high speed—the Tal drones would take care of it.

Still, he would like to know how the humans had overpowered Mingal Cham the 3012th and the Bo Taw. It was a startling victory for such base creatures. It would appear the Earther was the primary mover in that. The one named Cyrus Gant sought his own kind, heading for High Station 3.

No. Cyrus Gant *had* headed for High Station 3. With the Battle Fang's new acceleration, the hijacked ship would flash past the habitat as it sought to escape the Tal drones.

Dagon Dar had considered ordering the rest of the Teleship's Earth crew slain. He did not want them reuniting with Cyrus Gant. With the Special's death, he could reserve the other Earthers for further study on the political situation in the solar system.

In any case, Dagon Dar was not going down to Jassac. If he questioned enough primitives, he might find the location where the hidden aliens had met with the seekers. How could that help him against the present threat of the cyborgs or the Chirr?

Lashing his tail, Dagon Dar began to stride from one part of the chamber to the other. The Chirr had annihilated the Heenhiss gravitational system. Many Vomag armies remained on the planet, but the polar spaceports were radioactive ruins and the guardian fleet, drifting debris. No habitat remained. Chirr hordes had already surfaced, attacking the Vomags. The stubborn humans fought valiantly and with cunning. It would likely take the return of the Chirr space fleet before the insects could reclaim the entire planet as their own.

Why are the Glegan Kresh so foolish? Don't they realize the Chirr mean to destroy them too?

Despite his orders, the Glegan Kresh refused to recognize his elevation to FIRST. They dared to challenge his right as the primary philosopher king of the Fenris System.

Controlling the larger fleet—as the Glegan Kresh do—means nothing when that fleet is about to perish. Maybe the old FIRST made a mistake sending the soft thinkers to Glegan. The soft thinkers believe this is their hour. No. This is their end. Soft thinkers indeed, they would be better served to listen to me, the greatest intelligence left in the system.

A chime sounded. Dagon Dar halted, rotating until he faced a cunningly concealed screen. The chime sounded again. That meant an urgent message.

"On," Dagon Dar said.

A part of the wall shimmered, turning into a Kresh peering out of a screen. The Kresh had tattooed skin, proclaiming her a home-worlder heretic. They made excellent warship captains. The part of the heresy Dagon Dar found the most repugnant was the eating of human and Chirr flesh. He found the idea revolting, and quite unsanitary, too.

"FIRST," she said.

"Here," Dagon Dar said.

"The warships of our outer asteroid belt fleet have been accelerating for thirteen hours."

"That is in the accepted time limit," he said.

"You misunderstand, FIRST. I have called to tell you they are under attack."

Dagon Dar rose as he pushed off his talons. This was fascinating data, even if it came at such a grave expense. He was surprised the cyborgs would give away the range of their beams so easily.

"Are they using infrared laser beams?" Dagon Dar asked.

"No, FIRST. The cyborgs are destroying our ships with nuclear warheads."

Dagon Dar stared at the tattooed freak on the screen. She had green swirls around her eyes and a dagger tattoo down the length of her snout. The most egregious was the sun symbol of the *Codex of All Knowledge* tattooed in blue on her brain case.

"Give me your name," Dagon Dar said.

"Red Bronze the 232nd," she said.

"I see. You are a home-worlder heretic of the Red Metal School."

She dipped her tattooed head.

"You have feasted lately?" Dagon Dar asked.

"I am quite sober," Red Bronze said.

So, it was true. The Red Metal heretics indulged in the old passion of intoxication. What a revolting piece of dung. The heretics believed intoxication could bring sudden enlightenment. Wrong! Deep and abiding thought dissected a truth into chewable bits, allowing a Kresh to learn wisdom. It was no wonder the half savages ate sentient flesh.

"Do you mean to imply the cyborgs possess drones with fantastically greater acceleration than our warships?" Dagon Dar asked.

"By no means," Red Bronze said. "In point of fact, their drones are slower than ours."

"Yet you insist on telling me the cyborgs are using nuclear warheads to attack the accelerating outer asteroid belt Attack Talons and hammer-ships."

"Precisely," Red Bronze said.

"Show me the data," Dagon Dar snapped.

"I do so with reluctance, as I am unsure your staid intellect can absorb this chaotic reality."

Dagon Dar "pierced her features" with his stare. The Kresh idiom implied he would remember her later for harsh rebuke.

The image on the screen wavered. Red Bronze vanished from view. In her place, Dagon Dar saw an Attack Talon. It was a distant scope shot. The vessel's exhaust ports burned as hot as possible. The Attack Talon moved at maximum acceleration. That would give the shipboard Kresh terrible headaches for weeks to come. The superior Race of Fenris did not take well to high Gs for sustained burns.

The space ahead of the Attack Talon wavered as if heat generated there. Then the very fabric of reality seemed to tear, to open. Strange motes glimmered, and a dull, mind-wearying color expanded. Two missiles flared into existence.

No. I'm witnessing their exhaust burns. Are these chemically powered rockets? That seems unbelievable.

The rockets flew through the wavering space as if through a hole in reality. They sped toward the approaching Attack Talon. The rip in space closed behind them, and stars shone normally there once more. A beam lanced from the Attack Talon. This was a quick-acting crew. The beam struck the lead rocket, and it exploded.

The second rocket's warhead ignited into a nuclear pulse. Numbers superimposed over the image showed the magnitude of the explosion and its distance to the Attack Talon. The Kresh military vessel didn't have a chance.

The heat wave and the gamma rays and X-rays crumpled the warship. Seconds later, parts of the Attack Talon exploded. Pieces shed free. Secondary explosions shredded more of the vessel. There would be no survivors.

Dagon Dar sagged in his chamber.

The space image vanished from the screen and Red Bronze the 232nd reappeared.

"I am sorry to report this, FIRST. What you witnessed is occurring to the rest of the outer asteroid belt fleet. Since most of the warships were spread out in wildly varied locations, they journey inward by themselves. One cluster has fought off three such attacks."

"Describe it to me," Dagon Dar said.

"The cluster is composed of a hammer-ship, two Attack Talons, and three small darters. Altogether, they have destroyed six nuclear missiles."

"What are the present losses to the outer asteroid belt fleet?"

Red Bronze checked a panel. "Five hammer-ships, eleven Attack Talons, twenty-three Battle Fangs, and fourteen darters."

"How many remain?"

"One third of that number," Red Bronze said.

"What did you witness?" Dagon Dar asked.

"Exactly what you did except for the accompanying data," she said. "I have altered nothing."

"You mistake my question. I do not doubt the veracity of the data. I saw it. I accept reality."

"I am surprised."

"You will refrain from any form of insult."

"I am chastened," she said.

Dagon Dar grunted his surprise. "You follow the accepted form of courtesy and communication."

"You are FIRST. I recognize your rank and respect it."

"Under those conditions, we can work together. I respect your grade, 232nd. You have a high intellect."

"But not as high as yours," she said.

"I am FIRST."

"I have stated such."

"In the coming days, your rank may increase. In fact, I am sure it will."

"Why do you honor me?" Red Bronze asked.

Dagon Dar widened his jaws. "You have strange notions concerning the orthodox such as myself. I merely state facts. Most of the philosopher kings died at Heenhiss. The rest will likely perish or dwindle in number at Glegan. Among the survivors, a former 232nd will likely easily leap many categories, possibly into the Hundred, perhaps into the single digits."

"I see there is a reason why you are FIRST. You are decorous and swift in analytical ability. I will hold my inner objections at bay concerning the orthodox as we work together."

"I would expect no less from a 232nd."

"Ah, you are so correct and factual. Well, I cannot compete against your intellect. I can, however, avail you of my intuition."

Dagon Dar kept the shock from his features. An intuitive Kresh? The very statement revolted his core. How could a 232nd espouse such a doctrine? It amazed him.

"Let us reason through the data and seek working conclusions," Dagon Dar said.

Red Bronze nodded as a human might. "I state the first piece of datum. Whoever launched the missiles is an enemy of the Kresh."

"We will call that fact one," Dagon Dar said.

"Our enemy used a form of technology presently beyond us."

"Fact two," Dagon Dar said.

"Our enemy attacked the warships fleeing from the outer asteroid belt."

"Fact three," Dagon Dar said.

"The cyborgs possess a star-drive. They appeared suddenly in our system, in the outer asteroid belt."

"The humans used a similar technology."

"Do you think the cyborgs and humans are secretly allied against us?" Red Bronze asked.

"Given the historical information we have gleaned from the *Discovery*'s crew, no."

"The missiles used crude chemical rockets for propulsion. The blast indicates a fifty-megaton warhead."

"Given these facts," Dagon Dar said, "it would appear our new-technology-using enemies are the cyborgs."

"I agree with your analysis," Red Bronze said.

Dagon Dar had no doubt she would. It was an elementary deduction. Something else puzzled him about the attack.

"It would seem this is a devastating technology and tactic," Dagon Dar said. "According to the records, the cyborgs have not shown the capability before this."

"You have decided to proceed with our analysis with the cyborgs as the certain protagonist in this latest attack?"

"Yes."

"I'm not sure that I can—"

"I calculate the probability at eighty-nine point three percent that the cyborgs are indeed the protagonists of this new form of assault," Dagon Dar said.

"Oh," Red Bronze said.

"I can break down the probabilities for you."

"Later, perhaps," she said.

"As you wish," Dagon Dar said. Since she said nothing to that, he said, "Let me give you my observations."

"Please do."

"The new attack seems to work best against lone vessels," Dagon Dar said. "That is why the cyborgs use it at this time. They whittle our numbers to their advantage. It would appear they cannot open two . . . space warps close together."

"How did you reach that conclusion?"

"They would do so in order to destroy the Kresh cluster. Instead of taking that reasonable course, the cyborgs continue to make single space warp attacks against them."

"Instead of calling it a 'space warp,' might we name it a DW?"

"You mean use the human term?" Dagon Dar asked.

"What the cyborgs have done strikes me as a form of discontinuity window."

"I agree. DW is as good a name as any."

"And the most accurate," Red Bronze said.

"Well spoken. Now, the cyborgs pick apart our lone ships. Because they did not do so earlier in the outer asteroid belt, and since they did not do so to our ships here in the Pulsar system—"

"You have reached a fundamental conclusion?" Red Bronze asked.

Her excitement surprised Dagon Dar. The Red Metal heretics were a strange breed of Kresh. When advocating a fundamental conclusion, the accepted form of decorum mandated a cool and controlled manner.

"Indeed I have," he said. "From interrogating the humans, we know they cannot use a DW too close to a large gravitational source such as a sun or a planet. Compared to the humans, the cyborgs appear to have a refined DW system. They can create the DWs within a star system. The humans could not. It would appear the cyborgs create the DW near their ship, launch the missiles, and close the opening. We're likely safe near Pulsar and here in Jassac orbit. The Glegan fleet is likely safe near the third planet."

"As they cross from Heenhiss to Glegan," Red Bronze said, "the Chirr fleet is exposed."

"They move as insects in a large swarm. From our analysis, ships are safe while traveling together in packs."

"Not all of the Chirr vessels move in the swarm," Red Bronze said. "Would you like a confirmation of that by viewing their swarm?"

"No. I will take your word."

"Do you think this is significant?"

"The lack of cyborg attacks against the Chirr?" Dagon Dar asked. "Yes."

"It is critical," he said. "In fact, the timing of the Chirr surprise assault combined with the appearance of the cyborgs is conclusive proof that the two races work together against the Kresh."

"Ah," Red Bronze said. "Yes. Now that you point it out, it is self-evident."

"We are in dire straits," Dagon Dar declared. "With the cyborg fleet, the number of our enemies has doubled. Just as frightening, they possess a deadly new technology."

"What are we going to do?" Red Bronze asked.

Dagon Dar nodded. That was an excellent query. He did not know, but he would think of something. Otherwise, the Kresh in the Fenris System might soon become extinct.

27

Still traveling through the altered parts of his mind, Cyrus Gant was clothed in a billowing robe as he swayed atop a camel. Klane rode beside him on another beast.

The ungainly camel lurched with an obscene gait. Back on Earth at the institute on Crete, Cyrus had watched a nature show on them once. His beast acted just as the commentator said one would, which made sense, since this scene took place in his mind.

Cyrus watched the camel vigilantly while keeping a thin stick in hand. The ornery beast waited with evil patience. When it suspected that Cyrus no longer paid attention, it swiveled its head and tried to bite him on the thigh. A lashing strike across its nose was Cyrus's only defense.

Deep in his mind, a desert sun glared like a malignant eye. Burning dunes towered over them. Hot sand whispered down the slopes across the wasteland. The region was a parched sea of death, a desolate kingdom of doom and gravel.

Klane skillfully rode his own camel, having grown accustomed to it almost right away.

Sand ruled as far as they cared to stare. For days, no plant had appeared, no desert mouse, no vulture, no fox, no fly or gnat, nothing. This was a desert's desert, hot and waterless.

Cyrus pointed with his stick. "There," he said. He spat particles of sand from his lips. Then he turned back just as the evil beast gave him a crafty sideways glance. Cyrus raised his stick menacingly. The camel bellowed its complaint, but lurched toward where Cyrus wished to go.

Soon Cyrus and Klane crouched in a dune's feeble shade. They hobbled the camels. Leaning against sand, the two men passed a waterskin between them.

Klane seemed incongruous in his cloth headgear, scarf, and billowing robe, so different from his usual garb. He'd thrust a knife through his sash belt. Since leaving the barrier, he'd said little. Perhaps he thought about his death in the real world.

Cyrus capped the waterskin. Out of the corner of his eye he studied the morose Anointed One. "If it's any consolation," Cyrus said. "I think we're close."

Klane squatted, took the waterskin, squirted enough to dampen his fingers, and brushed his chapped lips. "Our water will only last another few days," he said.

Cyrus sat up. "Water is the least of our problems," he whispered.

Klane glanced at him.

Cyrus pointed at a metallic thing topping a dune. Slowly, Cyrus flattened himself onto the sand. Klane did the same thing. The two men crawled to the top of their dune.

The approaching machine looked like a giant armored spider fifteen feet tall. Instead of eight articulated legs, it had six. The sun reflected off the metal legs as the machine scuttled toward them.

"We mustn't move," Klane said.

"Why not?"

"It tracks by motion."

"And you know this how?"

Klane tapped his forehead.

"Does it belong to the Eich?" Cyrus asked.

"Yes."

"Is he in it?"

Klane closed his eyes. "No."

"The bastard. Where is he?"

"I think he flees while the machine attempts to kill us."

"What? Are you sure?" Cyrus asked.

"No. It is only a feeling."

"Great," Cyrus muttered. He squinted through the hazy heat, studying the approaching machine. Several things didn't make sense to him. Why did Klane know more down here than he did? It was his own mind, not Klane's. That bothered Cyrus, made him doubt Klane, the memory of Klane, just a little. The other thing that troubled him was the normality of the realm. It was like Earth. He'd expected something even more alien than the city and the sea of fire. What game did the Eich play? How would he know he came to the psi-parasite's fortress? Was the mind-rapist alien playing games with him, merely seeking time, or was something else going on?

"It's coming," Klane whispered about the spider machine.

Cyrus concentrated on it. A saucer-shaped body balanced at the top of the six legs. It had a bubble dome of glass in the center with a Saurian pilot. On the undercarriage was a swivel laser with a blinking red light on the end.

The spider machine halted. With a whine, the saucer rose a foot higher. Something clicked and the laser swiveled as if searching.

The camels had frozen at the machine's approach. Now, one of them bellowed. With its hobbled legs, it jumped.

The laser moved again as a loud whine went up an octave. The tip fired a red beam that pierced the camel's body, smoking as it went in and out the other side. The poor beast bellowed a second time, a forlorn sound, and crashed onto the sand.

The other camel went berserk and thrashed against its hobbles. Again, the laser beamed and the second camel soon lay dying on the sand.

"We're doomed," Klane whispered. "We lack the weapons to face it."

A harsh beep sounded from the machine, and the laser rotated back and forth, searching for them. With delicate grace, the spider machine used one leg at a time to approach the dead camels.

"Listen to me," Klane whispered. "We have one chance."

"Yeah?" Cyrus whispered.

"You must fight the machine."

"Care to tell me how?"

"You are the new Anointed One," Klane said. "I . . . died. It is up to you now."

"Listen, Klane—"

"There is no more time. You must fashion a creature out of the sand."

"What?" Cyrus asked. "How?"

"With TK," Klane said. "Fight it with telekinesis. Use your power to mold sand to create something for it to attack, and to attack it as well."

The saucer dipped near the dead camels. The beasts had run toward the machine. A dune still hid Cyrus and Klane from the controlling Saurian.

If the Eich was near, they had to defeat this thing quickly. Was that even possible? Cyrus concentrated. Klane had given him power the day he died. Now, it was time to use it fully. He willed the sand to take shape, pouring his psionic strength into it.

Why can I do this now and not at other times? I don't understand the laws governing my own mind. This is like a dream, where things are far too disjointed.

As the spider machine neared with its sensors beeping, particles of sand began to cling together. Quickly, the particles took shape. A thing reared upward as if something huge underground used the sand like clothing. It grew fast and took on a humanoid shape.

The sensor's beeping turned into a *ping* and the laser under the saucer swiveled toward the sand creature. A red beam shot out. It fused sand so glass slags sloughed off like chunks of flesh. That chewed up part of the sand creature.

Cyrus laughed harshly. With his TK, he gave the sand creature greater mass. It continued to grow even as the ray beamed.

The creature lifted huge sand arms. With ponderous steps and feet that shed sand at every step, the thing approached the mechanical spider.

The sand beast stood nine feet tall, so it was shorter than the machine. The beam smoked and glass slags tinkled as they shattered at the creature's feet.

The saucer rose higher on its six legs. A sand fist smashed and bent the undercarriage laser. A terrible whine sounded from within the belly of the machine. The TK creature reached and grasped the edge of the saucer. With a brutal yank and squeals of metallic strain, it forced the saucer lower, lower still. Then the creature raised a sand fist and smashed the bubble dome. With grainy fingers, it reached in.

The Saurian hissed with fear. The sand creature plucked it from its chair and hurled the Saurian twenty feet. A final snap and orgasmic jerks and flops told of the Saurian's death.

A winding-down noise matched the saucer's lowering. The bottom thumped against a dune. In seconds, the machine's whines and hums quit forever.

Cyrus exhaled. He hadn't realized he'd been holding his breath. His concentration weakened. He released the TK.

The creature lost coherence. Sand flowed until all that remained was a dry heap.

Cyrus stumbled and sweat dripped from his face. With a grunt, he sank to the ground.

"You destroyed the machine and killed the Saurian," Klane said.

"And it killed us," Cyrus whispered. "Our camels are dead and we're in the middle of the deepest, most haunted desert imaginable. I'd make a sand machine to carry us, but I lack the mental strength for it to go very far."

Klane blinked at the dead camels and blinked at Cyrus. "Let us inspect the machine before we admit defeat. Maybe we can cannibalize something from it."

Why not? With a grunt, Cyrus struggled to his feet. He rubbed his head, and he realized he didn't stay tired as long as he used to.

Maybe I am getting stronger. This ordeal is training me in the psi-arts. That's something, I guess.

First, they inspected the corpse. The Saurian could have been dead for years. At their touch, its clothes disintegrated. It had brittle skin and lacked eyeballs.

"Why did the eyes rot so fast?" Klane asked.

"I have no idea. I'd hoped you'd know."

The only substantial thing was the Saurian's belt with a hardened leather pouch. With his knife, Cyrus sawed through it and discovered peculiar tools and keys.

"Take those," Klane said.

The last item was a metal band that encircled the withered forehead.

"It's like a Bo Taw's *baan*," Cyrus said.

"We should take it, too."

Gingerly, Cyrus worked the *baan* free. It was light. He turned it over several times.

"What are you thinking?" Klane asked.

Cyrus shoved the *baan* onto his head.

"What do you feel?" Klane asked.

Cyrus grimaced. "Wait a moment." He closed his eyes but he felt no new sensations. He opened his eyes and stared at the machine. He willed it to rise. Nothing happened. He faced the direction the spider machine had come from. He concentrated.

A feeling began to take shape. Then it seemed he could see far into the distance. A hazy creature fled across the sand. It feared him. Cyrus willed a better look. The haziness grew into clarity. The creature had a python body with vestigial wings and a crown on its head. Was that the singing god? It looked more like a demon.

Come back, Cyrus told the Eich. He was sure that was the psi-parasite.

The wings flapped as the creature slithered across the sand. It screeched as if fighting back with psi-power of its own.

Foul beast of the field.

Who are you? Cyrus asked.

Desist. Accept what is. Submit to my control.

Cyrus concentrated. He realized this indeed was the Eich.

The creature did something then, and the vision ceased.

Cyrus removed the *baan* and secured it in his sash. He stood and dusted sand from his knees. In those seconds, he'd learned facts about the Eich. The mind contact had slipped information.

Cyrus laughed.

"What is wrong?" Klane asked.

"I know what happened to the Eich," Cyrus said. "I know why it's been on Jassac all this time."

"You touched its mind?"

"Yeah," Cyrus said. "Only that isn't the Eich, but its original Steed."

"I don't understand," Klane said.

"The parasite needs a psionic-talented person to exist. It's an energy creature, feeding off the psi-power. The snake thing with wings belonged to a very powerful psionic race. It had become a Steed and the Eich was its Rider. In some sort of psi-powered spaceship, they leaped thousands of light-years. It was an accident."

"You learned all that in the brief encounter?" Klane asked.

Cyrus nodded. He found that interesting. Maybe that's why the Eich used old memories to fight him. The parasite gave away too much of itself when they fought mind to mind. It was like two wrestlers grappling. They sweated and breathed on each other. In mind-to-mind fights down here, information sweated out.

"Something happened," Cyrus said. "The long jump stunned the Eich. The Steed knew mental freedom as it hadn't possessed for a long time. It used a process I don't understand and fled to Jassac. It hid the psi-spaceship. I think the parasite regained strength, but not in time to stop the Steed from killing itself."

"What?" Klane asked.

"The Steed wanted to kill the Eich. The parasite found the tubes under the mountain. I don't understand that part. The Eich has been surviving there, using its powers in ways that aren't clear to me yet."

Klane blinked thoughtfully. "You say the parasite needs psionic people to live in?"

"Yeah."

"Maybe it had something to do with Clan Tash-Toi and others developing seekers on Jassac."

"That's an interesting thought," Cyrus said. "You could be right."

"What else did you learn?" Klane asked.

Cyrus thought about it, shrugging soon. "I think that's it."

Grinning, Klane said, "Now we have to survive the desert long enough to use this new knowledge."

Together, they approached the deadly spider machine. The articulated legs lay askew. The sun continued to shine, to heat the metal.

"Hot," said Klane, when he put a palm on the saucer.

"I have an idea," Cyrus said. "The machine quit when I plucked the Saurian from its chair. Maybe if one of us sat in it, we can control the machine and make it carry us."

"I'll do it," Klane said.

Before Cyrus could disagree, Klane scrambled onto the saucer. He used a stone and smashed the jagged shards to make a safer passage in.

"The glassy substance is stronger than it looks," Klane shouted.

"You can help me over the glass," Cyrus said. He tried to climb onto the saucer. He snatched his hand back. Heat radiated from it. How could Klane stand it?

"I will assist you," Klane said.

With the Anointed One's help, Cyrus scrambled onto the saucer. He felt the heat through the soles of his sandals. His heart began racing as they approached the broken glass. If he could figure out how to revive the machine, they might actually travel in it and catch the elusive Eich.

"Careful," Klane said.

Gingerly, Cyrus eased over broken shards. His robe caught. Klane ripped it free.

Before proceeding, Cyrus studied the inner workings. The chair felt brittle but had a throne's armrests. Buttons and levers faced the open chair. On the sides, dull mirrors and colored controls were everywhere. He took a breath, eased onto the chair, and moved a lever. Nothing happened. He tried others with no result. Cyrus waited between each attempt. Then, one by one, he began to depress buttons. Sitting in the sun, in the black chair, sweat soon drenched him.

After a time, Klane said, "We should start walking."

"I must be doing something wrong," Cyrus said. Then he muttered a curse and withdrew the *baan*. He jammed it onto his head. "Lift," he whispered.

Nothing.

Cyrus tried other words. Then he began to move levers again and depress switches. Every attempt proved a failure.

"Why doesn't it work?" he asked.

"We're not Saurians," Klane said. "It could be as simple as that."

"You try sitting in the chair," Cyrus said.

Klane did. He even wore the *baan*. None of it made any difference.

Finally, the two climbed off the hot machine and jumped down onto the sand.

"It killed us," Cyrus said. The sting of defeat ate at him.

"We should start walking," Klane said.

Cyrus stared hopelessly at the machine. What had he forgotten? He couldn't think of anything.

"We could follow its tracks," Klane said. "Maybe that will lead us to something."

With astonishment, Cyrus turned to Klane. "Yes. We must hurry before the wind blows out the tracks. We have to find the Eich's tracks."

"We must travel," Klane said, "but we must not rush. In the desert, rushing anywhere kills."

28

Deep in his subconscious mind, Cyrus sank to his knees as the sun blazed heat.

It had been days since the spider machine had slain their camels. The landscape had changed from shifting sand to rocks, hardpan, rattling grit, and fused shards of metal and glass. Eerie pools of multicolored water had mocked them. One lick had proven the water's vile taste. Depending on the angle he looked at the pool, the water was red, green, or purple. A harsh metallic odor drifted on the wind. On his tongue, it tasted like copper or nickel.

From on his knees, Cyrus panted. His lips had cracked. Yesterday, they'd emptied the final dregs of the waterskins. Even knowing it was an illusion, he hadn't been able to make water.

Now merciless strength wrapped around his arm. Cruel power hauled him to his feet.

"Just a little farther," Klane said.

Cyrus mumbled words whose meaning he forgot the moment he spoke them. Why hadn't the spider machine heeded his efforts? What had he done wrong? How could the Eich stay ahead of them? Why couldn't he reach it with psi-power anymore?

They shuffled across the face of the desert, two insignificant motes. Time was agony. Life hurt. It was desolation, just wretched wasteland as far as he could glare.

"Down," Klane whispered.

Cyrus found himself lying on the hot ground. "What was that for?" he whispered.

"Another giant spider," Klane said.

Cyrus wiped grit from his eyes. He peered across the hazy desolation. Heat radiated there. "Where is it?"

Klane pointed into the distance.

Cyrus saw nothing. He glanced at the Anointed One, wondering if Klane saw mirages. The once pale face had darkened in the sun. The blue eyes watched as if Klane actually saw something. It was too bad the man had died on the Battle Fang.

"Up," Klane said, and he hauled Cyrus to his feet.

"The machine is gone?" Cyrus muttered.

"We can use its tracks."

Cyrus laughed. It came out a whisper. In this land, the sun sucked out water and vitality. He marveled at Klane's endurance. As Cyrus reeled, he began to feel that Klane had more in common with the spider machine than with him.

"Look," Klane said.

Cyrus raised his head. He hoped to see a cool lake. Instead, beside a cobalt-colored pool lay rusted armor, a rusted helmet, old shoes, and bones inside the armor. Other, larger bones lay scattered nearby.

They walked to the bones.

"Camel," Klane said as he squatted. He held up a bone.

Cyrus swayed. He eyed the cobalt-colored pool. He needed a drink.

Klane moved to the armored skeleton. "It has a sword. I could use that." Klane sawed through the ancient belt and lifted a jeweled scabbard. He tugged harder than he needed. The sword easily slid free. "No rust," Klane noticed.

The back of Cyrus's neck tingled. He rubbed it, and frowned. There was a memory . . .

With a hoarse sound, he dropped to his knees and pushed the armored skeleton. He rolled it over to reveal a pack.

With a slash, Cyrus parted the pack. Various contents spilled out. Among them was a flask adorned with odd symbols.

With a trembling hand, Cyrus picked the flask off the ground. It was surprisingly heavy. He used his teeth and pried at the stopper. It refused to budge.

"I'm not thinking," he muttered.

Cyrus stared at the flask and used TK to twist it. He tried with his fingers again. It easily came off. He put his lips to the edge and slowly tilted it. Cool water gushed into his mouth. He wanted to gulp. Instead, Cyrus swished the water in his parched mouth and let it trickle down his throat. He took two more swallows and passed the flask to Klane.

"How did you know about the flask?" Klane asked.

Cyrus realized it was a thought he'd pulled out of the Eich. That was interesting. He told Klane how he'd known.

Klane took several slow swallows from the flask before passing it back.

Cyrus pushed the stopper into place. With his thirst quenched, he fingered the pack's contents, packets of dried food. He sat down and ate one. Klane devoured the other.

Afterward, Cyrus scanned the hazy distance. He adjusted his headgear. Then the two set out to follow the Eich's python-like track.

||||||||||

Twice Cyrus spied a spider machine. Maybe it was the same one making rounds.

The two men lay flat or crouched behind twisted girders or chunks of fused glass. They passed metallic pools and spotted rusted girders that jutted out of the ground. They also came upon more bones.

The bones lay in a row: six strange skeletons. Each was a giant snake with vestigial wing bones. The wings had claws like a mutated bat. Each skeletal claw-hand clutched a staff of polished black wood. Neither grit, dirt, nor sand had piled on or around the staffs. Each pair of finger bones that gripped a stick contained a ring of jade. Each jade ring bore a skeletal tree stamped on its signet.

Cyrus squatted by one.

"Do you recognize them?" Klane asked.

"They are Steed skeletons. I remember now that most beings of their star empire called them Eich, even though the real Eich was the parasite inside them. The staffs and rings must have significance. I just don't know what that is."

Klane studied the skeletons. He pointed at neat little holes that had sliced through Eich bone. "The red beam," he said. "The spider machines killed them."

Cyrus pointed at a rusted girder. "These are part of a ruin. Klane, do you remember the ruins where we crossed the barrier?"

"Of course," Klane said.

"Is there a connection?"

Klane shrugged.

Cyrus rose thoughtfully. Some great disaster had destroyed the first city. Maybe in Eich history a terrible calamity had fallen upon the parasites or the host race. Did the Steeds war against Saurians? He had no idea. Did his journey do anything to the areas he went through? He'd never retraced his routes. What would he find if he did?

Scratching his cheek, Cyrus asked, "Do you remember the machine you first showed me? It moved on treads and used a scoop to toss bodies into the lake of fire."

"Yes," Klane said. "It marched in rounds."

"Just like the spider machines march in rounds here."

"I do not understand the significance."

"Neither do I," said Cyrus, "at least, not yet. But I plan on finding out. Keep an eye out for the machine." He laughed grimly. "We don't want to add our skeletons to the ranks of those who failed."

|||||||||||

Amid girders and fused glass, Cyrus created a second TK creature to destroy another spider machine.

I'm getting much better at this.

It was several hours since dawn, and the sun already heated the ground. By following the Eich's tracks, they came upon another set of bones, these two entwined in love. Klane spotted beam wounds. Cyrus walked around the skeletons in a widening circle. Behind a lump of fused glass, he found packs. They were filled with dust—and inside one was a vibrio-knife.

Hello.

Cyrus stepped to a nearby girder, flicked on the knife, and set the vibrating edge against it. As a hum rose in volume, the knife began to cut into the girder until it smoldered.

Cyrus yanked out the blade and flicked it off. "I like," he said.

Klane inspected the girder. "You did not hack. You only pressed the blade against the iron."

"Yep," Cyrus said. He wondered if the Earth blade meant he was changing these things to his way of thinking. Maybe his very presence down here defeated the psi-parasite. He didn't know that, but it was a thought.

"Let's go," Cyrus said.

They trudged in the growing heat. Perhaps an hour later, the girders and fused lumps of glass lessened.

"Although it doesn't look like it, we're walking upslope," Cyrus said.

Soon, the twisted girders vanished, together with the increasingly smaller lumps of glass. The slope also became more apparent.

"Wait," Cyrus said.

"Tired?" Klane asked.

"Wary," Cyrus said, pointing ahead. "Does it feel like we're approaching a valley?"

"A giant crater," Klane said.

"Excuse me?"

"I saw them . . . somewhere. Falling stars smashed into the ground, obliterating everything."

They resumed their trek. In another half hour, they trudged up the last of the slope and crested it.

A vast circular area of devastation spread out before them. It looked like fused and shattered crystal, a flat plain of it. Jagged lines radiated inward in a barren nothingness.

"The Eich," Cyrus whispered.

Some distance in the desolation moved a creature. He was too far for them to distinguish characteristics.

"He heads for the center," Klane said.

Cyrus shaded his eyes. The sun glared off the crystal, making it difficult to see. He squinted. "Yes, the Eich heads for a tall spire. We have to go there."

"Not during the day." Klane held out his hands. "The heat is already too much. We must retreat."

"The heat must not bother the Eich."

"At least not as much as it does us," Klane said.

"He's getting away."

"We'll catch him. It's just a matter of time now."

|||||||||||

By starlight, Cyrus and Klane worked down the sandy slope and reached the edge of fused crystal. It was eerie and lonely down here. A wind blew the fabric of their headgear.

Cyrus noticed that, like him, Klane hesitated to set foot on the cracked crystal. Far in the distance, in the center of the circular destruction, rose a silvery spire that beckoned even as it threatened. The Eich must be there.

Cyrus walked onto the crystal. It was warm like pavement at night. In it was a faint reflection of starlight. After several steps, Cyrus glanced behind. Klane still hung back.

"Coming?" Cyrus asked.

"Is this wise?" asked Klane. "I—" He touched his forehead.

"You can stay behind," Cyrus said. "I have to go on."

Klane's jaw tightened. He set foot on the crystal and followed Cyrus.

Soon, Cyrus felt as if he walked along the bottom of a desolate sea or across a dead moon. They crossed jagged lines. He glanced down each time. The openings went down farther than his eyesight could penetrate. They walked, and it seemed as if they walked off their world and onto another.

"This place is haunted," Klane whispered.

Once, Cyrus glanced back. The hairs rose on his neck. He couldn't spy the slopes. On impulse, he craned his head upward and discovered the stars had disappeared. Despite the lost stars, they still had enough light to see. He felt hope stir in him. The Eich kept fleeing. It must fear him, which would indicate he could defeat it.

I hope, he thought to himself.

In time, the spire loomed before them. It looked smooth, with a rounded top. After more steps, Cyrus realized it stood six stories high.

"Why does it stand and nothing else?" Klane asked.

"Be ready," Cyrus said.

"For what?"

"Anything."

They marched closer.

"There," Cyrus said. "I see an opening."

They hurried toward the spire and shifted leftward, circling it. An opening shimmered. The nearer they came, the less it shimmered, until they stood before a fifteen-foot opening. Within lay cables and to the side was a console of colored lights.

Klane made a sound in the back of his throat and clawed for his sword.

Cyrus blanched. There in the spire waited a giant spider machine. Cyrus stepped back, ready to use psionics.

"It's dead," Klane pronounced.

Sweat prickled Cyrus's forehead.

"Look," Klane said, pointing with his sword. "Cables are hooked into it."

Cyrus moved toward the opening. The cables, thick as pythons, snaked to the spider machine and to the bank of multicolored lights, several of which blinked on and off.

"Quick" Cyrus said, "cut the cables."

Klane rushed in, and fortunately Cyrus followed. As Klane's foot touched the metal floor, bright lights flooded the chamber. It made Klane's jaw muscles bulge. He swung—

Before the sword connected, a steel door slammed down behind them. The floor sank beneath them, which made Klane stumble and caused his sword to spark across the metal deck.

Cyrus sprawled onto the floor. This was an elevator. Did they descend into the Eich's lair? He hoped so. It felt as if time was running out. He had to get to the psi-parasite and finish this, regaining full control of his mind and the use of his altered psionic abilities.

29

Senior Darcy Foxe broke down in hysterical sobs as her body passed through a cleansing chemical bath to kill off the bacteria on her skin.

She didn't know the converting machine would soon peel off her epidermis and burn it in an incinerator. Perhaps it was just as well for her sanity that she didn't know.

The process was grim. The machine would remove her heart, lungs, and kidneys. Then it would extract her brain and spinal column, submerging them in pink programming gel. There the brain would spend a week, force-fed billions of pieces of data on tactical military situations and operant cyborg body handling.

Later, machines would reattach her augmented brain to a new and improved spinal column. She would receive an armored brainpan, power-graphite bones, artificial muscles, millions of microprocessing nanites, an armor-plated body, and better eyes.

Lastly, obedience chips inserted in her nervous system and a powerful governing computer would ensure her linkage in the vast cyborg mass.

Darcy's skin therefore meant nothing. Even so, the conversion program didn't want to contaminate its delicate equipment, the reason for the chemical bath. Afterward, Darcy would proceed to the skin choppers and the irreversible process would begin.

Darcy had done some hard arguing with herself. She wanted to be brave. The pain would only last for a little while. She kept telling herself that anyway. Yet she had begun to wonder. Did a model 6 cyborg retain some of its old memories? What if her identity remained in the core of her new cyborg being? Would she be trapped inside her own body, silently screaming in horror at what she had become?

There was another factor at work. Darcy was proud of her beauty. She knew men and some women loved to stare at her. How many thousands of moisturizers and creams had she applied to her face and skin? Her one mar had been a tiny scar on her left knee. She hated it, which was why she had undergone plastic surgery to remove the scar.

She ate sparingly of healthy foods, lifted weights, and ran many kilometers to keep her body fit and trim. Was that wrong?

Now the cyborgs would rip her down and rebuild her into a model 6 monstrosity.

That proved to be too much for her. As the harsh chemicals sprayed against her naked skin, Darcy howled for mercy.

The conveyor didn't heed her cries. It clacked remorselessly, taking her toward the skin choppers.

"No!" Darcy screamed. "You're making a mistake! You've made an error in calculations, Prime!"

She kept heading for the slicing area. In her panic, a moment of perfect clarity came. She had to appeal to the Prime's arrogance. That was the only way off this device.

She laughed like a maniac. Her eyes bulged outward as she did. The wild laughter came in frightened gales.

"You fool, Prime! I know your error! Hahahhahaha! I have bested you! The Prime Web-Mind of the Conquest Fleet will fail because you made a simple but quite reasonable error! I am wiser than you, Prime!"

The conveyer halted. It had only done so one other time with a human on the belt.

A slot in the side opened and Toll Three reached in, dragging Darcy Foxe off the conveyor.

Tears blurred her vision. She couldn't believe it had worked. They had listened. Now . . .

Can I hand humanity over to the cyborgs just to win a reprieve?

She didn't want to say yes. These beings were monsters, the worst sin in the universe. To think they originated from human stock was terror piled upon horror.

Darcy wasn't sure about time or distance. She found a cloak over her shoulders. Huddled in misery, she ate cold paste. It tasted like oil.

She wanted to ask Toll Three what he fed her. She was too afraid. Too soon, she found herself in the room on the chair staring at fading and reappearing triangles.

"You have dared mock me," the Prime said.

She nodded with her hair in stringy clumps from the chemicals.

"This changes nothing," the Prime said.

Hiccupping, Darcy stared at the screen. She had to harden herself and just do it.

"Quickly," the Prime said, "tell me how you think I've miscalculated. Then you will return to the converter."

"You must be joking," Darcy whispered.

"I never joke. I am the—"

"Yes, yes, I know. You're the ultimate male ego in the universe. You've made that abundantly clear." Darcy couldn't believe she'd said that.

"The human must receive pain for that," the Prime said.

Toll Three approached. Darcy shrank from his menacing stance, the device in his hand. The tip of the circular thing shone blue with electricity. The remorseless hand lowered as he applied the device to Darcy's neck.

She screamed, and she writhed. Pain flowed through her body. Nothing had ever felt like this. When the device lifted, she panted with sweat rolling down her skin.

"I am Prime. I rule here."

"You rule," she whispered. "I . . ." She waved her hand in a forlorn gesture. How could she outthink this monster? It was hopeless. Yet failing to try would lead to an impossible existence. "I want to become breeding stock. I can help you, you know, make it worth your while to be nice to me."

"The idea you can help me is mindless prattle. No. You will become a model 6 cyborg. I have spoken. My word is law."

"I have important information. I wanted to bargain with you. Now I see how foolish I was. You are too grand, too powerful and all-knowing for me to resist."

"You are wrong in one particular," the Prime said. "I do not know *all*. Otherwise, your statement is correct."

"Oh. You don't know everything? Then maybe I could know something you'd like to hear?"

"However remote, the possibility exists."

"Would it hurt you to hear it then?"

Three seconds of silence ensued. Afterward, the Prime told her, "You said you hold information. If you wish to feel more pain, keep the knowledge to yourself."

"No," Darcy said. She hung her head. The thought of going back to the chemical bath was simply too much. "You made an error about the others. By the way, they're called the Chirr."

"Explain Chirr to me," the Prime said.

Darcy told the Prime about the insect aliens. She spoke about the extended war between the Chirr and Kresh. Long ago, the Chirr nuked the surface of Glegan, burrowing deep into the planet to wait. The Chirr fleet she saw in space had only recently launched from the surface of Heenhiss, the second planet.

"A moment," the Prime said. "You claim the Chirr and Kresh are not allied?"

"Correct," Darcy said. "They're deadly enemies."

"Another moment," the Prime said. "If this is true . . . I must halt our coming attack. Yes. I must reconfigure the strategic situation."

Darcy wasn't sure how she could tell, but the Prime's presence departed. She looked around. Her clothes and vacc-suit were heaped in a pile behind the chair.

"When did those arrive?" she asked Toll Three.

The blocky cyborg ignored her.

She faced forward. The Prime had returned.

"I had planned to destroy the Chirr fleet," the Prime said. "I have annihilated most of the Kresh vessels fleeing the outer asteroids. The Kresh warships proved inept against my cunning ploy. My shift-sent missiles are a masterful tactic. This is the first time the cyborgs have employed the stratagem. I have already coded several volumes on new and improved procedures regarding such assaults."

Darcy nodded, having no idea what he meant.

"Naturally, I am too wise to simply take your word for this Chirr-Kresh war. I have begun a deep analysis of the situation. We will anticipate the outcome together."

Time passed as Darcy waited. She felt numb. If this didn't work . . .

"Attention!" the Prime said. "I have finished my analysis."

Darcy's heart thudded. She wanted to gain a reprieve. She didn't want to become a cyborg. She also dreaded becoming the worst traitor in human history. Would the Prime's Conquest Fleet win because she had given them this piece of information?

"I congratulate you, Senior Darcy Foxe," the Prime boasted. "Your information was correct. I almost made a category error. Fortunately, it seems my cunning runs deeper than I realized. By sending you to the chemical bath, I broke your resistance. By some calculus I do not yet understand, I must have known you held valuable data. I am to be congratulated on this. Yes. Because you helped me, Senior Darcy Foxe, I shall rescind my conversion order. This is a glorious moment in Prime history. We shall celebrate together."

Darcy was too exhausted to care. Just as long as she wasn't going back to the chemical baths. Tears began to tumble out of her eyes.

"Perhaps it is time to couple you with a breeding male," the Prime said. "I would enjoy the spectacle."

Darcy sat up, using the back of her hand to wipe her eyes.

"Jick is at hand," the Prime said.

"No," she whispered.

"What did you say?"

"Not Jick," she said, shuddering.

"He is repugnant to you?"

"Yes."

"I agree. Jick is repugnant. Besides, he is an inferior beast. Yet I do not presently have a breeding male. You will have to wait, Senior Darcy Foxe, which may be just as well. I have discovered through my century of existence that waiting for an event often proves more pleasurable than actually witnessing the thing. That is very strange, but I have concluded it is a universal maxim."

"You are wise," she said.

"Ah," the Prime said. "I also lack time for observing a vigorous coupling. Presently, my frame of reference is combat oriented. It is the attack phase. Since I deem the Kresh as the greater enemy, they will taste further defeats."

Darcy stared at the triangles. Now that she had momentarily escaped the chemical bath and a rape session, she had time to feel bad about what she'd done.

"I have already destroyed many Kresh vessels," the Prime said. "The remnant of their outer asteroid fleet flees, heading for the gas giant. There waits a second fleet. It is smaller than the Kresh force at the third planet. Logically, I should let the Chirr and third-planet Kresh fight against each other and weaken each fleet. I almost aided the Kresh by destroying the Chirr. That would have been a strategical mistake, lessening my chance of victory."

Darcy moaned. What had she done?

"Therefore, now is the time to attack the gas giant–placed Kresh fleet. They hide near the largest moon. Yes. It is credible to believe they have discovered my new shift-missile tactic. I shall have to go in and dig them out. My five dreadnoughts are more than a match for them. Still, it is possible I will sustain losses in the coming fight. Long-range torpedo and laser fire will be my primary tactic. That means I should appear . . . there."

Darcy watched. The screen showed space near Pulsar. Holes appeared millions of kilometers from the gas giant. The cyborg dreadnoughts moved through them.

"That is my immediate plan, Senior Darcy Foxe. Seeing the tactical blueprint before its implementation is my gift to you. I am seldom so generous with breeding stock, but this is a unique moment."

Darcy sat hunched on the chair, near tears again as she thought about her traitorous behavior.

"Sit up!" the Prime said.

Darcy blinked in surprise.

"Up, up, sit up!" the Prime said.

Toll Three stepped near as he readied the pain device.

In shock and sudden fright, Darcy sat up, throwing her shoulders back, which caused her breasts to rise.

"Much better," the Prime said. "Ah, you are beautiful indeed. I should point out that your sullen attitude was unbecoming of this glorious moment. The cyborgs cannot appreciate my vast intellect and martial cunning. It is odd, is it not, that a mere breeding beast such as yourself can marvel more intelligently than Toll Three?"

"I agree," Darcy said in a meek voice.

"Do not think you are smarter than Toll Three. He could defeat any twenty humans. Yet he lacks that independence of will that makes tormenting you so enjoyable. I will have to write a program concerning that. It is possible we Primes have made an error. I am beginning to believe we should each keep harem females to strut before our cameras and listen to our exaltations."

Darcy blinked, trying to make her sluggish thoughts work. "You are very wise to think of that."

"Yes I am."

"Why don't you implement your idea immediately?"

"I believe I shall. One can only communicate among one's own brain domes for so long. Many phases ago, I exhausted all new areas of conversation with myself. Hmmm. Likely, I will quickly tire of you. You are of limited intelligence after all. Yet, until that moment arrives, you shall become my first harem creature. I do you tremendous honor, Senior Darcy Foxe."

"I can hardly contain myself," she said.

"You will remain in these quarters. I shall instruct Toll Three to provide you with greater nutrients. Naturally, I expect you to maintain your trim condition. Perhaps, though, you could don small particles of clothing. One of my brain domes recalls that a female wearing panties and a bra can be just as erotic as one entirely nude."

Darcy told herself that being a stripper for a Prime Web-Mind would be much more pleasant than becoming breeding stock with her children destined to give their brains to these monsters.

Somehow, in some way, I must help to destroy these things. They are abominations against nature.

"In two hours we shall begin the grand attack," the Prime said. "It is therefore time for me to begin ordering and overseeing pre-assault maneuvers."

30

Skar 192 checked the controls from the pilot's chair of his Battle Fang. The ship accelerated at maximum, which strained its grav-plates. He didn't know how much longer they would hold.

Without the grav-plates, the Battle Fang wouldn't have stood a chance against the Tal drones. The Kresh missiles accelerated at twice the Battle Fang's speed. Still, by running away from them, he bought everyone aboard more time. With the grav-plates, they accelerated at twenty Gs. The Tal drones accelerated at fifty Gs. Without the grav-plates, the human occupants of the Battle Fang could have taken perhaps three Gs for an extended burn.

The Battle Fang had passed High Station 3 some time ago. The ship headed for the outer asteroid belt. Behind them, the Tal drones continued to catch up.

Skar opened a comm to medical. "Is there any change in his condition, Mentalist?"

"Negative," Niens said.

"How long will it take Cyrus to gain full control of his mind?" Skar asked.

"That is an extremely subjective question," Niens said.

Skar scowled. He didn't care for Mentalist Niens. The long-faced man enjoyed using large words and pontificating whenever the opportunity presented itself.

"What does that mean?" Skar said. "Time is time."

"You are profoundly wrong," Niens said. "Have you never been bored?"

"What does that have to do with time?"

"Why, everything," Niens said. "Time is an extremely subjective subject."

"Why can't you stay on the point? When will Cyrus wake up? If he doesn't soon, the drones will deploy their X-rays against us."

"If I could wake him, I would," Niens said.

"Why are you avoiding the question?"

"But I'm not. I'm answering to the best of my ability. The trouble is between you and me."

"What?" Skar asked.

"Your thought process is linear, very forward traveling. That is as it should be, of course. You are a Vomag."

"Soldiers fight in the Chirr tunnels," Skar said, nettled. "Do you have any idea what that is like?"

"Thankfully, no," Niens said.

Skar scowled once more. He didn't recall the range of the Tal drones. If only he could eke out greater acceleration from the Battle Fang.

"I believe time moves much differently for Cyrus Gant than for us," Niens said. "It's possible that in his subjective frame of reference, days or even weeks might have passed in his mind."

"What difference does that make to us?"

"None. I concede that. It's simply an interesting topic."

"Staying alive is more interesting to me," Skar said.

"No," Niens said. "It is more *essential*, yes, I grant you that, but it isn't more interesting. In fact, the subject bores me."

"You're tired of living?"

"Can't you understand that each of us faces our coming death quite differently from a Vomag? You strive against fate with every fiber in your muscular frame. I compose my mind, beginning to wonder what awaits us on the other side of death."

"How is that useful?"

A sigh came out of the speaker. "Skar, Skar, you are hopelessly—"

"Wait," Skar said. "I'm picking something up on the sensors." He bent over the panel. What did these readings mean?

"Are you seeing this?" he asked the other crewmembers.

"Is it a new long-range weapon?" Yang asked. He acted as the sensor operator, having relieved the regular crewmember so the woman could get some sack time.

"What transpires?" Skar asked, sitting back. A fantastically large spheroid moved through . . . what Skar thought of as "strange space." The soldier began examining the sensor information.

"That thing is five times bigger than a hammer-ship," Yang said.

"Cyborg," Skar whispered. "It's a cyborg military vessel." During their many journeys together, Cyrus had told him about the terrible beings and the war in the solar system over one hundred years ago.

"How can it do that?" Yang asked. "It just appeared in space."

More cyborg spheroids sailed through the strange space. The dreadnoughts moved slowly, majestically. They headed toward Pulsar, toward Jassac and High Station 3.

"I'm counting five dreadnoughts," Skar said.

"Affirmative here," Yang said. "Good thing they didn't appear twelve degrees closer to us. Then we'd be on an intercept course with them."

Skar nodded. He kept watching the panel. What else would come through the strange space? As he wondered, the oddities of the space vanished.

"I don't understand this," Yang said.

Skar sat back, thunderstruck. "While I do," he said.

"Tell me."

"Those were discontinuity windows," the Vomag said. "Cyrus has told me about them. That's how the Earthers reached Fenris."

"I thought DWs couldn't open inside a star system."

"Do you disbelieve your own senses?" Skar asked.

"No."

"The cyborgs are attacking," Skar said. "That is, they are maneuvering to attack."

"Uh-oh," Yang said.

Skar saw it on his screen. Powerful sensor scans struck the Battle Fang. They seemed to have originated from the cyborg vessels.

"What do we do?" Yang asked.

Skar was a Vomag: a genetic soldier. It was in his genes to fight to the end. How could he use the entrance of the cyborgs to their advantage in the present situation? The creatures from the stars had already attacked Kresh ships. He had witnessed some of the detonations near the asteroid belt, having watched on the long-range scope.

The enemy of my enemy is my friend. It was an ancient slogan from Earth, kept alive among the Vomags.

Skar turned around, looking at the others. "It's time we called Dagon Dar."

"Why?" Yang asked.

"Those Tal drones on our tail," Skar said. "Maybe we can convince the Revered One to retarget them against the cyborgs."

Yang thought about that, and he nodded. "It is worth the attempt."

"It will buy us a little more time," Skar said. "Maybe by then, Cyrus will wake up."

Yang shook his head. "I think our chances for survival are over. That game is up."

"I don't agree," Skar said. "While I live, I fight."

"No," Yang said. "You also hope for the best."

"None of that matters unless we can convince Dagon Dar. Hail him. It is time to bargain."

Dagon Dar understood the significance of the Vomag's offer. The low-grade creature had supped deeply of Resister creed. How could a human otherwise stare him in the eye without the obedience codes taught him in his youth taking hold?

Through the screen, the soldier managed to sit straight without any submissive bowing of the head. The codes were there in the man's brain. Dagon Dar recognized the signs.

This one has traveled with the Earther. The Sol humans are a disease to the body politic. After this is over, we must build a fleet and travel to Sol, eradicating all wilds.

"You can destroy us," the Vomag was saying. "But we are fleas compared to the cyborgs. Let us join forces and attack as one."

"Do you dare to believe the Kresh Imperium needs your help?" Dagon Dar asked. "I am the highest Revered One. You should bow low and beg forgiveness for your outrageous behavior."

The Vomag wavered. The struggle was writ large on his features. As a one-time Majestic Interrogator, Dagon Dar knew how to read the signs.

"The Chirr have run wild," the Vomag said in a harsh voice. "We have seen it through our scopes. The Chirr annihilated the Kresh fleet around Heenhiss. They must have killed many of my brothers and sisters in arms on the surface. I would avenge their deaths."

"Then you must obey my commands."

"I offer you an alliance instead," the Vomag said.

"You have dared more than I can tolerate—" Dagon Dar hesitated because Red Bronze the 232nd sent him an emergency signal. "Hold," he said, "while I confer."

With a touch of his claw, Dagon Dar erased the bothersome Vomag from sight. The tattooed Red Metal freak took the creature's place.

"I do not wish to presume upon our working relationship," Red Bronze said. "But I would like to suggest a possibility to you."

"Proceed," Dagon Dar said.

"Let us use the humans."

"They are Resisters. They are vermin. I desire to stamp them out."

"As do I," Red Bronze said. "Yet could we not put them to better use?"

"Explain."

"We do not know the range of the cyborg beams. Let us reroute the Tal drones and allow the hijacked Battle Fang to attack. Likely, we can learn the greater enemy's extreme range and beam intensity."

"Can the laser range be greater than those of our hammer-ships?" Dagon Dar asked.

"The cyborg vessels are larger, which implies a bigger engine. Does not a greater beam need a greater power source?"

Dagon Dar paused. He was aghast with himself. *I have let emotion rob me of my full analytical ability. A Red Metal heretic has kept her head better than I have. This is unseemly. Where does her icy decorum come from?*

"Your thesis has merit," Dagon Dar said.

"You are generous with your praise."

"No. I am practical and to the point. I have erred in letting my emotion color my judgment."

Red Bronze hissed, which was a form of Kresh laughter.

"I amuse you?" Dagon Dar asked.

"By no means," Red Bronze said. "I believe I understand your unease."

"Please, share this gem of wisdom with me."

"You believe I have sealed off my emotions and used strict logic," Red Bronze said.

"Am I wrong in believing this?"

"Yes."

"I fail to grasp where I erred," Dagon Dar said.

"I *use* my emotion to strengthen my logic."

"That is illogical."

"Yet I have done this, and you failed with your method," Red Bronze said.

"I have admitted my failure. Until proved otherwise, I do not believe emotions colored your thinking."

"But they most certainly have," Red Bronze said. "It is why we Red Metals strive for intuitive leaps."

"This conversation leads us nowhere," Dagon Dar said.

"Do you admit then that Red Metal doctrine has a noted supremacy over strict orthodoxy?"

"No. You spout theories without the proof needed to back them."

Red Bronze moved closer to the screen. "FIRST, my dearest desire is to close my teeth over the Resisters. I long to eat them chunk by bloody chunk, letting their meat digest in my belly."

"That is disgusting," Dagon Dar said. "It is worse than barbaric."

"It is a central tenet of Red Metal doctrine."

"Madness," Dagon Dar said.

"By focusing on this desire," Red Bronze said, "I tell myself, 'Let this Vomag believe he has tricked us. It gives me that much more of a margin of hope for his survival. If he survives, then I will feast on his flesh.' Because of that, I have logically seen his utility."

"Your reasoning has gaps," Dagon Dar said softly.

"I would appreciate you telling me where, FIRST. Let me learn from your superior wisdom."

She mocked him. At this unseemly moment—

Dagon Dar turned from the screen, stalking throughout his private chamber.

I am more emotional than I have realized. The Red Bronze teaches me, but not as she believes. I envision destroying her heresy, her cult. The joy of that moment will allow me to use her.

In some part of his incredible mind, Dagon Dar realized he utilized Red Metal heresy in his thinking. He would not admit it openly to himself, at least not at the moment. There would be time for that later.

Dagon Dar resumed his stance before the screen. He strove for reptilian ruthlessness.

"We will use the Resisters, these Humanity Ultimates," he said. "It would be wise to know cyborg capabilities before we engaged them. Still, we come to a critical juncture. Should we use the Tal drones and hijacked Battle Fang to test cyborg beams while we hide the fleet behind Jassac? Or should we accelerate now and thereby defend the Pulsar gravitational system habitats?"

"Do you believe our present warships can defeat the five cyborg vessels?"

"Would the cyborgs have appeared here if they believed we could defeat them?" Dagon Dar countered.

"Of what use is a military victory to us if our civilization is destroyed?" Red Bronze asked. "The Chirr will likely savage the Glegan Kresh. That leaves the habitats here at the Pulsar system as the last Kresh bastion."

"That is logically reasoned," Dagon Dar said. "I will now resume the conversation with the errant Vomag."

Red Bronze vanished from the screen. In her place, the blunt-faced Vomag reappeared.

"You will obey our instructions," Dagon Dar said.

"I cannot match your guile," the Vomag said. "I am a soldier. I only know how to tell bare truths. We will not obey your instructions as cattle. We are allies in a vicious war. As such, we will listen to your advice with careful consideration."

Dagon Dar studied the arrogant creature. He couldn't believe it would dare speak to him like this. Perhaps . . . Red Bronze had a point. If ever there was a human he could desire to devour—

Inwardly, Dagon Dar recoiled at this barbarity. What did it matter, this creature's arrogance? This was a war for supremacy in the Fenris System. He must use every article he could in order to drive for victory.

231

"For the moment, we are allies," Dagon Dar said. "I now speak as the FIRST philosopher king. I am taking the Tal drones off your scent. They are charged to destroy the lead cyborg vessel. You may do as you see fit."

"Skar 192 acknowledges your words, FIRST. We have a war pact. Let us fight our common enemy together."

31

Inside Cyrus Gant's altered mind, the elevator slowed. It had been traveling down for quite some time.

Cyrus massaged his forehead. "I feel the Eich," he said.

Klane sat cross-legged in the center of the elevator. The sword lay across his lap. He looked up. "It has been a long journey, my friend."

Cyrus nodded.

Klane looked away. "I . . . I don't think I'm going to be able to join you once the doors open."

This was surprising. "Why not?" Cyrus asked.

Klane made a groping gesture. "I exist in your mind. I am the memories of Klane. He—I died in the real world."

"Is that necessarily so?" Cyrus asked. "After this is over, all of it, I'll come back and visit you. In that way you will continue to exist."

"My friend, that isn't wise. I remember a memory of another seeker—he did as you suggest. It drove him mad because he could no longer tell fantasy from reality. No. Once you defeat the Eich—"

"If," Cyrus said.

"You must defeat the alien parasite. You must strip it of knowledge. Then you will become the Anointed One indeed and save humanity. I wish . . ." Klane looked away.

The elevator grounded. The doors opened and dense jungle growth greeted the two men. Cyrus recoiled at the screeches. A musky, damp odor drifted into the elevator. A pink sky showed through the leafy foliage. He'd never seen trees or clouds like that.

"The Eich's home world," Klane said. "This is the stronghold it created in your mind. Here, it is powerful. Here, I cannot go because I will lose coherence."

"Will you wait for me?" Cyrus asked.

"I do not know if I will exist by the time you return."

Cyrus moved up to Klane. He held out his hand. The two clasped, shaking.

"It has been my privilege knowing you," Cyrus said.

"I'm glad you came to the Fenris System, my friend. Without you, humanity here would have lost. As long as you live, I believe we have a chance."

"I hope you're right," Cyrus said.

"You have become much stronger," Klane said. "Use your power. Destroy the Eich. There is no other way."

"Good-bye, Klane."

"Good-bye, my friend. Remember me."

With moisture in his eyes, Cyrus stepped out of the elevator and into the memory of the Eich home world.

‖‖‖‖‖‖

Cyrus moved cautiously, slowly. Once, he looked back, and he could see Klane staring after him. Would he ever see Klane again?

Something inside him said no. This was it. Could a memory cling to life?

The next time Cyrus glanced back, fronds and leaves hid the elevator. He was in the Eich's world, with its odd odors and gigantic insects. The pink sun made everything look wrong. In some ways, this was more alien than the atomic-blasted city. This was an alien world, or the memory of one.

Here, the Eich, the psi-parasite, would be at its strongest.

Several more steps brought Cyrus to a steel wall. He scowled and looked up. It curved inward. Was this a giant terrarium? Did the Eich live in a tiny slice of its home world? That might make more sense. Everything was in his own mind, after all.

Cyrus moved along the wall. Then he heard a noise, a faint squeak. His heart rate increased. Sweat prickled his neck. He could feel the alien's nearness.

Swallowing a lump down his throat, he took out his vibrio-knife and moved inward, pushing aside fronds.

A horrible creature slithered into view. It was huge and serpentine. The swaying made it difficult to focus on its mottling. A crest of bone like a crown topped its python head. Vestigial bat wings with claws gave it hands of sorts. Inhuman intelligence swirled in its flat reptilian eyes.

Even here, the psi-parasite had to use a disguise, Cyrus realized. It rode a long-dead Steed.

The Eich spread its wings and screeched.

Pain exploded in Cyrus's head. He moaned. As the creature glared, the pain throbbed so his eyesight blurred. Uncontrollable and unreasoning fear filled Cyrus.

The Eich slithered closer as its gaze bored against him. Cyrus dropped his knife, clutched his head, and sank to his knees. Moisture oozed through the fabric over his knees from the damp soil.

"You should have submitted long ago," the Eich said in its reptilian speech. "Then you would have retained more of your personality. Now, rash human, I will take full control of your mind."

Cyrus clutched his head, trying to concentrate. "What . . ." His mouth had become dry. "What are you, really?"

The snake-creature hissed triumphantly. "I am the Rider. I came to this star system many cycles ago in my ship. Yes, I realize you learned something about me. Our empire lies in the core of the Milky

Way galaxy. There I will return, a long journey so I can heal from the damage I took eons ago. Your body will go there, but I will devour your mind."

"Did you . . . ?"

"The Kresh almost discovered me several times," the Eich said as it watched Cyrus with malevolent intent. "Their intelligence is amazing. Then you humans arrived, the first colony ship. Oh, what malleable clay your kind proved to be. I have molded the seekers for many cycles. Slowly, I readied the one who would revive my ship so I could go home again. But no, Cyrus Gant of Earth. Your Teleship crew and those vile cyborgs have upset my timetable. Now I will have to move quickly to survive."

The Eich struck his mind with a psi-bolt.

"No," Cyrus whispered. His mind shield strained under the assault. He had fought against Jasper and practiced with Venice until he'd gained better understanding of psi-shields. Klane had taught him even more.

The Eich screeched, flapping its wings. The power of its attack grew.

Cyrus's vision faded. His mind throbbed with agony. He tried to shield, but the creature had immense strength. He saw it as a ball of pulsating energy. The thing was alien and slippery, sucking off the psionic power of others.

"How . . . ?" Cyrus whispered.

"Yes," the parasite said. "Fight me. Let me feed off your enhanced strength. The glow of your shield warms me."

In that moment, Cyrus remembered a rule of knife combat. Trying to match strength against strength seldom brought the best results. Cunning, ruses, and tricks worked better. The Eich absorbed his power, feeding off it.

The null. I need to use a null.

As his vision darkened and his thoughts began to fade, he built a null, particle by particle. He shielded himself just enough to keep the Eich from controlling him.

Cyrus could see the pulsating slippery thing. Then the Eich as a snake-creature appeared before him.

The thing no longer flapped its wings. It didn't screech with joy either.

Cyrus completed the null, slipping the Eich's attack to one side.

"This is impossible," the Eich said. "This is my fortress. Here, I rule."

Cyrus shouted the Latin Kings' battle cry. He picked up the vibrio-knife where he'd dropped it. With a flick of his thumb, he turned it on.

The Eich focused on him. Cyrus grunted as something hit his mind, but he kept moving forward, setting his feet on the damp soil one ahead of the other. Perhaps the Eich increased whatever its attack did. Cyrus exhaled sharply and stutter-stepped as he almost lost his balance.

Then Cyrus used the stubbornness that had helped him survive in Level 40 Milan. He burrowed deep into himself. He kept the null in place even as pain throbbed in his head. He howled like a Berserker. Sweat glistened on his face. He regained his balance. With leaden steps, he closed the distance between them.

The Eich slithered back. It screeched as if in mockery.

Cyrus moaned as his head slumped forward. It seemed so heavy. He could no longer breathe and realized he'd black out soon. In a last attempt, he leaped at the Eich.

Instead of retreating, the creature slithered at him. It tried to enfold Cyrus in a leathery winged embrace. Cyrus stabbed straight. The vibrio-blade hummed and shrieked, and the point exploded out of the Eich's back. The knife man from Milan went wild, hacking so gore jetted as if in a slaughterhouse. In moments, the Eich was smoking meat and pools of body fluid.

The psi-parasite was dead. He had done it.

Around him, the strange plants and fronds faded from view. Then the bloody Eich parts vanished. Cyrus roared in agony as new memories flooded into his mind. He saw the Eich piloting its special craft. It was unlike Kresh, Chirr, cyborg, or human craft. It ran off psi-power and possessed unique weaponry.

Much of the Eich memories were too strange and too detailed. They flooded into his mind nonetheless. As that happened, other memories slammed into him. Past seekers, other Eich, even the Saurian slaves of the star-spanning race of psionic parasites rammed home into his mind. The Sa-Austra, the vat-changed humans—everything poured into his conscious and subconscious. He understood new ways of using psi-bolts and psi-shields.

How long have I been inside my own mind?

In his mind, Cyrus saw himself flying upward through the darkness of his id. He sailed for the light, for consciousness—

And he opened his eyes in time to hear the Battle Fang's klaxon ringing its alarm.

32

"Cut acceleration," Cyrus said. He sat in the control chamber with Skar and Yang, having raced there from medical.

"I don't trust Dagon Dar," Skar said. "He might use one of the Tal drones and just take us out."

"I'll be able to tell," Cyrus said.

"Tell what a warhead is going to do?" Skar asked, sounding skeptical.

"It's not that hard really: a smattering of TK and telepathy to put me there at the warhead. But I'll know if the Kresh sends a radio message or uses a laser link."

"You finally figured out how to use your extended powers?" Skar asked.

"Enough for now, I hope," Cyrus said with a grin.

It felt wonderful to be out of his mind and back in reality. He never wanted to go down there again. The darkness, the aliens, the weirdness—no thanks, he much preferred normality.

His thoughts strayed to Jana. He would attend to her soon. This was the moment to act, though. The Prime Web-Mind of the Conquest Fleet had made his move, and they needed to counter it.

Cyrus remembered Klane's mental voyage to the cyborg fleet. With Klane's memories and his own past Earth knowledge of cyborgs, Cyrus had a good idea what he faced. The big vessels seemed familiar—like Doom Stars from one hundred years ago during the era of Marten Kluge. The kilometer-huge warships even had collapsium plating. The defeat a century ago must have stung pretty badly if the cyborgs copied their enemy's greatest weapon system.

He put everything out of his mind: the Teleship crew in confinement on High Station 3, Jana, past history, all of it. If he didn't act fast enough, High Station 3 would become either cyborg booty or charred pieces of debris. He had to do something now to save his Earth friends, his Fenris friends, and the Kresh warships in the Pulsar system. Even with his enhanced psionics, he didn't know if they had a chance against the combined foes.

Would the Eich ship in the cyborg vessel still work after all these centuries? Could he make it run for him? Those were big ifs. He didn't even know if the Battle Fang could reach it.

Cyrus exhaled. In those few seconds of psi-contact, the Eich had done something to the captive on the cyborg vessel. What was her name: Senior Darcy Foxe? It had been a brief connection. Through it, the subtle Eich had begun a process that had brought the cyborg warships from the outer asteroids to the Pulsar gravitational system. The Eich had wanted its ship, of course, the sooner the better. Cyrus had to get there so he could win this war.

Skar finally cut acceleration. The ship noise immediately changed to something friendlier, not so fraught with high-pitched whines. The vibrations in the bulkheads lessened as well.

"The Tal drones will reach firing position against us in ten minutes," Skar announced.

"I'm going to need quiet," Cyrus said. "This is all new to me and I have to concentrate."

The control chamber members shut their mouths, including Yang and Skar. Cyrus could feel their fear. They knew the Battle Fang was in an impossible situation, and yet it was in the perfect position thanks to the Eich.

A tight grin spread across Cyrus's face. The Eich had been the hidden hand behind much of the Fenris System's history. The Eich had been clever and subtle. The parasite had guided the psi-seeker breeding program on Jassac. The alien had even been the unseen hand behind human resistance against the Kresh.

Cyrus had all the parasite's memories, although he still worked on deciphering the majority of them. The Eich had feared the Kresh intellect. With enough clues, the mighty raptor aliens could possibly have deduced his existence.

Cyrus took a deep breath, holding it before exhaling. He did this several times, slowing his heart rate. He needed a relaxed state. There would be time enough for frantic action.

I am the null.

"The Tal drones are five minutes from firing range," Skar said quietly.

Cyrus frowned.

"Shhh," Yang said. "What are you thinking? Let him concentrate."

No one spoke again.

Cyrus allowed his body to relax against the back of his chair. He gathered his psi-ability. The altered part of his brain was now at balance with the rest of him. Fortunately, he had practiced during the inner journey. If he hadn't—

Don't think negatively. Let your mind flow. Let it gather resolve.

He did, and like a man exhaling air from his lungs, Cyrus Gant let his consciousness lift from his body. He saw the material form resting in the control chamber. The rest of the crewmembers sat stiffly at their stations. Yang and Skar glanced at his body from time to time. They looked nervous, frightened, and, because of that, angry.

I can't blame them. The old laws bind their thinking. I mustn't judge their actions, but help them in this incredibly dangerous universe.

In many ways, it was inconceivable humanity had gotten as far as it had. He had to become their protector against the threats waiting out there for them.

With his consciousness, Cyrus readied himself. The solar system and Fenris had become his Level 40 Milan. Humanity was *his* gang, and he would do everything in his power to protect his people.

Don't get arrogant. Don't let the Eich's memories take over your personality. You're just a man with a talent. Remember that, and practice humility. Pride goes before the fall, and I want to keep standing, baby.

With psionic power, he began to weave a modified null around the Battle Fang. This one would be hard to pierce. It wouldn't last forever, but it didn't need to. He had to reach the cyborg vessel, the Prime's craft. Then he had to reach the Eich vessel. He was going to need every fighting man and woman aboard the Battle Fang to do it, too. Cyborgs were terrible foes, more than a match for humans in face-to-face encounters. And yet, he had to do it this way. With the Eich ship, he could win. Cyrus was certain of that. Getting to the alien vessel was another matter.

We're going to have to board like pirates. First, we're going to have to survive a fight.

Cyrus put the final changes on the Battle Fang. He examined his handiwork and declared it not bad. It should work.

As Cyrus looked around in space with his psi-vision, he noticed the Tal drones. He'd forgotten about them. One of the big missiles activated its warhead.

No! Dagon Dar lied! He's targeting the Battle Fang. Why didn't I sense his treachery? Cyrus sent his consciousness racing at the drone, wondering if he'd reach it in time.

|||||||||||

Each Tal drone had an advanced AI targeting-flight computer.

Four of the AIs had accepted the radioed change in targeting data from the main Kresh hammer-ship. They reconfigured their flight paths, ignoring the sensor blip representing the formerly targeted Battle

Fang. None of the four reacted as the hijacked vessel disappeared from the sensor feeds.

The fifth AI had other ideas. It received the radio message. A long burn and high acceleration had damaged a linkage in the main AI core. Backup systems reacted as if enemy jamming had struck. The altered AI regarded the new targeting data as enemy sabotage.

The AI held a microsecond's debate with itself. It applied mathematical weights to each possibility, ran calculations, and realized the truth. It had to launch an immediate attack—the vanishing Battle Fang had upset the targeting certainties. So it had to strike fast if it was going to hit.

The AI reconfigured the situation and realized the enemy ship possessed an advanced cloaking device. After a swift assessment, the AI concluded, obviously—why cloak unless the pilot was an enemy? That meant a new heading for the Battle Fang. Yes, yes, the AI realized it had to outwit the crafty pilot.

Before the warhead could ignite, however, the AI knew it had a battlefield obligation to give its sister drones a greater possibility of survival. The Tal drone AVR-312 braked.

At this range, the Battle Fang couldn't flee fast enough to escape. But if it—the AVR-312 drone—decelerated . . . one, two, three, four, five, six, seven seconds . . . that would allow the other Tal drones to gain enough distance to avoid the negative effects from the coming nuclear blast.

At the cone tip of the warhead, AVR-312 thrust its targeting rods into possible cones of probability. Each rod pointed in a slightly different position. What the AI didn't do was waste one rod on the Battle Fang's former heading. It would need every rod to ensure a higher hit probability.

The AI did not possess common sense, but weighted numbers and odds.

A strange sensation burst through the neural net. The AI recognized the sensation as enemy interference. Thus, it speeded ignition.

The warhead exploded its nuclear core. The atomic blast destroyed the missile. Before the heat vaporized the targeting rods, speeding gamma and X-rays reached the rods. That concentrated them in a deadly beam. At the speed of light, the gamma rays and X-rays speared into the void. Then the thermonuclear blast annihilated every particle of AVR-312. The AI had fulfilled its reason for existence.

|||||||||

Cyrus's consciousness wailed in despair. To have come so far, to beat the Eich, and now to lose to Kresh treachery—it sent him spinning in defeat back to the Battle Fang. Better to die in his body than live like the Eich had.

In seconds, Cyrus opened his eyes. He expected anything but what he found.

Skar, Yang, and the others in the control chamber laughed wildly.

"What happened?" Cyrus asked.

"The Anointed One is back!" Yang shouted. The big man rose to his feet, rushing near, pounding Cyrus on the back, propelling him forward with each strike. "Well done! You just saved our lives!"

"But I—"

"That was amazing," Skar said. With both of his, he shook Cyrus's right hand. "I've never seen anything like it. Dagon Dar betrayed us, but your psi-power proved greater. Clearly, there has never been anyone like you."

"I don't understand," Cyrus said.

"The Tal drone exploded and the atomic pulse sent X-rays in every direction but ours," Skar said. "Once, I would have called this a miracle. Now I know that you engineered the event."

Cyrus nodded woodenly. He wanted to know how this had come to be. *Is there something I'm missing?*

"The other drones are heading for the cyborgs," Skar said, resuming his seat. "Does that mean we're invisible to them?"

Cyrus wasn't sure about anything now. This didn't make sense. Standing, shaking his head, he figured he'd better wake Jana while he had a chance. Too many imponderables still made this an iffy proposition.

33

Sometime later, Cyrus smiled as he walked back into the control chamber with Jana. They had spent two hours together, talking, making love, and touching afterward.

The situation had changed considerably since Cyrus had left the bridge. The Tal drones approached the cyborg warships. The five mighty vessels had accelerated for a short time, and then seemed content to drift toward the Pulsar gravitational system.

The Pulsar Kresh fleet had come out from behind Jassac—in relation to the cyborgs. They also accelerated slowly, at two Gs.

Skar had counted the Kresh, watching on the passive scopes. The Battle Fang appeared to be invisible to the Kresh and cyborgs.

"I count seven hammer-ships," Skar said, "fifteen Attack Talons, twenty-six Battle Fangs, and forty darters."

The darter was a fighter-bomber with a Kresh commander and several human crewmembers. They weren't deep-space vessels, but could reach what the Kresh considered Pulsar's gravitational border. Bigger than Earth fighters, they were more akin to patrol craft.

"I've been computing tonnage," Skar said. "The cyborgs have one and a half times the Kresh mass."

For a time, Cyrus studied the situation. He asked Skar about the Chirr fleet headed for Glegan. He wondered how much damage the cyborgs had done in the outer asteroid belt. Slowly, an overall star system picture emerged.

ALIEN WARS

"It looks bad for the Kresh," Cyrus said. "Heenhiss is gone. The bugs have destroyed the space habitats and fleet. Who knows how many Kresh remain on the planet with their Vomag armies?"

"I would say a considerable number," Skar said.

"I'm sure you're right. How many Kresh will survive in the Glegan system?"

"That will depend on the Chirr in Glegan," Skar said. "If they can launch a similarly sized fleet as the others did on Heenhiss, the Kresh are doomed."

"I'm surprised the Glegan Kresh haven't begun bombarding the planet."

"Maybe the underground ports are buried too deeply," Skar said. "The Chirr are clever. They must have realized the Kresh would expect a second launching after witnessing the first."

Cyrus pursed his lips. "I think we're missing something. Klane saw it when his mind went to the nests."

"Are you talking about the Chirr adepts Klane once faced?" Skar asked.

"Yeah. They'll have a big effect on the space battle around Glegan."

"Don't forget," Skar said. "The Kresh have their Bo Taw."

"True. Maybe it will depend on what the Chirr have underground in Glegan. So that leaves the first planet and Pulsar as the major Kresh population centers. If Glegan falls, the first planet won't be able to resist the Chirr. You said the cyborg ships split up in the outer asteroid belt, destroying habitats. Pulsar might be the last refuge for the Fenris Kresh."

"That's why the Kresh Pulsar fleet is coming out to do battle," Skar said. "They want to save the habitats."

"Yeah." Cyrus glared at the screen.

"What troubles you?" Jana asked. She stood behind his chair as she rubbed his shoulders.

"I wanted to trust the Kresh," Cyrus said.

"You did?" asked Skar, looking outraged. "For what possible reason?"

"Uh, the Eich Empire, for one," Cyrus said. "Maybe the Chirr for another."

"We can't trust Dagon Dar," Skar declared.

"He made that pretty clear," Cyrus agreed. "The Eich craft has some unique powers, but I don't know if it can take on every alien fleet in the system. That's one reason I wanted to make an alliance with the Kresh."

"I don't see how this ship you describe can take on even one enemy flotilla," Skar said.

"I'm still wondering that myself. The Eich's memories are difficult to decipher. I'm hoping being there in the silver ship will fully unleash the old thoughts."

As Skar watched his panel, he stiffened. "The cyborg ships are doing something."

Everyone in the chamber fixated on the main screen. It was slaved to the passive sensors. The Tal drones still had a long way to go to reach their optimum firing range.

Gigantic laser focusing systems poked out of the armored dreadnoughts. The tips began to glow. Then, on one cyborg vessel after another, vast beams speared outward. They traveled at the speed of light, reaching many millions of kilometers.

"Impressive," Skar said.

"I'd say," Cyrus agreed.

The Tal drones were heavily armored. Even so, one after another winked out, annihilated by the cyborg beams.

Afterward, the laser systems withdrew and the ports closed. The five dreadnoughts continued to drift toward an engagement with the Kresh fleet.

"Well?" Cyrus asked Skar. "Do the Kresh have equally long-ranged beams?"

"The hammer-ships will," Skar said. He'd spent much of his time during their stay in Pulsar's upper atmosphere studying military information. He had scoured the ship's computer banks. "Yet how do we know the cyborgs fired at their maximum range?"

"We don't," Cyrus said.

"The Kresh are gambling everything."

"All right, let's do some computations. We're going to have to assume the cyborgs don't sense us. If they do, it's all over anyway. Luckily for us, they're not accelerating. That would have made things very difficult. As it is, we're going to have to not only slow our velocity, but try to gently land on the selected dreadnought's outer hull."

"How will we get inside the ship?" Skar asked.

Cyrus tilted his head. "You know, I'm not sure."

"So you've just admitted that you haven't thought everything through," Skar said. "I suggest we use the Battle Fang as a ram, smashing through the outer hull. Preferably, we should get as close as we can to the Eich scout. Can you sense where on the dreadnought it is?"

"I can," Cyrus said.

"We must ram them there."

"And how are we going to survive the impact?" Cyrus asked.

Skar looked thoughtful. "Ah. We have construction foam. I suggest that we build crash cocoons for each of us. Before we ram, we will secure ourselves in the cocoons. Those of us who survive the crash will boil out and help you fight your way to the silver ship."

Cyrus thought about that.

"It's better than trying to break through the hull in vacc-suits," Jana said.

"Yeah, I think you're right," Cyrus said. He was thinking about High Station 3. Too bad he hadn't been able to spring the space marines and Argon. He could have used them. Instead, he had Skar, Yang, Jana, a few other seeker-augmented Berserker Clan warriors,

Niens, and the shuttle and Attack Talon crew who had finally thrown in their lot with them. Only Skar and the Berserker Clan members had really trained for combat.

"Interesting," Skar said. "Look."

Cyrus glanced at the main screen. Five hundred and thirty Tal drones launched from the Kresh fleet. The big missiles accelerated at fifty gravities. Then, dark gels began spraying out of the hammerships that had remained behind.

"What are they doing?" Jana asked.

"Creating a space shield for the fleet," Cyrus said.

"With gels?"

"Those will absorb the enemy lasers," Cyrus said. "At least, that's what something like that is supposed to do in theory. I used to read about the Doom Star War. Such gel clouds used to be quite common in the solar system. I'm surprised the cyborgs haven't already done that."

"Maybe they will," Skar said.

"Okay," Cyrus said. "We're going to have to reconfigure our approach. Because of our super-null, we're invisible to both sides. That doesn't mean we have shielding against their weapons. If enough Tal drones explode close enough to us as they pump their rods, it's possible the heat or radiation will wash over our Battle Fang. That might end it for us."

"What do you suggest?" Skar asked.

"I'm open to ideas."

Skar scrunched his brow, putting lines there. "I suggest that the sooner we reach the cyborgs the better."

"So . . . ?" Cyrus asked.

"If you can mask our acceleration," Skar said, "I think we should speed up."

"That means massive deceleration near the cyborg ships later," Jana said.

"Will that use of our thrusters affect the super-null?" Skar asked Cyrus.

"Maybe."

"Accelerating is a risk then," Skar said.

"One among many," Yang said. "However, concerning combat situations, I think we should listen to the Vomag."

"I'm inclined to agree," Cyrus said. "But if the cyborgs see us too soon, they'll shoot us down. Better to accept the right number of risks and make it to the prize."

They glanced at each other, obviously wrapped in their own private thoughts. If he wanted to, Cyrus could have read them. Klane used to do that. Well, that had more been the Eich in Klane. The old rules from Earth still held for Cyrus. He didn't like to read people's thoughts because it seemed wrong. Since he'd never done it much in the past, it wasn't difficult for him to rein in the desire now.

"I think you should make the final decision," Skar said. "You know more about the individual risks than we do."

"Okay," Cyrus said. "Let's try it your way. If I have to strengthen the null . . . I think that's better than gambling about getting caught in the middle of a shooting war between the cyborgs and the Tal drones."

"So be it," Skar said. "We will ready the ship for acceleration."

34

From a central node on his hammer-ship, Dagon Dar watched a monitor. Darters maneuvered Tal drones just behind a gel cloud.

The gel wouldn't stop the mighty cyborg lasers for long. The gelatinous substance had a different duty. It was a sensor screen. The main Pulsar fleet readied for acceleration. It would leave twenty drones behind. If the Pulsar fleet failed to annihilate the cyborgs and, instead, perished, these final drones might save the Pulsar habitats.

The last twenty Tal drones would wait behind the gel cloud. The cyborg sensors probably would not be able to pierce the gels. If the enemy dreadnoughts moved near the cloud, the drones would ignite their warheads behind it and fire X-rays, at a hopefully arrogant, unsuspecting, and heavily damaged enemy.

"The Tal reserve drones are fully deployed, FIRST," a Kresh subcommander informed him.

"Begin acceleration," Dagon Dar said.

He already leaned his bulk against a padded board. The grav-plates hummed, the great engines began creating thrust, and the hammer-ship gained velocity. He pressed against the board. Grav-plates didn't work as well on a big ship as on a small one. An inverse square law meant they needed too many grav-plates to make the hammer-ship react like a Battle Fang. That limited the size of a major Kresh warcraft, the hammer-ship the ultimate in possible mass.

The rest of the Pulsar fleet followed Dagon Dar into battle. The plan was simple. Actual war maneuvers always were. Logic dictated a maximization of firepower at the critical point. That point would be the first engagement with the cyborgs.

When the five hundred and thirty Tal drones reached firing position, he wanted the hammer-ships to begin long-range laser fire. The cyborgs would no doubt attempt to destroy the drones. As they did so, they would also have to deal with the Kresh heavy lasers.

The Kresh would lose space vessels, likely many of them. The existence of the Race was at stake. The Chirr sneak attack combined with the outer space assault—

The universe conspires against us. Dagon Dar knew that wasn't true. The universe was made of inert matter. Such substances did not reason. Therefore, it did not act with a will. No. That mandated intelligence. The timing of the Chirr meant they had an alliance with the cyborgs. That was fascinating for several reasons.

How had the Chirr communicated with the cyborgs? What commonality did the two races possess? Chirr were uncommunicative and aggressive. Cyborgs devoured others to make more of their species. That made the machine-flesh melds incredibly dangerous. They could feed off the defeated and grow. Chirr could only feast off the dead.

Just like Red Bronze the 232nd desires to eat her foes.

As the hammer-ship accelerated toward destiny, Dagon Dar considered the implications of the Red Metal heresy. Even with the most sophisticated species in the universe—the Kresh—barbarians thrived among them. How important would stamping out the heresy be . . . if they survived the coming battle?

What will mark my rule of the philosopher kings? Perhaps this was the wrong moment to think about such matters. Maybe, though, times like this focused one's thoughts. The universe was a dark place, filled with unknowns.

It is good we seek the Codex of All Knowledge. *How sad will be the day of our passing. It is imperative we win.*

A low-ranked Kresh turned from her station, indicating she wished his attention.

I must learn to isolate myself more. As FIRST, I have an obligation to the Race to give myself time to think. None here can match my intellect. After this is over, I will begin to modify my daily structure. Without deep thought, how can I guide the Race with precision?

The low ranker made another wave.

"Yes?" Dagon Dar said.

"Red Bronze the 232nd would like to speak to you."

"Put a hologram here," Dagon Dar said, indicating an alcove. He would speak to her in as much privacy as possible.

As Dagon Dar took up a station, a holoimage appeared in the alcove. It showed the Red Metal freak's head.

"Does your hammer-ship proceed on course?" Dagon Dar asked.

"FIRST?"

"Your hammer-ship—"

"Of course," Red Bronze said. "Yes. We are accelerating."

"Excellent. Your heavy lasers are ready for extreme range?"

"I have asked for this communication to report a troubling possibility," Red Bronze said, "not to discuss trivia."

"Proceed," Dagon Dar said.

"The original Tal drones, the five, I mean, irked me."

"In what manner?" Dagon Dar asked.

"I have made an imprecise statement. I mean the malfunctioning drone troubled me."

"The one that destroyed the hijacked Battle Fang?"

"That is the question," Red Bronze said.

"What is?" Dagon Dar asked. Had he missed something?

"Did the drone destroy the hijacked craft?"

"I fail to appreciate your humor," Dagon Dar said. "Perhaps it is because I'm so busy."

"Red Metal doctrine encourages laughter," Red Bronze said. "However, that was not my intent here. I speak to you with absolute sobriety."

"Frivolity aids logical thought?" Dagon Dar asked.

"Yes."

"Absurd," he said. "That is illogical."

"In a strict sense, you are correct."

"In a total sense I am correct," Dagon Dar said.

"Please allow me to profoundly disagree with you," Red Bronze said.

"You need never agree with me ever."

"I am not your enemy, FIRST. I seek our Race's survival."

"As do I," Dagon Dar said.

"We are not at odds."

"Yet apparently we are."

"FIRST, frivolity or laughter helps logic by acting as an emotional release. I believe orthodox doctrine forces its practitioners into rigid modes of behavior. That builds tensions within the person, who is unable to find release. Red Metal doctrine takes our . . . imprecision into account."

"You skate perilously near an insult," Dagon Dar said.

"That is not my intention. Rather—"

"Enough!" Dagon Dar said as he lashed his tail. "I have pressing matters to attend to. Please, state your opinion concerning the Tal drone and the hijacked Battle Fang."

"As you wish," Red Bronze said. "I have gone over a recording of the encounter many times. I believe the warhead's AI must have malfunctioned. Unless you sent a second signal I am not aware of."

"I gave the humans my word as FIRST. I sent no secret signal."

"Ah. Forgive me, please. I had forgotten about your solemn word."

"Perhaps if you placed more value in extended mnemonic training . . ."

"Now *you* attempt to insult *me*," Red Bronze said. "May I ask why?"

Dagon Dar held himself still. He realized Red Bronze irritated him. What could cause such an emotional reaction? Disgust filled him as an idea formed. Could he find Red Bronze sexually alluring? Did he wish to procreate with her?

Foolishness! My progeny will not be Red Metal heretics.

As with most reptilian forms of life, the Kresh young either fended for themselves or survived under the watchful eye of their dam, never the sire.

"Please continue with your observation," Dagon Dar said. What a time to find sexual allurement.

"As you wish," Red Bronze said. "The Battle Fang vanished seconds before the Tal drone ignited. Because of the distances involved, none of us must have noticed this, at least initially. Something kept bothering me about the sequence. Following this unease—as our doctrine encourages—I studied the encounter."

"What is the significance of your find?" Dagon Dar asked.

"Why, the Battle Fang cloaked itself before the Tal drone fired its X-rays. That is critical."

Dagon Dar thought about her logic. "Yes. I see what you mean. The drone would have still destroyed the Battle Fang, though."

"That is an assumption. If your thought is correct, where was the Battle Fang's debris?"

"The debris is cloaked, of course, just as the vessel found itself."

"What produced the original cloaking?" Red Bronze asked.

"I have no idea," Dagon Dar said.

"I believe you do. The humans, the psi-able, used a null earlier to help them hide in Pulsar's atmosphere."

"True. Now we understand this null. Our Bo Taw would have sensed the use of the null to hide."

"Perhaps this was a new form of null."

Dagon Dar analyzed the concept. She was right. It was amazing he hadn't seen this. "Of course," he said. "The cloaking could not have been mechanically applied, as there is no indication of new technology. Therefore, whatever cloaking occurred, with our known givens, would have probably originated with human psionic abilities."

"Such is my own conclusion."

"So wouldn't the debris have remained cloaked?" Dagon Dar asked.

"Possibly, given the psi-operator remained alive after the ship's destruction."

Dagon Dar hissed. He fully appreciated the logic now, the purity of it. "If the psi-able human is alive to practice his new null, reason indicates the Battle Fang still remains intact. That means my word is yet whole."

"Will the humans agree? After all, the warhead pumped the X-rays that fired at their craft."

Dagon Dar lifted the upper skin flap protecting his teeth. "No. They will not agree. They will surely believe we attacked them on purpose. We must send them a communication stating that—"

"No!" Red Bronze said. "Radio transmissions would alert the cyborgs of the craft's existence."

"Why would that matter to us?"

"If you help the cyborgs destroy the Battle Fang, you will have broken your oath to them."

"True." The words came hard to Dagon Dar. His pride and orthodoxy forced it from him. "You are wiser than I realized, 232nd. I am also forced to conclude you still suspect more."

"I do. Something strange is in play with this Battle Fang."

"You think the Creator's hand is at work?" Dagon Dar asked.

"I would not be so rash as to propose something of such magnitude," Red Bronze said.

"What then?"

"I do not know. It must have something to do with the psionic Anointed One."

"You believe in their Humanity Ultimate rhetoric?" Dagon Dar asked.

"Until I know more, I observe and make conjectures. I am seeing unusual things such as the Chirr space fleet, humans acting deceivably, and, of course, the cyborg battle fleet. Because of these things all acting at once, I suspect an unusual cause."

"That is logical," Dagon Dar admitted. "Further, it is interesting."

"There may come a time when we must communicate with these humans. Excuse me. That was imprecise. I mean we may have to deal with them in a manner suggesting equality. I do not mean to imply they would ever be as wise or as moral as we are. I wonder, however, if they might stumble upon . . . methods to give them an equality of power."

"Ah," Dagon Dar said. "That is the thrust of your message, isn't it?"

"It is."

"I do not agree with your analysis regarding an equality of power. I find the very words and concept repugnant. Yet you have made startling insights. Therefore, I will remember your argument in the eventuality that we find ourselves in this impossibility. Was there more?"

Red Bronze hesitated. She dipped her head. It almost might have been a shy gesture. "There is one more truth."

"I am listening."

"You are an incredibly handsome male," Red Bronze said. "I felt you should know how I feel."

With that, the holoimage wavered and vanished. It left Dagon Dar with a peculiar feeling in his abdomen. What a strange sensation. He wondered what it portended.

35

Cyrus lay on a pallet beside Jana. He rubbed one of her legs. The skin was so smooth, the shape of her thigh so enjoyable to see and touch.

Given the Battle Fang's acceleration and the distances involved, it would still be several hours before they had to get ready.

As his fingers trailed up her leg, a great lurch threw Cyrus off the pallet. He slammed against the deck plates harder than seemed right. A crack sounded and sharp pain flared in his hip. He roared. The bulkheads quivered, and klaxons began to blare.

A terrifying whine spread through the ship. The engines cut out, ending thrust and stopping the acceleration. Incredibly, Cyrus began to float. So did Jana. It meant only one thing: the grav-plates had stopped working.

Remembering his space training in Earth orbit, Cyrus shoved off the deck plates with his hands. His left hip throbbed. What had just happened to him?

"Cyrus," Jana said.

"Just a minute," he said. He reached a comm station and opened channels with the control chamber. "What's going on?" he asked.

For a few moments, no one answered. Then Skar's voice came out of the speaker.

"The grav-plates ruptured," the soldier said. "That began emergency engine shutdown procedures. It's a miracle we're still alive. The heavy Gs could have torn the vessel in two."

"The grav-plates are broken?" Cyrus asked.

"Enough that we have weightlessness," Skar said. "Since it will be easier to move equipment like this, I suggest we keep all of them offline. They're unbalanced right now as it is."

"Can we fix them?"

"That is the question," Skar said.

Cyrus clicked off the comm. Moving to a computer link, he used it to make some calculations. It would have been better if they could have kept accelerating longer. They would have stopped the engines in another hour. At their present velocity, they would reach the cyborg dreadnoughts before the Tal drones reached their optimum firing distance, but not by much. The extra hour of thrust would have given them a greater margin.

In growing disbelief, Cyrus stared at the terminal. Could the techs fix the grav-plates soon? They needed the Battle Fang to decelerate long enough to allow them a hard ramming instead of obliterating the ship with a destructive collision.

It feels like we're right back where we started, Cyrus thought. *No more grav-plates.*

Floating, Jana bumped against his hip.

Cyrus groaned at the pain.

"You are hurt," she said.

"When I fell off the bed, I landed with too many Gs pushing me down. I think I might have a hairline fracture."

"That is bad," she said.

If he couldn't walk in the cyborg dreadnought . . .

"I have to get to medical. Now," he said.

"Let me help."

"No. Follow me. You're not trained in zero-G maneuvering. My hip—"

"I understand," she said. "I might hurt you more. Go. We must repair you as quickly as possible."

Repair, he thought, *not heal, huh? Either way, I have to get my hip looked after.*

||||||||||

Mentalist Niens was all the Battle Fang had in lieu of a doctor. That meant as Cyrus lay on a pallet in medical, Niens examined him.

"Does this hurt?" the mentalist asked, probing the hip.

Cyrus clenched his teeth, nodding.

"Hmmm," Niens said. The mentalist clumsily moved a machine near, scanning the hip with it. After a few moments, he said, "It is broken."

"Bad?"

"A faint line," Niens said.

"On Earth, we call that a hairline fracture."

"Ah. That is an apt term. I shall call it the same thing."

"I have to use my hip," Cyrus said. "Can you give me a painkiller?"

"Certainly," Niens said, "but I advise against it."

"Why?"

"The painkiller might interfere with your psionic abilities."

"I have to do something," Cyrus said.

"I could hypnotize you."

Cyrus snorted. "You don't think that won't interfere with my mind powers?"

"You're right. We cannot hypnotize you. I can affix a brace. Then you will have to ignore the pain."

Cyrus stared at the mentalist. "I have another idea. Can you leave medical?"

"I can. Why would you wish this?"

"I have my reasons," Cyrus said.

"What about me?" Jana asked.

"I want you to stay."

Niens shrugged. "You are in charge. If you need me, I will be in my room."

"Thanks, Niens. I appreciate it."

The mentalist nodded and floated out of the room.

"Why didn't you want him here?" Jana asked.

"I'm not sure I trust him. Don't ask me why, because I don't know."

"Why not read his mind?" Jana asked.

"Maybe I will," Cyrus said, "later. First, I want to try a new talent."

"Psionic healing?" Jana asked.

"Now you're reading my mind."

"No," she said. "Sometimes, our seeker did this on Jassac when a warrior received a terrible hunting injury."

Cyrus snapped his fingers. He must have sensed the Jassac memory. Now that she'd told him about it, he sought a seeker recollection in his mind.

Suiting thought to action, Cyrus closed his eyes. He probed the hairline fracture with TK and telepathy. With a combination of both, he aided the bone's repair, speeding the process. That increased his metabolism. Before he went too far with the healing, his eyes snapped open.

His stomach rumbled. He was ravenously hungry. He told Jana and she fetched him some food. He wolfed it down and drank several bottles of water. Then he resumed his trance, repairing his bone a little more. In this manner he fixed the break, healing the hip as good as new.

That as much as anything else he'd done let Cyrus know he wasn't just a regular Special from Earth anymore. He'd become something different. Therefore, it was time to start thinking differently. He had a gift. It didn't matter how he'd come to receive it. With Fenris humanity and likely Sol humanity threatened by multiple alien races, he needed to use his gift to the max.

I have to stop the cyborgs. Then, if I can, I have to help the enslaved humans throw off the Kresh yoke and keep the Chirr from annihilating everything nonbug.

||||||||||||

The next four hours were grueling for everyone aboard the Battle Fang. Skar led many, supervising construction of Vomag crash pods.

When the time came, everyone would don air masks and Skar would seal them in. If anything could help the crew survive a collision of Battle Fang and collapsium plating, it would be these foam pods.

The techs slaved on the grav-plates.

Meanwhile, Cyrus and Jana gathered weapons. Each invader would wear a vacc-suit. Over it, he or she would wear a Vomag vest. They would carry Vomag pistols with exploding pellets, hatchets, and mag-grenades.

"We need heavier weapons," Cyrus said. "Doesn't this ship carry plasma cannons or las-rifles?"

"Just these," Skar said.

"We're going up against cyborgs," Cyrus said. "They have better weaponry than pistols, I can assure you of that."

"Need does not produce the result," Skar said. "If these creatures truly fight as you have described before, *you* will have to make the difference."

"I'll have to stay in my body."

"What does that mean?" Skar asked. "We all have to stay in our bodies."

"Never mind," Cyrus said.

At last, the chief tech informed them the grav-plates would work for a time.

"I wouldn't turn them on just yet," the tech said. "Save them for the critical moments."

"Will the grav-plates hold under intense deceleration?" Cyrus asked.

"I give you odds of fifty-fifty."

"We need better than that."

"The grav-plates have never received major overhauls," the tech said. "I cannot change that. In my estimation, we should tear them out and install new ones. I'm surprised these have worked for as long as they have."

"We don't have new ones," Cyrus pointed out.

"This I know."

"So they may quit just when we need them most?" Cyrus asked.

"In our circumstances, we have always needed them most."

Silently, Cyrus agreed. This had always been a long shot. It was simply a longer one than before.

Soon, he, Jana, and Skar returned to the control chamber. The soldier brought up the main screen.

The five dreadnoughts loomed large. The Battle Fang would have to begin braking maneuvers in fifteen minutes. Behind them, rushing past High Station 3, accelerated five hundred and thirty Tal drones. A wall of missiles firing X-rays appeared on the screen—the deadliest flock Cyrus had ever seen in his short life. Even his many memories had never witnessed something like that.

From a much farther distance, the Kresh fleet accelerated, although not as fast. Nearly one hundred warships would soon engage the cyborgs in a long-distance duel.

This was turning into something similar to the major battles of the Doom Star War. He was living through history in the making.

"Do you know which dreadnought we must attack?" Skar asked.

Here it was: the moment of truth. Once, Klane's consciousness had traveled to the cyborg fleet. Cyrus had also done that earlier for a brief moment. It had been a grim sensation. He had been able to sense all those horrors on the vessels. What mad genius had invented cyborgs?

Cyrus hoped that that man or woman was roasting in Hell. They had given the universe the worst of humanity, transformed into something like aliens. Marten Kluge had hoped he'd killed them all. He'd failed.

It's our turn to try, Cyrus told himself. *If we win, if I can get back to Earth, we have to start an interstellar war to eradicate the cyborgs.* Either this kind of menace was destroyed, or it destroyed. There was no middle ground, no peace and no neutrality. It was a struggle to the death for one side or the other.

Cyrus Gant composed himself. This time, he didn't need to shut his eyes. The psi-power had come upon him with greater ease each time he used it. He realized more profoundly than ever that his inward mind journey had readied him for the fight better than anything else could have.

In his mind against the Sa-Austra and the Eich, he'd practiced his new powers for days, for weeks. Yet in reality, only a short time had passed.

Cyrus raised his arm, pointing at the screen. "The one in the middle," he said.

Skar sat at the controls. He applied thrust, turning the Battle Fang's nose toward the selected vessel. "Where on the ship should I aim?"

Cyrus felt for the silver ship. He found it right away. For him, it blazed like a beacon. Incredibly, it was in an outer hangar bay. The Prime should have taken it into the center of his vessel.

Cyrus told Skar the coordinates.

After a few adjustments, the Battle Fang aimed for the sealed hangar bay.

"It is time to decelerate," Cyrus said.

"That means it is time to seal you up in the foam pods," Skar said.

Even the techs would go in. If the grav-plates failed now, nothing was going to matter. Cyrus and Skar oversaw everyone's entombment.

In the third-to-last pod, Cyrus leaned in, removed Jana's mask, and kissed her on the lips. "Good luck, beautiful," he whispered.

"Good luck, my love," she said, and then put her mask on.

Cyrus grinned. Then he sprayed foam over her, sealing her in the crash cocoon.

Soon, it was his turn. He lay in the foam pod, put on his mask, and turned on the air. He breathed deeply.

"Ready?" Skar asked.

"I am."

The soldier aimed the sprayer at Cyrus. Foam boiled out of the nozzle, sealing the Anointed One inside. They were almost ready to attack.

||||||||||

Skar 192 sat alone at the controls of the Battle Fang, gloriously contemplating the fight of his life. Skillfully he turned the craft so the thrusters aimed at the enemy. He would enter his foam pod at the last minute. Someone had to steer them in.

Lifting his weapon hand, Skar examined it. The hand, the fingers, they were rock steady. He had been born and bred for this moment. He was a soldier.

Skar flipped the switch, and gravity returned to the Battle Fang. The grav-plates worked, at least right now. He tapped a control and the engines applied power. Mass thrust spewed from the ports. The Battle Fang decelerated and the grav-plates whined with complaint. The bulkheads shivered and the ship threatened to come apart.

With remorseless courage, Skar continued to decelerate. His kind went deep into the tunnels of the Chirr to seek battle. That took courage. This? Bah, it was nothing.

A red light appeared on his panel. One of the grav-plates had just blown. The whine increased, and the Battle Fang still decelerated.

"Last a few more minutes," Skar said. "Then I will grant my first kill to your memory."

The words barely left Skar's lips when a tremendous explosion shook the Battle Fang. Red lights flared on his panel. Several grav-plates ruptured at once. Worse, the shocks caused the vessel to tumble end over end.

Skar barely twisted around in time and clung to his chair. Because the grav-plates were gone, enormous gravities yanked at his body. His grip slipped, but the tumbling ship gave him a moment's reprieve. He managed to pull the crash bar down and snap buckles into place. The spinning Battle Fang threatened a blackout as more Gs caused blood to drain from his head. The hijacked vessel tumbled out of control as it raced at the cyborg dreadnought.

36

Darcy shuddered as the chamber's bulkheads glowed with heat. She didn't know what caused that. Toll Three had left, locking the hatch. The Prime was occupied by his duties, whatever they might be, and his presence had departed.

Darcy wore panties and a bra. It was too hot to wear anything else. She was tired of being naked, though, and had to put on something.

Suddenly, she faced the one wall. The triangles had reappeared. It meant the Prime focused on her.

"What is the meaning of—" the Prime stopped talking in midsentence.

Seconds later, the room quit glowing and it began to cool down.

"I fixed your heat problem. The chamber is too near a main coil unit. I have been pumping the lasers, readying them for distance firing. The aliens rush at us, eager to die. It is quite amusing. Perhaps you would like to see what I face."

The first try, Darcy croaked her words. She was thirsty and frightened. Clearing her throat, she said, "Yes, please. I would like that."

The triangles vanished. In their place was a picture of hardburning spaceships, hundreds of them. A moment of hope leaped in her breast.

"So many," she whispered.

"You speak about the number of missiles?" the Prime asked.

"Aren't those spaceships?" Darcy asked.

"No. Your former alien overlords attempt an elementary combination assault. I suppose it is the best they can do under the circumstances. Perhaps they do not realize the power of my dreadnoughts."

"Have they faced your ships before?"

"No indeed," the Prime said. "This is their first taste of a full cyborg invasion. Before, we sent heavily armed scouts. One limped back with the data we needed. From the information, I know this fleet will annihilate the reckless aliens. This is a great day. The universe will witness the extent of my military power. It is awesome to behold."

"You've already impressed me," Darcy said.

"Have I? Good. It means you are suitable harem material. Your body has excellent proportions. I had begun to wonder, though, about your mind. I am mostly vast intellect and brainpower. True, I have armies ready to fight at my command. And I control these five dreadnoughts. Soon, I will launch the orbitals and then the boarding-party vessels. Senior Darcy Foxe, this is a day of destiny for me. That your intellect is sufficient to understand my amazing might and superior tactical ability allows me to gratify myself with your honest praise. It is honest, is it not?"

Darcy swallowed uneasily. "I never lie about things like this."

"Excellent. You would be too afraid to lie, yes?"

"None may deflect you from your purposes, Great Prime. Oh, they might try, but your superior brainpower will uncover their schemes every time. My few hours in your presence have given me a glimpse into cyborg greatness. Although, I would hasten to add that among the cyborgs, no one is like you."

"I am the Prime. I am the intellect of this fleet. Now, as much as I enjoy our honest conversation, I must attend to combat matters. Do you realize that the aliens have made a critical error?"

"I did not."

"They believed I showed them the full range of my heavy beams. Perhaps they thought I feared their missiles. No. I used half the range in order to lure them closer into destruction. Still, they have given me pause. I wonder if there might be a sly ploy afoot that I have not foreseen."

"Is such a thing possible?" Darcy asked.

"My poor dear beautiful creature," the Prime said. "While you have enough intellect to realize my supreme greatness, most of you is still physical beauty. These are aliens. I have yet to capture one and study it in depth. They may have unknown quantities and qualities. The simplicity of their weapons leads me to believe this isn't so. Yet the mind creature earlier gives me some pause."

"Oh?"

"Perhaps I should sweep space with my AI-brain shift mechanisms. They might pick up psionic waves. Yes. The mind alien acted upon you before. Oh, Senior Darcy Foxe, this is truly a marvel."

"I don't understand."

"While basking in your praise and examining your body, military programs of mine received stimulation. This has caused several of my brain domes to explore new avenues of speculation. I suspect this is another parameter of my genius. Sometimes, Senior Darcy Foxe, I believe I act with cunning without realizing how clever I really am. Fortunately, my great intellect allows me to analyze truths others would miss. In addition, I lack any form of false modesty. I know I am great, thus I always see the signs of my extreme prominence."

"Ah."

"So then," the Prime said, "I awaken the sluggish shift-dedicated bio-brains. They thought they could relax after the inner-system shifts. No, no, I spike them with urgency drugs. Ha, ha, they squirm. Now, I will fuse them with the AIs and—let the psi-scanning begin."

"What are you searching for exactly?" Darcy asked.

"A moment while I calibrate. Hmm, I suppose it makes the best sense to begin scanning near the dreadnoughts. I will—WARN-ING!" the Prime shouted.

Darcy screamed, clapping her hands over her ears as she fell off the chair. She struck the floor and curled into a fetal position. The sound hurt her head.

"My AI-brain shift mechanisms have spotted a previously cloaked object," the Prime said. "It is tumbling at me in close proximity. It will strike—"

The deck plates shuddered. Darcy heard shrieking metal and tearing steel. The bulkheads shook. The screeching sounds lessened, and then there came silence.

Gingerly, Darcy lifted her hands from her ears. She was ready to clap them back in place.

"Prime?" she asked.

"Treachery," the Prime said. "The aliens were craftier by far. Intruders have breached the main hull of my dreadnought. I will summon cyborgs and capture them. They cloaked a vessel. Yet do not fear, Senior Darcy Foxe, I will crush these vermin. Afterward, I will smash the Kresh fleet into tiny particles."

37

Cyrus blinked several times as something wet stained his eyes. Where was he? What had happened? He felt groggy, disoriented.

Have I returned to my mind, fighting the Eich?

No. That didn't seem right. He . . .

I'm in the cyborg dreadnought. We made it. Why don't I hear Skar giving us commands over the headphones?

Cyrus tried moving an arm. He groaned. His muscles felt twisted, misused. He hurt everywhere as his body throbbed.

That must have been some crash. Why don't I remember it? Had he blacked out? What would have caused that?

Some of the wetness trickled past his eyes, over his upper lip, and into his mouth. He tasted it, and realized it was blood.

I'm bleeding.

He used his psionics, healing the gash on his forehead. Then he strengthened his limbs. His stomach rumbled. *Boy, I'm hungry.*

Clenching his teeth, he forced his arm to shift around his body. He found the vibrio-blade, turned it on, and began cutting his way out of the construction foam.

Several minutes later, as he sat up, he found the main control chamber a shambles. A quick analysis at a sensor board showed him the cyborgs had covered the main breach. There was a breathable atmosphere in here. He opened his vacc-suit helmet, ripped open food concentrates, and devoured them. He crammed so fast that he began to hiccup. He needed the protein and fats for the healing.

Everywhere he looked were crushed bulkheads and smoking, sizzling debris. After taking a long drink of water, he sealed his helmet and began searching through the chamber.

With the vibrio-knife humming at full strength, he cut open crash cocoons. The blade slashed through the hardened foam with ease. The first pod revealed a dead tech with a broken neck. The second also showed death with a metal strut pierced through the corpse's chest.

Are they all dead, even Jana? He hesitated, but soon began to cut again. Whatever had happened was. He didn't have time to become queasy or afraid.

The third cocoon gave him an unconscious Jana with blood trickling past her lips. Jamming the knife point-first into a deck plate, his hands roved over her body. The vacc-suit was intact, thank God. He took several breaths, composing himself, using telepathy. With a sigh, he realized she was okay. He shook her awake.

Her eyes snapped open. She stared at him with fear.

We made it, love. Now I need your help.

After a moment, she nodded. He gave her a hand, helping her stand. He retrieved the knife. She checked her suit, tested a rib, and licked the blood off her lip. Finally, she faced him, mouthing the words "I'm ready."

They tore open more cocoons, gathering the survivors, Yang among them. The horror was Skar. The soldier sat strapped to his chair, his head hanging forward.

A knot tightened in Cyrus's gut. They'd gone too far together for him to lose Skar now. Without hesitation, he used telepathy, mind probing the man. The soldier was alive, but he was dying fast.

"No," Cyrus said. *That's not going to happen.*

Taking a wide stance, he gathered his power. Then he mentally dived into the Vomag's battered body. He began rebuilding ruptured organs. It was delicate work. Cyrus made two mistakes, but recovered in time. Afterward, he repaired bones, forcing them to knit back together. All of that ate up Skar's interior reserves. Even so, the man's eyelids flickered.

With great care, Jana removed his helmet.

"Go," Skar whispered. "Leave me to my fate. Get the silver ship while the cyborgs are surprised. You don't have time to fuss over one man."

"Shut up, you fool," Cyrus told him. "I need your help to defeat the cyborgs. Jana is going to feed you. Your body is screaming for protein. Eat even if you think you're going to vomit. You desperately need the nutrients to aid with the repairs."

Skar stared hard, and comprehension entered his eyes. He must have felt wretched, but he was a Vomag. He obeyed orders even though he almost gagged several times as he swallowed the food concentrates.

Cyrus bent over him, grabbing Skar's shoulders. Cyrus didn't know why, but touching the subject made it easier. He continued the process, healing the tough soldier. A moment later, Cyrus released Skar, stumbled backward, and sagged to his right knee.

"What's wrong?" Jana asked, concerned.

"Give me a second," Cyrus said. "I feel disoriented. I'm not used to that."

The others watched him. Their frightened gazes were eloquent. If he went down . . . nothing else mattered.

Come on, Cyrus. Get it together. You can't fail your friends now. Skar brought you here. Now suck it up and use what you've been given. It's your time to go to the limit.

He straightened and said, "Put on your helmets. It's time to go."

Everyone sealed back up. Then Skar shouted a warning over the headphones. The noise crackled in Cyrus's ears. Metal screeched to the left, and three tall cyborgs squeezed into the damaged control chamber. The enemy had made it onto the Battle Fang!

With a soft *phuft,* Yang fired his pistol. The exploding round struck a cyborg on the armored chest, shedding bits of debris and producing a slight gouge but otherwise having no effect.

The three creatures moved with impossible speed. Unless the cyborgs stood utterly still, their bodily details were hard to see. With the vicious swipe of a hand tool, one creature gutted a tech, spilling the man's innards, splashing blood and guts against a bulkhead. A second cyborg smashed the helmet and then the brains of a Berserker Clan warrior, causing the top half of the head to disintegrate.

The violence stunned several people, who froze in shock.

More cyborgs squeezed into the wreckage, making seven of the killing creatures. The new ones carried rifles.

"You have to mind-blast them, Cyrus!" Jana screamed over the headphones. "Otherwise, we're dead."

Cyrus watched the new cyborgs lift their rifles. Gunfire smashed three people, pitching them onto the deck plates. The cyborgs swiveled, retargeting.

Cyrus shut his eyes. He was getting faster at this, and he knew what to do now. A mind blast would be easier. He had to keep his friends alive, though. At the speed of thought and with deadly precision, Cyrus psi-stabbed each cyborg mind. That part of each creature was fully human. Before the cyborgs could pull the triggers, their brains hemorrhaged.

In the confines of the wrecked control chamber, the seven cyborgs convulsed. Two got off dying shots. One missed. The second smashed a helmet, grazing a woman's head, but leaving her alive. Then the creatures went inert, crashing onto the wreckage, becoming part of it.

The grazed woman moaned. Skar reached her, checking her and helping to take off the damaged helmet. He took a good one from a dead tech and attached it to the woman's suit.

"Is anyone else hurt?" Jana asked.

"Woman," Yang radioed. "What are you thinking? If they are hurt bad enough to be unconscious, how will they be able to respond? If not, they can fight."

"Count off," Jana said.

Cyrus let the others worry about numbers. He had to figure this out fast.

I have to kill the cyborgs faster, and I have to reach the silver ship.

What was the best way to do this? With a psi-scan, he saw that more cyborgs were on the way, several hundred of them. Okay. Where exactly was the prize? He scanned farther, saw it, and found the passageways that would take him there.

"Grab the cyborg rifles," Skar said. "They're better than our pistols. We have to protect Cyrus the best we can. He can't do everything. And I expect the cyborgs are going to make him try to do everything at once."

Cyrus had opened his eyes and he was mentally with them again. "Okay, people," he radioed.

"Our comm lines may be monitored," Jana warned.

That was a good point. *Listen, people,* Cyrus said via telepathy. *I know which way to go. I'm going to put it in your minds—now.*

He gave them a mind map of the passageways to the silver ship.

"I see," Skar said. "We know our destination. You will all follow me. You will shoot to kill, and you will give your lives to protect Cyrus Gant. The salvation of humanity depends on him. This is the moment of destiny and we are the vanguard."

So saying, Skar moved toward the spot the cyborgs had used to crawl into the wreckage.

Cyrus hurried after him. So did the others as they rushed out to storm the cyborg dreadnought.

|||||||||

Senior Darcy Foxe shrieked as the room's speakers blared into life.

"Attention!" the Prime shouted. "I spy humanoids instead of the dinosaur aliens. What is the meaning of this?"

"I don't understand?" Darcy said in a weak voice.

"Observe," the Prime said.

On the wall screen, Darcy saw people in vacc-suits racing down a dreadnought corridor. Some carried rifles, others pistols. They moved past downed, no, dead cyborgs. That was amazing. She counted seven intruders altogether. How could so few hope to capture a cyborg military vessel?

"You will tell me about these invaders," the Prime said.

"Yes," Darcy said. "I will gladly do that. The creatures you're seeing are human."

"I already know that. Tell me what I don't know."

"How can I do that?" Darcy asked. "You are supreme. I am a harem woman."

"Do not attempt word games with me, Senior Darcy Foxe. You know the creatures of this system. Tell me what I am seeing."

"Oh," Darcy said. She looked more closely. "The one in the lead is a Vomag."

"Explain the word to me."

Darcy did, telling the Prime about the genetic soldiers.

"Why is there only one of them?" the Prime asked.

"I have no idea."

"That is not acceptable. You must know more. Speak while you are able. Have they come to rescue you?"

"No," Darcy said. "That's impossible." *Wouldn't it be wonderful if that were true, though: that they're here to take me home.*

"Do you want to be rescued?" the Prime asked.

"Of course not," Darcy lied, as she trembled. "No one could give me as great an honor as you do. No one is as awesome as you are. Serving others after realizing your greatness would only lead to my sorrow."

"I knew this to be true, even if I hadn't said as much among my brain domes. I had thought just now to execute you, Senior Darcy Foxe. I find the idea of others possessing you as maddening in the extreme. You are mine and no one else's."

"Thank you for reassuring me of this," Darcy said. "I thought maybe you wouldn't want me any longer."

"Why would I think this?" the Prime asked.

"Humans are doing this to you. I'm human. I wondered if you would hold it against me."

"Never," the Prime said. "Humans are independent agents. The action of one does not mean anything concerning another."

"You're so right," Darcy said. "I wish I could help you stop them."

"Yes, yes, that is why I speak with you. I seek knowledge about them. I want to know their strengths and weaknesses. Perhaps as important, I must know why they are here."

In an instant, Darcy knew. There couldn't be any other reason. In that moment, hope flared, and she began to plot furiously.

Can I even try? Yes, I must. This is my last opportunity. Grab it, Darcy, or I'll hate you for the rest of my life.

"I am monitoring your bodily functions, Senior Darcy Foxe. My instruments inform me you are agitated. Why is this?"

She swallowed, knowing this would never work. The Prime was too intelligent. Yet if she didn't try to bluster, to lie—*Yes, I must feed him what he wants to hear. By stroking his ego, I might be able to blind him to the truth.*

"Speak to me, Darcy."

Full of anxiety, she said in a weak voice, "I fear for you, Prime." He didn't answer. Her fright boiled into terror. She almost moaned. Her knees grew weak.

"Why do you fear for me?" the Prime asked. "How can these creatures possibly defeat me?"

"I-I don't know." *Can't you come up with something better than that? I'm so stupid. I have to think.*

"Don't lie to me, Senior Darcy Foxe. I can punish more severely than anyone else in the universe."

She did moan, and she clutched her stomach. This was never going to work. Even so, she nodded, plunging ahead. "I-I need to know something before I can tell you the danger."

"Speak faster, harem woman. I do not like these creatures running loose in my main ship as the enemy missiles approach. Soon, the battle will begin. By then, I must know what these seven are trying to do."

Realizing the Prime feared—even in some small way—helped calm Darcy. "How did the humans cause all the cyborgs to go to sleep?" she asked.

"Not sleep, you stupid, beautiful woman," the Prime said. "Those cyborgs are all brain-dead. I will have to find new minds to put into their brainpans before I can use them again."

The information startled Darcy. She'd seen over one hundred cyborg dead. "How did the seven humans kill them?" she asked.

"That is what infuriates me," the Prime said. "I do not know."

If the seven could brain-kill one hundred cyborgs, they might have a chance. Darcy couldn't see how, but they were doing it, right? *If you're going to trick someone, you have to sprinkle in truths.*

"Have you used the AI-brain sweeps to examine them?" Darcy asked.

"Ah, for such a beautiful harem thing, you are surprisingly cunning. How marvelous for you to sense that statement. Of course, one or several of those humans must be using psionics. I will train the AI-brain shift mechanisms against them."

"Can you do that in the dreadnought?" Darcy asked.

"I will do what I must. Possibly, that will destroy my craft. I will have to transfer to a different dreadnought before that happens."

This is it—an opening. I have to say this just right. "What about me?" Darcy asked. "You're not going to leave me behind, are you? Prime?"

"No," the Prime said shortly. "I am sending Toll Three to escort you to my main brain dome chamber. You will ride with me, Senior Darcy Foxe. So don your vacc-suit."

Darcy could hardly breathe, but she forced out the words. "Toll Three might be too late. Can you tell me which corridors to use in order for me to run to him?"

The Prime was silent for two seconds. They were the most agonizing moments in Darcy's life. Then the speaker sounded.

"Yes," the Prime said. "Your idea has merit. And you have shown your loyalty to me. Listen carefully, Senior Darcy Foxe, and I will give you the route."

Darcy nodded even though it was difficult to think. She felt numb and light-headed. This would be her last chance for freedom. Once the hatch opened, she would try to find the invading humans and die with them. She hated the Prime. And if there was one chance in a million she could help the invaders destroy the monster, she would take it.

The Prime finished showing her on the wall. Darcy faced the hatch. She doubted it would open. Something at the last second would cause the Prime to change his mind.

A *click* sounded, and the hatch swung open. With a fast-beating heart, Darcy rushed to it. After everything that had happened to her, she actually had a chance to try to save herself even though it was as remote as the moon of Jassac.

|||||||||||

Cyrus panted as he moved one boot ahead of the other. The air flowed through his recyclers. The dreadnought must be accelerating, because it had become hard to lift his feet.

"Slow down," Skar radioed. "We must walk. The Gs are too strong for us to run for long. People will begin tearing their muscles."

So far, Cyrus had psi-slain several hundred cyborgs. He hadn't let them get close enough to fire their rifles. That had taken concentration and the heavy use of his mind, which had speeded his metabolism. He'd eaten all his helmet's concentrates—the paste—and he'd just about sucked down his water supply. He breathed harder than anyone else did. They just had to move. He had to move and think—

Uh-oh, here came some more of them.

"Just a minute," Cyrus panted. He halted and sensed Jana steadying him. He focused on the cyborgs rushing toward them, using a new set of corridors. Maybe the creatures thought this would surprise him. He'd be the one handing out nasty wonders.

One, two, three, he used selected psi-pricks in their minds. He'd learned about a critical vein. Cutting it caused them to die instantly. The bodies clanged against distant deck plates.

"Okay," Cyrus whispered. "It's safe again."

The heavier Gs no longer hindered them. Weightlessness came to the giant vessel.

"This will make it easier," Skar said. "Cyrus, which way do we go?"

With a burst of telepathy, he refreshed their mental maps.

"It's near," Jana said.

"No," Skar said. He faced them, and he gave an exaggerated wink. "It is very far from us."

"That's what I meant to say," Jana replied over their headphones. "I was hoping it was near. That came out wrong."

"It happens to everyone," Skar said. "Yang, do you know a shortcut?"

"What?" the big man asked.

Skar stepped near Yang, winking exaggeratedly again. "Do you know a shortcut to the long-distance spot?"

"Oh, of course," Yang said. "Follow me."

Cyrus was fifth in line as the old hetman led them toward the selected hangar bay. The silver ship was almost in sight.

In the next section of corridor, nothing new happened. Cyrus wondered what the Prime had in store for them next. Because of the multiple brain domes, the Prime was impossible to read telepathically.

Yang opened a hatch and went through.

Cyrus was the fourth person in the hangar bay. Lights bathed the spacious area. He saw it right away: the silver ship. They had almost reached their goal.

38

Cyrus made it to the silver ship without incident. The others flanked him. He examined the alien Eich vessel. Skar, Yang, Jana, and the others looked everywhere else, watching for cyborgs.

"It's beautiful," Cyrus said.

"It is?" Jana asked. "I think it looks menacing."

He knew the Eich memory gave him a different perspective. It was too bad they couldn't see what he did.

The silver ship was bigger than an Earth fighter, but not by much. It had a perfect teardrop-shaped design, with a point at the end. What he hadn't observed before with the psionic view were the lacing and swirls on the skin of the vessel. Those had purposes. No ship had ever been designed for psionic use like the *Shy-Nar-Sithya*.

Cyrus's jaw dropped. Merely thinking the craft's name brought goose bumps to his skin. At last, after long eons of time—

No. We're going to do this my way, Cyrus thought at the remnants of others in his mind. *I'm in charge. I will rule the memories because I defeated each of you in mortal combat.*

He could feel the memory of the Eich make a last struggle for dominance. Then he controlled it. *It's time to examine the* Shy-Nar-Sithya.

Cyrus circled the silver ship. It was an Eich Empire mind-scout-ranger, the newest of the new breed eons ago. That empire was far away in the center of the galaxy.

Is the ship alive?

No. That was merely an Eich idiom. The thing enhanced psionic power, but only if one used the craft with precision.

This is going to be dangerous.

Cyrus took a deep breath. He continued circling the craft, searching for the entrance. None of the machinery, if it still worked, could help him from out here. He had to get inside.

Why don't I see a hatch?

He knew the Eich had gone in and out of the ship. Hmm, he was missing something.

"Well?" Skar radioed. "I hate to interrupt you, but do you have any idea how you're supposed to use the ship?"

"Give me a few more minutes," Cyrus said.

"I will obey. Yet I think you should do your magic now instead of waiting for the last second as usual."

‖‖‖‖‖‖

Darcy ran through corridors as the tiny hairs on the back of her neck rose in horror. She'd escaped the monstrous room. Tears threatened to spill from her eyes. She told herself *no*. There wasn't any time for that. She had to be brave if she was going to make it to the humans.

What did it mean that seven intruders could kill hundreds of cyborgs? It made no sense. Yet she realized that if she was ever going to avoid a cyborg-future fate, she had to reach them.

She tried to remember exactly what the Prime had shown her on the wall. The seven were obviously here for the silver ship. How could the Prime not see that?

Think, Darcy. What route did Toll Three use when he took you there the first time? Can you retrace it?

Her stomach knotted as she came to the first nexus. Either she could follow the Prime's instructions, living like his pet, or she could dare to go—left!

That's the route. I'm sure of it.

Her legs felt weak. She went left just the same, and now she ran. The steel corridor went on forever, or so it seemed.

"Senior Darcy Foxe," the Prime said in her headphones. "You stupid harem woman, you went the wrong way."

Her mouth was dry and the fear too overwhelming for her to give him a sarcastic comment.

"I'm sorry," she whispered.

"You must turn around, Senior Darcy Foxe. My brain domes are deep inside the vessel. Toll Three will reach you any minute."

Darcy kept running as a stitch of pain knifed in her side. She wasn't used to sprinting like this.

"Senior Darcy Foxe, do you hear me?" the Prime said.

"I'm afraid," she said.

"Stop, harem woman," the Prime said. "Toll Three is running faster. He will reach you soon."

Darcy threw a glance over her shoulder. The corridor was still empty. Tears began to trickle from her eyes. The Prime had put her in the convertor. He would have made her a model 6 cyborg. In time, he would get angry again and do the same thing. Next time, he wouldn't stop at the last second.

"Are you trying to escape from me, Senior Darcy Foxe?" the Prime asked.

"I love you," she whispered.

"Can this be true?"

"Dearly, dearly love you," she added.

"Then you must stop."

Inspiration struck. "I hate those evil intruders. How dare they hurt your precious cyborgs! I will stop them, Prime. I will show you how much I love you."

"You seek to deceive the greatest mind in the universe. How did you think to get away with it? I perceive your petty lies. You're attempting to join the humans. You're willing to throw away the most prized location in human history, at my side as a sex object. I will teach you hard lessons, Senior Darcy Foxe. I will make you rue the day you deceived my noble heart. Senior Darcy Foxe, I am angry with you. No one plays me false as you just have. Look—Toll Three is right behind you."

Darcy glanced back. The blocky cyborg ran with impossible leaps and strides, eating up the distance, coming down the corridor after her.

"You will weep ten thousand tears, Senior Darcy Foxe. You will—"

Darcy reached a hatch. Frantically, she tried to open it, but it was frozen shut.

"No," Darcy sobbed. "Why are you doing this?"

"Run, little harem woman," the Prime gloated. "Oh, I am thoroughly enjoying this. How funny you are, how sadly pathetic."

Darcy realized she moved the bar the wrong way. She looked back. Toll Three was less than thirty meters away. With a scream, she shoved the bar, opened the hatch, and ran into the hangar bay. She spied the silver ship.

Darcy ran. A clank of metal told her Toll Three had made it through the hatch. She moaned with dread.

Don't worry, a voice said in her mind. *I know you, Darcy. I saw you before. He is going to die—now.*

Darcy looked over her shoulder. Toll Three leaped. She screamed as the cyborg dived at her with his gleaming metal fingers outstretched.

An invisible force slammed the cyborg. He hit the deck plates hard, bouncing, sliding toward her. When he came to a halt several centimeters from her feet, the meld's orbs stared at nothing. Toll Three was brain-dead.

She had reached the seven humans at the silver ship.

39

Dagon Dar waited tensely in the main control room of his command vessel. The five hundred and thirty Tal drones approached optimum firing range. Far behind, the seven hammer-ships readied their lasers. The nuclear-pumped X-rays had a far shorter range than the larger and more coherent hammer-ship lasers.

Dagon Dar lashed his tail. Now the Kresh would smash these cyborgs. He would obliterate the attackers. Afterward, he would begin a long curve, taking the Pulsar fleet as fast as possible to Glegan.

The Heenhiss Chirr were three-quarters of the way to the third planet. Still, no new bug ships had lifted from Glegan.

"FIRST, look," a subcommander said.

Dagon Dar studied the main viewing screen. His eyes grew larger. Incredibly wide beams reached out from the cyborg dreadnoughts. The laser moved downward, cutting through the Tal drones.

"How long does the laser stay on target?" Dagon Dar asked.

In the hammer-ship, Kresh personnel studied their sensors. At last, the subcommander spoke up. "Three seconds per drone, FIRST. The intensity of the beam—it is intolerably hot."

Dagon Dar could see that. Incoming data showed a swath of destruction to the drones.

"Initiate the Tal firing sequence," he ordered.

"But—"

"By the time they reach optimum range, the drones will no longer exist. They must fire now."

"At once, FIRST," the subcommander said. "It will take several seconds for the message to reach them."

"Order the hammer-ships to begin firing on the lead cyborg vessel," Dagon Dar said.

"Our lasers cannot match their intensity."

"I understand," Dagon Dar said. "Yet we must do what we can. Now is the moment. Fire the lasers! Send the signal: all hammer-ships must attack!"

||||||||||

Millions of kilometers separated the two fleets. The Tal drones were seven hundred thousand kilometers from the enemy ships. Optimum distance was five hundred and sixty thousand kilometers.

The hammer-ships could reach many millions of kilometers with their heavy lasers. The cyborgs could return the favor. The dreadnought lasers, however, were five times as powerful as the Kresh rays.

As the five cyborg beams cut through the mass of missiles, Tal drones slagged into molten pieces. Over half of them had ceased functioning by the time Dagon Dar's message reached the AIs. They configured distances, enemy speeds, range of X-rays—five more drones were destroyed in that time.

The remaining Tal warheads ignited. The nuclear blasts pumped the rods and flashed X-rays at the speed of light. They struck collapsium plating, incredibly dense armor, and did negligible damage to the dreadnoughts.

Now the main battle began between the cyborgs and Dagon Dar's Kresh.

The seven hammer-ships concentrated on the central cyborg dreadnought. At the moment, the hammer-ships were the only Kresh vessels able to attack at the extreme distance. The speed of light was three hundred thousand kilometers per second. Seventeen seconds after leaving the hammer-ships, seven heavy lasers began to boil and burn into collapsium plating.

At the same time, the cyborg lasers burned against a Bo Taw psi-shield of the selected hammer-ship. Space there glowed with a weird and brilliant color. The mighty lasers simply halted. Such was the awful power of the lasers, however, that they began to push against the glow, forcing it closer, closer to the targeted hammer-ship.

The seven Kresh lasers burned against the central dreadnought. Although the hammer-ships had greater numbers, the strength of their beams dissipated to a greater degree. The cyborg laser was larger, more powerful, and had tighter coherence at extreme range. Even so, the collapsium plating on the targeted vessel began to rupture in places. The cyborg vessel braked, slowing its velocity. The other four dreadnoughts moved beyond the targeted craft. One slid downward, coming between the dreadnought and the Kresh lasers.

That took the central dreadnought out of the fight, at least for the moment.

Now, four cyborg dreadnoughts beamed their great lasers toward the selected hammer-ship. Unknown to the Prime, the Bo Taw onboard the targeted vessel cried out. Most clutched their elongated foreheads, dropping unconscious to the deck. That further weakened the psi-shield, which went down seconds later.

Four great beams smashed against the hammer-ship. The outer armor did little against the cyborg lasers. They sliced sections of hammer-ship into various pieces. Debris and beings spilled out. Explosions vaporized most of the mass. The hammer-ship was gone, destroyed by the annihilating rays.

Because the cyborgs used advanced teleoptics instead of radar for targeting, the Prime knew about the destruction seventeen seconds later. Commands flashed between the dreadnoughts. Soon, the cyborg beams retargeted, shifting toward the next hammer-ship, beginning the process anew.

||||||||||

Despite the agonizing loss so soon in the fight, Dagon Dar observed the situation with reptilian calm as he made his calculations. He did not like what he found. What should he do? Retreat seemed out of the question. His only consolation was that battle was seldom a mathematical application of certainty. Random factors could intrude—luck. Could he count on that? No. Likely, the Kresh were doomed.

"We can hurt them," he told the others. "We must continue accelerating toward the cyborgs. Once we close the distance, the Attack Talons and Battle Fangs will engage in the fight, improving our odds."

"At our present velocity," the subcommander said, "that will take over two hours."

"Yes," Dagon Dar said. "Likely, we face catastrophic defeat. Yet there is a slim chance of victory. The key is destroying one of their dreadnoughts soon enough. That will reduce their percentages by one fifth. Therefore, we will grasp at this hope and continue to attack."

||||||||||

Cyrus watched the vacc-suited woman stumble toward them. Through the helmet, he could see the tears streaming down her face.

"Is this a trick?" Skar asked with his rifle aimed at the woman.

"No," Cyrus said. "She's an ice hauler. The Web-Mind has been abusing her."

The woman stopped short. She had dialed into their comm net. "How can you know that?" she asked.

"I read minds," Cyrus said.

"This is all very well," Skar said. "Can't you access the machine? What are you waiting for?"

Cyrus turned away from Darcy Foxe, from the others. He regarded the perplexing silver ship. "I'd love to go inside," he told them, "but there's no hatch."

"Touch it," Darcy said. "You're supposed to touch the outer skin."

Cyrus regarded her. "How did you know that?" He didn't need her answer. He saw that the Eich had left it in her mind.

Removing a gauntlet, Cyrus stepped closer and let his fingertips brush the cool outer hull. A shock buzzed his hand. He jerked it away.

"What's wrong?" asked Skar.

"Shhh," Darcy said. "Leave him alone." To Cyrus, she said, "Touch it. You know you have to."

Gathering his resolve, Cyrus pressed his palm against the silver ship. A shock went up his arm, neck, and head and seemed to pop inside his mind. He knew now. *I must teleport inside. That's the only way in.*

He frowned with distrust. Why would the Eich have left the message in Darcy's mind? Was it a last trap? What would it be like inside the *Shy-Nar-Sithya*?

"We don't have much time," Skar said. "Whatever you're going to do, my friend, do it now."

In case this was the end, Cyrus wanted to shake the soldier's hand. He wanted to hug Jana and bid farewell to Yang and the others. Instead, in the interest of time and humanity, he bent his head, closed his eyes, and concentrated.

Cyrus Gant accessed the entirety of his transfer memories. He saw how Klane had teleported once. It had left the former Anointed One with a nosebleed. Drawing a lungful of air, Cyrus repeated the teleportation mind sequence.

In the blink of an eye, he vanished—and he reappeared inside the *Shy-Nar-Sithya*.

It was dark inside, the air thousands of years stale. Fortunately, he wore his vacc-suit. With a click of a button, he turned on a helmet lamp. The inside of the silver ship was constructed for an Eich Steed, a snake creature. It had a curving couch, a crystal for a screen, and nubs for controls.

Cyrus tore thoughts and ideas from the memory of the Eich. *Ah. Okay. I think I see.*

He tapped nubs. After thousands of years, engines purred to life. That was incredible. How could it be in such good condition and work immediately? Before he could ask himself more, the *Shy-Nar-Sithya* spoke to him in Eich. Instead of attempting alien speech—Cyrus's throat could never have pronounced the majority of the words—he used telepathy.

The dialogue between him and the silver ship was brief and pointed.

Lights gave illumination, and stored psionic power poured into Cyrus Gant. It was similar to Klane's experience in the Chirr nest. Here, however, the *Shy-Nar-Sithya* allowed him to utilize the psionics with perfect control. What's more, the banks were full to capacity. Over the centuries, the craft had naturally recharged with driblets of Kresh and then human thought. When the Eich had crashed the ship, it had nearly zero psi-energy.

Even with the Eich memories, the technology was beyond Cyrus's grasp. He knew how to use the *Shy-Nar-Sithya*, but he didn't understand why it worked as it did. It would have been like a caveman turning on a light switch but having no clue about hydroelectric turbines, transformers, and the intricacies of electricity.

Stand back, he told the others outside the vessel.

Skar was worried about more cyborgs showing up.

I'll take care of the cyborgs on this dreadnought before I leave, Cyrus told them.

Each of them wanted to know where he planned to go.

Cyrus had no more time for the others. He lay down on the Eich couch, closed his eyes, and let himself fully integrate into the *Shy-Nar-Sithya*.

His psionic abilities increased a hundredfold. It bewildered him for a moment.

No. I'm going to do this a single step at a time. First, let's settle with this ship's cyborgs.

He used the same killing TK, eliminating nine thousand and sixty-four cyborgs aboard the vessel.

Ah, look at this. The Prime had already lifted in a shuttle, heading for a different dreadnought. With a swift thought, Cyrus began shutting down the Prime's life-support systems. The multibrained creature wailed, attempting to issue commands. Cyrus fused the life supports, knowing the Prime Web-Mind of the Conquest Fleet would be dead in minutes.

A controlled thought caused the *Shy-Nar-Sithya* to teleport from the hangar bay. It reappeared outside and behind the dreadnought in relation to the approaching Kresh.

Cyrus expanded his psi-vision. Four dreadnoughts continued to beam the hammer-ships. The hammer-ships returned the favor. Another cyborg craft had reached the limit of its collapsium armor. If the Prime had been running the fleet, he would have surely ordered that vessel to move back behind the others. Instead, the damaged dreadnought continued to beam.

That allowed the cyborgs to annihilate the third hammer-ship.

Then the great cyborg vessel took Kresh laser beams in the gut. The rays of killing light slashed through bulkheads, burning cyborgs, shower stalls, food refractors, oil bins, coils, water, more bulkheads— until the Kresh beams reached a fusion core. It went critical. Explosions in the dreadnought killed two thousand and fifty-seven cyborgs. The great vessel shuddered. Still the enemy beams chewed into the craft. One reached inner armor plate on the other side.

At that moment, a terrific thermonuclear explosion ruptured the great craft. It began to break apart, causing secondary breaches. Air, water, and debris surged outward into the vacuum of space. The rest of the cyborgs died, washed with atomic heat and radiation.

Three dreadnoughts now poured their titanic rays at the fourth targeted hammer-ship. The fight entered its critical phase.

Cyrus saw all this, and he made swift calculations. With the *Shy-Nar-Sithya*, he could create a Bo Taw rebellion by shifting their love conditioning. He also saw the Chirr approaching Glegan. Worse, he counted the numbers of Chirr vessels hidden inside the third planet. It was double the size of the original Chirr fleet that had lifted from Heenhiss. Perhaps as important, Cyrus recognized the psionic strength of the Chirr. It was incredible.

He lay inside the silver ship, wondering—then it struck him. He knew what he had to do.

40

The silver *Shy-Nar-Sithya* vanished from its location behind the cyborg dreadnought. It reappeared in Dagon Dar's hammer-ship, in the main hangar bay.

Cyrus readied himself. According to Eich memories, the Kresh made difficult telepathic partners. The dinosaur mentality hated mind-to-mind linkage. Nevertheless, that's what Cyrus planned to do. He couldn't risk leaving his ship.

Dagon Dar, Cyrus said. *I have a deal to make with you.*

"Who is this?" the FIRST asked from where he stood in the hammer-ship's control chamber.

Cyrus would have told the creature he merely needed to think the thought, not talk, but the Eich memory let him know the Kresh would refuse to do that.

I am the Anointed One of the human race. I am very real. Oh, this was interesting. Dagon Dar had a theoretical knowledge of the Eich. *Your former FIRST was right about a hidden alien influence. It was a danger, but no longer. I have killed it. The cyborgs and even more the Chirr will exterminate the Kresh and the humans from the Fenris System.*

"So you force your way into my mind, trying to demoralize me. I don't accept your statements."

Believe your senses then. Cyrus showed the FIRST what the Chirr had in store for the Kresh.

"These are mind forgeries that I reject," Dagon Dar said.

I'm in your hangar bay in a psi-driven vessel. That is truth. How did my ship get here? I will tell you: I teleported from the cyborgs. They found this ship hidden in an outer asteroid. I can just as easily teleport nuclear bombs onto your vessels, destroying them one by one.

"Why don't you then?"

Because I want to make a deal with you, Cyrus said.

"After we attempted to destroy your Battle Fang?" asked Dagon Dar.

I already see in your mind what happened. The AI malfunctioned. I also sense that the Kresh keep their word. You are different from how I first conceived you. Yes. You dinosaurs think of yourselves as very moral.

"What bearing does your last statement have on us?"

Even as we bargain, the cyborgs are destroying your fleet. I can destroy them in minutes. If I do, however, you would either destroy their ships or capture them.

"Why would you care?" Dagon Dar asked.

Because I claim those dreadnoughts for the human race, Cyrus said. *Your Bo Taw are going to rebel against you soon. They can hate you instead of love you. Then where will you be?*

"You spout vain threats."

Ultimately, you must realize I don't. The silver ship in your hangar bay proves I speak the truth in your mind.

"I see your ship on my screen," Dagon Dar said. "You are in our hangar bay. This is . . . profoundly unsettling. Very well, there is truth to your statements. The silver ship proves as much. I am rational. I am logical and go where the facts lead. So then, what is the nature of your bargain?"

I will slay the cyborgs, staffing their ships with humans. Together, we shall defeat the Chirr. Then the Kresh and humans will split the planets in the star system. Together, we will begin a league of sentient species, united against the Eich Empire, if it still exists after all this time.

"What are the proofs for your statement? Specifically, I mean this so-called stellar empire of snakes?"

*Prepare to be amazed, Dagon Dar. I will unfold in your mind what
I know about the Eich.*

Cyrus did so, explaining in a sweeping panorama, and showing
what a single Eich had achieved in the Fenris System.

"I am stunned," Dagon Dar said at last. "But I cannot agree to
your proposal."

Cyrus groaned.

"Hear me out, human. You must seek out Red Bronze the 232nd
and expose her to what you've shown me. Then we shall talk again."

During that time, more of your ships will perish.

"Yes. But I cannot make such a decision as you ask when this conversation may be a sheer delusion. Speak with her, and then we shall
talk again."

||||||||||

Dagon Dar paced, and he came to a swift conclusion. He began
ordering Battle Fangs to dive into the cyborg laser beams. One by one,
the craft began to obey.

A Battle Fang had less armor than a hammer-ship, and a fraction
of its mass. Soon, the first small vessel became red hot, exploding,
killing everyone onboard.

In such a manner, however, the FIRST kept more of his hammer-
ships in the contest longer than otherwise.

A second cyborg dreadnought fell before Kresh beams. That left
two of the mighty spheroids in the fight. The third cyborg warship
continued to hide behind its brethren.

Battle Fangs dwindled in number, and another hammer-ship disintegrated under the cyborg beams.

"FIRST!" a subcommander shouted.

Dagon Dar whirled around, saw where the subcommander
pointed, and rushed to an alcove. A hologram of Red Bronze the

232nd appeared. The FIRST realized with shock that the tattoos added to her beauty, not the reverse. How remarkable that he should notice at a time like this.

"Dagon Dar?" she said.

Expectant, he waited for her to continue speaking.

"The Earther has spoken to me," Red Bronze announced.

"Do you believe in his apparitions of the mind?" Dagon Dar asked.

"Red Metal doctrine—"

"We have no time for the niceties of philosophical thought," Dagon Dar shouted. "Just give me your conclusions."

She gave the briefest of nods. "Yes," she said. "I believe Cyrus Gant. The Kresh Race is in mortal danger."

"Above all else," Dagon Dar said, "we must retain our integrity so we can add to the *Codex of All Knowledge*."

"The species must survive," Red Bronze said. "I would make the bargain."

"Humans are notoriously fickle. To grant them the dreadnoughts—"

"We must certainly take safeguards," Red Bronze said. "Yet I trust Cyrus Gant."

"Why would you? Has he befuddled your mind?"

"I trust him for the most logical of reasons. He has acquired a ship of awesome power. Did he destroy us with it? No. He seeks to bargain because danger lies in the stars. Danger seethes underground in the hives of the Chirr. Without his help, we will lose to the bugs. We can survive and grow in alliance with the humans."

"An alliance with our servitors?" asked Dagon Dar.

"Times change," Red Bronze said. "The Kresh must adjust to realities if we desire continued existence."

Dagon Dar nodded thoughtfully. The Pulsar fleet disappeared ship by ship to the cyborg rays. That weighed on him. Yet he did not think to lie to the human in order to gain temporary help. If he gave his word, he gave it as FIRST.

"Yes," Dagon Dar whispered. "I will make the pact. Where is Cyrus Gant?"

"I will summon him," Red Bronze said.

|||||||||||

With the *Shy-Nar-Sithya*, Cyrus teleported. He appeared behind the cyborg dreadnoughts. His friends would live or die according to Kresh trustworthiness.

He sat up in the ancient craft. His vacc-suit was running low on air. He would need a new tank soon.

Don't worry about that. Get the job done.

Cyrus concentrated, and the silver craft shifted into the first dreadnought. He radiated a death command, and ten thousand cyborgs perished. With telekinesis, Cyrus shut the lasers down.

Using the silver ship, he popped into the last dreadnought and did likewise.

Blood trickled from his nose, over his lips, dripping off his chin. He would have liked to wipe it away. He couldn't do that with the bubble helmet on.

He was weary. The silver ship's psionic levels had dipped dramatically. He had half the psi-cells remaining. After that, it would take years to refill. Maybe he could do what the Chirr did, stealing life forces.

Cyrus shook his head. No. He wasn't going to turn into a cosmic vampire. He would be legitimate.

As the cyborg lasers stopped firing, he waited. The Kresh beams still burned into the pitted collapsium armor. If they were going to cheat—

Even as he thought that, Cyrus watched the rays flicker out. The battle between the Pulsar Kresh and the cyborg invaders was over.

Seven humans besides Cyrus lived aboard the huge ships. Which humans would he recruit? Would he turn the Bo Taw love conditioning into hate for the Kresh? Might he be able to make a different kind of mental virus? Could he switch the Bo Taw's love of the Kresh into a love of human survival?

I like that. Cyrus shook his head. His thinking was becoming confused with fatigue. Such a thing was in the future. *I'm very tired.*

He made a last teleport, reappearing in the first cyborg hangar bay. Then Cyrus popped out of the *Shy-Nar-Sithya*, appearing two inches off the deck plates. He landed badly, stumbling, crumpling onto the floor.

One of the vacc-suited people raced to him. She ran swiftly, with grace. Jana twisted off his helmet.

The air inside the hangar bay was tainted but breathable.

"Cyrus!" she cried. She used a rag, wiping his nose, sopping up blood.

"What's happening?" Skar said, standing over him.

Cyrus looked up. He grinned, blood speckling his teeth. "You're not going to believe this. I think we won. What's more, I may have just freed Fenris humanity from under the Kresh talon."

"How is that even possible?" Skar asked.

Jana rubbed Cyrus's forehead as he rested his head on her lap.

"Let me close my eyes a few minutes," Cyrus said. "I need a break. Then I'll tell you everything. We still have a lot to do before this is over."

41

One hundred and fifty-three hours later, a former cyborg dreadnought reached High Station 3.

"I still say you're taking too great a risk going there yourself," Skar told Cyrus. They stood in a hangar bay near a cyborg shuttle.

"Dagon Dar is still shocked by recent events," Cyrus said. "You should also remember that I was in his mind. I know he means to keep his word."

"Minds change," Skar said, "especially if given enough provocation."

"Do you want to come with me as my bodyguard?" Cyrus asked.

"Take Jana and Yang," Skar said. "They've never been forced to love the Kresh. In this, I trust them more than I trust myself."

Putting his hand on the Vomag's shoulder, Cyrus leaned near, whispering, "I have another reason for going."

"Yes?"

"It's time to start changing the Bo Taw. We're going to need them."

"Won't that make Dagon Dar angry?" Skar asked.

"I guess we're going to find out."

Twenty minutes later, Jana piloted the shuttle, lifting from the hangar bay and guiding the craft toward the space habitat. Cyrus sat beside her, watching a dot become the great rotating cylinder.

It seemed like a lifetime ago that he'd fled this place. How many of the others from *Discovery* still lived?

Cyrus squirmed in his seat as he thought about Chief Monitor Argon and First Sergeant Mikhail Sergetov. He dearly hoped they had survived Kresh captivity and interrogations. Everything was different from those desperate days. Instead of being nobody, he was someone important.

Cyrus smiled at Jana.

"We will be married soon," she said.

"You'd better believe it."

She leaned over and kissed him. He grabbed the back of her head and made it a good one.

"I love you, Cyrus Gant."

"And I love you, baby."

She gave her attention back to the controls. Too soon, she brought them through a hangar bay entrance. Thrusters whooshed and they settled toward the docking lock.

Is this the same bay I entered when I made my escape the first time?

A clang and a shudder told him they'd landed.

"Ready?" he asked.

Jana and Yang nodded. Both of them had Vomag pistols strapped to their sides. Each wore a helmet. They would protect him with their lives. It made him feel strange. Without him, everything would falter. If he lived, Fenris humanity could come out equal and possibly even on top.

Maybe I am taking a big risk coming here like this. I have to start the Bo Taw rebellion, though. We need the psi-adepts to make this work.

The agreement between Dagon Dar and him included the immediate release of the Earth captives.

Cyrus exited the ship, walking down a ladder. On the deck, he found himself face-to-face with three tall Bo Taw and a squad of Vomags behind them.

The oldest Bo Taw stepped forward. He wore a purple robe and a scarlet band around his head. He bowed in a formal manner with his hands hidden in the folds of his long sleeves.

"Where are the Kresh?" Cyrus asked, glancing around. The place looked deserted.

"They tasked me with the meeting," the Bo Taw said. "We will—" The older man squinted, and the two other Bo Taw began mentally testing Cyrus with harsh mind probes.

The former gang member from Milan grinned, blocking what he now considered their feeble attempts. The old Cyrus Gant could never have done this. Swiftly, Cyrus practiced psi-judo, turning the assault around. He saw the love conditioning in their minds, and he dialed the emotion to a new setting. He didn't make them hate the Kresh, but love the idea of human freedom more.

He wasn't sure he could have done this so quickly if they hadn't tried their little assault. That was interesting to know. Would he have to provoke attacks in the future?

The lead Bo Taw blinked, and he massaged his cranium. The man studied Cyrus as if seeing him for the first time.

"You . . ." the Bo Taw said, his tongue seemingly becoming too twisted to continue talking.

"Be careful before you speak," Cyrus cautioned. "Think it through first."

The three Bo Taw exchanged glances with each other. The oldest one faced Cyrus, asking, "What did you do to us?"

"Gave you a new perspective on things. What do you think?"

"I . . . I would like a berth on one of your dreadnoughts," the oldest Bo Taw said.

The others murmured their agreement.

"You have a task here first," Cyrus told him. Mentally, he showed the Bo Taw how to influence his friends in a similar manner as he'd been affected.

"I understand," the Bo Taw said. He smiled, showing perfect teeth. "Thank you, Cyrus Gant. I think for the first time in my existence I feel as if I'm doing something noble."

"Good. Now how about taking me to my friends?" he said.

"A splendid idea, my lord," the Bo Taw said. He clapped his hands.

The Vomags stood straighter, saluting the man from Earth. "Come," the Bo Taw said, "follow me."

||||||||||

The door to the first cell opened. Argon sat on a pallet. The giant had lost a lot of weight. He looked gaunt, and fear made him flinch.

What have they done to you to make a Highborn do that? Cyrus wondered.

Instead of waiting for a greeting, Cyrus used telepathy. He saw exactly what had happened. In mind-numbing horror, he saw each proceeding torment. The callousness of Argon's treatment infuriated Cyrus. The Kresh thought they were moral, huh? It seemed inconceivable to Cyrus now. Although he didn't want to, he made a small adjustment to Argon's memories. He psi-pushed the Chief Monitor back to the man he used to be.

For a moment, Argon looked confused. Cyrus could see it in the Highborn's eyes. Then the Chief Monitor straightened. "Cyrus," he said, in a deep voice. "Why are you here?"

"I've come to take you away, Chief Monitor."

"Away to where?" asked Argon.

"First, to my dreadnought," Cyrus said. "In time, you will captain the Teleship back to Earth."

Argon frowned. He glanced at the Bo Taw behind Cyrus. Then he scowled. "You just adjusted me, didn't you?"

"I've grown in abilities," Cyrus said, instead of answering.

Argon truly looked at him then. The Chief Monitor nodded. "Yes. I see. Thank you, Special. I-I believe they broke me."

"What was broken has been mended. You're back. I'm taking everyone who survived with me."

"How can this be possible?" Argon asked.

"Do you want to remain in your cell? Or do you want to come with me to my ship?"

Argon rose to his towering height. Anger began to smolder on his face. He flexed his big hands. "The things they did to me—" He took several steps toward the nearest Bo Taw. There was murder in the big man's eyes.

"Don't do it, Chief Monitor," Cyrus said. "They've learned some new things as well. They're on our side now."

The words made the Chief Monitor pause. He seemed to consider what Cyrus had said. "Yes," Argon muttered in a thick voice. "I want to get back to Earth where I belong."

Cyrus could have told him there wasn't any place safe in this universe. But he didn't think Argon needed to know that just yet. It was time to get Argon, Mikhail, and the rest of *Discovery*'s crew out of there and to an all-human zone.

After all this time, they were going to go home to Earth.

EPILOGUE

With the defeat of the first cyborg invasion, Dagon Dar strengthened his position as FIRST among the Kresh. With the announcement of human equality, the Glegan Kresh repudiated him.

No plea or warning of what was coming up out of Glegan convinced the third planet Kresh of their impending doom.

"We must aid them," Dagon Dar said. "We cannot afford to lose their ships or their persons."

"Aid them how?" asked Cyrus.

"Use the intersystem shift ability of your dreadnoughts. Lob missiles at the approaching Chirr."

"I don't have enough crewmembers yet to even run one of my vessels."

"Let the Kresh board them then. We'll know what to do soon enough."

"Your word is golden," Cyrus said, "but these are human vessels now. Give me free rein of High Station 3, and I will be able to recruit more crewmembers quickly."

"Is your word golden?" Dagon Dar asked. "Our Bo Taw are deserting us there. What did you do to them?"

"They're human," Cyrus said. "They're on our side now. I told you what I was going to do."

"Yes, but—"

"You're betting your Race's existence on my word," Cyrus said. "I realize that. What you must also understand is that we're going to need each other if we're going to defeat the Chirr. That as much as anything else means I'll keep my word. Despite your belief that humans are inherently chaotic, I am rational."

"Defeating the Chirr, yes; that is why we need the Glegan Kresh. Can't you understand *my* logic?"

"Oh, I understand it all right," Cyrus said. "Before I can help you with the Glegan Kresh, I need more people. That should be as clear as a bell to you."

Dagon Dar swished his tail. Finally, he said, "I will consult with my consort on your proposal."

Later, Red Bronze agreed to the idea of a mass influx of humans to the dreadnoughts. That included the Resisters on High Station 3 and the humans on Jassac and elsewhere. Unfortunately, the Chirr reached Glegan before the first vessel became fully operational with its human crew.

The battle started right away. The Glegan Kresh had seeded the system with hidden thermonuclear warheads. They took a dreadful toll of the advancing Heenhiss Chirr. Then the Glegan bugs launched a hidden fleet from under the surface.

The Kresh had a plan for that, too, and it came close to working perfectly. Chirr subterranean lasers made the difference. From their superior orbital height, the Kresh dropped asteroids on the third planet. The raining rocks took out half the Chirr vessels before they could leave their docking bays. The underground beams broke up enough asteroids to let the rest of the Chirr spacecraft reach orbital height.

Afterward, one of the bloodiest space battles in the Fenris System took place. The Glegan Kresh performed excellently, but it wasn't enough against the Chirr masses.

The bugs destroyed everything in their path. A hammer-ship and five Battle Fangs made it out of the Glegan gravitational system, but that was all. The remaining Chirr smashed all the habitats until only their craft remained around the planet.

"Your people did better than I thought they would," Cyrus said later.

"I mourn for our losses," Dagon Dar said. "We are ruined."

"No, we're not. It's time we decided on our allied plan to destroy the Chirr."

"You must gather your personnel for your dreadnoughts," Dagon Dar said.

The Chirr fleet remained around Glegan for six weeks more. During that time, the Heenhiss planetary-bound Chirr began surface assaults against the polar regions.

Cyrus decided the dreadnoughts could use some veteran Vomags as human marines. Several cyborg AI-brain shift mechanisms still worked. With Argon and the space marines manning the dreadnought, Cyrus used a shift opening to slip ten heavy landers from High Station 3 into orbit around Heenhiss.

The vehicles screamed down through the atmosphere, the thrusters shaking the rocky ground where they landed. Using telepathy, Cyrus brought Timor Malik and five hundred survivors of the equatorial army to the landers. Everyone boarded. The heavy vehicles promptly roared for space, and soon another shift opening appeared in Heenhiss orbit.

The ten shuttlecraft raced through as Chirr vessels lifted from the other side of the planet. The opening closed behind the last lander, and they found themselves near High Station 3. The new Fenris space navy received a draft of five hundred marines, fresh from the horrors of Heenhiss.

The true test came two months later. The Glegan Chirr split their space fleet, sending one quarter of the swarm back to Heenhiss.

Dagon Dar and Cyrus waited until the vessels were three-quarters of the way there and beginning to decelerate.

Then Cyrus used his best dreadnought, creating shift portals. Instead of a few missiles, the entire Kresh fleet jumped into position before the bugs. A swift battle of annihilation began, the Chirr caught by surprise.

It was the most lopsided victory to date. It also began the great exodus from Heenhiss of Kresh and Vomags alike. The Chirr were too strong for them to think of remaining on the planet. Eventually, the main Chirr fleet might return. The majority of the Heenhiss survivors moved to Jassac. From there they separated, each species leaving for its own territory.

A year later, Teleship *Discovery* left the Fenris System, heading back to Earth, with Argon as captain. Five former Bo Taw would power the newly constructed discontinuity window AI.

Every dreadnought had its allotment of human crew. No Bo Taw served under the Kresh. The two species had separated, each to its own half of Jassac.

Fear kept them together; fear of the deadly Chirr and the even more dangerous Eich Empire that waited out there in the center of the galaxy.

Cyrus Gant had become the guarantor of the Fenris humans, with new habitats under construction in the outer asteroid belt. The Kresh and humanity rebuilt at a furious pace, readying for another cyborg invasion. In the meantime, they kept watch of the Chirr, readying an invasion fleet of their own to wrest Heenhiss back from the bugs. Afterward, they would seal the Chirr on Glegan for the next several hundred years.

The first interspecies alliance had taken form. As interesting, after a solid year of cooperation, they remained at peace with each other. Considering all the bad blood between them, that was a fantastic achievement.

Cyrus wondered what Premier Lang of the solar system would make of all this. The guarantor of the Fenris System awaited the next Teleship, knowing that this was only the beginning of a new era for humanity and their Kresh allies.

ACKNOWLEDGMENTS

Thank you, David VanDyke, for the first round of editing. Many thanks to Jennifer Smith-Gaynor for her excellent editing advice. She always made me think. I'd also like to thank my copy editor, Jon Ford, for his hard work. As always, I'm very thankful to the 47North Team, a great group of people who are a pleasure to work with. I want to give a special thanks to my beautiful wife, Cyndi Heppner, and to Madison and Mackenzie, two super, young ladies. Lastly, but most importantly, thank you, Lord God, for letting me publish my work.

ABOUT THE AUTHOR

Photo © 2013 Cyndi Heppner

Vaughn Heppner is the author of many science fiction and fantasy novels, including the Invasion America series and the Doom Star series. He is inspired by venerable sci-fi writers such as Jack Vance and Roger Zelazny, as well as by *The Nights of the Long Knives* by Hans Hellmut Kirst. The original *Spartacus* movie and its themes of slave rebellion color much of his work. Among his contemporaries, Heppner counts B. V. Larson's military science fiction novels as the most akin to the Fenris series. Canadian born, Heppner now lives in Central California. Visit his website at www.vaughnheppner.com.